Valentina Cebęni was born in Italy. She is a passionate reader with a background in the classics. Since her teenage years, Valentina has cultivated her love of writing with the discipline of a Tibetan monk, determined to explore the recesses of the human soul through her characters. She currently lives in Rome.

'Set on a beautifully evoked Italian island, this atmospheric story is full of friendship, love and the most wonderful characters – a true feast for the senses. I thoroughly enjoyed it. I can't remember the last time a book made me feel so hungry!'
Jenny Ashcroft, author of *Beneath a Burning Sky*

'A bit of sunshine and romance and a whiff of ethereal mystery. What's not to like?'
Trip Fiction

'A feel-good read'
Hello!

VALENTINA CEBENI

The LITTLE Italian BAKERY

ABACUS

ABACUS

First published in Italy in 2016 as *La ricetta segreta per un sogno* by Garzanti
First published in Great Britain in 2018 by Little, Brown
This paperback edition published in 2019 by Abacus

1 3 5 7 9 10 8 6 4 2

A CIP catalogue record for this book
is available from the British Library.

ISBN 978-0-349-14198-5

Printed and bound in Great Britain by
Clays Ltd, Elcograf S.p.A.

Papers used by Abacus are from well-managed forests
and other responsible sources.

Abacus
An imprint of
Little, Brown Book Group
Carmelite House
50 Victoria Embankment
London EC4Y 0DZ

An Hachette UK Company
www.hachette.co.uk

www.littlebrown.co.uk

To women and their extraordinary strength

PROLOGUE

Summer 1940

Leaves rustled in the distance and the promise of summer was on the wind.

'Look, Joséphine, the sky's just magical this evening.'

A pair of blue eyes followed the line of Edda's slender finger as it pointed up towards the sun.

'You're right, and look at the clouds, aren't they huge!' said Joséphine.

'They're like enormous lemons, as big as the ones growing in the garden,' Edda added, fishing a lemon jelly sweet out of the basket she'd placed between her and her friend. The sweet was a piece of sunlight not much bigger than a sugar cube, a concentrate of pure sugar and lemon zest left to dry then briefly plunged into boiling honey, the product of an entire day's work. Studying the golden glow of that sugar-crusted fragment of the Mediterranean, Edda felt proud of her efforts. She popped the sweet between her lips and squashed it against her palate. Her eyes widened as she marvelled at the taste of the island summer, with its perfumes of wild flowers and salt, white towels left to dry in the sun and jugs of iced lemonade to sip. The sweet was like a journey encompassing everything the last three magical months had given her and the promise that the years ahead would be the best of her life, as long as Joséphine stayed by her side.

Edda kept sucking, thirsty for the jelly's citrusy summer flavour while her friend watched her. 'The jellies I made with Sister Anne yesterday really are delicious – you absolutely have to try one,' Edda said, smacking her lips, before rummaging around in the basket again to get one for her friend. 'Go on, Joséphine. I made these just for you, I know you're crazy about lemons!'

'I know, but these are for the lunch with the bishop tomorrow, Edda! The nuns will be so angry when they find out, and they'll punish us again.'

'If they find out,' Edda corrected her with a wink. 'I told Sister Anne they hadn't turned out very well and I made an extra jar of candied lemon peel. I made these ones just for us. For you, because I know how much you love them.'

Joséphine nodded happily as she accepted Edda's gift, smiling as Edda squeezed her hand.

'You're right,' Joséphine agreed.

Silence fell, interrupted only by the chirruping of the crickets. The easterly wind rippled through the leaves of the lemon tree that stood on the terrace, filling the air with their irreverent perfume. Down in the fishermen's village a distant radio sang an old song about a betrayed lover; the woman's voice was like velvet to the ears of the two girls who lay stretched out on the convent's terrace.

'Joséphine?'

'Yes?'

Edda turned onto her side, propping herself up on her elbow. On her face was the serious expression of someone about to say something important. 'Do you think it's possible to love someone like a sister even if they're not your sister? I mean, even if you don't have the same parents?'

The other girl sat up, wrapping her arms tightly around her sore knees. Sneaking out with Edda during evening prayers had earned them an exemplary punishment – an entire day locked in their respective cells at the convent, separated and fasting. At least until her best friend had arrived on the terrace with a basket full of sweet treats.

And yet she would have done it again; since Edda had arrived at the convent she hadn't felt alone any more.

She rolled up the sleeve of her cotton habit and showed Edda the semicircle of pale skin on her wrist. 'Of course. We made a pact, remember?'

Edda nodded and uncovered her own little scar, showing it off like a trophy. 'Sisters for ever,' she said quietly, as if it were a magic spell.

'Sisters for ever,' Joséphine agreed, breaking a piece of sugary gold in two.

Gelée al limone

200g sugar

100ml lemon juice

2 spoons of lemon peel, candied in honey

12g sheet gelatine

1 spoon natural vanilla flavouring

Sugar to decorate

Place the gelatine in cold water and leave to dissolve for at least ten minutes. Meanwhile, finely chop the candied peel.

Pour the sugar and lemon juice into a bowl and place over a medium heat until the mixture begins to boil.

Carefully wring out the gelatine and arrange pieces of candied peel in the bottom of a set of plastic chocolate moulds.

Once the lemon and sugar mixture has been boiling for about two minutes, add the gelatine and mix until completely combined. Turn off the heat and pour the mixture into the moulds. Leave the sweets to cool.

Once cool, remove the jellies from their moulds, dip in the sugar and serve.

1

1983

Elettra stood, arms folded, in front of the closed door with the sign 'The Dream Kitchen' swinging in front of her. One of the hinges had broken, but there was no longer any point in trying to fix it.

She steeled herself and went in one last time: it really had been a day to forget. She would have done almost anything to strike it from the calendar, but that was impossible. The sun had risen again as normal, bringing the familiar memories with it.

'Baking was never my choice, and you knew it,' she said, turning to the photo of her mother which hung on the otherwise bare wall of the shop. It was the photo of an intensely private woman whom Elettra had thought of by her given name rather than as 'Mamma'. She had called her Edda. Now Edda was in a coma, almost as if destiny was determined to put miles between them, to continue their lives as they had started, with Elettra's mother and her past remaining a mystery to her daughter. With her olive complexion and long, dark hair, Edda looked like Elettra in the photo on the wall. Of all her features, only Elettra's blue eyes came from their unknown source.

Elettra had tried to hold it together for the past few months but now she was unravelling. She began to sob and continued speaking to her mother's photo. 'If I'd been half as good as you at making pastries and bread I wouldn't be here now. People would be queuing up to the bakery, just like when you were in the kitchen. But you never wanted to admit that I wasn't like you, that I simply didn't want to be shut up inside the four walls of a kitchen.' She wiped her tears. 'You tried to make me follow in your footsteps, even though you knew very well that I dreamed of something else, that I wanted to go to New York and do that journalism Masters.' Elettra moved closer to the photo. 'You were somehow convinced that you had a gift to pass on to me, and that by learning to bake I would be able to heal people like you did. You spent years telling me that there is a magic to food, that even the simplest biscuit can mend a broken heart. I tried to tell you that I didn't have your gift, but it didn't work. And look at me now. The bakery has folded and here I am on my own, because you're all I've ever had.'

Back in the street, Elettra turned up the collar of her coat and began to walk without a fixed destination. Her head was empty and her legs simply felt the urge to take her far away. She thought about calling Walter, her ex-boyfriend. Their break-up was recent and she still felt raw inside: he had put his parents' wishes before his love for her. Dialling his number would have been easy, but she couldn't bring herself to do it.

What she needed was a friend. She turned towards the phone box in the middle of the square and dropped all the loose change she could find in her pockets into the little silver slot.

'Hello?'

There was a lump in Elettra's throat and her voice was a whisper. 'Ruth?'

Just one word in that wavering voice was enough to make the other woman take charge straight away. 'Tell me where you are, I'm coming to get you.'

'No, don't worry. It's late and Sarah needs to spend some time with her mum.'

'Don't you start trying to play superwoman with me, you know it won't work. Tell me where you are,' Ruth insisted at the other end of the line. They'd known each other since they were tiny.

'I feel like I'm suffocating, Ruth, like I'm going mad,' Elettra whispered. 'The bakery's closed down and Edda's medical fees keep going up, especially now the doctor wants to try a new treatment. They're doing all they can to keep her alive but there never seems to be even the slightest change and I don't know how much longer I can afford it.'

'Elettra . . .'

'I don't have a job any more, Ruth. I don't know what I'll do tomorrow, or how I'll manage to pay the bills, and I'm not even brave enough to visit my mother and see how she is. Just the thought of seeing her in that bed surrounded by tubes leaves me paralysed. I don't know what to do any more . . . I . . . I don't know, Ruth, I don't know. I just wish she was here with me, that she'd tell me what to do, but there's no one here. *No one*'s here, Ruth.'

'I'm here,' her friend pointed out. 'And so is Edda, she's there with you, Elettra; your mum can hear you when you talk to her. A mother never abandons her child, so go and see her and then come straight over to my house, I need to talk to you.'

Elettra used the cuff of her coat to wipe away the mascara that had run down her cheeks; she knew that tone of voice well. 'I can't accept any more money from you, you know that.'

'There's no need to be like that; I've sold most of the equipment from my dad's old business, the money will start to come in soon.'

A sigh filled the silence on the line. 'Really? I would have to pay you back – I mean it, Ruth.'

'Yes, okay,' Ruth said, smiling, knowing their friendship was too close to ever hold her to that. 'But you've got to promise me something else.'

Elettra fished the last coin out of her pocket and fed it into the slot. 'What?'

'That you'll use some of it to go on a holiday.'

Another sigh came down the line. 'I've lost my job, my mother needs drugs that cost an arm and a leg and I'm on the verge of a nervous breakdown. I don't think this is the right time for me to go on a holiday.'

'As I was saying, the payments will start coming in next week, so money isn't a problem at the moment. And a holiday is always going to be better than years of paying to see a therapist, isn't it?'

'Ruth . . .' Elettra began, but her friend interrupted her.

'I'm begging you, do as I say, just this once,' she said sweetly.

Elettra wasn't convinced by what her friend was suggesting, but when she thought about the here and now, her only wish was to get as far away as possible: Ruth might not be entirely wrong.

2

As she sat in the waiting room of the clinic where her mother was receiving treatment, Elettra found herself thinking once again that she didn't even have the guts to be in the same room with her. Her fingers clutched a necklace depicting Saint Elizabeth of Hungary. Edda was so devoted to the patron saint of bakers that she kept a small shrine to her at home. Elettra didn't know why she'd brought the necklace with her that day: she'd seen it on the bedside table and felt an urge to take it with her. The saint in her hand had a dreamy expression that instilled Elettra with a sense of peace, an inner calm she had rarely known in all her thirty years. She turned the necklace over in her fingers, lingering over the inscription around the edges of the medallion hanging from it: *Île du Titan*. She had never paid it any attention before. The name didn't mean anything to her, but she imagined it was one of the mysteries of Edda's past that she'd kept from her. Even after all these years, there was so much about the past that her mother had held back.

'One of many mysteries,' she said out loud in a tearful voice. Days, clouds, smiles: everything had been lost with Edda, swallowed up by her empty sleep.

9

Elettra took a deep breath in the waiting room and realised she couldn't do it, she wouldn't see her mother today, and picked up her bag. As she stood up, she found herself enveloped by a familiar smell. It was the warmth of an intense, familiar fragrance. It seemed to come out of nowhere.

She frowned, trying to connect the fragrance with a memory. She knew that scent of flour softened by a hint of sugar, but she couldn't work out what the playful background smell was. Then a gentle draught brought to mind a memory that made her knees go weak. The fragrance was unmistakeable. There was no doubt about it: it was the smell of Edda's aniseed bread.

Elettra used to be crazy about those special aniseed rolls, and she still remembered how as a child she used to love dipping them in warm milk until the icing turned clear. She could remember the exact consistency of the aniseed seeds that released their summery flavour like exploding fireworks. She always looked forward to the evenings when Edda prepared the mixture, the slightly alcoholic aroma of the rising dough, its good, clean smell.

'Oh my God,' she murmured. She looked around the corridor cluttered with trolleys full of bedsheets and drugs; what she had just experienced was not real, merely fantasy or nostalgia.

'No, sweetheart, it's all real,' a voice behind her corrected her.

Elettra swallowed carefully.

She took a deep breath and turned round; behind her was a woman in a wheelchair, an old lady who looked at her with small eyes.

'I'm Clara, a friend of Edda's. It's a pleasure to meet you, Elettra,' she added.

'You know who I am?' Elettra asked, feeling uneasy as she faced the small woman who was wrapped in a turquoise blanket.

'Of course, you're the only thing Edda ever talks about!'

Elettra's whole body tensed. She wondered what the woman was after.

She had read plenty of stories of people tricked and defrauded by phony clairvoyants; of being preyed upon when vulnerable. She came out with it: 'Look, if you're trying to make some money, you've picked the wrong woman.'

'Listen to me: your mother is thinking of you, sweetheart.' The woman's hand seemed to caress the air. 'She doesn't want you to worry about the bakery, there was nothing that could be done to save it. She'd rather you took better care of yourself.'

Elettra drew back. She held the woman's gaze. 'I'm sorry, I think you've confused me with someone else. My mother's been in a coma for a year and she's in no condition to hold a conversation. As for me, I'm absolutely fine, thank you.'

'I beg to differ, you don't look fine.'

Elettra gasped, wrong-footed by the woman's irreverent tone. She'd had enough of her pretensions. 'I'm sorry, I really must go.' She clutched her bag and turned away, but the old lady moved in her chair as Elettra started to leave.

'Wait!' she called. 'Edda asked me to tell you to make aniseed bread, but not to go overboard with the orange peel like you usually do!' she shouted after her.

Her words brought Elettra to an immediate halt part way down the corridor. 'How did you . . .' she asked, turning round, but the old lady spoke over her.

'Remember, Elettra: just two spoonfuls of coffee per cup. Once you've prepared the rolls, wrap them in the cloth on the kitchen sideboard, the one you spilled juice on when you were eight, and take them to the Convent of Saint Elizabeth on Titan's Island. Unless I'm mistaken, you've got something of your mother's with you which will show you the way,' she said, touching her neck. 'A very special compass.'

11

Elettra rubbed her eyes: there was no way the woman could know about Edda's necklace, it was impossible: she hadn't worn it since she had arrived at the clinic, but had held it in her hands.

'You'll find all the answers you're looking for on the island, my girl, but don't let anything or anyone intimidate you; close your ears to what the inhabitants of that hostile land may tell you. Leave your rolls at the feet of the Saint. Offer them up to her and pray for your mother, the Saint will hear you. She will heal both of you. And don't be afraid,' she added, 'everything will work out fine. Everything.' Elettra listened avidly. Faced down by that little old woman, her resistance had crumbled.

'I have to go, child,' Clara bid her farewell in a whisper.

'Wait, Clara!' exclaimed Elettra, rushing to crouch at her feet as the ward sister appeared in the corridor and took charge of the wheelchair. 'What exactly should I pray for? What will I find on that island?' she asked, but the nurse gave her a disapproving look and turned her back on Elettra with a couple of brisk manoeuvres. Elettra jumped up and grabbed her by the shoulder, keeping a firm grip. 'Please, please: let me talk to her. It's important.'

The nurse tugged herself free and looked Elettra up and down. 'This lady is seriously ill. Please show some respect and be kind enough to leave her in peace,' she dismissed her as she moved away. The wheelchair rolled along silently, carrying the old lady and her secrets with it.

The answers, the past: once again, everything was slipping away from her.

Elettra stood helplessly in the middle of the corridor, watching the ward sister escort Clara back to her room.

The spell was broken, the aroma of aniseed was gone.

Pane all'anice

1kg flour

200g sugar

25g yeast

600ml milk

1 spoon honey

1 egg yolk

1 spoon oil

4 spoons aniseed seeds

1 orange (peel only)

1 pinch of salt

For the icing:

1 egg white, sugar, lemon juice.

Dissolve the yeast in a little warm milk with a spoonful of honey and leave to stand for at least ten minutes.

Mix together the flour, sugar, salt, aniseed and orange peel and heap on a flat surface. Make a well in the centre, add the egg yolk and oil and combine.

Gradually add the remaining milk, then, finally, add the yeast mixture.

Knead the dough vigorously for several minutes until it achieves an elastic consistency.

Place in a large, oiled bowl and leave to rest until it doubles in volume.

Shape the dough into balls the size of oranges and place them on a baking tray. Cover them with a tea towel and leave to rest for an hour.

Lightly brush the rolls with egg white, put them in an oven pre-heated to 170°C along with a small pan of water and bake for about 30 minutes.

To ice: mix the egg white and the sugar until you have a thick, pale paste and add several drops of lemon juice. Brush onto the cooled bread and leave to dry completely.

3

Elettra spent hours staring at the small statue of the Saint that stood in the house she and Edda had shared for years. What had that woman meant by finding answers on the island? What had she meant about her being able to heal herself and her mother? She was searching for an answer in the statue: in addition to spending her life working to help the needy, the story went that in order to disguise the bread she was taking to the poor and sick, Elizabeth, the young widow of Louis IV of Thuringia, transformed them into roses, thus earning herself the title of patron saint of bakers and nurses. It was a fascinating story, which Elettra had made her mother tell her every evening when she was small, but it was of little help in alleviating the doubts crowding her mind. All that Elettra knew about her mother was that she had been brought up by nuns. Edda's parents couldn't afford to look after her, so one morning they had entrusted her to the care of their parish priest who had taken her to a convent where she had been employed as a scullery maid. It had been pure luck that she had also been educated and loved during her time with the nuns, whom she had unexpectedly left in order to move to the city where, after a number of years, she had managed to open the bakery.

But none of that explained what connects me to the island that Clara mentioned, or what connects the island, the convent and my mother's life, Elettra reflected. Her mother had been more guarded than most people, and of course Elettra was now genuinely concerned that her past would disappear with her.

Edda was stubborn, she always had been; never offering a single concession to Elettra's need to know about her own father, for instance. She shook her head at the memory of their disagreements, the silences that had divided them for years. She turned to the small altar in the hall to replace the burnt-out candle and as she held out a new one, she asked the young queen of Thuringia to help her mother, to bring her back to her in some way. There was nothing more that Elettra needed than healing – for herself and for her mother.

'Please, please, I beg you,' she repeated through gritted teeth. Then she stopped. Was she really praying to a statue in hope of a sign? That wasn't like her at all.

I need to stop letting others influence me, she scolded herself as she looked at the scared woman reflected in the mirror, before heading to Edda's room and the drawer where her mother kept the tranquillisers that helped with her chronic insomnia. She tried not to think as she opened the drawer, not to see the clothes which were still perfectly ironed and arranged by colour. She picked up a jumper and inhaled her mother's scent.

Elettra realised she was suddenly sick of waiting – waiting for her mother to get better, waiting for her own life to begin. She'd waited so long that she'd passed up on her dreams and run a business into the ground. Everything that had happened already was enough of a sign – she decided that there and then. She was ready to take matters into her own hands and to act herself. If the woman had said that an offering to the Saint was what was needed then she would do it. Maybe she was truly losing her mind and simply running away, but it had to be better than standing still and remaining here.

She barely gave herself time to gather the ingredients together on the table before running to the telephone.

'Hello?'

'It's Elettra. I need some aniseed seeds.'

'Hi, Ruth, it's great to speak to you!' Ruth said sarcastically.

'Please, don't lecture me. This is important,' Elettra insisted.

Ruth snorted. 'What do you need aniseed for at this time of night?'

'It's complicated, Ruth. Please.'

'You're not really trying to tell me that you've dragged me out of bed because you've had a sudden urge to bake, are you?'

Elettra sighed. 'Listen, I can't explain it all now. All I want to know is whether you can give me the seeds. Do you have any at home or not?'

Her friend exhaled. 'We'll see, when do you need them?'

Elettra gripped the telephone tightly. 'Right now.'

'Elettra, are you okay?' Ruth said softly.

'Please. Just now.' Elettra said and hung up.

A short while later, a bag in her hand and polka dot pyjamas poking out from underneath her raincoat, Ruth arrived at the doorstep. She let herself in with her spare key.

Elettra was up to her elbows in soft, sticky dough. 'Here's the aniseed you asked for.' Ruth placed the bag on the table. She watched her friend energetically kneading the dough. 'Are these the aniseed biscuits that you're in such a hurry to make?'

Elettra grunted in reply; combining all the ingredients took effort and concentration, and she couldn't afford to make mistakes. Not this time. She had found Edda's recipe in the old biscuit tin on top of the fridge, but she'd had to stop herself from cursing; it didn't give a single measurement, just a list of ingredients.

'My mother and her damned mysteries!' she had exclaimed, screwing up the piece of paper, her fingers rigid with tension.

So she'd had to rely on her memory for the details.

Elettra took a handful of flour and sprinkled it over the pastry board. 'No, they're not biscuits,' she replied after a while, giving in to Ruth's silence. She folded the dough in half and twisted it into a plait which she slapped against the table, repeating the process until she was exhausted. She remained tight-lipped all the while, despite the temptation to confide in her friend; she could have told her about the old woman and the scent of aniseed that appeared in the hospital, but Ruth wouldn't have understood. No one would.

She opened the bag, releasing a cloud of fragrance, and used her hands to stretch out the dough ready for the seeds. 'I've decided to follow your advice. I'm going away,' she announced finally.

Ruth was busy making coffee and she gripped the pot tightly as she turned round to face her. She looked relieved. 'That's great! You really need to take a break,' she said, giving Elettra's shoulder a squeeze. She punched her gently on the arm and reached out to light the hob. 'So tell me, where have you decided to go?'

Elettra smiled; Ruth might be ready for the idea of a trip, but she certainly wouldn't be prepared for the destination. 'Just to a small island.'

Silence. Elettra had surprised her and now she needed to give her time to process it.

Ruth shifted her weight from one foot to the other. 'An island?'

'Yes, it's a small island in the Mediterranean, between Corsica and Sardinia. I've been reading about it.'

'Don't they all speak French there? How are you planning to communicate?'

'You're right, there used to be a small French community on the island, but luckily they're all bilingual there nowadays, so I won't have any trouble making myself understood. It's called Titan's Island.'

'Wait. *What* is this island called?' Ruth asked.

'Titan's Island.'

Ruth bit her lip. 'Oh, Elettra. I've heard about that place. I was told about it when I went to Sardinia last summer.' Ruth's look of bemusement turned to worry. 'Elettra, are you really sure you want to go there? From what I heard it's really isolated, and not at all easy to get to. It's ideal for someone who likes nature and the wilderness, but if I know you at all, it's not the place to go.'

'But it *is*. It really is,' Elettra replied, her head still full of Clara's words and her warning not to let herself be swayed by hearsay about Titan's Island or its inhabitants.

Ruth cleared her throat and folded her arms across her chest. 'Elettra, I heard really strange stories about it last summer, and I'm not comfortable about the idea of you going there alone.'

'What sort of stories?'

Ruth looked anxious but it was clear she was going to humour Elettra. 'Okay, we got really close to the island on a day trip from Sardinia, and we were told that it's a bit of a prehistoric place. They've had some trouble, historically; the island is split into two, and the people on one side don't mix with those on the other side. Apparently, there was a tragic storm there a couple of years ago, and lots of people lost their husbands and loved ones. There's a colony of widows or something who separate themselves from everyone else. That's what it's best known for. Our crazy tour guide mentioned a curse, and something to do with spirits who haunt the coast. To be honest she was completely away with the fairies.

The point is it's not a good place to go, you'll be on your own and you won't know anyone.'

Elettra burst out laughing. 'Are you serious?!' she exclaimed. 'Since when have you believed the nonsense that crazy people tell you?'

'Since my best friend took it into her head to go to a remote island full of strange people. Not to mention the fact that I'm sure your mother and your obsession with the past have something to do with this plan.' She tilted her head, trying to meet Elettra's suddenly elusive gaze.

'Partly,' she admitted, aware she was backed into a corner. 'I feel like I'll find answers there. Perhaps the ones Edda has denied me for all these years.'

'I knew it, I knew it!' Ruth exclaimed, shaking her head. 'When will you stop resenting her, eh? Edda is in a coma, she's ill. She needs you, here and now.'

Elettra plunged her hands into the dough. 'And what about what I need?' she burst out, letting the pain and anger spill out of her mouth in a fit of bitterness. 'Where was my mother when I asked her about my father, her life, when I begged her for a single memory about her past? And where was she when responsibility for the bakery came crashing down on my shoulders, before I had time to think, time to try and live the life I'd always dreamed of?'

'Elettra, this has nothing to do with . . .'

'Oh, really? You think this has nothing to do with the fact that in the end I've had to set my life and my dreams aside and do exactly what she wanted? Nothing to do with the fact that I longed to be a journalist and instead I've found myself baking cakes and biscuits just like my mother intended?'

'Elettra . . .'

'You don't think this has anything to do with the fact that my mother has sabotaged every effort I've ever made to build myself a life independent of hers?' Elettra interrupted her, fuming.

'No!' exclaimed Ruth, exasperated by the incandescent rage that left her friend red in the face. 'For heaven's sake, Elettra, of course I don't; nobody knew your mother was going to have a stroke, she didn't plan to leave you alone to run the bakery by yourself!'

'I don't know!' shouted Elettra with her arms in the air, her voice coloured by the pain of a disappointed daughter; with the pain of someone forced to live a life she hadn't chosen. 'I don't know anything any more, that's the point.' She collapsed onto a chair and covered her face, her whole torso shaking with repressed, dry sobs. She wanted to cry, but she couldn't.

Ruth watched her, confused and worried, then knelt down in front of her and took her hands. 'How long will you stay there?' she asked in a small voice.

'I really don't know, as long as I need to,' Elettra replied, glancing at the table, embarrassed by the violence of her outburst, 'but I wanted to ask if you'd keep an eye on the house and Edda until I come back.'

'Have you already planned when you're leaving?'

'Yes.'

'Okay.'

'I'm not running away, Ruth.'

'I didn't say you were.'

'But that's what you think, I can tell from your face.'

'Perhaps.' Ruth gave a half smile. 'But I understand why; this is a difficult time for you.'

And she was right. Elettra needed to get away from there, but she hadn't decided to run away from her mother, quite the opposite. After what had happened she was more determined than ever to go and find her, to seek the answers to her questions about Edda, and why they had both found themselves here with so much pain and heartbreak.

She looked down at the dough that was now rising under a tea towel then washed the flour off her arms. 'Too many strange things have been happening recently, and now I don't need to take care of the shop any more, I want to find the answers I've never been given,' she remarked as she dried her hands.

Ruth sighed and took two cups off the shelf. She added sugar to each as her friend poured the coffee. 'So when are you leaving?' she asked, helping herself to a pastry from the tray by the sink.

Elettra brought the coffee up to her nose to smell the rich aroma. 'Soon,' she replied.

'Is this aniseed bread for the journey?'

The timer went off, announcing the end of the first proving. Elettra now needed to shape the rolls and leave them to prove for another hour before baking them and icing them with sugar and coloured sprinkles.

She prodded the rough surface of the sweet dough, looking at it with hope in her eyes. 'It's for the journey of a lifetime.'

4

The weekly ferry service was the only connection between the island and the mainland and it left a trail of golden spray behind it as it entered the sheltered waters of the bay. A huge rock greeted the ship as it arrived at the port, which was overrun by broom and wild irises. Elettra could see a lighthouse up above. She stood on the deck of the ferry, wrapped tightly in her jacket, clutching a cup of coffee and feasting her eyes on the island's wild beauty. She gave a sigh of relief as she heard the motors cut out and the ramp at the back of the boat open with a groan. She went down the still-swaying gangplank, even more determined to enjoy the view in front of her. There was a small tourist marina, a dozen berths separated by long decks; and the fishermen's port, a walkway of cracked wood littered with lobster pots and crates left out to dry in the June sunshine, beyond which rose a series of hills covered in heather, juniper and arbutus trees.

She smiled; she felt like the whole island was welcoming her. She brushed a lock of hair out of her eyes, her other hand gripping the bag that held the bread. She took a deep breath, her first on that small stretch of land in the middle of the sea.

She surveyed the scene and allowed herself some time to soak up the port town and its atmosphere. She was surrounded by the chaos of the market, its stalls, improvised from pallets and beach umbrellas, selling fish and fresh fruit. Just as she was taking it all in, she noticed something from the corner of her eye: on the other side of the stalls was a line of women dressed in sombre, black ankle-length cotton skirts and matching shirts, clutching paper bags bulging with vegetables and tomatoes and orangey peaches to their chests. Their hair was spun like silver, and contrasted with the sun-darkened skin of their faces. They were dressed in mourning clothes, and walked with their heads down, weighing up the fruit and vegetables on display in silence. The exchange of bank notes was a mute transaction: none of those present spoke a single word to them, and nor did they seem to acknowledge the faces of the women in front of them.

A procession of ghosts, Elettra thought, shadows that defy the position of the sun, as they moved through the small crowd, which opened a passage as they passed by, treating them like lepers. How strange, she thought. She wanted to follow them, feeling they might be able to help her get to her destination on the island, but before she could reach them, they seemed to disappear into the town's small alleyways.

She unzipped her bag to check the bread. Despite her fears, it didn't seem to have suffered from the journey. On the contrary, the aroma of aniseed was even stronger than when she had first baked it, little comets of scent lighting her way to the truth.

She had left in such a rush that she hadn't even thought to book a cheap hotel – the only kind she could afford – but she was feeling impatient and wanted to dive right in.

Elettra stopped an old lady in the square and hesitantly followed the direction indicated by her hand. She didn't let the woman's confused look, or the harshness in her voice when she mentioned the convent, get to her.

'The convent? The one where those unfortunates live on the other side of the island?' the woman had asked, looking her up and down. Elettra wasn't entirely sure how to respond.

'The Convent of Saint Elizabeth?' she had repeated, as the woman had pursed her lips and started a coughing fit.

'Go then, and may the Lord protect you in that hell,' she said drily, continuing to cough while turning away and leaving Elettra alone and disconcerted in the dusty street between the houses.

'What a warm welcome,' Elettra murmured to herself as she set off uncertainly, losing herself in the woodland left parched by the sun. She had laughed at Ruth's warnings regarding the island and its strangeness, but she started to think that perhaps her friend's concerns weren't so far-fetched after all.

She walked along dirt tracks and steep paths trying to remember the woman's harsh words. She had been sure she would reach the convent in less than half an hour, but she'd been walking for much longer than that without meeting another living creature, apart from a lizard and a stray dog. She stopped and found herself studying the countryside, completely out of breath.

There was still no sign of the convent. She mopped her brow and turned back, trying to retrace her footsteps to the point where she'd got lost. The paths all looked the same and she couldn't work out where she'd taken a wrong turn. Each trail was a tongue of earth and rocks worn into the vegetation, just like all the others, and the glare of the sun had only made things worse.

This place really is like a hellish paradise, she thought. She decided to try to trust her instincts and turned around another bend. In the distance she finally spotted the outline of a building on the top of a hill. It was old and in rundown condition. As she got closer she could see its flaking plaster and tufts of green poking through the roof tiles. The nearer she got, the easier it was to see that the building was in fact the convent she was looking for. The woman with harsh words hadn't given clear directions, but at least she had indicated the approximate right direction.

Once she reached the top of the hill she turned to look at the landscape that had suddenly appeared beyond the curve in the path: a cobalt blue bay whose beauty made her forget all her troubles. The sun's rays were reflected in dazzling sparkles bright enough to bring tears to her eyes, but the colour of the sea in the coves sheltered by the rocks was as deep and dark as the night sky.

In front of her she could suddenly see the reason for the island's mythical name: it was a large rock formation, a sort of geological formation that was shaped very clearly as a statue; a giant Titan lying on one side, stretched out on an enormous green bed. The rock seemed to be a sort of dividing line or point between the two sides of the island: the port side, which was picturesque and animated, where she had just come from; and the other, where she now was, on which the convent stood. This side was more rugged and wild, where nature ruled, the woods were inaccessible, capable of swallowing up houses and trees, and the paths were winding. This was where Elettra had seen the women in mourning clothes go, a handful of silent silhouettes with their eyes downcast, balancing baskets on their heads, until they were suddenly swallowed up by the winding streets that eventually led to this untamed area of shrubbery and isolation.

Elettra smiled at the sleeping giant, the guardian of an island shrouded in mystery, then approached the convent. She rang the bell and noticed that the gate, which was flanked by two huge lemon trees, was half open and would let her in with a gentle push.

Elettra walked through, straight to the cool of the cloister which suddenly re-energised her. It was nice to feel the fresh air on her back and to absorb the calm atmosphere that lingered amongst the columns surrounding the central courtyard. She gazed upwards as she walked along the portico, and stumbled over the uneven marble paving slabs more than once as the bread suddenly seemed to start pulsing like a living heart against the sides of her bag.

Not now, thought Elettra, giving the bag a smack: she knew she seemed crazy, but these last few days had taught her that the line between the rational and the irrational is not always clear.

Elettra kept an ear open for any sounds, a noise that would suggest she wasn't alone in the cloister and courtyard – but any voice that the convent might possess seemed to be to shut off behind a series of closed doors that led off the cloister. One, however, was slightly open. Elettra moved closer but could detect no sign of life behind it, not even the swish of a nun's habit.

Looking back to the courtyard, something in one of its corners caught her eye: a patch of grass was adorned with blooming hydrangeas and lemon trees heavy with golden fruit. She felt as though her heart was in her mouth. There, in that very corner, stood the Saint.

Elettra's bag fell to the floor and her lips suddenly were dry. She felt an intense heat run over her skin, like a caress at the end of a tiring day. Breathing deeply, she clutched Edda's necklace in her hand and picked up her bag. After all, it was Edda she was looking for; her history, their history.

She pressed her clenched fist against her chest, reciting a prayer from memory, then slowly walked towards the Saint, her hand stretched out towards the statue.

'You,' she whispered gently as a waft of sweet, citrusy fragrance caressed her hair. Clara's instruction to go to the island and the convent as soon as possible echoed in her head, and she knew this was where she was meant to be – almost as if destiny or some other hand had compelled her here. She felt as if she had been drawn to it with an inevitability, she and this place attracted like two magnets.

'Can I help you?' a voice suddenly called out.

Elettra jumped, and quickly lowered her hand.

She took a step backwards, clearing her throat. 'Yes, I think so ... to be honest, I was looking for the statue of the Saint,' she stammered, wishing she could pull herself together. She tucked her hair behind her ears, but looked around with the air of someone who's been caught stealing; her legs were shaking and her heart started beating hard.

'I rang the bell when I arrived, but nobody answered so I came in. I'm sorry, I didn't mean to intrude,' she stuttered, flapping her hands. The woman before her merely shook her head and smiled the sweetest smile Elettra had ever seen, hypnotic and magical. Elettra's heart rate slowed down a bit.

'It's no intrusion, really; anyone who wishes to pay homage to the Saint is welcome,' the woman explained, walking up to the statue and brushing it with the tips of her fingers. Her voice was low and gentle, like the early morning mist on a distant horizon.

Elettra studied the woman's long golden-blonde hair, which was held back behind her ears with two hair grips and stood out against her simple lilac dress. She couldn't have been much more than a couple of years older than Elettra, if that, but they looked like they came from completely different places in time. And yet, there was definitely something that drew her to the woman's face, her eyes, her open, reassuring smile.

'I've come a long way to get here,' Elettra explained as the woman moved towards her, suddenly embarrassed to have shared the moment with a stranger.

She looked Elettra up and down. 'I guessed as much, you don't look familiar. Where exactly are you from?'

Elettra shook herself. 'Not all that far in distance, to be honest, but it was quite a journey getting to the island,' she replied, thinking back to her travels. 'At one point I thought I would never make it.'

'We all arrive where we are destined to go.'

Elettra repeated those words under her breath, trying to memorise them; she was creating her own destiny, even though she had never felt ownership of it before. She felt the need to remind herself of it in this moment, even if the decision to set off on her journey had been prompted by Clara's words. 'Anyway, I'll only be a few minutes, then I'll leave the convent and the sisters in peace.'

A slight blush coloured the cheeks of the woman next to her as she stretched out her arm and pointed to the surrounding cloister and doors. 'There are no nuns here; you can stay as long as you want.'

'But you . . .'

'I'm not a nun,' the woman replied with a flash of her white teeth.

Elettra studied her carefully: she wasn't wearing a traditional nun's habit, but the woman's lightness of step and modest dress had misled her. She looked her up and down, a puzzle to decipher.

'Lea Coureau, it's a pleasure to meet you,' the woman introduced herself, holding out her hand to Elettra as if to dispel any uncertainty.

Elettra shook it warmly. 'Elettra Cavani,' she replied, as the harsh voice of the woman from the town ran through her head. She squeezed Lea's hand, pausing to study her further; there was something elusive about her eyes and heart-shaped lips. As Elettra met her gaze she became aware of something unsettled too, but the thought evaporated before she could put it into words.

Suddenly there was a sharp noise from above – the crystalline sound of something shattering into pieces, which drew Elettra's eyes to the windows on the upper floors; someone was up there. Elettra looked up and clearly saw a curtain closing; the smudge of a handprint left on the glass. She turned to ask Lea for an explanation, but the woman was walking off towards the columns that flanked the cloister; Elettra could hear the echo of her footsteps. Elettra was slightly shaken, but decided to make her offering to the Saint without further delay. She opened her bag with a decisive action and the cloister was suddenly full of the perfume of Edda's baking.

'Edda!'

Elettra spun round.

She had heard it distinctly, a voice had called her mother's name. About to kneel at the feet of the Saint, she looked up again: all the windows were closed, she checked them one by one. The voice didn't sound like it had belonged to Lea. I may be exhausted, but I'm not crazy, dammit, she told herself. Her eyes meticulously raked every inch of the courtyard and cloister, but it was no good. Everything seemed to be unchanged and in order, therefore opening the door to the unpleasant possibility that she'd imagined it. She mopped her forehead and rubbed her eyes. Could it all be in my head? she asked herself, looking at the bread wrapped in the white cloth. It had been a long and puzzling day, and she was afraid she might be losing her grip on reality. With her fists clenched against her thighs, she thought back to Clara's words and her warnings about the journey. She would never be able to uncover the truth if she continued being frightened of things. She had come here to make her offering.

She placed the bread at the feet of the Saint and bowed her head, with the prayer for new hope in her heart. She concentrated on the image of Edda, her lively smile. She knelt down on the chipped marble and, as Clara had suggested, prayed to the Saint to wake Edda from her coma, to heal her mother and herself. In front of that statue, in an old convent, on an island in the middle of the sea, she felt at ease for the first time, despite her tiredness and the propensity of her mind to play tricks on her. In that moment she felt much closer to Edda than she had felt when holding her hand during the past year.

This island was having a strange effect on her, she told herself, but couldn't continue with the thought. Lea had returned, and she could feel her powder blue eyes on her back. She stood up again, and felt compelled to ask: 'Did you hear that noise?'

Lea brushed some hair out of her face. 'What noise?'

Elettra looked upwards, pointing towards the closed windows that faced onto the cloister. And now what do I tell her? She'll think I'm crazy, she thought. She gripped the handle of her bag so tightly that her fingers turned white. 'I thought I heard a voice . . .'

Lea shrugged her shoulders and rubbed her arms. 'What kind of voice?'

Elettra felt self-conscious. 'I just thought I heard something . . . something smash, or maybe a voice. I'm tired. It could have been anything.'

'The magic of the convent,' Lea replied without batting an eyelid. 'It seems like time doesn't exist here, like you could sit on the edge of the pool and look at the water and wake up ten years later, just like that.' She looked around the courtyard. 'I've often had that sensation, but time never does seem to stop. It runs faster and faster, taking both tears and happy memories with it.'

Lea's voice was tinged with a touch of bitterness and only a faint trace of the smile that had lit up her face remained. Elettra nodded. She had placed one hand on a column and she could clearly feel the faint pulse of the building: the place was alive, an age-old lifeblood ran along and through its walls, the memory of things.

'What brought you here?' murmured Lea.

Elettra glanced briefly at the woman and the empty bag, repressing a shiver; she had completely lost track of the time since entering the convent and the temperature was starting to drop. 'I owed it to my mother,' she replied instinctively.

Lea looked at her curiously. 'Is she particularly devoted to Saint Elizabeth?'

'Yes, but it's more than that. I have the feeling that my mother has some kind of connection with this place, but I'm not quite sure how to find out what it is.'

'Why, does your mother have trouble with her memory?' guessed Lea, lowering her voice, empathising with the pain she saw appear on Elettra's face.

Elettra felt overcome with emotion at this kindness and smiled at her gratefully. The idea of unburdening herself to someone was extremely tempting, and she reassured herself that if something went wrong, she would be going home within a fortnight and would never see the woman ever again. 'My mother's been in a coma for the last year,' she whispered. That was always the hardest part, to think that the woman who had given her life was no longer the person she had fought with and loved. The blow felt harder every time, despite her efforts to hide it. 'She had a stroke and I don't think she'll regain consciousness; the doctors aren't optimistic.'

Elettra shook her head, saddened and angered by a truth she no longer knew how to face, but Lea squeezed her hand tightly. She was just a stranger, but in that moment Elettra felt a familiarity, a sense of something that she had been missing. She felt both uncomfortable and embarrassed by it, and tried to pull her hand away but Lea spoke with a smile.

'There's no need to look for somewhere else. You can stay here if you like.'

'But I . . .'

'As long as you haven't already booked somewhere in the port, of course.'

'No, it wasn't that,' Elettra replied. 'I wouldn't want to disturb you at all.'

'Don't worry, it's no trouble. The convent is deconsecrated and it belongs to me. There haven't been any sisters here for years, so you can imagine that there are more rooms than I could possibly use myself.' She gestured to the buildings around the cloister while Elettra tried to reorder the chaos of her mind. It had been liberating to speak without thinking, and without weighing up each word, but she still felt gripped by doubt, perpetually conflicted.

'Stay here tonight,' Lea repeated. 'You're exhausted, and it's too late to go back to town now; the path down to the port is dangerous in the dark and it's very easy to get lost,' she added, pointing to the sky streaked with violet. Elettra's gaze continued to move between Lea and the empty bag. The woman wasn't wrong; the likelihood of getting lost in the dark was rapidly increasing. What she needed right now was a shower and some clean sheets: and this need momentarily quietened the fears and doubts in her mind.

'If you're worried about the price, you should know that I have absolutely no intention of asking you for money, and if you're happy here with us you can stay as long as you want. All we'll seek in return is a hand with the housework,' Lea said.

'Us?' Elettra echoed.

'Exactly. Two other women, Nicole and Dominique, have also lived here for the last couple of years; you could say that together we're a little female community. We're a family.'

'But . . .' she murmured, surprised.

'Shall we go, then?' Lea encouraged her. It was an offer that Elettra didn't know how to refuse.

'I don't know how to thank you,' Elettra gave in, stretching out her arm. She put her hand in Lea's cool one, following in her footsteps.

During the brief walk through the convent she couldn't help noticing the rundown state of the structure: the marble paving was worn with use, the wooden window frames were blistered by the sun and overgrown creepers covered the façade. The walls inside were covered with the greenish traces of damp. There was even crumbled plaster lying in tiny piles around the edges of the rooms.

The smell of mildew dogged their every step, but Lea didn't seem to pay it any attention; she continued walking briskly along corridors, opening doors and changing direction until Elettra was completely disorientated. They crossed an unused wing and went through a small chapel that Lea said was still visited by elderly women in search of comfort. They went up a staircase to the first floor, and Lea explained that this was where the nuns used to live. The sight of the bare walls and the worn wooden doorframes surprised Elettra; she wasn't used to such austerity and started to feel a little trapped and claustrophobic.

Lea stopped in front of a closed door and pushed it open firmly.

'Here we are,' she said, holding it open for Elettra. 'I always keep a room ready, just in case, but I'll give you some clean sheets later, and some blankets in case you get cold in the night. As you can see, it's not luxurious, but it is clean and neat.' Elettra peered through the doorway and walked in; there was a table and chair, a small wardrobe and a bed directly below the window which had a view of the sea, and a crucifix to watch over her dreams. It was rather spartan, but it seemed clean and fairly comfortable.

Elettra walked over to the window in search of the Titan rock she'd noticed during the day, but she couldn't see it. It would have offered her some comfort.

'You can't see the port from here,' Lea said. 'The convent faces the other side of the island, the part I imagine you haven't visited properly yet. In my opinion, it's the better part, the real Titan's Island,' she added with a wink.

Elettra ran her hands over the salt-crusted shutters, watching the dark silhouettes on the sea.

'At least I can see the fishermen's boats from here,' Elettra replied, trying to hide her disappointment at not being able to see the statue and the lively port. It was so secluded around here and she felt a little unnerved. She looked curiously around her, searching the clean furnishings for some sign of the lives that had been spent between these walls. She put her bag on the table and her small suitcase by the door.

'I noticed something strange today,' Elettra continued, immediately catching Lea's attention.

'What?'

'When I arrived I saw a line of women, dressed in mourning, walking in this direction. I don't know who they were, and I thought they might be here but they're not.'

'Yes, they were coming to this side. The two sides of the island are very different, poles apart in so many ways.'

'What do you mean?'

Lea looked straight at her. 'For example, there are no men here, but there are in the town.'

'Why is that?'

'It's just the way it is.'

'Why? There must be a reason,' Elettra pressed her a little.

Lea seemed to consider for a long time before answering. 'It's a long story that nobody likes to remember, because it's caused a lot of pain and has led to the division between the people who live on either side of Titan.' Lea turned away from her and clasped her hands impatiently.

'I see,' Elettra replied, sensing Lea's reluctance to explain from her body language.

Lea remained distant and rigid, her hands clenched tightly at her sides. It was clear that she didn't appreciate Elettra's curiosity about the islanders.

Elettra looked away, seeking refuge in the panoramic view of the sea. But after a while she ventured to break the silence. 'Did I say something wrong? If so, I'm sorry, I didn't mean to.'

Lea shook her head and cleared the clouds from her face with a smile. 'Don't worry, you didn't say anything wrong,' she reassured her. 'Why don't we go and find something to eat? I'm absolutely starving and I'd like to introduce you to the others.' With that, she linked her arm with Elettra's and guided her out of the room.

5

Except for the gusts of wind, Elettra's first night on the island was cloaked in silence. She tossed and turned between the lavender-scented sheets but she didn't sleep a wink.

But at some point in the night, a loud voice unexpectedly broke the silence.

'Edda!' she heard someone shout again.

Elettra sat up immediately, her eyes wide. She pressed her hand against her chest, which was clammy with tension. She remembered the voice she'd heard when she was by the statue of the Saint, pushed back the covers and rushed to the door. Out in the corridor there was nothing but a long dark passageway and bare walls.

She heard the sound of light, hurrying footsteps and then finally Lea's face, lit by the flickering light of a candle, peered towards her from the stairs.

'Did you hear it? A voice shouted a woman's name just a moment ago.' Elettra blocked her path, but, waxen-faced, Lea shook her head.

'No, definitely not. Nicole and Dominique are in their rooms, and I've just been to close the shutters upstairs. It must have been the wind that frightened you.'

Elettra raised an eyebrow. 'The wind?'

'Exactly.' Lea looked at the candle flame, a gentle smile on her lips. 'On the island we have a story about windy nights like this one: it's said that the heavens send out the voices of those we love on the wind so we can feel them close to us, and I've often noticed it. It's just a story, of course, but sometimes it seems true.'

Elettra shivered as she heard Lea's words: something didn't quite ring true about that story, but Clara's warning echoed in her mind. Don't let anything or anyone intimidate you, she reminded herself. Back in her room, Elettra felt as though the walls were talking to her, she could hear their breaths responding to her heartbeat.

All I need is a bit of courage, she told herself, her head filled once more with Clara's words and her hopes of learning more about her mother. I should stay here, voices or not, she decided, I'm not going to be scared by a silly story.

Having made her decision, she slowly relaxed as the shadows left her mind, making room for her memories from earlier that evening. It had been a really lovely evening, she thought, allowing her mind to drift back to dinner just a few hours ago.

It had been pleasant to let the chatter around the table envelop her, to feed off the exchanges of Lea, Nicole and Dominique between courses. The youngest in the group, Nicole had translucent skin, a fragile sweetness and a delicate physique. Her soft voice and fine features made her the complete opposite of Dominique, an older woman who had sat at the other end of the table. Dominique had thick coppery hair and a powerful build from working outdoors. She had almost entirely ignored their new arrival and continued her meal in silence while Nicole, in contrast, had bombarded Elettra with questions. Elettra had tried to strike up a conversation with Dominique, but it had been impossible.

It didn't matter, anyway. With Lea and Nicole on either side of her, Dominique's icy welcome had been a minor concern, as had the burnt toast, because she had been given a greater gift than a good meal. After a year of silent suppers, Elettra had basked in the warmth of friendly conversation and felt joy at being around women so different from her in many ways, but also more similar than she could imagine.

After dinner Elettra had stayed to chat with Nicole. Dominique had gone back to her room as soon as they'd finished eating.

'It's nothing personal, that's just how she is,' Nicole had reassured Elettra, placing a hand on her shoulder to dispel any disappoint-ment: Dominique hadn't even turned round or responded when Elettra had wished her goodnight. Nicole picked up a cleaning cloth and slung it over her shoulder. 'If you want to go up and rest, go ahead. I need to take care of my weekly duties,' she'd explained, while leaving the table to fill a bucket with soapy water.

'What duties?' Elettra had asked.

'Cleaning,' Nicole had replied. 'We try to share out the chores at the convent so that life is easier for everyone, and it seems to work. But you should go to bed now. Really, you must be exhausted.'

Elettra remained stubbornly where she was; she didn't want the evening to come to an end so fast, not yet. 'I'm not that tired, I'll give you a hand,' she had said, picking up a broom. Together with Nicole she cleaned the whole room, then waited in the doorway until the floor was dry.

'Can I ask you something?' Elettra asked, leaning her chin on the broom handle.

'Of course.'

Elettra had taken a deep breath, looking her new friend in the eye. 'On my way here I noticed that this part of the island is almost uninhabited, apart from the convent and a small group of women dressed in mourning I met on the way, but I didn't see any houses.

Or men for that matter – there aren't many of them around here, are there?'

Nicole looked down. 'You're right, there are very few men on the island, but there haven't been any on this side of the island for almost two years.'

'Why?'

Nicole took a deep breath. Her small chest rose inside her pale blue dress, and Elettra was aware of a note of bitterness as it expanded. 'It's because of a tragedy that struck the island two years ago, a storm that killed many friends and loved ones. It took my husband away.'

'I'm sorry, I didn't mean to ... Truly, please forgive me,' Elettra had stammered, mortified by the shadow of pain that darkened Nicole's smile. But Nicole just shook her head, her smile still in place.

'Don't worry, you weren't to know. But that's why I live here,' she said, gazing around the room. 'Lea offered Dominique and me a home; Dominique's husband was at sea too that night, and when we lost everything nobody in town wanted anything to do with us. She saved us.'

'I don't understand: why wouldn't anyone in town want to help you? You'd just lost your husbands and your homes at the same time. Why would they push you away?'

'Because we're widows, and the islanders here consider it unacceptable for a woman to outlive her husband; here, widowhood is seen not just as a punishment of the soul but of the body. People avoid speaking to you unless they're widows too, and when you walk in the street they cross to the other side, as if losing the love of your life were contagious. All the other widows decided to shut themselves away in the loneliest and most forgotten part of the island. More than that, the people of the town hate Dominique and me because we have chosen, in some ways, to continue living.'

She'd shrugged her shoulders. 'As if Fabien's death wasn't difficult enough.'

Elettra had felt herself reel; she had not been ready for that kind of confession, and she was stunned to discover that someone so young had already known and lost the joys of married life. 'Were you very much in love?'

Nicole had sniffed. 'He was the one for me. More than a husband, he was my family and best friend all in one. He was my everything, and he was taken away.'

'I'm so sorry,' Elettra whispered quietly and put a hand on Nicole's arm. 'It must have been terrible for Dominique to experience a loss like this too.'

'I know; as you've seen for yourself, her personality is different from mine, she reacts to the pain with hardness, silence and work, but while I sometimes despair, I won't give in to other people's cruelty. That's why I thank heaven that I met Lea. She's different from the others; she's lived on the margins since she was a child. She's had her own struggle with the islanders and she's been ostracised for her own reasons. Because she's an orphan.'

'But why? Being an orphan isn't anyone's fault!' Elettra was starting to feel outraged.

'It is here, because we all belong to someone from the day we're born: first, we belong to our parents, and if we're women, once we're married, we belong to our husbands, so no one has forgiven her for her origins. Over the years she's had to put up with all kinds of gossip and nastiness about both her and her parents; there are those who even say that she's the daughter of one of the nuns. She knows what it means not to be accepted, and that's why she's made us welcome in her home.'

'Does the entire convent really belong to her?'

'Yes. But what about you, what brings you here? I mean, the convent's not exactly mentioned in the guidebooks they sell in town.'

'It's a long story,' Elettra said, not wanting to continue that line of conversation. She had a great deal of sympathy for Nicole, but in reality she had known her for less than three hours and it didn't feel right to open up about her mother. She had felt strange enough about telling Lea, but it had been different in that case. Elettra cleared her throat, determined to regain control of the conversation. 'But it's strange that an orphan should have enough money to buy a whole building like this.' She watched Nicole as she went back into the kitchen and started to arrange the chairs around the table.

'She bought the convent directly from the Roman Curia for half its worth, paying for it with money she'd been left by the nuns who raised her.'

'That seems like a very good deal, even though it's a costly investment,' Elettra had commented, looking up at the mildew stains on the ceiling and the spider webs that filled every corner. The building was in a terrible state, but a small part of her envied Lea. She would have needed a similar stroke of luck to save the bakery, perhaps only half the money needed to purchase the convent would have been enough, but destiny had turned its back on her. She'd tried to shake off those thoughts by asking Nicole what the usual rate was per night for a bed. Nicole stared at her, speechless for a moment.

'The price?' Nicole repeated, her doe eyes widening. 'I don't understand.'

'You mean that Lea really doesn't charge a single cent to stay the night here?'

'That's right. Neither Dominique nor I have ever paid her anything for her hospitality.'

Elettra couldn't believe it but almost smiled to herself; here was a woman whose business sense was even worse than her own. 'This place is huge; how does she pay for its upkeep if she doesn't charge rent?'

Nicole twisted the cloth in her hands, her gaze evasive. 'Until now we've managed to get by on exchanging fresh produce and things we've made, little things, but Lea has always refused to charge people money to stay here. She's very firm that she'd feel terrible if she did.' Nicole's voice had got lower, as if talking about money made her uncomfortable.

And therein lies the problem, Elettra had thought, turning to look at the wet patches on the floor; if Lea continued to offer hospitality in return for nothing more than a little help with the housework she would find herself in the same position as Elettra. Maybe Lea couldn't see it right now, but Elettra could. At least her mistakes had given her that insight.

At Lea's invitation, Elettra remained at the convent, in thrall to the traces of lemons and aniseed that drifted through every single room.

She couldn't explain it, but there was something magnetic about this group of women, this small female community; all of a sudden the crumbling plaster on the walls was no longer an alarming feature, and the low water pressure and the tiles missing from the roof had become details that could be overlooked. It took twice as long as normal to run a bath or do the laundry, but nothing could compete with the view of the bay, with the bright yellow of the lemons which grew on the terrace, or with the scent of laundry left to dry in the sun. And Elettra still needed to uncover the connection between her mother and this place, a connection that seemed to grow stronger and stronger, as each day she spent with the women passed.

Being here will do me good, she repeated to herself, putting her return ticket back amongst her papers. She was sure that her spirits were benefiting from the little kindnesses that Lea showed her each day, which included a glass of fresh goat's milk with her breakfast.

'I don't help out enough to be pampered like this,' she commented one morning while Lea was energetically beating an egg yolk and some sugar. Sometimes, if Elettra closed her eyes while Lea mixed the ingredients, she felt as if she could hear each grain of sugar crunch between the metal of the spoon and the ceramic bowl before sinking into the doughiness of the egg in a soft, swollen, velvety mixture. The addition of the coffee and the boiling milk was pure theatre; the egg yolk and the sugar seemed to open up, welcoming them with a creamy embrace.

The voice she had heard on the first night had fallen silent, and Elettra had settled on the fact that she had been disorientated, and probably filled with grief and fatigue on those first few days in the convent. Her mind had probably been playing tricks, and she was willing to dismiss it as a flight of fancy – for now, anyway. She had mentioned it to Lea and Nicole, but they just shrugged their shoulders and claimed, 'I didn't hear anything,' a phrase which was repeated numerous times during the early part of her stay.

There was still an uneasiness in Elettra when it came to their silences and their assurances that everything was normal. The more they evaded questions about the widows or the islanders, the more Elettra felt compelled to discover the reasons behind their behaviour. She could sense there was a story trapped within the convent walls, and her suspicions only grew when it came to Lea's murmured conversations with Nicole and Dominique, which would sometimes stop when Elettra entered a room. There wasn't any hostility involved, she certainly hadn't felt that, but rather a need to protect something. Elettra felt herself drawn to whatever it was.

Lea gathered the empty cups from the breakfast table as Elettra savoured the flavour of the bittersweet *caffellatte*. 'I'll have to polish the entire convent to work off all this sugar,' she joked.

After a few days inside the building, Elettra decided to venture outside with her chores, and try her hand working on the vegetable garden beside the convent, a plot partially cultivated by Dominique. She began to work beside Dominique, under her watchful eye, also in the hope of coaxing a few words from her ... her hope was in vain because Dominique always took care to maintain enough distance between them so as to prevent conversation.

Between arriving in the convent and settling in, while getting used to its rhythms, an idea had grown in Elettra's mind. She'd thought of some ways to bring in money for Lea and she wanted to try the ideas out on Dominique. She felt instinctively that Dominique was the person to talk to over Nicole, despite her initial reticence.

Elettra worked up the courage to approach Dominique and to finally ask a question, shading her eyes with her hand. 'Do Lea or Nicole help you in the garden from time to time?'

Dominique dug her hoe into the ground next to a bush and broke the earth before meeting Elettra with a sharp gaze. Her skin was tanned by long days in the sun, and she kept her lips determinedly closed. Dominique was unlike Nicole: there was not a hint of sweetness or candour in her, but something deeper and darker, like a rage, a grief, a mourning unexpressed that she had been unable to release.

Elettra continued about the matter at hand. 'I thought we could ask someone in town, or perhaps from one of the neighbouring islands if they would be prepared to do a few hours of labour in exchange for a share of the harvest, given the urgent repairs that need to be carried out.' She paused briefly to gauge the temperature of Dominique's response. Elettra was trying, she really wanted to make herself useful, but Dominique's lips remained sealed and motionless in the face of Elettra's enthusiasm. 'I think it's a good idea, don't you?' she pressed on in her attempt to coax an answer out of Dominique, but all she earned was a shrug.

'As you like,' Elettra finally gave up, rubbing her aching back. She promised herself to spend the afternoon on less demanding chores. She studied Dominique's profile carefully and guessed that, in spite of her impressive energy levels, she must be at least ten years older than her. Nobody either inside or outside the convent knew what was going on behind those troubled eyes. Pain and loneliness, that was what Elettra read in her face, in her calloused hands and in those robust silences, like boulders forming a wall that Dominique had built up between herself and the rest of the world.

This whole thing about the widows is absurd, Elettra thought at lunchtime, as she used her spoon to stir the colourless broth dotted with pieces of onion. Nicole had done her best, but surprisingly she was a near disaster in the kitchen.

'Would you like some more soup?' she offered, dipping the ladle into the broth, but Lea and Elettra shook their heads, exchanging a complicit glance.

'We decided a while ago to take month-long turns at cooking and cleaning to make life at the convent run more smoothly and it's currently Nicole's turn,' Lea explained while they waited for the potato gratin which their friend was spooning out of the pan. Elettra watched it slop onto the plates and instinctively wrinkled her nose. The potatoes were barely cooked, the cheese hadn't melted and the béchamel was like salty buttermilk, gathering in yellowing pools speckled with nutmeg.

'I could take care of the cooking,' Elettra offered once the dinner was over, laying her fork on her plate. 'I don't know how long I'll be staying yet, but I'd like to help out until I go. I'm not much good at manual tasks and I don't know anything about horticulture, but I'm pretty good in the kitchen. I ran a bakery until recently, so the least I can do to thank you is to cook for you. It would be my pleasure,' she added, one hand on her chest.

Cooking for Lea and the others would also leave her enough time to find out a little more about the convent and islanders. For now, Elettra was happy to not be desperately overwhelmed by thoughts of her unwell mother and not to have the urge for answers that had brought her here. She had faith that they would come in good time. What she needed to do was spend time with this community of women. Now the bakery had folded it was important for her to feel stable and useful and to spend a few days without thinking about her own problems.

Lea played with the edge of her plate while Elettra nervously twisted her napkin in her hands; she hated to feel like she was under scrutiny, but nothing made her feel more alive than the rush of adrenalin while she awaited the verdict. It had been like that when she had worked as a journalist and submitted her articles to the editor.

'Well?' she asked, tapping her toe against the table leg. 'What do you think of my taking over the cooking?'

Lea's eyes met hers and Elettra tried to read the answer she wanted to hear in them.

'I think that's a good idea,' Lea replied. 'As long as Nicole doesn't mind.'

'No, no, not at all,' Nicole said quickly. 'It's not something I enjoy very much.'

'Thank you,' Elettra murmured, happier than she had felt in a long time. Too long a time.

Once the table had been cleared, Elettra hurried into the larder; she wanted to make a list in a notebook of all the ingredients available to her and their quantities. She had just lifted a metal jar of cinnamon down from the shelf when she saw a dusty jar at the back. She reached out to lift it down but as soon as she caught sight of its rounded side and the label that had been stuck onto it her heart skipped a beat; on the side of the glass, behind strips of sellotape that protected the yellowed paper, was some decidedly familiar handwriting. She swallowed.

Her hands began to shake, and her heart started to race like mad.

'No,' she murmured, 'can't be.'

But it was, her eyes were not deceiving her; the old-fashioned handwriting with its elegant lines and curves was just like Edda's. The jar contained candied lemon peel and Elettra wondered what it signified.

But the more she looked at the yellowed paper, the firmer her conviction that it really *was* Edda's handwriting. It had to be hers. She could recognise this handwriting anywhere. Anywhere. She sighed, her hand gripping the dusty glass.

'Oh my God, Clara was right, and so was Lea: this place is magical,' she stammered, clutching the jar to her chest and reliving all the emotions she had experienced since crossing the convent's threshold, which had often been strong enough to make her doubt her own sanity. Ever since the very first time she met Lea, Elettra had felt surrounded by an unusual energy; it vibrated in the warmth of the walls' embrace, in the Saint's arms and in the shadows that the convent concealed behind heavy curtains and abrupt silences.

But this silence was more eloquent than any words could be.

The truth was there, before her very eyes; in the jar which she clutched in disbelief, in the confirmation of a strange feeling she'd had ever since she had first laid eyes on this building.

She placed her hand on the wall. 'Perhaps my mother has been here,' she murmured, euphoric and frightened at the same time. A clue, at last, that wasn't a voice in the darkness or a stranger in the waiting room of a hospital.

She gripped the handle of the lid tightly, but resisted the temptation to turn it and immerse herself in her mother's world. That very moment brought back memories of when Elettra was a child and Edda would entertain her by getting Elettra to identify spices based on their fragrance.

'If my mother has really been here, maybe even lived in this convent, I swear I'll find the answers that she denied me and that Clara promised. I'll rediscover my mother here, I can feel it,' she said, looking at the saucepans on hooks which hung from the wooden beam above her head.

Edda had always spoken to her through food, and Elettra had found her through food again. But to really find her here, Elettra would need to relate to this place in the same way that Edda had. She needed to weave the threads of their past back together again. She would need to connect with the island, filling her soul and her lungs with the perfumes and smells which Edda had once inhaled, to inhale them for herself, many years later, and dive into a new time, her mother's time.

'Here's to us, Mamma,' she said while the convent's rusty gate groaned on its hinges behind her.

The early afternoon air was still, but she didn't mind; these hours, the hottest ones, gave the countryside a unique heat and perfume. She needed to get out a bit, even just for a walk in an aimless direction after having made her discovery; and by venturing out in the quiet of the afternoon, Elettra felt like she could see the island at its most authentic, wild and uninhibited – perhaps just as her mother had seen it.

The land of the widows, she thought, searching the stony paths on the lookout for black silhouettes.

With her heart beating hard in her chest, she took the stone path in the opposite direction to the one that went down to the town. It was marked by the slow passage of the worn shoes of the women who lived there, hidden from the eyes of the community. In that part of the island there was nothing but chalky cliffs and the wreckage of old ships amongst the rocks.

Elettra saw a few wooden houses hidden amongst the pine-wood, but she didn't meet a single person along the way. 'A ghostly place to live,' she murmured, observing huge holes in the storm-damaged roofs and the crumbling tableau of a village that seemed to have been abandoned overnight.

Then she turned towards the sea, and that's where she saw him, the first man she had come across on this side of the island. Through the muggy afternoon haze she could see the bright outline of his shirt standing out against the seemingly endless backdrop. He was sitting on a rock waiting for a fish to take his bait, a pad of paper on his lap and a canteen of water by his side.

An artist, Elettra thought, as he held out his closed fist to take the measure of the countryside he was transferring onto his paper. She watched in amazement as he quickly scribbled down a tangle of charcoal lines. She couldn't help but notice he was rather good-looking, too, as his broad shoulders moved up and down, and his muscular arms emerged below his rolled-up sleeves. When she looked up to observe the stranger again, their eyes met. His were as dark as toasted hazelnuts and blond stubble speckled his well-defined features. It only lasted a moment, then Elettra stepped backwards, seeking shelter in the bushes. He had seen her and knew what she was doing. She was well aware that spying on a man was the sort of thing a teenager would do, but she had been unable to resist the temptation. She turned away, embarrassed.

A little while later, on her way back to the convent, she saw Dominique walking through the long grass carrying a pair of wooden boxes: beehives. Dominique wasn't wearing anything to protect her from the bees and she was whistling an old folk song that Elettra had often heard her own mother sing. Elettra could vaguely remember the words. As she pushed her way through the undergrowth to get back into the convent grounds, Dominique suddenly turned round to face her. Her whole body moved as if she was ready to run, but she quickly looked at Elettra with disapproval.

They exchanged just one brief look, but in that moment Elettra thought saw the trace of a tear running down Dominique's face.

6

A flash of silver crossed the dark sky, offering the stargazers a wish.

Sitting side by side on the terrace with Lea to enjoy the silence of the evening, Elettra had tied Edda's old shawl around her shoulders to stop herself shivering from the cold. It was nice to talk to Lea about her day, but what she most appreciated about her companion was the freedom to remain silent. With Lea she didn't need to fill empty silences with words, and although she couldn't explain why, they somehow seemed to understand one another; their bond was growing, although there were still some things that Lea was guarded about.

'Everything seems so poetic after the sun's set,' Elettra observed.

'Mmm, languid.'

Elettra nodded, delighted they were on the same wavelength. 'Exactly,' she agreed.

The night and the terrace seemed enchanted. It was just about possible to identify the horizon thanks to the huge shadow of the pinewood, but beyond that their eyes struggled to focus on anything except the bike lights belonging to the kids in town who were out in search of adventures – they danced in the darkness like fireflies. The wind carried the distant echoes of radios and the sounds of the simple, relaxed life of the port to them.

'There's something I wanted to ask you,' Elettra said, picking at the paint on the sun-scorched railing on the terrace.

Lea turned her head just slightly, still enraptured by the dazzling light of the stars. 'Yes?'

'You've always lived here, haven't you?'

Lea nodded. 'I was practically born in the convent.'

Elettra took the jar of candied peel out of her pocket and handed it to her. 'Do you know who wrote this label?'

Lea bent down to look at it. 'It seems very old, where did you find it?'

'In a corner of the larder when I was doing the inventory.'

'It must have been sitting there for a long while, then. It might have been before my time.'

'That's exactly what I'm trying to find out. You must know the history of the convent. It seems such a fascinating place; who knows how many stories there are about this building?' she said, staring dreamily at the moon, as Lea drew back a little. Elettra could sense a little tension in Lea's back and arms.

'Growing up between its walls doesn't make me the custodian of the convent's history,' she replied, but Elettra didn't let Lea's reticence stop her, and she took her hand to bridge the gap her friend had created between them.

'I'm only asking you for a little help, nothing more.'

Lea breathed loudly. 'I'm not sure why you're so interested in the history of this place. It's just an abandoned building.' Elettra sighed: Lea was avoiding her questions again, just as she had done when Elettra had first heard her mother's name called out in the courtyard of the convent. Elettra might now be more open to the idea of magic and the power of suggestion, but on this evening she was finding it hard to accept that hearing someone call her mother's name was a figment of her imagination. Since discovering the jar of candied lemon peel she had felt emboldened, and it had awoken a new sense of determination in her.

She turned the jar over in her hand; it was possible that thousands of people had handwriting like Edda's, but she was sure that this was something more. 'This handwriting is really similar to my mother's.'

Lea swallowed. 'I understand, but . . .' She stopped short and pushed herself away from the railing, a fleeting shadow in her eyes.

'Maybe I should ask Dominique, perhaps she knows something.'

'I doubt it. She hasn't lived here long, and that label looks very old. It's probably from just before the war, when the convent was still fully functioning. I'm sorry I can't help you.'

'Perhaps you could try and contact one of the nuns, one of the old sisters I read were transferred to the mainland.'

'Impossible,' Lea said brusquely.

'Why?'

'They died years ago. All of them.'

It was an unexpected blow that left Elettra stunned. It was a dead end, literally, the key to a safe that was already empty. 'Well, at least I tried,' she said despondently. 'It's strange, but sometimes I feel like she's with me, you know? My mother, I mean. It's as though she's here, right next to me.'

Lea turned round suddenly, a stray lock of hair falling across her face. 'Mothers are our real cornerstones, they represent the historical memories of our souls. I don't think there's anything more sacred than the love between a mother and her child.'

They were silent for a long time until the hooting of an owl caught Elettra's attention. 'There's something else I wanted to ask you,' she continued, turning to face Lea, who nodded at her to go ahead. 'Walking around the convent over the last few days I've noticed that a lot of the rooms seem to be closed up, an entire wing in fact, and I was wondering ... '

'What exactly do you want to know?' Lea interrupted her with a frown.

It was late at night and the only light was that from the sky, but Elettra could have sworn that there was something uncertain in her friend's look. Lea turned away from the view, folding her arms across her chest.

'Well, first that story about the voices ... '

'I told you, the wind here plays tricks on you.'

'I've tried to believe it, but it's just ridiculous,' replied Elettra, suddenly frustrated. 'What next, a ghost that haunts the convent? We're all a bit too old to believe in fairy stories.' She saw her friend's reaction and tried to change the mood, smiling lightly, to relieve some of the tension, but Lea just leaned forward and gripped the railing.

'The closed rooms need to stay that way; believe me, they really don't contain anything important. When the nuns still lived at the convent they were used as store rooms and archives, but then they were emptied and closed up. According to the elderly locals, the Nazis used them to interrogate and torture local partisans, and nobody wants to go anywhere with that history. They still hold a lot of pain.'

Elettra nodded, shaken by the incident of cruelty revealed by Lea's story. 'Okay,' she murmured as Lea turned to look at the horizon.

The mugginess of the last few days had been blown away by the mistral wind, which continued to blow above the choppy sea. It would continue for another three days; Elettra had now begun to understand the rhythms of the island. Lea continued to stare at the view. Something in her behaviour just didn't add up, but Elettra let it lie. She still wanted to ask about the jar of candied peel, but the questions stuck in her throat. She sensed she wasn't going to get much more out of Lea tonight and went back to her room to rest.

Elettra was woken in the middle of the night by a ruckus in the hallway, soon followed by footsteps in the corridor outside her room.

Her eyes flew open and she sat up; there was someone outside her door, but whoever it was had stopped at the first creak of Elettra's bedsprings. She cursed them silently and slowly freed her legs from the sheets; if she was careful enough, she could find out who was there. She crept across the room on bare feet, her breathing uneven and heart racing, and reached out to turn the door handle, but just as she did a small rectangle of paper slid through the gap between the door and the floor.

Elettra froze. A note had appeared at her feet. She knelt down to read the message.

Don't ask questions.

Elettra's heart thumped like mad.

What does this mean? she thought to herself, holding the paper between her fingertips. She found the courage within herself to shout out, 'Who's there?' but the person on the other side of the door, if anyone was there, didn't reply. Elettra refused to be scared and cowed, and grasped the handle and opened the door with a quick, decisive move. She was sure she would catch the messenger in the act, but there was nothing outside but darkness, and the shadowy tunnel of the corridor was silent, just as the note suggested she should be.

There was absolutely no sign of the messenger, who seemed to have been swallowed up by the darkness that now fell over Elettra's thoughts, too.

She closed the door and leaned her back against the wood.

Who wants me to keep silent? What kind of sick joke is this? Elettra thought. She felt more sure than ever there was a kind of mystery hidden between the walls, and if that was the case then someone clearly felt it needed to be protected by a threat. Elettra looked back down to the words written on the paper. She held the note to her chest. What is this place hiding, and how do I fit into it all?

These questions would keep her awake throughout the long wait until dawn.

7

Edda always said that there was a specific science to bad days: the air would become heavy when there was one on the way; the light would seem too bright and objects would start to give off signals warning you to keep away from them.

This had happened to Elettra ever since she was a small child, but she was reluctant to pay attention to the signs that morning. She had put bitter arbutus honey in Nicole's milk instead of asphodel honey and burnt Dominique's omelette while making breakfast, earning herself curious looks and whispers from the two women. Then, when she decided to pour the milk Lea had brought into a bottle, the boiling pan slipped out of her hand, resulting in a huge, sweet puddle on the floor.

'Today is not my day,' she grumbled, flinging a cloth onto the floor. The mysterious message, now hidden from prying eyes between the pages of the novel she had brought with her, was at the forefront of her mind. She had spent the entire night ruminating over those words, tossing and turning and worrying. Who had sent her that warning and why? Was it a threat? Along with the jar of candied lemon peel, this was evidence that something was going on. She wasn't going mad, and she'd made a decision not to be intimidated, either – whoever was behind this didn't scare her. Elettra had an instinct that confiding in Lea was useless given the way in which she avoided her questions, and the same was true of Nicole and Dominique, who didn't know anything about her mother. In fact, it was obvious that the history of the convent was a difficult subject for all the women who lived there; every attempt to raise the topic ended swiftly, either by being ignored or, worse, blocked.

It would be better if they just told me, Elettra thought, as she began to clean the kitchen. Then, when she went out to refill the bucket from the well she noticed that the door of the old chapel was open. She slipped inside, feeling the need to retreat from the whole world for a few moments, and the atmosphere of peaceful calm amongst the huddled pews of the small and now obsolete room seemed ideal. She tiptoed across the floor, her body gradually getting used to the coolness of the place, but all thoughts of composure disappeared immediately when she turned towards the altar: there was a man balanced precariously on a stepladder in front of the painting of the dying Christ, paintbrush in hand and his shirt speckled with paint. As far as she knew, no men lived on this side of the island so she was completely startled.

'Who are you?' she exclaimed. Her loud voice was amplified menacingly along the small aisles, scaring the man on the ladder, who wobbled dangerously before saving himself by grabbing hold of a pillar and pulling his weight back towards the wall.

'Who the hell are you?' he replied. When he turned round Elettra recognised him immediately. It was the artist she had seen on the cliffs. There was no way she could forget his eyes, even if she'd wanted to.

She didn't know what he was doing there, whether he had recognised her or what his link to the convent was, but despite the chaos in her mind, she couldn't move a single muscle. She remained motionless in the middle of the central aisle, her thoughts paralysed, before clenching her fists and regaining her combative manner. 'I'm a guest of Lea's, if you must know, but I'd like to know who authorised you to touch that painting,' she continued, pointing towards the artwork and ready for a confrontation.

'I'm here to restore it,' he replied. 'What's it got to do with you?'

'How do I know you're not vandalising it?' Elettra challenged. She realised she was really on edge, probably still from the night before.

'It's all right, Elettra,' a voice called out from by the chapel door. It was Nicole who had heard the exchange and had joined them. The man quickly jumped down from his ladder and exchanged a look with her. Nicole continued: 'Christ's face needed a bit of work. The salt in the air attacks the paint to the point of destroying it completely and he's the only one in the whole archipelago capable of doing such a delicate job.'

'Oh,' was all Elettra could say.

'I'm going to get some fresh air for a moment. If that's all right with you, of course,' he said, passing smoothly between them. He glanced quickly at Elettra, who saw no resentment, but more an air of amusement in his eyes. Irritated, she turned first towards Nicole, who remained where she stood in the middle of the chapel, then towards the sound of the footsteps that echoed off the walls.

'That's Adrian,' Nicole said. 'He can be a bit moody sometimes, but he's a nice guy once you get to know him. He helps us out a lot; he only moved to the island recently but he's become the local Mr Fixit. He makes a living from doing whatever odd jobs are going because, unfortunately, earning a living from fishing isn't exactly profitable,' Nicole told her. 'It takes effort, sacrifice and a good dose of luck, which few fishermen have,' she added. Elettra had stopped listening, struggling to take her eyes off the door through which he'd just walked out. His scent was still in the air, a mixture of white musk and the sea which had enchanted her.

She closed her eyes for a moment, trying to imprint the smell onto her memory; she liked it, it smelled of summer.

'Are you okay?' Nicole asked her after a while. She tapped the metal steps of the ladder with her index finger.

'I just came in here for a few minutes of quiet, but I didn't want to disturb anyone. I'll come back later when you've finished.' She said goodbye, remembering the bucket she had left by the door before she came in.

She went over to the well in the middle of the cloister where, with a few practised motions, she attached the bucket to the pulley and lowered it inside. She waited until she heard the impact of the bucket on the water, then began to pull on the rope, but raising a full bucket took more energy than she had. She pulled and pulled, her hands gripping the rope that rubbed against her palms, but all she did was make herself breathless.

'Do you need a hand?'

Elettra released her grip on the rope, which was caught just in time by the worn hands of the woman beside her.

'Slowly, my girl, I'm too old for tricks like that!' she protested, giving Elettra the rope back, impassive in the face of Elettra's gaze. Elettra was trying to remember the faces of those who had come to the convent to pay homage to the Saint over the past few weeks, but none of them matched the old woman's. She was around seventy, with a stocky figure and a severe expression that matched her steely character.

'Is Dominique here?' she asked in a hoarse voice.

Elettra secured the rope and turned to look at her, perplexed; she hadn't understood much of what the woman had said. The woman was speaking the island dialect, too quickly for her to follow.

'P-pardon?' she stammered, leaning towards the woman, who frowned impatiently.

'I asked you whether Dominique is in, I need to speak to her. Dom-in-ique, understand?' She spoke loudly as if she talking to an inattentive child, then, faced with Elettra's look of confusion, she took a deep breath and ran her hand through her silver-streaked hair, as if searching through the last shreds of her limited patience. 'You're a foreigner, right?' she asked, giving up on dialect, confident that she would get an answer this time.

'Exactly,' Elettra replied, relieved to understand at least one word. 'I've only lived here a fortnight or so, I'm not from the island. I'm from the continent, as you say around here,' she continued, looking towards the coast, as though there were an imaginary border in the sea which separated these two realities, dividing places and people.

The woman nodded, bending down to pick her basket up from the ground. 'You must be Elettra, then,' she said, studying her out of the corner of her eye to see if she could confirm any of the stories she'd heard about her, while wiping her hands on her sun-bleached skirt. 'I'm Isabelle Fouchet, the island's midwife and an old friend of Lea's.' She shook her hand with more force than Elettra had expected from a woman her age, continuing to stare at her unperturbed. Isabelle looked at her as if she saw or recognised something suspicious in her, but Elettra was sure that she wasn't as surly as her severe expression suggested. There was warmth in her gaze, and an aroma of violets floated around her imposing figure.

Isabelle continued before she had a chance to say anything. 'Right; now that we've introduced ourselves, could you answer my question, please?'

'I think you'll find her in the vegetable garden,' Elettra replied. 'In any case, be careful when you go and look for her. She's set up some beehives around the edges, and the bees might sting you,' she warned. But Isabelle had already started walking before Elettra could finish speaking, heading towards the garden with the heavy steps and curved back of old age. 'How bizarre,' Elettra thought as Isabelle pushed her way through the weeds.

As she watched the woman walk away, she chewed her lip and thought: if Isabelle's the island's midwife, she must know a lot about its history. I could ask her a few questions about my mother. Then she thought about the note, the threat. She had been told to keep silent and to preserve the secrets that someone was determined to protect. But the morning wasn't even over yet and the island was already revealing more of itself and its inhabitants.

It had been a surprising morning and at lunch Elettra decided to ask Lea about Isabelle and her role, despite not getting her hopes up with the expectation of any concrete answers.

'What do you want me to tell you? Isabelle has always lived here, ever since I was born,' Lea had commented, stirring her spoon through her soup.

'Then do you think she might have known my mother, might be able to tell me something about her and her life at the convent, assuming she really lived here?'

Lea nodded, breaking her bread into pieces with impatient movements. 'But first you need to find out whether Edda actually set foot on this island ... I wouldn't be too sure. Even if Isabelle did know her, I don't think that she'd remember her. I love Isabelle, and she's the closest thing to a mother I've ever had, but because I know her so well I should warn you that her memory's starting to go, and even her remaining recollections aren't as reliable as they were. I wouldn't believe everything she says, if I were you,' she said, stopping short, breaking the bread into crumbs before letting it fall onto her plate.

The wall had risen up before Elettra's helpless eyes yet again. She had learned that there was no point persevering.

After lunch, Elettra was feeling restless again. The island had seemed to open itself up to her a bit more today, and she was curious as to where else it might let her in a little – it was clear that no new information was going to come from Lea. She went for a walk towards the small village not far from the convent. Seen from a distance, it was little more than a handful of houses clustered around the church which overlooked the bay beside it. The remains of a religious devotion eroded by the sea, thought Elettra, as she approached the majestic wooden door of the church, finely sculpted by local artisans, and saw the paint peeling from the walls in big white flakes.

She had thought hard about who might have a knowledge of the island's history, who else might have been here as long as the nuns who had all now gone? The answer lay in the parish priest. Perhaps he knew something about Edda; in small places like Titan, the religious authorities often served as the community's memory.

With her heart pounding in her chest, Elettra pushed open the huge door with all her might, and glanced around the interior of the cool, quiet church. There, in front of the altar, was a man in his thirties wearing a long black cassock with a milk-white collar hiding a scar on his neck.

He turned round. 'Can I help you, *signorina*?'

Elettra looked at his face. With his light colouring – reddish beard and pale skin – the parish priest looked like he could have arrived on Titan's Island just a few days ago. All her hopes seemed destined to drown in the young man's curious gaze, but she decided to try anyway.

You're here anyway, so at least try and ask about his predecessor, she told herself with little conviction, but she was soon prevented by the arrival of an elderly woman, probably the priest's housekeeper. Elettra had seen her only once before, briefly at the convent; she had been bringing flowers for the Saint and she had spent almost two hours in the chapel before their paths had crossed again in the cloister. Now, Elettra remembered picking up the handkerchief she had dropped on the floor and giving it back to her, and that the woman had taken it and walked stiffly away without even deigning to thank her.

Elettra felt a wave of hesitation as soon as their eyes met; the housekeeper spared her a single glance, just enough to acknowledge who she was, but Elettra could see a palpable hostility there. 'We should go, *mon père*, it's the postman's widow's funeral and we still need to arrange the schedule for visiting the sickly. Rosa needs extreme unction, the family have asked for you twice already since this morning.' She spoke to the man, turning her back on Elettra as though she wasn't standing in the church too.

Elettra wasn't prepared to accept such treatment passively. 'Excuse me, *mon père*, could you tell me how I can get in touch with your predecessor, please? Does he live here?' she asked, closing the gap between them created by the woman, who glared.

'He's in Paris, if you really must know. At the bedside of his seriously ill sister,' the woman replied on the curate's behalf.

Elettra ignored her and continued speaking directly to the priest: 'Do you know if there's any way of getting in touch with him. It's just I—'

The woman interrupted her. 'Nobody with the slightest bit of conscience or intelligence would dream of disturbing him at such a difficult time.'

Another wall. That was what Elettra saw in the housekeeper's

65

words, in her rigidly straight back, in her two small hands balled into fists. She was not welcome, and her questions even less so.

She swallowed her frustration and smiled at the priest who seemed relieved, as though the woman had somehow saved him from an awkward situation.

'Thank you so much for your time, *mon père*, have a good day.' With that, she took her leave.

Elettra followed the winding street and had no trouble locating the local bar and tobacconist; the only place with a public telephone, it wasn't far from the church and, like any other local bar, she found a group of men gathered outside the door, each with a glass of wine and an easy smile. They froze on her arrival, apart from a man with a green apron tied around his waist – presumably the owner – who continued puffing on his cigarette as though nothing had changed.

'Can I come in?' Elettra asked. The bar was dark and contained old wooden tables and stools and a bar full of half-full bottles.

There was no reply.

She cleared her throat and repeated the question more loudly, but the closer she got to the bar the more suffocating the combined smell of tobacco and wine became. She swallowed a mouthful of smoke and put her hand to her throat, and then she walked right into the back of the bar. 'Is anyone there?' she asked impatiently.

A crash of breaking plates broke the silence, and a breathless young woman emerged from the door that led to the kitchen. She had a pale face and a fringe that covered her forehead and her eyes remained resolutely fixed on the floor tiles.

'I'm sorry to have made you rush, but I thought—' Elettra said.

'How can I help you?' the woman interrupted her, the words stumbling out before Elettra could finish.

Elettra stiffened, her hands gripping her bag; there was something about this situation that made her feel uneasy. The bar owner outside had barely looked at her, and the woman who'd had to take his place at the bar seemed a bundle of nerves, her hands moving all over the place and her lowered gaze flickering towards the door at regular intervals. Elettra guessed she must be afraid of being told off by the owner for the broken plates, or perhaps she was just inexperienced, but, whatever the reason for her behaviour, she seemed determined not to draw any more unfavourable attention to herself.

'A *caffè freddo*, please,' Elettra asked, noticing a jug of ice next to a teapot as she looked for the telephone. She spotted it at the end of the room on the right, beside the toilet, which had an 'out of order' sign hanging from the door handle. 'Do you mind if I use the telephone?' she asked, gesturing to the corner of the bar while the woman stood with her arms wrapped tightly around herself, staring from under dark eyelashes. She didn't utter a word, just nodded her assent.

It was a brief call to Ruth, just long enough for Elettra to reassure herself that Edda was OK and that her best friend hadn't forgotten her.

'Your letters only arrived yesterday, all at once; you know what the post is like,' Ruth apologised, before Elettra stunned her by announcing the extension of her holiday. Silence. Elettra stared at an advert for a miraculous anti-wrinkle cream on the wall in front of her. 'What do you mean you're staying longer? I don't understand, when you left I thought you were only planning to stay for a couple of weeks.'

'I know, but so much has been going on,' Elettra said. She gripped the handset, scanning the room out of the corner of her eye; she didn't want anyone listening in. She took a deep breath, imagining Ruth's foot tapping impatiently. 'The fact is, there's something special about this place, I don't know how to explain it to you,' she continued quietly. 'I feel closer to my mother here than I ever did sitting next to her in the hospital for all those months;

67

it's like I can live her, breathe her in the air; I feel like I can finally clear things up and find the answers she's refused me all my life.'

'Have you gone mad, Elettra? What do you mean you feel close to your mother, what's Edda got to do with this mysterious convent?' Ruth went on the attack a little. 'And what's all this destiny nonsense, is it some kind of spiritual revelation? Please, don't be so ridiculous, Edda needs you here, stop running away from her.'

Elettra sighed. She couldn't mention the candied lemon peel or the warning note to Ruth; with her hyper-rationality there was no way she would understand something Elettra herself struggled to explain, but did exist and was real.

'I'm not running away, we've already talked about this,' she countered, but it was all she had time to say before the call was cut off, leaving her with the sound of the monotonous dialling tone. She rummaged in her pockets in search of more coins, but she barely had enough to pay for her drink. Defeated, she replaced the handset and went back to the bar where her coffee was waiting.

'Here you go,' the woman said, pushing the cup and saucer towards Elettra, who looked at her in surprise. She hadn't heard the woman moving about or the sound of a coffee machine, so she'd imagined she must have forgotten her order, but here it was, waiting for her, filling the room with the powerful aroma of roasted coffee beans.

Elettra let the strong, creamy liquid slide over her tongue. 'This is the best *caffè freddo* I've had in years,' she said appreciatively, raising her empty glass, coaxing a smile from the woman. She slowly ran her finger around the damp rim of the glass and looked up at the woman on the other side of the bar. Elettra saw a melancholy but beautiful face hidden behind the stained apron and the frizzy hair; her eyes were the colour of chocolate and so languid and intense that they seemed to be unusually expressive – but suffocated by that reverential expression; eyes hidden by long dark lashes.

'Do you know if there's a bakery near here?' Elettra asked her.

'No, there's not,' the woman replied curtly, but when she saw Elettra's quizzical look she bit her lip. 'The bread arrives every morning from the nearest island, there's a little bakery there,' she added, tapping the buttons on the till. She gave Elettra the bill and started wiping the bar again; it was as if she wasn't expecting conversation and didn't seem keen to encourage one.

But Elettra drummed her fingers on the wooden bar. 'So there's only a morning delivery each day?'

'Unless you take a boat and go and buy it yourself.'

'I'm not from the island, I'm staying at the convent.'

An unexpected sparkle lit up the woman's face, colouring it with sweetness. 'You're lodging at Saint Elizabeth's convent?'

'Yes, I have been for a while now,' Elettra replied, starting an unexpected chat with the woman, who she learned was Sabine, the wife of the bar owner who had stayed outside to drink with his friends. She'd hit upon some common ground by chance: just mentioning Lea's name was enough to get the woman to open up.

'You know Lea pretty well, don't you?' Elettra asked her, trying to find a crack in the island's wall.

'Yes, of course, poor Lea.' Sabine nodded. 'If I think about the things they say about her ... The gossips say she must have got a discount on the price of the convent because the Curia wanted to buy her silence,' she told Elettra, pouring her a second cup of coffee. 'It's on me,' she said, ignoring Elettra's raised hand. Her curiosity piqued, Elettra pulled up a stool. 'Her silence? Why?' she asked, making herself comfortable.

Sabine gave her a quick glance. 'It's a long story, and by no means a happy one.'

'I've got all the time in the world,' Elettra replied, 'and I might roast to death if I go outside,' she joked, looking towards the door.

Sabine held back a calm smile and arranged the tea towel over her shoulder as bursts of laughter drifted in from outside. 'Lea has never had a happy life, never. She's been an orphan since birth, the poor thing. The nuns raised her, but the convent began to empty after the war and when even the few remaining nuns left a few years ago, the Curia put the building up for sale and Lea bought it with the money the sisters had left her.'

'Yes, that's what Nicole told me.'

'But it didn't end there,' she added. 'Lots of people around here think that Lea is the daughter of the last abbess, and that's why they accused her of taking advantage of a special price to buy the building, but I've never believed that story. She's just an unlucky girl who's never had any family to rely on apart from a small group of nuns; it's cruel to talk about her like that.'

Elettra pushed back her hair, which had gone limp from the humidity, and took a deep breath. 'Perhaps it's jealousy rather than cruelty, but, to be honest, I'm not sure there's much to envy. It's hard work to keep a place like that going,' she replied, as Sabine sighed bitterly.

'You're right; it's a miracle it's still standing. It hasn't been restored for years.'

Elettra straightened up on her stool. 'I heard the Germans used it as a place for torturing prisoners,' she said, but Sabine shook her head.

'You're wrong; not a single German crossed the convent threshold, the island's Resistance went to great efforts to protect the Saint,' she said.

'I see.' Elettra nodded with a strained smile. Lea had lied to her; Sabine's words had turned a suspicion into a fact, but Elettra didn't understand why Lea had done it, what she needed to protect. 'Tell me more about the story of the abbess,' she asked.

Sabine frowned, surprised by the interest that story had aroused in the young stranger. 'It's just a legend. Some say the abbess is the last nun still alive and that she's hidden in a secret room, others claim she's an extremely beautiful woman who made a pact with the devil to gain immortality, and others still that she died many years ago and that her spirit wanders the abandoned rooms of the convent. It's a shame, though, that nobody's ever seen her. I don't know what she looks like, even though I was born and raised on this island.'

A bell rang somewhere out in the street, but neither of them paid it any attention.

'There's one thing I don't understand, though,' Elettra continued quickly, 'how is it possible that nobody's ever seen the abbess? I didn't think the convent belonged to a closed order.'

'You're right, but the last abbess was never seen in public; she didn't even take part in the festival of the Saint during her tenure. She always lived shut up in the convent.'

Elettra licked her lips, ready to ask further questions, but she fell silent when she saw the owner come in with a couple of empty bottles and signal to his wife to hand him some more. The air suddenly seemed to thicken and Sabine's behaviour changed radically; her voice became little more than a whisper and her shoulders were so hunched that Elettra had the impression she wanted to curl in on herself. She waited motionless until the man left them alone again, then returned to her enquiries.

'But why did she shut herself up in the convent?'

'Nobody knows,' Sabine replied. 'Then time passed and the convent gradually emptied, until Lea became the owner. And we all know what happened next.'

Elettra's whole body leaned towards the woman. 'What?'

'A storm,' Sabine replied tersely. She turned reluctantly to face Elettra, continuing in spite of what was clearly a desire to forget. 'The night that changed the face of the island. It's a terrible story. Awful. One second—' She stopped short, disappearing into the back, returning quickly with a crate of beer. 'Two years ago the island was struck by a terrible storm, the worst it's ever experienced. The fishermen's village on the other side of the hill was washed away and so were all the men who'd gone out fishing. Like I said, it was truly awful.' Her hands shook and her breathing was faster, as if she could still hear the raging sea in her ears.

She picked up one of the bottles, glanced towards the door and pressed it to her chest, hugging it as if it were a newborn. 'It was January and it was devilishly cold. To be honest, I can't remember much about that afternoon, just that the sky suddenly turned black and then there was a wall of water,' she told Elettra in a shaky voice. 'It was everywhere, in the houses, in the streets, in the fields. I did nothing but empty buckets of water out of the cellar; it was so freezing cold my hands were red and swollen, but every time I went up the stairs I knew that worse was waiting for me outside when I opened the door. Every time I poked my head out of the door I felt the mixture of wind and water snatch at my face and hands, it was impossible to do anything.'

She held her hands against her face, her gaze absent, distant. 'I couldn't even keep my eyes open, so I shut myself up in the house. My husband Gustave, on the other hand, was determined to open the bar that evening. He said nobody would be alone out of choice during a storm like that, and he was right. Soon half the islanders were in here.'

Sabine told her story in a detached manner, as if those memories belonged to someone else, yet Elettra could still feel the cold trapped in her words, in the fingers she frenetically twisted together.

'Night fell early that evening, it was soon dark. I remember that almost as well as the sea, which grew rougher and whiter as it pounded against the shore. We're lucky on this part of the island because the port and the bay protect us from the biggest storm surges, but God knows what happens on the other side of the Titan; that's the most exposed area, where the currents are always very strong. But it's just there, in that cursed patch of sea, where there are the most fish to be found, and that's where the fishermen always used to go. They'd set off in high spirits that morning, guessing how much they would earn from their catches, but not a single one of them returned. There was no trace of them, not even a piece of wood or a broken net.'

Sabine's eyes were devoid of any light; they had seen too much horror, too many of other people's tears to shed any more. 'We were all in the bar when the mayor, Vincent Leroux, arrived. Some of the fishermen's wives had crossed the island on foot in spite of the storm, looking for news; they had arrived with sodden clothes and their hearts on their sleeves, but their prayers were worthless. Just after midnight the authorities told the mayor they'd given up the search; they explained that it had been too long since there'd been any sign of the fishermen and, with a storm like that still raging, continuing would have meant putting the rescuers at serious risk, too.' She rubbed her arms, the memory of that dark night still in her eyes.

'Vincent, the mayor, came in through that door, I remember it as if it were yesterday. His face was dark and his hands shook as he clutched the bulletin from the coastguard. He pushed his way through the people until he reached the middle of the room, then he began to read. He read and reread the message aloud several times, so even those sitting right at the back could hear him, but none of us understood what he was saying; we all just stared at him blankly, some clasping rosary beads in their hands, others gripping bottles of wine. But then we understood, and how we understood! It all became clear the next day, when the sun rose above the debris on the other side of the Titan. There were entire families where only the women had survived.'

Elettra learned that in just a few hours the storm had redesigned the geography of a land which had been robbed of an entire generation of men. Sabine told her about women who'd wandered the streets of the island in search of shelter and their missing husbands. Many of them, including Dominique and Nicole, had found themselves at the bar a few hours later, their faces soaking and their souls broken. Their hair was dirty with mud and their clothes were weighed down by fragments of the homes the wind had blown away, of a life that had been torn away. Their eyes were empty, their lips open but utterly unable to give voice to the horror into which their existence had sunk.

'In town everyone started to call them "the widows of the sea", but their presence was a thorn in the side of the island's memory. It was such a painful time that no one wanted to be reminded of it. It's sad that human beings react that way but there's nothing you can do to change it. So some of the women went back to the ruins of the houses knocked down by the storm: in one sense they had to, because nobody here could look them in the eye without feeling pain and heartbreak. And that's also why they won't accept Nicole and Dominique – they didn't go back to their houses, but simply chose another way of living.'

Elettra rubbed her forehead, amazed. 'This is all ridiculous,' she exclaimed. 'Surely the most difficult times are when a sense of community should be felt most strongly?'

Another voice suddenly rang out from beside the front door. 'A sense of community with those savages, you mean? Believe me, it's impossible.' Elettra turned round as the woman continued. 'And it's obvious that nobody wants to have anything to do with that gaggle of no-hopers, given their behaviour.' The woman started to walk towards the bar, her designer heels clipping across the dark floor, which was dirty with dust and saltwater; above her heels were two stocky legs whose imperfections were only half hidden by a

74

knee-length pastel skirt. The woman quickly checked the state of her hair in the mirror behind the bar, and a powerful odour of hairspray combined with rose water filled the room with a nauseating femininity. She had the innocuous appearance of a fifties housewife, dressed in pale colours with a pearl necklace hanging off her slim neck, but Elettra felt an impulsive dislike for her sharp eyes, which were expertly softened with a peach-coloured eyeshadow.

The woman opened the clasp of her Chanel handbag, barely sparing a glance for Elettra, who was sitting on the neighbouring stool. 'Cigars for my husband, Sabine. Immediately,' she ordered, her index finger in the air, further studying her reflection in the mirror. She continued to ignore Elettra, only turning to face her when she heard her sneeze loudly.

'Excuse me,' Elettra stammered, her nose buried in a tissue, while the other woman ran her fingers around her necklace, 'strong fragrances always have this effect on me.'

'Oh, really?' the woman replied, looking her up and down, without smiling.

'Here are the cigars for Monsieur Leroux,' Sabine said, handing the woman a dark box.

'Thank you, my dear, but go and get another packet; we're expecting guests this evening, we need to celebrate,' she added, tapping the toe of her shoe on the floor while she waited for Sabine to come back with a second packet. Beside her Elettra kept her gaze fixed on the grainy residue of her coffee, unsure about engaging with this woman.

'Things will be changing soon, in any case,' the woman announced to Sabine, her chest swelling, as Sabine listened to her with her hands tight and her back as rigid as a soldier's. 'Soon the convent will no longer be a refuge for no-hopers and this island will finally be able to put the past behind it. This whole saga needs to come to an end and Lea needs to accept that. Everyone knows that she hasn't kept her promises about maintaining the building and the Saint in good condition, so she can pack her bags, too. This time my husband is fully within his rights to throw her out,' she continued loudly, so Elettra could hear her too. She stood with her handbag pressed against her generous bosom and when she turned to go soon after, gave Elettra only a quick glance. 'Goodbye,' she cooed on her way to the door, disappearing into the bright light of the afternoon.

Elettra waited until she heard the woman's smooth voice saying farewell to Gustave, who was still outside with his friends, then, preoccupied, she immediately turned to the barmaid. 'Who was that?'

Sabine tucked a lock of hair behind her ear. 'Sylvie Leroux, the mayor's wife. She's the most powerful person on the island. Even more powerful than the mayor and the priest combined.'

'She dresses like she's just stepped out of a magazine from the fifties – she doesn't look that cunning and evil!'

Sabine smiled and came around the bar to close the door Sylvie had left open. 'So you wouldn't believe me if I told you that she was the one who had the priest replaced a few months ago? It seems that old priest's sermons about brotherhood and his unwillingness to take the mayor's side in the business with the convent cost him his position,' she added, tipping the dregs of a bottle down the sink.

Elettra was shocked as the real picture came into focus; according to Sabine the mayor's wife was an extremely influential woman. Lea was at risk of losing the only home she'd ever known to the caprice of a bored rich woman. She jumped off her stool and snatched her bag up from the bar, waving goodbye to Sabine. She needed to get back to the convent, and quickly.

8

It had taken Elettra less than a second to decide whose side she was on, her instincts left her in no doubt. A voice from within urged her to defend Lea and the others, rebelling against a situation similar to the one which had cost her her own future just a few weeks ago. She hadn't had a choice about closing the bakery – the money had run out and the competition was ruthless – but it was different for Lea; she could still fight. Even if she had lied to Elettra, even if she continued to avoid her questions, it didn't matter.

It didn't matter because in spite of everything that may have happened between them, silences included, there was something powerful and mysterious connecting them.

Elettra clenched her fists and took a deep breath, running up the path that led back to the convent.

There was barely any air left in her lungs by the time she reached the gates, but she froze on the threshold when she saw Lea arguing with a middle-aged man who was menacingly brandishing a fistful of papers.

'You won't get away with this much longer, *signorina*, you can be sure of that!' he shouted, red in the face. He had just walked out into the small piazza in front of the gates and was wiping his bald head with a tissue when Lea emerged from the shadows. Her normally perfect hair was in a static cloud around her shoulders and her pale skin had turned an unhealthy red. She was unrecognisable, her face distorted with anger.

'You can't do anything to me. The convent is mine, I bought it with my own money, and you will never take it away from me, never!' she screamed at the top of her voice, her arms stretched out to point at the walls around them. 'This is my home, get that into your head for once and for all, and leave me alone!' she thundered.

An amused smile was visible beneath the dark hair of the man's moustache, as he waved the roll of paperwork at Lea.

'We'll see who comes out of this on top, we'll see!' he repeated, retreating to the car parked by the gate, which he drove away at top speed.

Elettra brushed herself clean of the dirt cloud the man's hurried exit from the scene had generated and went over to Lea, wrapping her in a hug; her friend was panting heavily, like an animal exhausted from a fight.

'Who was that?' she asked, nodding at the departing trail of reddish dust the car had left behind.

'Vincent Leroux, the mayor; the biggest snake on the whole island. Excuse me, Elettra, I need to be alone,' Lea replied, walking quickly away.

'Incredible,' said Elettra, shaking her head. Undeterred, she followed Lea inside and headed for the only place she was sure to find her: the kitchen, surrounded by bags of dried herbs and infusions to calm her nerves.

She made her way through the scents of dog rose, orange blossom and chamomile and stopped opposite Lea on the other side of the table. 'Sit down,' she said seriously, 'we need to talk.'

She told her about meeting Sabine and Sylvie's plans for the convent, but Lea wasn't prepared to hear the truth from her friend. Elettra had had no idea that Lea's financial situation was verging on poverty.

Lea drank her boiling tisane in big sips, while Elettra tried to reorder her thoughts and concluded, 'What I don't understand is why they're so very determined; why are the mayor and his wife so attached to the convent – what does it mean to them?'

She kept asking, but Lea never gave her a clear answer; each time she would end up staring bright-eyed at the table, her fingers covering her flushed cheeks as she fled from who-knew-what terrible vision. Elettra reached out her hand towards Lea, just as Lea had reached out to her when she had arrived on the island with dozens of questions in her head. But the warrior who had just confronted the mayor seemed to have turned into a defenceless puppy. A person who needed protecting, whom Elettra swore to herself she would defend at all costs; it was unusual for her, but all it had taken was a look, just one look.

'I want to help you, Lea, but you have to let me,' Elettra murmured, searching her friend's blue eyes, but seeing only the same dark shadow on Lea's face that she still saw on her own when she looked in the mirror each day, and then she understood. They were both suffering the same illness, but she had decided to overcome it – that was the point of her journey.

'Why does the mayor want to throw you out of the convent? And, more importantly, why does he say he can?' she repeated slowly, but firmly, while Lea looked at her with her shoulders hunched as if to protect her secrets. She tried to escape, but Elettra's gaze continued to follow her wherever she tried to hide. She was trapped.

'There's a clause in the contract for the sale of the convent: the buyer has to commit to taking care of the structure, otherwise the building will pass to the ownership of the commune which can then hold an auction to sell it. And Leroux knows this only too well.'

Elettra's fist clenched in the pocket of her dress. 'What a bastard. I bet he was the first to sniff that out; he'd love to see you in trouble.'

'That's for sure, but also because he wants to gain control of the convent to turn it into a luxury hotel with a golf course attached,' she confessed, 'and he would relocate the Saint. Hundreds of years of tradition just gone like that.'

'What do you mean? Surely Leroux can't touch the statue without the permission of the Curia?'

Lea sighed. 'It's a very complex situation, Elettra, but Leroux knows the right people to have the Saint moved if she were to become an obstacle to the realisation of his plans. And believe me, he'd do it. After all, this convent is deconsecrated now; nobody's come here to celebrate Mass in years and the women who come here to pray only do so because they have a connection to this place, to the Saint herself. He's already decided to put the Saint in the church in town, uprooting her from the place she's always stood, from her sea. From us. From me,' she finished, her eyes clouded and her voice spent.

Elettra stared at Lea, incredulous. 'But there must be a way out of this,' she began tentatively, 'and are we completely sure that Leroux wants to go that far, as far as moving the patron saint of the island from her historic home?' she continued with Lea's eyes on her all the while, as heavy as clouds before rainfall.

'You don't know him, you don't know what he's capable of. I've discovered that he's already come to an agreement with a businessman from Paris. It's a done deal; as soon as that man sets foot on the island, he'll destroy everything this place represents: its history, its traditions, everything. And all with the support of the mayor, obviously.'

Elettra nodded, making a mental note of this new information. Everything was taking on a new significance. 'Right,' she agreed, 'the mayor is a despicable person; but why are you so sure this plan of his isn't just hearsay or gossip? How did you find out about it?'

'Isabelle isn't a gossip,' Lea replied, gripping her empty cup. 'I trust her absolutely and if she says the mayor is in cahoots with that man then he is,' she said.

Elettra sat back in her chair. Property speculation and corruption; she finally understood the manoeuvres to marginalise Lea and the widows, to force them to leave. The mayor needed a clear field for his dealings and Lea was an obstacle in his way. Lea explained that in order to free himself of her and get his hands on the convent he had proposed to move her to a house on the edge of town; it had a vegetable garden and was near the sea, everything she might need was close at hand, but Lea had been unmoveable. She would never leave the convent, but when she showed Elettra the accounts book – the same exercise book that Elettra had seen her leafing through despairingly on several evenings – it became blindingly clear that, as things stood, she couldn't hold out for long. And that was without the fact that winter was nearly upon them and there were still a number of repairs to complete.

'There's one more thing,' Lea said. 'Now even the payments from a mysterious benefactor that have been arriving for years have stopped.'

'What payments?' Elettra's ears had immediately pricked up with curiosity.

Lea got up and took a metal box down from the sideboard, the kind that locked with a key. She turned the accounts book so it was facing Elettra and removed dozens of yellowing photocopies from the box.

'Look, here,' she replied, fanning the pages across the table. 'For years this person with an indecipherable signature has been sending this money, always the same sum. I'd receive their payment at the end of every summer, and it would be enough to get through the winter, but the payments stopped last year. I don't know what can have happened, or who this benefactor was; perhaps they died, or perhaps they just decided to stop making donations. In any case, I've had to do without their support since then, but I won't pretend that money didn't keep me going. I used it to pay for the heating, but now ... ' She stretched out her arms in a shrug, while Elettra, paralysed, stared at the photocopy of one of the payment notices.

'It's not possible,' Elettra stammered.

'What's not possible?'

Elettra swallowed slowly, her heart beating like a drum. She knew that signature; even though it was almost illegible, she knew it very well; she had filled entire pages of her diary with that name during her school years, and since the day of the accident she'd had to sign it on the rent contract for the bakery, on everything, while she waited for the courts to name her as legal owner.

And now the same signature was popping up in a convent hundreds of kilometres from their home, where she had lived a happy life. There had been a secret or two, of course, like any other family, but now Elettra was opening chasms at every step which were taking her back to a past which Edda had never wanted to share with her.

She refolded the photocopy of the document and gave it back to Lea, who was watching her in silence. Thoughts were whirling around in Elettra's head at a thousand kilometres an hour, flashbacks and images of a distorted past and the way it would affect her present; she struggled to recognise herself in all of it.

'My mother is the convent's mysterious benefactor,' she told Lea gloomily. 'It may be illegible, but it's her signature on the documents. There's no doubt about it,' she said quietly.

Lea shook her head. 'It can't be,' she said.

Elettra went quiet for some time and then spoke. 'I set off on this journey in search of my past because I was told that I would find all the answers I've always been denied here; I was told there was a link between my mother and this place, and that link was already becoming more apparent to me every day; she's always been devoted to the Saint and there were other signs. And now these payments . . . ' She fell silent again.

Her thoughts then turned to the threatening note. She couldn't mention it to Lea, who was already in enough of a mess, so she decided to keep it to herself for now.

'I'm sorry, Elettra; I really don't know anything about this,' Lea told her again. She slumped into a seat, her eyes flitting around the room, unable to settle on her friend. 'I had no idea that your mother . . . that you . . . oh, God, I don't even know what I'm trying to say.'

'That's simply because there's not much to say,' Elettra replied, looking down into her empty hands. 'My mother kept me completely in the dark about this. Don't you think that's strange?'

'Very,' Lea agreed, chewing on her nail as Elettra became lost in memory, in the tangles of an unravelling past.

'The name of the island didn't really mean anything to me, and I couldn't understand why that woman, Clara, had told me to come here in particular, but I just felt compelled, like a magnet. So I took a risk and set off, and now look at me, in this place that is full of my mother, her cooking, a history I wanted to discover . . . I would never have imagined my mother had secretly taken it upon herself to support the convent for years even after she'd left it, even if she did grow up here. And it's even more of a surprise that she would have kept it secret from me.'

'Elettra, I don't think she wanted to . . . ' Lea began, but was interrupted.

'I would never have opposed her wish to make herself useful, to help you. Never, believe me. But as her daughter, don't you think I should at least have been told? I'm blood of her blood, but she preferred to keep me completely out of it, as if I were too stupid to understand.' Elettra's cheeks went red and her fists clenched in an effort to contain her rage, the bitterness she could taste every time she thought about her mother's silences, the way Edda would turn her back when Elettra asked about her mysterious father, her mother's childhood or the place where she'd grown up. It had all come to the surface like a bubble of magma, bursting and releasing fiery cinders into the air.

Elettra was furious; she felt humiliated, deceived by the only person she had ever trusted. Had she even really known her mother?

Burrowing into her memory of the terrible days immediately after Edda's stroke, Elettra suddenly remembered finding some anomalies in her mother's bank statements. But she'd been too overcome by worry and grief to investigate closely, and had put them back in the drawer, dealing with only the essentials to carry on the business, while her mind was whirling. The payment hadn't been a huge amount per year, but in total over the years would have been substantial, and Elettra had just put a stop to them as the bakery started failing and her attention was needed elsewhere. Now, a year later, sitting in the kitchen of a tumbledown convent in the middle of the Mediterranean, she finally understood their significance.

'Why didn't she ever tell me, why didn't she confide in me?' she asked out loud, looking Lea straight in the eyes even though she was talking to herself.

'Elettra, I can't answer that, but believe me: there is no history to uncover here,' Lea insisted, a sudden blush colouring her cheeks and her voice choking up, becoming quieter and quieter.

But Elettra had stopped listening to her. She took a deep breath, a void opening in her chest to accommodate the new pain, and looked down at her hands again until she felt the gentle touch of Lea's fingers against her burning skin.

'I don't know what to say to you, and I'm sorry; all I can think is that your mother seems to have lived here and must have remained very attached to this place, and that must be why she kept sending money for so long, probably with no ulterior motive. To be honest, it seems like you desperately want to find something, some kind of holy grail that can answer all your questions, but perhaps you need to look inside yourself. Perhaps everything is more straightforward than you imagine, with no dark secret to uncover. Perhaps the key to unlock the door to the past isn't here, but in the words your mother said to you, in the silences you've buried in your heart. But believe me, it's not here,' Lea repeated with a tense smile.

Elettra moved away shaking her head, a caged animal in a room suddenly too small to hold all her questions. 'No, Lea; there's something about this whole story, about the convent, that doesn't add up. I don't know how to explain it, but I can feel it. It's real, as real as you and me,' she insisted, clenching her fists. There was the jar, and now the documents, but it was still all hazy, and she didn't have even the smallest clue as to a starting point.

She needed to look for information about the years her mother had spent here. Perhaps there were archives that went back to that period. She needed to find them. And perhaps her search should start in those very rooms that Lea was so determined to keep her away from. There was something suspicious about the way Lea had avoided her questions so far, but Elettra didn't have time to ask herself why. And she was going to keep some of the information to herself, like the note under the door, at least until she had a few more answers. She had her mother's life to reconstruct in order to try and make some sense of her own.

'Perhaps I'd find something more if I didn't always end up at dead ends,' she burst out, rebelling against her apparent destiny. 'It feels like I don't know anything any more, as though my life were a photo album with half the pages blank: I can only save the years I can remember, the rest is lost.'

She exchanged a look with Lea, but neither of them had any answers.

Nobody did, apart from Edda.

Elettra pushed her chair back, her legs full of an urge to leave. 'I'm going to get some fresh air, otherwise I'll drive you mad,' she said, running a hand through her hair.

Getting away from the convent was the only way to avoid the crashing weight of disappointment, her rage towards a life full of half-truths. It was impossible to think between those walls, so she left the gate behind her and, following the scent of the herbs, took the path that led down to the port.

She's taken money from us and from the bakery for years and sent it here, to a stranger. But why? she kept asking herself, but the words sounded worse and worse. 'What is there here that's so important, what was there here?' she asked the wind, in search of an answer that it couldn't give her.

Edda's feelings and actions were a huge black hole for Elettra, who had actually felt as though she was growing much closer to her mother over the last few weeks. Her feeling that this convent was where Edda had lived before moving so far away to the mainland had been growing, but the discovery of those documents, of a life that didn't run parallel with their shared life, was a blow from which she wouldn't recover quickly. Elettra walked until she reached the port where the ferry was docked. She was filled with rage and considered getting on it there and then, leaving this mess behind, but as soon as she spotted two men pushing through the crowd she felt breathless. She didn't need to go any closer to confirm their identity: even at that distance Elettra could smell the musky scent of men's aftershave that accompanied the first arrogant figure. Beside him hurried the mayor.

It was the businessman from Paris, there was no doubt about it, and she felt the bitterness at the life she'd wanted to put behind her bubbling back up to the surface in response to that realisation.

'I won't let it happen,' she murmured, watching the pair disappear in the mayor's car.

A shiver ran quickly up her back to the base of her neck, radiating into every cell of her body. She was so angry that she felt as though she had gathered the very clouds that were threatening to spill overhead.

She couldn't let it happen, she owed it to her mother. After all, Edda wasn't so inconsiderate as to withdraw all that money from the family finances without good reason, and Elettra was benefiting from the generosity. Perhaps the convent might be the only place she would be able to rediscover Edda and find the roots she had been seeking for years, so she wouldn't let a stranger rob her of her chance. This could be an opportunity for her to set things right with her mother, and to set right what had happened to the bakery.

This time she would fight to prove her worth to both her mother and herself.

She turned her back on the port and returned to the convent. She scratched her knees on the prickly heather as she cut across the fields, the sea washing against the cliffs in the background, and arrived breathless at the feet of the Saint. She was the only person Elettra could turn to for help.

She needed a sign, nothing more, but the Saint didn't seem to be listening to her.

Disappointed, she studied the statue's porcelain face and jumped when she heard Isabelle's laughter echoing in the cloister. She was walking arm in arm with Nicole, carrying a basket full of jars of honey. What an old woman who lived alone was going to do with all that honey was a mystery, but Dominique's bees seemed to have magical productivity so they were unlikely to miss a few jars.

Elettra followed the two women, but she stopped transfixed on the cobbles when she saw Nicole take a jar from Isabelle's basket and admire its contents. Gentle drops of rain marked the pale shoulders of her dress and the sound of a storm rumbled in the sky. Now she knew what to do.

Pane perso al miele di zagara

4 slices stale bread

200ml milk

50g sugar

1 vanilla pod (seeds only)

1 whole egg and 1 yolk

4 spoons of orange blossom honey

1 handful wild strawberries (optional)

Butter

Beat together the eggs, milk, vanilla seeds and sugar in a large bowl until completely combined, then dip the bread into the mixture for a few minutes on each side so that it is well soaked.

Heat a knob of butter in a frying pan and cook the slices of bread until golden on both sides.

Warm the honey in a bain-marie, drizzle it over the warm bread and serve immediately, garnishing with wild strawberries or a sprinkling of icing sugar to taste.

9

Elettra didn't sleep a wink that night. She couldn't. She felt an overwhelming urge to dive into the ghosts of an unknown past, and if that weren't enough to keep her awake, there were also Lea's attempts to put her off her research.

At dinner that evening Lea had told her again that it was pointless to keep on searching for a history that didn't exist. Words Elettra was tired of hearing.

'You should stop chasing ghosts, Elettra. The convent is becoming an obsession that is at risk of distracting you from the real reason you came here: your mother,' Lea had told her, her voice dangerously close to a reproof. 'Edda once lived here, you've found proof to confirm that theory, from the jar to the documents, but it doesn't seem to be enough for you. Why? Why are you so dead-set on digging into this place's past rather than enjoying the closeness to your mother, breathing in her perfume in the places where she herself lived many years ago? Who knows how long this convent will remain here; you should enjoy it for what it is for as long as you can.'

'Answers, all the ones I've never had and have been searching for my whole life. I want answers, Lea, I don't expect any more of this place or of my mother.'

'Then you should know that when we search for things we don't always like what we find out, and perhaps they've been hidden from us to protect us, to shield us.'

Elettra had frowned, doubt in her eyes. 'I don't follow you, what are you trying to say?'

'That the truth isn't always the right option. Sometimes forgetting is an act of love.'

'No Lea, you're wrong: the truth is always the right option, and I'm going to uncover it at any cost,' she had said. She had walked out of the door in the heat of her need to know, leaving Lea tense. Elettra had walked quickly towards her bedroom, in need of some time to think, but she had stopped outside the door. Beneath it was another white sheet of paper. She had looked around cautiously before bending over to pick it up, and she had felt her knees give way as she read the contents of the message.

Stop chasing ghosts. Stop asking questions. Stay silent and all will be well.

A real, genuine threat. The second in a short space of time, she had thought, tearing up the paper as her pulse pounded wildly in her head. The handwriting was the same as the previous note, and she would ignore this threat too, just like the last one, because she needed to get to the bottom of her mother's story; the mysterious messenger would do better to leave her alone, because she had no intention of backing off. A warning like this wasn't going to stop her.

'None at all,' she had repeated aloud, although there was no one around. She checked the corridors and then stood in front of a window, with the moonlight falling over her as her thoughts flew to Edda and her childhood memories of her. 'I'll fight for them,' she had decided, offering her prayer to the stars. 'Even if someone's not so keen on the idea.'

Elettra went down to the kitchen the next morning and arranged everything she needed to make fried bread soaked in orange blossom honey, one of Edda's special recipes. But when she went out to the garden in search of Lea and Dominique, she found herself enveloped in an intense cloud of aniseed and a spontaneous laugh crept upon her tired face.

She was on the right track, she knew it. This wasn't her imagination.

She waited impatiently for the others to come in from the vegetable garden, gathering everything she needed for the small banquet she wanted to make for breakfast. She rehearsed the argument she had come up with during the night while sleep evaded her once again, but when she found herself sitting at the table with the others, she felt herself falter. Her conscience told her she should talk to Lea, Dominique and Nicole in a frank manner about the mayor's plans and what they should do about them, but when the moment came to speak it was as though her lips were stuck together; speaking would reopen an old wound, she could see it in the way in which Nicole was picking at the sugary bread she normally wolfed down, tracing patterns in the honey on her plate, and in Dominique's gloomy gaze, but she couldn't avoid it. They needed to understand that if they didn't take action they would lose what little life had been left to them, just like she had lost her bakery.

She pushed her fork through the golden crust of the honey-soaked bread, inhaling the fragrance of warm butter that rose up from it, that sweet scent that reminded her so much of her mother. Since she had arrived at the convent cooking had no longer represented a challenge, rather it had offered the possibility of rediscovering both Edda and herself, that relationship she had fought for such a long time. She had declared war on her mother because Edda had forced her to learn her language, the language of doughs and lengthy bakes in the oven, but she was gradually rediscovering the magic at the convent. Elettra could slowly feel herself making peace with her mother and her family's history. Edda showing her the way to the convent, to that past which she had refused to speak of for so long, was a final act of love.

But she still had to save the convent from Leroux and his plans in order to do so.

She closed her eyes and opened them again slowly, her heart and her gaze full of her need for the truth.

'I know what it means to lose everything; I've already experienced it, I know how devastating it is. You feel empty, everything good you ever thought you'd been or done is taken away,' she began.

Silence fell in the room. Suddenly all eyes were on her, and she felt her palms become clammy with nerves. She didn't like remembering those days, the nights spent on the sofa in front of a blur of images on the television screen, her blouse covered with crumbs and her hair uncombed; she had hit rock bottom back then, a pain which came flooding back beneath the gaze of the women in front of her.

'It didn't go well for me, and now I know that the failure was my fault: I should have had more belief in Edda, in her love of cooking that she tried to pass on to me, instead of digging my heels in,' she admitted, hunching her shoulders, her eyes veiled in bitterness. She swallowed, exchanging a look with Lea, and clenched her fists. 'But it doesn't have to be like that for you. So the mayor's set to work on throwing you out of the convent? Fine;

you show him that you're not the compliant women he believes you to be. Show him your strength, fight for your home. You've got every chance of sending Leroux and his gossip crawling back to where they came from.'

'Rousing words,' Dominique interrupted her, pouring coffee into her mug, but Elettra didn't let her cynicism put her off and continued unperturbed.

'I had an idea last night, but I need you to help me put it into action. All of you, no exceptions,' she replied. Fists still clenched, she looked at the women around the table one by one; she read apathy, disillusion, bitterness in their eyes. A disenchantment that only served to strengthen her feeling that she was in the right. 'You've got the skills, I've seen them, and it would be stupid not to use them to save this place. We all owe something to the convent,' she said. 'This place has protected you and shown you hospitality when everyone else turned their backs on you: now it's time to return the favour.'

'What are you suggesting we do?' Dominique interrupted her, looking up, searching for a weakness, the crack that would bring down Elettra's optimism and vision.

'We can't do all that much at the moment, there isn't enough money in the bank, but we can start by selling our produce at the market. The tourists love things like this, convents always hold a fascination for outsiders, and I don't want to see any more fruit rotting on the branches like last Sunday,' she said, thinking back to a few days ago when she had gone for a walk in the orchard and come across the peach tree surrounded by fruit mouldering on the ground. 'With what we gather from the earth we can sell cakes, jams, candles and honey, which the bees produce in huge quantities; in a place like this where the electricity comes and goes, people will always need candles, and as for pastries made with honey ... well, I get the impression they're already highly appreciated,' she added, remembering Isabelle's bag full of jars. 'We need to make ourselves known, show these people that the convent isn't inhabited by wild women as Leroux's wife is always claiming and gossiping about. All we'll need is a stall to display our produce and the will to save this place,' she concluded.

'It does sound like a good idea,' Lea admitted, albeit cautiously; Elettra could sense an openness in her, and perhaps a little energy and determination in the words that were emerging. Lea wiped her lips with her napkin, as if savouring the velvety taste of honey and crispy bread. 'I could make infusions and herb-based creams, but it's unlikely they'd let us sell our produce in town. Don't forget, they hate us here.'

'Exactly,' Dominique chipped in. 'They see us as lepers; nobody would buy from us.'

'That might be the case on Titan's Island, but if we widen our client base to the neighbouring islands, there's nothing Leroux could do to stop us.'

'That's what you say: that bastard wouldn't hesitate to confiscate the fuel for the boat if he were to find out,' Dominique claimed.

Elettra snorted; Dominique's obstructiveness was starting to frustrate her. 'And if he did, we would all learn to row,' she replied, spreading her arms. 'But before we raise the white flag, as Dominique is suggesting, I think we ought to at least try and save this place, don't you?' she persisted, as stubborn as Edda; she couldn't believe that Sylvie Leroux's poison had infected Lea and Dominique too.

'I could help you with the biscuits, if you want,' Nicole offered, breaking the silence and prompting general astonishment; they all knew how limited her culinary skills were, and even Lea's own optimism wavered when it came to tasting her creations. But Elettra welcomed her offer. Finally a constructive suggestion, exactly what she needed.

'Of course, that would be great.'

'And I'm quite good at embroidery,' Nicole added. 'I could sew some little bags or doilies. If we bought the fabric we could sell the pastries ready packaged in little canvas bags, it would be cute. What do you say?'

'That would be amazing,' Elettra replied, infected by Nicole's enthusiasm. She looked around the table again, her eyes full of the promise of a bright future: they were all there, ready to share in that great ball of energy put in motion by an idea voiced over a piece of bread and honey and a glass of milk.

Everyone except Dominique, who continued to drum her fingers on the table.

'Don't take it personally that she's not jumping for joy, she just needs some time to get used to the idea,' Lea reassured Elettra under her breath, noticing Dominique's hunched shoulders while Nicole whistled as she cleared the table. 'Let's start off by working out what needs to be done. How about we put it down in black and white?'

Elettra took her hand. 'I'd say that's an excellent idea,' she murmured as the adrenalin started to give way to rationality, highlighting the potential weak points in the plan.

'How are we going to maintain constant productivity, have you thought about that?' Dominique quibbled. 'The equipment we have is useless, and a lot of it – what I use in the garden, for example – is rusty. And that's without mentioning those ancient ovens from when the convent was fully operational – those creaky old things haven't been used for years, but they'd be essential for the kind of production you're talking about. If we don't at least get the basic equipment in working order, we won't save anything at all. In fact, that bastard will kick us out with even greater satisfaction.' She placed the coffee pot down on the tablecloth with a bang as Elettra's eyes flashed at her. Elettra then looked over to Nicole, whose gaze was fixed on her plate, and who seemed to have suddenly lost her liveliness.

'Unfortunately, Dominique is right,' Nicole said. 'Elettra's idea is fantastic, but we need equipment in a good state of repair to prepare produce to sell in the market, and how can we manage without enough money to repair it all?' she asked the others in alarm.

Lea had listened to Dominique's complaints and Nicole's fears in silence without taking her eyes off her friend, sitting motionless with her fingers steepled in front of her face. Elettra's idea was a good one. 'I wouldn't give up that quickly,' she declared, her mind searching for a solution. Looking around she saw the sharp outline of the toolbox in a corner of the room. There was only one person who could help them, the very person who had forgotten it there. She smiled, satisfied, and slowly turned to face the table.

'We'll sort out the equipment that's still usable ourselves, we can buy what we need to mend it with the last of the savings. And I've just had an idea of how we can fix the ovens,' she continued enigmatically.

10

Elettra folded her arms across her chest, her chin jutting out as she observed the cascade of bougainvillea that framed the house. It was an old stone building with blue window frames ingrained with brine, nestled like a jewel in the pinewood that cut it off from the rest of town. It enjoyed breathtaking views; the bay lay below like the arm of a sleeping lover, and a warm wind rustled the low bushes. 'Is this where your contact lives?' she asked, pointing at the building. Lea suddenly turned towards the back entrance and Elettra followed her breathless, pushing a branch of jasmine out of her face and wiping her hands on her skirt. 'Who is it?'

Lea grumbled, her hands clenched against her legs. 'Someone who isn't home,' she replied, staring at the closed door.

After a few seconds of silence, interrupted only by a herring gull which spread its wings above their heads, Lea clicked her fingers. 'How stupid of me not to think of it sooner!' she exclaimed. 'There's an isolated cove near here where he moors his boat; that's where he goes to fish when work's thin on the ground,' she added.

'So what shall we do?' asked Elettra.

'We'll wait for him to come back,' Lea replied, scanning the horizon.

They waited for a while that felt like for ever to Elettra. Lea's feet tapped on the dusty path, then she looked at Elettra and turned her back on her, towards the beach. 'Follow me,' she ordered, setting off. She walked quickly along pebbly paths that led down to the sea, untroubled by the uneven ground, unconcerned for her companion lagging behind her.

But as soon as she found herself by the sea, Elettra felt all her fatigue vanish in an instant. The view of that patch of emerald water held in the embrace of the white, chalky cliff walls made every drop of sweat running down beneath her clothes seem worthwhile. 'It's stunning, words can't describe it,' she stammered as the wind played with the hem of her skirt and Lea continued walking quickly onwards ahead of her.

But Elettra couldn't take another step; she was hypnotised by the beauty of that wild panorama; she wanted to enjoy every moment of this discovery, every splash of the sea, of the waves which washed against the shore and seemed to reach out to her with arms of soft white foam. They called to her, they wanted her.

She checked out of the corner of her eye to make sure Lea was far enough away, slipped off her shoes and walked into the cold water up to her ankles, laughing at the salty splatters that marked her dress. She leaped into the water to play with the waves, finally dancing free. The sound of her laughter soon reached Lea, who was deep in conversation with a man sitting on a small boat pulled up onto the sand several metres further down the beach. He had been at sea when she and Elettra had arrived at the beach, but he had returned to the shore as soon as he had seen them.

Elettra walked quickly across the wet sand, reaching Lea in just a few strides.

'This is Elettra Cavani, a dear friend of mine. Elettra, this is . . . '

Adrian, she thought, him again.

For a moment their eyes met.

Elettra blushed and looked down, while he gave a smug smile, hidden by his sun-bleached beard. She noticed Lea look away, excluded from this secret, from moments known only to the two of them and the island.

'Adrian,' she greeted him under her breath.

Lea nodded, perplexed.

Elettra offered him her hand. He barely glanced at her, but when their hands touched for the first time and Adrian wrapped his fingers around her palm she felt something crackle in her chest. Something had broken at the exact moment of contact, an unexpected collision.

Once again, like the time she had seen him in the chapel, Elettra felt her horizons tilt.

She noticed Lea step back, her mouth closed in silence. Then the moment was disturbed by the appearance of Isabelle, making her way through the thick green woods and waving to catch their attention. Elettra sensed Lea's relief at the distraction as she left them to see what Isabelle had come to say.

'They need me at the convent, Elettra, right away,' Lea explained.

'Okay, I'll come with you,' Elettra said at once, but Lea shook her head.

'There's no need, you stay here and talk to Adrian about what needs to be done. I won't be long,' Lea said.

'Are you sure? I can help you sort out the problem and then we can come back together,' Elettra said, determined, but Lea shook her head.

'It's not something you can help with, believe me. And let's not waste our time.'

'I can try.'

'No, really, it's fine for Lea to handle!' Isabelle cut Elettra short, raising her voice and surprising Lea, Elettra and Adrian.

'Honestly, it's fine, Elettra, really, thank you. Anyway, talk to Adrian about our plans. I'm sure you'll be able to explain the details just fine and, like I said, we don't have time to waste.' Lea turned to follow Isabelle who was already walking swiftly away. She looked back and reassured Elettra. 'Don't worry, Adrian knows our situation and we've been consulting him on how to save the convent for some time. I only hope you manage to drag him away from the sea; he's a tough one to persuade.'

Lea turned to Adrian. 'We need your help, otherwise we wouldn't have disturbed you, you know that,' she insisted, and disappeared into the pinewood.

Elettra sighed. Now that Lea had gone she felt uncomfortable there with a stranger, no matter how attractive he was; she could see at a glance how the simple life had really strengthened Adrian's arms and back, but there was something unspoken in his eyes, stifled by the sting of loneliness that seemed to accompany his days, reflected in the deep silence that was now between them.

She waited patiently while he arranged his nets then slowly went over, her eyes fixed on the tangles he was unravelling; his fingers moved with the same certainty as hers when she made shortcrust pastry, small quick touches so as not to heat the butter too much. Adrian seemed to know every fibre of his net.

She cleared her throat, passing a broken shell from one hand to the other.

'Lea told me you're not from around here. Have you lived here long?'

'A year.'

'And you're happy on the island?'

'Yes.'

'Mmm.'

This was proving more difficult than she'd expected. She picked up another shell from the beach and threw it back into the sea. 'Listen,' she said, dragging her foot through the sand, 'about that day in the chapel, I want to apologise. I shouldn't have had a go at you like that.'

'Don't worry, it's water under the bridge,' he cut her short.

'Okay,' she murmured.

A gust of wind blew a handful of sand towards them, but it didn't seem to bother Adrian; he continued to repair his nets in front of a quiet Elettra. It was impossible to speak with the wind whistling in their ears, and she didn't want to wait all afternoon until he decided to listen to her, so she grabbed the nets that still lay on the beach and dragged them over to the boat. On his knees examining the hull, Adrian watched as she created long tracks in the sand. Once he had stowed the oars in the boat he jumped to his feet and gave the slippery wood a pat. 'Everything seems to be in order here, shall we make our way back to my house? We can talk there. The wind's getting up, which isn't a good sign.' He pointed to the building nearby, while she brushed her hands against her dress, trying to get rid of the sand caught in the fabric.

For a moment, just the blink of an eye, he stopped to look at her, to study her tanned face with its proud lines, as Mediterranean as her low voice, and invited her to follow him. Once out of the sun in the pleasant cool of the kitchen, he took a bottle of wine and a couple of dark-coloured glasses down from an old sideboard. She collapsed exhausted into a chair.

'Just water for me, please,' she said, raising a hand as she saw him dig his knife into the cork to open it.

'Are you sure?'

She looked up. There was something magnetic about Adrian, she thought to herself as she examined his clean lines and the shape of his eyes; he wasn't statuesque like her ex Walter, but she couldn't stop staring at him. 'I'm sure,' she nodded.

He put the wine down and filled a jug with water. 'Do you want ice?'

'That would be perfect.' Elettra saw him rummage in the drawers of the freezer, pulling out a plastic bag, taking a knife from a different drawer, and plunging it into the coloured bag to make a little hole. He squeezed colourless cubes into the glass and finally added the water from a jug.

Elettra smiled. The slice of lemon he added last of all made her smile even more.

She drank a couple of sips, giving him time to fill his own glass with red wine. 'I assume you already know about the mayor and his colleague's plans,' she began, tensely tapping her fingers against the glass.

Adrian pulled his wicker chair alongside hers. 'Do you mean Bernard Morel?'

'Who?'

'The businessman who's just arrived from Paris. He's a big player in his field.'

'You know his field?' she asked, curious.

'Not really, but then it's not my home the vultures are circling.'

Elettra sat back in her chair; Adrian had hit the nail on the head. 'That's why I'm here: I need your help. Me, the convent, all of us,' she explained. She could sense him weighing up her every move, every change in her expression; he was studying her, trying to decide whether he could trust her, she imagined. He held his glass, warming the wine with the heat from his palms. 'Lea did mention some trouble with Leroux, but I didn't realise that it had become so serious.'

'Yes, it has. It's much more than scheming: Isabelle has told us that Leroux plans to throw Lea and the others out by taking advantage of a clause in the contract of sale so that Morel can acquire the building for only half of its true value and transform it into a luxury hotel. But the worst thing is that he seems prepared to go to any lengths to achieve his goal,' Elettra said in a rush. She tried to maintain a measured tone, but the memory of the mayor's latest visit heated her voice. It was inevitable, she couldn't stay calm when faced with such cruelty; just thinking of Sylvie Leroux's self-satisfied smile turned her stomach.

'Lea told me things were serious,' Adrian confirmed as Elettra knocked back her glass of water, 'but I didn't know the details of it.'

'She has an unfortunate habit of downplaying problems. The situation is beyond serious. It's desperate.' She refilled her glass and put the jug down. She started to tell him their plan. She took a sheet of paper out of her bag on which she had made a list of all the urgent repairs and the ones that needed to be completed before winter, hoping he would agree to help them.

'Well, that's everything,' she finished half an hour later, taking a deep breath.

She waited with her fingers entwined under her chin while Adrian worked out an estimate, but his face was an indecipherable puzzle. Tired of waiting, she started to look around the room, a modest kitchen which he alone seemed to use; there were a couple of peaches in the fruit bowl and the only thing she could smell in the house was paint. She guessed that Adrian must have taken advantage of a quiet spell to repaint the walls of some of the rooms beyond the kitchen's half-open door.

Once he was finished, she refolded the sheet of notes with the sums circled in red and put it back in her bag.

'I want to be honest with you,' she added. Her hands were shaking and under the table her feet just wouldn't stay still. His eyes still fixed on her, Adrian unnerved her, and she was even more worried by what she was about to tell him.

He looked at her attentively. 'I'm all ears.'

Elettra clutched her glass, drying the moisture that had formed on its surface. It was difficult, saying those words took an immense effort. 'Since Lea doesn't have much money, she was planning to ask you to work for free, at least for the moment, but it's clear that that's not possible. It wouldn't be fair to you. And it would also be a big sacrifice for Lea to ask it of you.'

Adrian responded, 'Lea and I are friends, and friends help each other in times of need. Of course, if I had to do everything for free I would need to find another job to pay the bills. But I want to help and we'll find a way to get it done.'

'Given the state of the convent and the limited time available, I'm trying to avoid any kind of delay. That's why I've decided that I'll be the one to pay the costs in advance. I can start with a small sum now, if that's all right with you, and you'll receive the rest from the income from the sales.'

'I think you ought to discuss this with Lea.'

'That's the thing, the whole point: Lea mustn't know the terms of our agreement for the moment. I want her to have a chance to catch her breath, to focus entirely on our project. That's my only condition,' she added, imagining how Ruth would react when she told her that she had pledged her remaining finances to restore a ruined building: there was something left over from what Ruth had given her which she hadn't used in rent here, and there was the last of her savings too. Ruth would tell her she was crazy, but then, it had taken a touch of madness to bring her this far.

She swallowed the lump in her throat as her gaze returned to rest lightly on him. 'What do you say?' she continued hesitantly.

Adrian looked up and smiled at her for the first time since they'd met.

'It's a deal,' he said. 'And, for the sake of honesty, you should know that I had already decided to help you the moment Bernard Morel set foot on this island.'

Focaccine alle mele

500g flour

1 cube brewer's yeast

100g sugar

300g milk

5g salt

2 spoons acacia honey

Calvados

3 apples

1 vanilla pod (seeds only)

Cinnamon

Oil

Dissolve the yeast and the honey in 100ml of warm milk and leave to rest for ten minutes.

Peel, core and grate two apples.

Combine the flour, sugar, vanilla seeds, salt and a generous sprinkle of cinnamon in a bowl then gradually add the yeast, grated apples and the remaining milk until you have a well-mixed and elastic dough. Shape it into a ball and leave to rise overnight until it doubles in size.

The next day, cut the remaining apple into thin slices and soak them in Calvados. Take the dough, divide it into balls the size of mandarins and flatten them with your fingertips, then arrange the liquor-soaked apple slices on top of them.

Heat the oil in a frying pan and cook the focaccine one at a time until golden.

Dust with sugar and cinnamon and serve hot.

11

Adrian kept his word. He arrived promptly at the convent gate every day ready to make his contribution to the cause.

And to devour the *focacce alle mele* that Elettra made. He was crazy about them and had never tasted any so good before.

Elettra would have given anything to be like him, for that air of independence and detachment he seemed to wear, as if he didn't need anything that ordinary people sought; he got on perfectly well with everyone, but without getting close to anyone. She saw it as an emotional detachment, reflected in his need for solitude, which also prompted him to seek contact with animals and the wild nature of the island and take refuge from the company of his own kind.

Just a few days earlier she had gone to find him to take him some biscuits and some of the money Ruth had given her. It was enough to cover the initial expenses, but as she had guessed, Adrian wasn't home. He rarely spent his free time between four walls, either his own or the bar in town: he loved open spaces, freedom in all its guises, as Elettra had learned from watching him work through the kitchen window.

Like her, Adrian needed a life without fixed boundaries, so that day she had decided to look for him in the only place she thought he might be, just where she herself would have gone: the beach. She had set off along the earth and stone path that led from his door to the shore with her basket on her arm and there she had found him, busy rolling around on the edge of the surf with a stray dog who ran away as she approached.

'I'm sorry I scared your friend away,' she had murmured in his ear.

'Who, Brioche? That dog's afraid of his own shadow.' He had leaned towards her, his neck stretched to peer into the basket that hung from her arm. 'What have you got there?'

'Just some honey biscuits, but that's not why I came.'

He had smiled, slipping his hand into the basket to steal one. 'No?'

Elettra had watched him stealthily as he enjoyed the fruits of his petty theft, before rummaging in the basket again and taking out a white envelope. 'We have a deal, remember?'

Adrian had barely looked at the outside of the envelope before his mind strayed back to the beach, his eyes coming to rest on a boat moored a few metres away from them.

'I don't like talking about money, not with you.'

Elettra stood up taller; the situation was becoming interesting. 'Because I'm a woman?'

'Yup.'

'Well, I can see that the island attitudes have infected you, too,' she had mocked, giving him a pat on the back. 'Come on, this is strictly business, it's not personal; it's not like we're discussing who should pay the bill at a restaurant!'

He had looked at her, shaking his head. 'Can we talk about it later? The sunset looks completely different from the sea.'

He had smiled at her, playing with the words and lowering the tone of voice to sound more convincing, and she hadn't been able to tell him no; less than ten minutes later she had found herself in the boat with him as he rowed energetically away from the coast to take advantage of the calm sea. He had rowed until the lights of his house were little more than specks, then pulled the oars into the boat.

Her hands folded on her knees, Elettra had stared at the distant coast. Little red patches had broken out on her skin, heating her face. She felt uncomfortable: they were completely alone in a couple of square metres, far away from everything and she wasn't sure she was ready to trust a man again. Not yet.

'It's the first time I've ever been in a boat. One this small, I mean; I arrived on the ferry, of course,' she had said after a long silence and the odd cough while Adrian lay down with his arms folded behind his head to watch the sunset. Elettra remained upright with her hands clasped. Adrian had nice hands, big and strong, if always covered in paint; his square palms radiated security, and, even marked by cuts and calluses, they seemed capable of unexpected tenderness which she had witnessed a few minutes earlier watching him play with Brioche. They were masculine yet delicate hands which must have caressed countless women, she imagined with a flash of annoyance.

'How far are we from the coast?' she had continued, trying not to look at Adrian's tanned skin beneath the fabric of his shirt.

'Why waste time talking? Enjoy the moment, the ephemeral beauty of the night as it falls over the horizon; is there anything more intense than a sunset?'

'So you're a poet too, then?' Elettra had goaded him, and he had smiled at her and pulled himself up into a sitting position to look at her. He had his own particular way of looking, running his eyes over the skin of whoever was in front of him. Not everyone, though, and not in the same way.

'I'm many things.'

Elettra had suppressed a smile, folding her arms. 'A Don Juan, too? Is that why you brought me out here?'

That was when Adrian had stared at her, without saying a word for almost a whole minute. He had rested his arm on his knee, leaning forward, his mouth slightly open and his hair falling over his eyes. 'If I'd wanted to seduce you I wouldn't have brought you so close to the shore, in fact I wouldn't have brought you out in this wreck of a rowing boat,' he had said, tapping the side of the boat with a laugh.

His gesture had wrong-footed her. For a moment she had thought he was trying to seduce her, in which case she would at least have known what to expect from him, but Adrian kept avoiding every attempt to define him. He was an abstract painting, a complex tangle of coloured lines.

'Then why are we here?'

He had lowered his head, wiping his hands on the rough fabric of his trousers. He had looked around as the encroaching darkness swallowed up the faint lights of the town preparing for the night. 'Because I've seen interesting stories in your eyes, places and flavours that I haven't experienced,' he had said quietly. 'And a melancholy that fascinates me.'

'Wow,' Elettra had stammered, disguising her embarrassment with her usual gesture of tucking her hair behind her ear. But Adrian didn't want to let her off the hook. He had leaned towards her, brushing the back of her hand with his fingertips. His hands radiated heat, hands which thrilled her.

'I also thought you needed a change of perspective; you've spent ages, perhaps too long, looking at the sea from the shore. It's time for a change of scene, don't you think?'

*

'A change of perspective,' Elettra repeated, tying the apron around her waist. Adrian's words, his sweet voice and the way he had of looking at her, almost as though he saw the soul beneath the clothes and flesh, still surrounded her like an embrace. He had been nice to her despite his original standoffishness; he had given her her first starry night at sea, stretched out on the opposite side of the boat to look at the sky with no need to speak, without that gauche awkwardness between them.

'What madness,' she said in a low voice as she searched the sideboard for the bowl she had left on the table the night before. It contained the dough for the *focacce alle mele* she was making for Adrian and she needed to hurry if she wanted them to be ready by the time he arrived. She carefully sliced a couple of apples and put them to soak in a blend of sugar and Calvados which would go perfectly with the mixture she was about to knead on the pastry board. Every push of the dough was a wave from the past that came back to wash against her memories. She thought about the *focacce* she used to make in the bakery after Edda's stroke, the toughness of the dough she was always kneading, her impatient hands. There was no love in it, that was why she lost customers, who began to prefer the ready-made pastries from the supermarket next door. She had stopped loving either herself or the baking, busy with her fight with Edda, which she regretted now that she felt her beside her.

All it would have taken to save us was a little bit of love, telling me about the convent, perhaps, Elettra thought; to feel her nearby like I do now, to feel her touch on this dough, between these walls that are impregnated with her. To be close to one another, body and soul, as we can only be here now, in the space between the table and the oven, in the doughs in which I gradually seem to be rediscovering her. Elettra reached into the bag for a handful of flour. Difficult as her relationship with Edda was, it had flourished in the connection between flour and water, in the rise that she had finally got just right in the bread that she had begun baking with joy again, the pastries she finally wanted to cook, which had acquired additional, more intense flavour. It was complicated, as tricky and twisted as a ball of dough during kneading, but warm and welcoming like the scent of the olive batons she had left rising under a cotton cloth, as sweet as the apples she had left to soak in the liquor. Like this dough, she thought, slipping a morsel into her mouth.

She still needed to incorporate more air into the dough so it would achieve a good rise during baking, just like her mind needed time to absorb the news about her mother, but she had barely plunged her hands into the soft mixture when the worries about her future surfaced once again, sticking to her good mood like the dough to her fingers.

'Don't you start, too,' she murmured to the pale-yellow dough that was slowly expanding on the floury table. She stroked its rough surface, sprinkled some more flour onto the pastry board and continued kneading, finishing up a few minutes later with ten little rolls, on which she arranged the apple slices while the oil in the iron frying pan started to heat up. She checked the flame under the pan out of the corner of her eye, wrinkling her nose as she saw the surface of the oil start to bubble. She had hated frying ever since she was little; she had never once managed to catch the oil at just the right moment. She would always do her utmost to spy those elusive little waves in the frying pan but she rarely managed to see them, so one day many years ago Edda had told her to stop relying on fortune-tellers' tricks and drop a little bit of dough in the pan. If it sank then the oil wasn't ready, if it floated then she could start frying.

It had been at the time of the city's carnival, Elettra could still remember it.

At that time of year her mother always prepared sweet fried

ravioli with almonds, and then there were the mountains of saffron fritters and *mostaccioli* biscuits covered with coloured sprinkles. Every carnival was a festival of colours and fragrances, the bittersweet taste of candied orange, of dough rolled in warm eucalyptus honey, of almond brittle wrapped in lemon leaves that crunched between her teeth. Elettra could still remember how the window display would fill with joy between Epiphany and the start of Lent, the splendour before the long period of penitence during which, in contrast, Edda wouldn't let her go anywhere near a biscuit.

'Don't you worry about what other people do. Lent is Lent, and Christians do penance; those who gorge on sweet things all year round wouldn't even know a church if it was right in front of them,' Edda would say, gesturing at the passers-by when Elettra demanded a pastry. Edda was inflexible, with a rigidity Elettra had often criticised during their arguments.

She was right, though, Elettra thought, placing the first fritter, always the ugliest and never properly cooked, onto some kitchen paper. Her mother's inflexibility had helped her not to lose her way like some of her peers, although all too often the rigidity she had imposed had asked too high a price of a young girl with a wealth of childhood dreams. There were no Saturday nights at the disco for Elettra, never an unauthorised absence from school or a holiday at the beach with a friend's family. Her place was in the bakery with Edda who had only really been half a parent, in terms of being emotionally present, although Elettra had never had the courage to say it aloud.

A parent with secrets, way too many secrets, she thought, running through the list of clues she had found along the way.

'That's what I could smell all the way down the road!' Adrian exclaimed from the doorway, as a fritter slipped from Elettra's hand and into the frying pan, splattering drops of boiling oil everywhere.

He rolled up his sleeves as he came over to where Elettra stood, his nose overcome by the smell. '*Focacce alle mele*, my favourites,' he continued, rubbing his hands at the sight of the piping hot pastries.

Her *focacce* looked bronzed by the sun of a magical season.

'I hope they've turned out well,' she said as she fried the last one. She switched off the gas and rolled the last fritter in the cone of spiced sugar, then placed it in a wicker basket with the others. Adrian watched in silence as she dusted them with more spiced sugar, moving the fritters so gently she barely seemed to touch them.

'Don't let me disturb you,' he said with a smile, but Elettra didn't reply, lost in her own little world. He leaned against the wall and folded his arms, watching her move. The pastries were extremely hot and steam danced in the air, but Elettra didn't seem to notice. Adrian continued, 'I came early because I wanted to show you something. If you want to see it, that is; you seem a bit distracted today,' he said.

Elettra's gaze turned to him. Her hands were covered in white crystals, her fingertips glistened with oil. She still held a pinch of sugar in her fingers and her hair was falling into her eyes. 'What do you want to show me?'

Adrian stretched a hand towards her, a determined smile on his face. 'A *focaccia* first. Everything in this world has a price.'

She took one from the basket, a playful light in her eyes. 'If a *focaccia* is your preferred price I can pay you in them from now on.'

'A thousand of these and you could consider it a done deal. Not one less, mind, or the deal would be off,' he shot back jokingly. He raised his fritter in a toast to Elettra and sank his teeth into it, giving a moan of ecstasy while she laughed as she dusted the remaining *focacce* with sugar.

She covered them with a cloth and wiped her hands on the apron she wore tied around her waist. 'I'm ready, we can go,' she said as the walls around them started to come to life. The rumbling in the water pipes suggested that Nicole was awake; in a few minutes she would appear blinking through half-closed eyes with the imprint of her pillow still on her cheek, while Lea and Dominique would return from the tool shed and the garden within the next quarter of an hour.

Adrian swallowed the last bit of his *focaccia* and wiped his hands on his jeans. 'OK, come with me,' he said, leading her to the wing of the convent where he was working, the one that housed the old bakery.

Elettra had been left breathless the first time she'd set foot in the old bakery: the room was as big as her mother's bakery, perhaps even a tiny bit bigger, but the passage of time and Lea's limited means had quickly reduced it to an abandoned workshop. There was clutter everywhere, even inside the ovens, and the damp had risen almost a metre up the walls, tracing a layer of green the whole way round the room. Most of the doorframes were riddled with woodworm and the floor was chipped in several places.

But Elettra could feel Edda's presence intensely there, confirmed by Lea, who had told her how the rooms used to be the centre of convent life. This was where the first bakery on the island had been built and it had remained functional until the fifties, thanks to the work of the nuns who were known throughout the archipelago for their culinary skills. Wrapped in the room's silent embrace, Elettra had imagined that it was in this very place that Edda had taken her first steps in the art of pastry. She liked to think of herself as determined to follow her footsteps on a new path towards self-discovery.

'Unfortunately, a few years after the end of the war a terrible fire destroyed the whole kitchen complex and that marked the start of the convent's decline,' Lea had told her. The fire had ruined everything, she had explained, and soon afterwards the bakery doors had been bolted and the nuns had withdrawn into silence.

The convent kitchens had died that night, and then come back to life several decades later at the hands of Adrian, the first to go back into those rooms.

He had opened the windows once more and swept away the cobwebs, painted the walls white and restored the doors, and that morning he wanted to show Elettra the fruits of his labour; he wanted her to notice his efforts and see that the money she had invested had been well spent. He said he wanted to see her smile, because he liked the way she smiled, the way her cheeks coloured and her eyes crinkled to make room for the lips folded into a happy crescent moon. He wanted Elettra to be pleased with his work, pleased with him.

'Come in, come and have a look,' he insisted when he saw her stop on the threshold, taking her by the hand as though it were the most natural gesture in the world. He showed her the newly cleaned and levelled floor, the woodworm-infested fitttings repaired and treated with products that had restored their former glory, the walls painted a dazzling white to cover the huge black smudges that had deprived the room of light for so long. Elettra blinked, her mouth half open in astonishment, but it was the smell of wood and aromatic herbs filling the room that really caught her unprepared. She looked around, walking on tiptoe, struggling to recognise the space she had been in just a month earlier, like a child on Christmas morning who finds the garden covered in snow and a Christmas tree surrounded by presents with their name on.

'Adrian,' she murmured, her hands clutched to her chest, while her bright eyes reflected her emotions on finding a past that seemed to be coming back to life between these bricks, in the imperceptible pulsing of memories, the fragrances she felt belonged to her, even though they lived in a time long ago, distinct from her own.

He walked past her in just a few steps and headed towards one of the ovens. He pulled back the bolt and opened the cast-iron door to show her inside. Her heart thumped and she had goosebumps. Images of an unknown past danced in her mind, the hazy profile of a woman, little more than a girl, who moved agilely through the room, pots full of ingredients and spices spread about on the enormous table. For a moment she smelled fresh menthol on the air, but Adrian, brushing against her, was enough for it all to vanish. Somehow she was sure she had seen her mother, or a girl who looked like her, perhaps, or maybe she felt herself to be Edda.

'I don't know what to say,' she murmured with her hands pressed against her lips to protect the words and images she wanted to keep for herself.

'"Thank you, Adrian" would be a good start,' he joked, closing the oven door again and breaking the spell.

Elettra moved towards the window, turning her back on him. Her heart was hammering in her chest and she was suddenly overwhelmed by an intense heat that took her breath away. She undid the top button of her shirt, her fingertips tingling with agitation.

Everything around her suddenly seemed alive.

She leaned her forehead against a wall in an attempt to cool down a bit, but that seemed to have come to life beneath the whitewash too, so she pushed away again and turned back to face Adrian, who was watching her with folded arms. 'You really surprised me,' she apologised with an embarrassed smile. 'I hadn't realised that you were working on this wing of the convent,' she murmured to the floor, her voice shaky and rough with emotions.

He dug his hands into his pockets. 'I didn't do it all by myself, but I wanted to be the one to show you. The day after our meeting I came to take a look and have a word with Lea; she was the one who told me to start here and that it was really important to you.'

Perhaps Lea had wanted the work to start with the bakery because it might be a link to Elettra's mother: she regretted doubting her. Her friend wasn't obstructing her, she understood; perhaps, given Lea's past and the gossip she had had to withstand herself, she had been afraid that trusting Elettra would expose her to yet another danger. There was also the chance that Lea had simply done it so they could start using the larger ovens in the bakery for their business, although it was wishful thinking that the stall in the town would sell so much. They wouldn't need anywhere other than their main kitchen for a while.

Lea's lived here marginalised ever since she was born, it was insensitive of me to doubt her, she scolded herself.

'Well, are you going to have a look or not?' Adrian continued, snapping her out of her doubts.

'Of course,' she stammered. She went over to the oven and cautiously put her hand on the stone that covered it. She imagined Edda there cooking dozens of loaves of bread before building herself a life elsewhere, and now, more than thirty years later, Elettra was in the same place, on the trail of Edda's life.

Fragments of her mother surrounded her like a blanket worn threadbare but still redolent of home, a warmth into which she wanted to disappear. It was energy, Edda's energy, that Elettra now felt stirring gently inside her.

Are you here, Mamma? She surprised herself with her question, swallowing quickly to avoid being overcome by emotion. She stroked the oven walls, remembering her mother's profile in her mind, unconscious in a hospital bed hundreds of kilometres away, but when she looked through the oven door she saw something at the back of the tunnel carved through the stone.

'What's that?' she asked Adrian, beckoning him over and pointing into the darkness.

'I've no idea.'

Elettra eyed up the baker's peel. 'Let's see,' she said, grabbing hold of it then handing it to Adrian, who looked at her in puzzlement. 'You look, if it's a dead animal I might go into hysterics.'

He narrowed his eyes, took the peel and poked it decisively into the oven cavity. 'It's strange, I didn't notice anything unusual when I cleaned it, but it's lucky you saw it; once you lit this oven whatever's in here would have been reduced to ashes.'

'Let's see what it is before you start talking about luck,' she corrected him, drying her palms on her skirt. She felt full of adrenalin, a powerful energy she hadn't felt for ages, and she tapped her foot impatiently while she waited for Adrian to extract the mysterious object.

'Here we are,' he said, manoeuvring the handle with the skill of a snooker player, but as he pulled the peel out Elettra saw a hint of disappointment on his face. 'All that effort for a notebook. And who the hell hides a notebook in an oven anyway?' Adrian asked.

Those few words set off an alarm bell in her head.

Elettra immediately bent over the small bundle of papers, their edges burned, and found what she somehow knew already: it was her mother's handwriting again, and her name written in the childish script of a teenager.

'Oh my God,' she murmured, leafing through the pages incredulously, while her eyes filled with tears and her pulse pounded in her temples. 'Oh my God,' she repeated, shaking. It was an indescribable feeling, for her, to hold the time-stiffened paper in her hands and find her mother's comments in the margins of each recipe, between a butter mark and the grains of sugar that had been trapped in the tangles of time. That notebook was Edda, her mother; there she was in those recipes, in those rough measurements, in the comments, everywhere. She was in recipe 'Number 1', which she had written with her own hand, in the instructions for shortcrust pastry that graced the first page, in the béchamel recipe, corrected a couple of times, and there again in the nutty bread, the same kind she had baked the day she had her stroke.

Edda, little more than an inexperienced child, as awkward as Elettra herself used to feel when they cooked together. But still the same Edda, the mother she loved, she could shout it out loud now without embarrassment.

'Here you are at last,' she said, stroking the imprint of an aniseed trapped between the pages, its fragrance pungent and fresh. She had spent nights on end awake, waiting for a sign, something to show her which path to follow, and now here it was, irrefutable proof. There was no doubt that Edda had lived at the convent, and it was most likely that she had worked for the nuns.

She clutched the notebook to her chest, her chin pressed against the stiff cover, her imagination lost in the spirals of time.

So it really was her connection with these walls that made her send money to the convent. She probably spent some of the best years of her life here, but presumably she'd still had the courage to move away. But why, Elettra kept asking herself, if everything was so clear cut, had Edda kept the truth from her?

With her eyes and heart clouded, she flicked carefully through the pages, her fingers flying through mountains of recipes of every kind, some of them completely foreign to her palate, to her hands.

Over the years the total sum Edda had given towards the upkeep of the convent would have been significant; a sum which would almost certainly have paid for the journalism Masters in New York that Edda had denied Elettra.

'You were afraid I'd get angry with you, weren't you?' she whispered, stroking her mother's handwriting, immersed in an imaginary dialogue with her, in the magical meeting of two different times through the yellowing surface of the paper. Through that notebook and the documents that Lea had shown her, Edda had revealed her character once again; a bittersweet woman and mother. She loved her daughter, Elettra didn't doubt that, but Edda was obsessed with the idea of losing Elettra, without understanding that, in fact, the love that binds mothers and their children is a subtle but indestructible thread, capable of resisting even great distances. But Edda hadn't seen this, she didn't understand it; Elettra needed to stay with her, always by her side, because that was the only place her daughter would be safe.

Over-protectiveness, insecurity, fear: Edda was a maze of worries with distant roots, an enigma that perhaps only the walls of the convent were capable of solving.

How many more secrets do I still have to uncover before I reach you, Mamma? Elettra asked herself, pressing the notebook against her chest, her arms folded to protect something, a fragment of the past that had burrowed into her skin like a splinter. Her heartbeat had gradually returned to normal and so had her breathing. In spite of the fire in her eyes, her temperature was back to normal, too.

She had been speaking quietly but now realised that Adrian's eyes were upon her. She saw that he was tapping his foot lightly, looking at her with curiosity. He smelled of bergamot and paint and his very presence soothed her. 'You've done an amazing job, Adrian, thank you,' she murmured, looking up to see his smile, her attention caught by the light tapping of his footsteps. 'You've given me back a piece of my mother, part of a story that I've always wanted to know.'

'Well,' he downplayed it, looking slightly perplexed and rubbing his forehead, 'I just gave you a hand, that's all.'

'No, not at all. What you don't know is that I came to this island because my own mother might have grown up here. The name of this island was engraved on the medallion she always wore. My mother and I have always had a very difficult, argumentative relationship; for years I asked her to tell me about our family, about my father, but she always refused. Not a sign, even a snippet of information. That's why I came straight here when I realised this place might be connected to her past. And now I'm certain she lived here. For weeks all I've had were doubts and unanswered questions, until today, until the moment we found this,' she said, showing him the recipe book as though it were a trophy. 'And it's all thanks to you,' she added, her cheeks alight with joy, unsure why she'd shared such confidences, because she'd just told him part of a story she had continued to hide from the others.

'If it's that important to you to trace your mother and her past, I hope you can find what you're looking for here,' he whispered, rubbing her slender arms.

Elettra closed her eyes, soothed by the sweet sound of Adrian's voice in the background; she was ready to let go, to give in to the need for protection and comfort that had been burrowing inside her for months, the need which she felt more than ever in that moment, but when she turned, ready for that moment of madness, Adrian had already begun walking along the corridor, far from her voice, from her. He had moved away immediately; their contact had been fleeting, barely long enough for her to voice a wish.

She shook her head to rid herself of that thought, and stayed in the old bakery, walking through the room with the same reverence as a tailor taking a customer's measurements, but with the determination required for a war that needed winning. She could be reborn there, and the convent with her; and although she found it difficult to look at it at the moment, the notebook would be her secret weapon.

12

After finding Edda's recipe book, not a day went past when Elettra didn't visit the old bakery where the ovens were. She felt in her restless hands that the moment was approaching to light the ovens once more, to take up the challenge and try to follow the path her mother had laid out on those pages, but she was afraid to do so.

But life, Clara and the necklace with the medallion reminded her that the time for fears was over, and that if she really wanted to rediscover Edda she would have to confront them.

'I thought it would be a good idea to try out one of the ovens. I was thinking of making some biscuits, nothing special,' she said in a rush one morning while Lea yawned as she buttered her slice of toast. 'Dominique brought in two full baskets of almonds just yesterday and it would be a crime not to use them for biscuits,' she continued, immediately receiving enthusiastic agreement from Nicole, who was sitting next to Isabelle who had dropped in to visit. 'Would you like to join me and Nicole?' she asked Lea, who gulped down a mouthful of scalding coffee, distracted. Lea seemed pleased for Elettra, the smile with which she had greeted her happiness surely sincere, but Elettra also noticed a bitter note in her clouded eyes, disturbed by some new melancholy.

'I'd love to, but I can't; I need to dry the herbs for the tisanes and make the violet syrup. I've had so much to do recently that I've fallen behind with things.'

A loud and sudden thump from the floor above froze the whole table.

Elettra jumped to her feet. 'What was that?'

Lea, who had also jumped to her feet, looked worriedly towards the ceiling and exchanged a look with Isabelle. Isabelle had been joining them for breakfast at the convent more and more often, particularly since Elettra had confided to her, one late evening, the reason for her journey to the island.

It had happened by chance one night over a cup of milk when Elettra was facing too many unresolved doubts. She had gone down to the kitchen in search of something to calm her thoughts and instead had found Isabelle, a willing listening ear for her story. It had felt natural to tell her about her mother, her bakery and her special link with the convent, but when Elettra had asked Isabelle whether she had ever met her, Isabelle had given her the same answer as all the others.

'I'm sorry, unfortunately I can't help you. I've always had a pretty good relationship with God, but I've always had problems with the Curia and its representatives, and there were plenty to be found at the convent at that time, so I made myself as scarce as possible,' she had quickly explained, crushing Elettra's hopes.

This response had prompted Elettra to keep her guard up around Isabelle, especially since Isabelle also stubbornly denied the existence of the voice that cried out in the middle of the night.

The same presence that had just made itself known.

Lea and Isabelle looked up, both wide-eyed and holding their breath.

'What's going on?' Elettra broke the silence, following their gaze.

Isabelle swallowed, her lips dry as she slowly lowered her raised hand towards the table. 'It must be a mouse or something, the roof is full of those creatures.' She played it down, barely looking at Lea who signalled almost imperceptibly to her.

'Exactly, I'd better go and take a look,' Lea responded, wiping her hands on a tea towel. 'It's always best to check before they cause some kind of disaster,' she added, hurrying to the door.

'Wait, Lea, I'll come with you,' Elettra exclaimed, ready to follow her into the corridor, but Isabelle's rough grasp held her back.

'Leave her, Lea's not afraid of a couple of mice, is she? That girl's dealt with plenty of worse problems!' she said, relaxing her grip once she was sure Lea was far enough away.

'Yes, but what if they weren't mice?'

'If it wasn't mice then it was the door falling off that old wardrobe in her room yet again. In fact, I'd stake my life on it; I've told her it's dangerous, but she never listens to me,' Isabelle added, returning to her seat at the table and spreading a generous helping of butter on her bread while Elettra looked at the ceiling, perplexed.

'The wardrobe door?'

'Yes, the wardrobe door,' Isabelle replied impatiently. 'Why on earth do you two ask so many questions? First you, then Lea; it's just too much!' she burst out as Elettra continued to look sceptically at the ceiling.

Wardrobe doors don't just fall off by themselves, Isabelle, she thought, shaking her head at yet another mystery. And Lea's hiding something. But what?

There were footsteps above their heads and the air was full of the sound of the swallows flitting amongst the branches of the fruit-laden trees.

Nicole gathered up the crumbs from their breakfast and scattered them on the windowsill, then turned to the two women sitting at the table with feigned cheerfulness. 'Right, Elettra, shall we go and find the ingredients for the biscuits?'

The sun was at its highest when Elettra and her assistant reached the bakery.

They had gathered and weighed out all the ingredients together and, although she watched her apprentice's every move, Elettra was always careful not to invade her space; she wanted to leave Nicole free to feel the dough with her own hands. She was the one who needed to tell from the texture of the dough that she had added too much flour, to 'speak' with the mixture she was mixing until she achieved the perfect balance.

Nicole made a little crater in the mountain of flour and sugar and filled it with the eggs and milk, while the butter softened on a saucer. The only sound in the kitchen was the metallic noise of the utensils that swayed on hooks hanging from the ceiling.

In the distance they could also hear the repetitive sound of Dominique's hoe and Lea coming and going in the herb garden, where she was picking ingredients for her infusions.

'Did you know Fabien used to love almond biscuits? He was just crazy about them,' Nicole confessed, breaking the porous egg shells against the table and dropping a couple of yolks into the mouth of the sweet volcano. She took a piece of butter from the saucer and rubbed it between her fingers.

When she heard that name again Elettra stopped, her hands buried in the pale mass of the dough she was preparing for the next day's bread. She hadn't been able to find a way to talk to Nicole about the tragedy she had suffered since her first night at the convent. Nicole had been madly in love with her husband and Elettra, who had barely experienced love, could only imagine how devastating her pain at the loss must be.

Nicole watched in silence as the dough crumbled. For a moment Elettra thought she had stopped breathing, so slight was the movement of her chest beneath her shirt, but perhaps she was just trying hard not to remember. Nicole added a bit of milk to combine the crumbs into the mixture, which became smooth and elastic. Elettra turned to look at her, her arms covered in flour. 'He must have been a very special person.'

'Yes,' Nicole nodded with a strained smile while Elettra suggested with a glance that it was time to add the baking powder.

Disorientated by their conversation, Elettra groped for the bag of toasted almonds she had left to cool and poured a couple of handfuls into Nicole's dough. The young widow plunged her hands into it, smiling at the memory of her Fabien. She divided the mixture into two long snakes, like Elettra had shown her, brushed them with a beaten egg and slid them into the oven, turning to her friend who was watching her in concentration, a smudge of flour on her cheek.

'It was his cousin Luc who persuaded him to go out to sea the day of the storm,' Nicole started to tell her story, closing the oven door. 'He kept going on about it until he finally convinced Fabien, even though I was against it. At the port that morning the mother of one of the fishermen, one of the oldest women on the island, was like a wild animal, as if she could sense that something wasn't right; she kept telling her son that he shouldn't go, that he'd be able to scrape together the money to pay the bills some other way, but he paid her no attention,' she added with a hint of frustration. She dragged a chair across to the oven and curled up in front of the flames. She put a hand against her cheek, enchanted by the tongues of flame that danced in the oven's black mouth. 'They never listen to women here any more,' she murmured as Elettra turned to look at her, 'and the sea didn't spare them.'

Elettra looked down. She was having a hard time keeping her eyes on the small woman who was such a scatterbrain in the kitchen, yet so stoic in the face of tragedy, and who maintained the smile that lit up her face despite the storm and its legacy. Pain had stripped her heart of the promise of a happy life with the man she loved, but, unlike Dominique, Nicole had not relinquished her sweetness.

'It must have been terrible,' Elettra said.

Nicole smiled slightly as she slowly squashed a ball of dough between her fingers. 'Yes, it was, and it still is every day, but I know that I haven't lost my Fabien. He lives and he'll live for ever, because in my heart he's immortal. There, no one can take him away from me, not even the sea.'

Elettra nodded, her gaze downcast to hide her emotion at these words; they were stronger than anything she had ever felt. Elettra continued working the dough, then set it down on the shelf next to the oven. 'You're a very wise woman, Nicole.'

'You're wrong,' her friend told her, her voice suddenly rough. 'I'm just like any other woman.' She turned to check the biscuits which were darkening in the oven, breathing in the scent of her memories.

A ray of sun, the last one before the storm that was brewing in the sky, struck the half-open window, and caressed Nicole's cheek; it carried the scent of the sea, that distant and silent world where Fabien was at rest.

'Elettra?'

'Yes?'

'Do you think we'll manage to save the convent?'

Elettra set aside the spatula she was using and put her hand on Nicole's shoulder. 'We have to, we don't have a choice. We have to,' she repeated.

She stayed by Nicole's side until, together, they took the biscuits out of the oven, the first her friend had ever made in her life.

Elettra showed her how to slice them diagonally, and together they put them back in the oven to toast. They saved them for after dinner that evening.

Later, in front of a melancholy fire sweetened by the subtle notes of juniper wood and a glass of liqueur made from wild berries, Elettra and Nicole brought out the biscuits.

'Elettra?' Nicole said, her face illuminated by the flames. 'Do you want to try one?'

Elettra smiled back at her, distracted, and put her drink on the table. 'I'd love to.' She took a biscuit from the plate, examining it carefully before biting into it under Nicole's nervous gaze. The taste reminded her of ice-cold nights in her home town, when the heater in Edda's apartment would break down and she would make space for Elettra in her warm bed. Elettra now felt the warmth of that embrace envelop her, as her fingertips were perfumed by the spiced dough, and as if everything else had vanished and her mother was still there.

She placed the rest of the biscuit on her napkin; she felt fortunate to have relived that small fragment of the past. Nicole was twisting her hands as she waited for Elettra's response. It was Nicole's hard work that had made Elettra's journey back in time possible.

Nicole had that gift, she knew how to evoke happy memories.

'Well?' Nicole asked, fidgeting impatiently in her seat.

'Perfect,' Elettra decreed, patting Nicole's hand.

Later that evening, alone in her room, Elettra thought about the power of memories and of a past that is difficult to escape. All her friends had that sort of past. Her life had always been a journey along slippery paths where nothing is stable, but she was tired of it. She needed certainties, to understand where her family came from in order to understand who she was. And to do that she needed to understand why her mother had abandoned the convent, yet had continued to support it for years in great secrecy.

The reason must be hidden right in those forbidden rooms, from which Lea was still determined to keep her far away. Elettra was sure of it. That's where she would start to search for the truth, and there was no time like the present.

It's time to take action, she repeated to herself, walking quickly along the corridor. She turned to look at the moonlight pouring in from the windows and held her breath; she could hear the wind howling.

She pulled her dressing gown tightly around her and set off up the first flight of stairs towards the truth. She went up them one at a time, her blood pumping faster with every step until she reached the door to the archives. She slipped a grip out of her hair and took out of her pocket a pair of pliers she had borrowed from Adrian's tool box, remembering a game she and Ruth used to play at school as children, picking the locks of their enemies' secret diaries with whatever was to hand. The same trick took longer with an ancient lock, and required a calm that her fingers could not achieve. They were shaking, the combined result of excitement and terror.

She slipped the metal pin into the lock, keeping her wrist soft like Ruth had always told her, but a sudden thud from the stairs left her paralysed.

Then a voice snapped the fragile thread of her courage.

'Why are you doing this to me, Edda? Why, Edda?' the voice shouted. Then there was a second thump, then another, and a shower of broken glass and someone crying out.

Elettra jerked suddenly, breaking off the spoke of the hairgrip inside the lock, her breath caught in her throat. She swore – it wouldn't be easy to get it back out – as she started to hear weeping, a sad litany.

Her eyes raked the deep darkness of the night, her sweat ran cold on her skin.

'Elettra, Elettra, is that you?'

A shadow appeared, coming towards her, steps dragging with fatigue.

She moved away from the archive door, the pliers and what remained of the hairgrip buried deep in her pocket. She took one step, then another, until she came face to face with Isabelle's silhouette. She had a long wound on her arm, a cut that ran from her shoulder to her elbow, colouring her white shirt a deep red. Little specks of glass, sharp and irregular, rained down around her worn sandals.

'Isabelle, what happened?' Elettra asked, hurrying towards her with her arms outstretched, heedless of the other woman's hesitation as she backed away.

'For heaven's sake, stay back or you might hurt yourself. My skirt is full of glass.'

'Don't worry about that ... how on earth did you get that cut ... and more importantly, what are you doing out at this time of night?'

Isabelle pressed her hand against the cut, covering her fingers in blood. 'I fell, and this is what happened,' she mumbled, avoiding Elettra's gaze as she tried to meet her eyes in the darkness.

'Right, come with me to the kitchen. I'll find something to clean that cut and I'll check that there's no glass in it.' She gave a last glance towards the closed door to the rooms which she believed and hoped contained the archive, and escorted Isabelle downstairs with a sigh. She checked carefully that there were no fragments of glass in the cut and bandaged it up while she waited for the water to boil for a tisane.

'Well, are you going to tell me what happened?' she pressed, but Isabelle shrugged her shoulders, staring her down as if she were a stubborn child.

'I've already told you; I fell and bumped into a window.'

'A window? Where?'

'For God's sake, Elettra, you're worse than a policeman!' she grumbled impatiently. 'It's not enough for you to know that I've hurt myself, now you want to know how many pieces the window broke into?'

Elettra crossed her arms. Here we go again, she thought, irritated. She turned and added two spoonfuls of dried herbs to the boiling water; after a few minutes she poured the infusion into two mugs. She didn't say a word, just sat down opposite her friend and sipped the tisane.

She was well aware that Isabelle wouldn't be able to bear the silence for long.

'Fine,' she gave in at last, spreading her arms. 'Yesterday evening I came by to see how Lea was doing, and we chatted for a while. I hadn't planned to stay long at all, but then I realised that it was very late and I wouldn't be able to make my way home across the island at night.'

'Why not? There are people around, and you know the paths well; you couldn't get lost even if you wanted to,' Elettra thought aloud, but was silenced by the look Isabelle gave her.

'You can go and tell that to the wild boars that come down from the Titan by night. I only know how to deal with them when they're in pieces, in a stew, with a nice pile of potatoes on the side, other than that I don't care to make their acquaintance,' she replied, pulling her shawl across her chest. 'As for you, what are you doing wandering around the convent at this hour? Old people like me don't need much sleep, but you should rest.'

Elettra looked down guiltily; mentioning the archive to Isabelle

133

was out of the question. And then there were the threats; someone didn't want her to ask questions. She was still shaking at having heard the voice. She needed to do this by herself. She tightened her grip on the steaming tisane, her eyes reflected in the mixture of chamomile, orange blossom and hawthorn. 'I couldn't sleep.' It was a lie, but only in part; even if she'd stayed in her room, she wouldn't have fallen asleep easily.

'Mmm. You see?'

'What?'

'I haven't nagged like you, always exhausting people with questions; I contented myself with what you told me. You should learn to do the same.'

Elettra said, 'Perhaps I should, but I can't. Because just before we met I heard that voice again. It was calling my mother,' she pressed on when she saw Isabelle shifting in her chair. 'It's the truth, Isabelle: I heard it. And you must have heard it too.'

'I didn't hear anything at all, and if you weren't so obsessed with all this history, you would understand why.'

'What are you trying to say?'

Isabelle put down her tisane, reaching for Elettra's hands.

'That at a certain point you have to let the past go, before it takes over your present.'

Elettra kept repeating these words of Isabelle's to herself in her room later. She had offered Isabelle her bed, but she had said she was more comfortable in the armchair in the kitchen beside the embers.

'I like the smell of cinders, it reminds me of my childhood,' she had said just before they said goodnight.

'And my memories, my childhood?' Elettra had said, asking the stars, looking for her answer in the corner between Andromeda and Cassiopeia. But all that remained of her wishes and hopes that night was a patch of spectral light.

13

Summer suddenly left the island overnight, hiding the sun behind a layer of fine mist. The whole countryside faded under the steely shadow of the clouds and the wicker chairs disappeared from the few inhabited roads, along with the cats and the bicycles. Only the elderly, the memory of the island, remained outside, tending their gardens and the small patches of land snatched from the sea where they gathered food to live on; a storm was encroaching upon the streets which were usually filled with tourists.

The area around the port wasn't the only place where the air got colder every day; the sun-scorched paths where Elettra loved to lose herself and think of Edda soon became muddy rivulets.

So the kitchen and her mother's recipe book became her only refuge.

Elettra had done nothing but knead, bake and ice since Edda's notebook full of recipes had appeared in her life. The old jam- and butter-stained exercise book was, in her eyes, more precious than a photo album, because in the pages full of spelling mistakes, numbers and notes in the margins, she had rediscovered her mother, and the power of a memory that no roll of film could ever have captured. The pages full of notes and stains had restored a passion she thought she had exhausted, that she was sure had been washed out of her blood a long time ago. But she had been mistaken.

She was mistaken because in following her mother's instructions she rediscovered Edda's voice, she could feel her warm breath on her skin again, almost sense her next to her.

Everything in the convent, everything now, spoke to her of Edda. She went for walks in the garden by herself more and more often, to think, especially when she found herself arguing with Lea about even the smallest things. In fact, since she and Adrian had found Edda's notebook, she had found it impossible to talk to Lea. Lea had started behaving strangely towards her: she seemed colder every day, and sometimes even standoffish, but when she was with the others or Adrian she seemed to return to normal.

One day, after her umpteenth argument with Lea, Elettra had sought refuge from her mental turmoil under the thick canopy of the old lemon tree at the end of the garden and there, with her head against the trunk, rich with the smell of grass and damp, she had noticed a scar in the bark. Annoyed by Lea's words that still crackled like electricity in her mind, her heart had stopped for a moment when she made sense of the scar: they were words carved with a knife decades before.

The name legible on the trunk was her mother's. And underneath that was something that had been crossed out.

At some point long ago her mother had also sat beneath this lemon tree. Perhaps she, too, had had a day as bad as Elettra's, or perhaps she'd argued with someone and had come out here out of frustration too.

We've never been as close as we are now, Elettra thought a few days later, as she stroked the cover of the notebook and waited for the dark that would hide her from the eyes of the world. She had decided she wouldn't stop at the first failed attempt and, in fact, her meeting with Isabelle had raised her suspicions even further. That part of the convent, those rooms, were hiding something.

And so, when the sun gave way to darkness, Elettra ventured into the deserted corridor, the only sound the dripping of the drainpipe. She slowly put one foot in front of the other, holding her breath every time she passed one of her friends' rooms, and prayed that Lea wouldn't be suffering from insomnia that night.

She used a set of pliers to extract the hairgrip that had snapped off in the lock the other night, and immediately inserted a new one. She released the deadbolt with a quick jerk, ignoring the sweat gathering on her forehead, but as the door opened she felt all her level-headedness desert her and collapsed to her knees with relief.

She took a candle from her dressing gown pocket and its warm light lit years of abandonment. Finally, a bit of luck: she had found the archive straight away. It was a small room, crammed full of papers; there were ledgers everywhere, completed in an elegant script that seemed to belong to a time many centuries past, but in fact went back only seventy years or so, and hundreds of books in dusty towers. The surface of the desk was completely covered in sheets of paper; documents and bundles of correspondence were everywhere, making it difficult to even walk through the labyrinth, and Elettra began to feel uncomfortable. Finding information about Edda would not be that easy, and would surely take more than one night of searching.

Why on earth did Lea want to hide such a mess? she wondered, holding back a sneeze. She decided that if she wanted to learn anything it would be best to take a few ledgers at a time so as not to raise suspicion. She took the first volumes within reach, huge tomes that she would only be able to hide under her wardrobe, where she knew that nobody would find them even when cleaning, and carried them to her room. She dropped them onto the bed, turned on the light and started to leaf through them; inside were columns full of names, with dates and figures written in the margins.

These look like the endowments the families gave to the convent to provide for their daughters, Elettra guessed, noting how much difference there was between the donations. Some had placed great riches into the hands of the then abbess, some had even given land, and others had only offered a couple of animals, which Elettra imagined must have been all they had.

'Let's see where you are,' she murmured, searching for her mother's name amongst the columns. She examined the vast majority of the registers she had brought with her, but there was no trace of Edda. No name recorded, not a date as a starting point. She closed the last book with a thump, placing her elbow on the cover. She would need to further her search soon, but would have to do it quickly, because if the mayor had his way the time she had left on the island would soon run out.

Another few weeks and not much would remain of the flowery cloister Nicole had tended to so devotedly; soon they would have picked the last peaches, made the plums into jam and preserved the black figs Dominique ate for her solitary lunches, laying in supplies of food for the cold season ahead.

The next morning Elettra felt as though the air had the same flavour as the mushroom soup bubbling on the hob, a flavour that reminded her of Sundays in autumn when she would go with Edda and Ruth's family to gather mushrooms in the forests around the city. She would return from those outings covered in mud and absolutely starving, but she remembered with nostalgia the garlic and rosemary flavour of Edda's soup and her voice telling her not to leave the garlic on her plate because it was good for her heart. As if those fleshy morsels were amulets against all ills.

'What did they do to you, Mamma, to drive you away from here and make you keep the truth hidden from me for all these years?' she wondered, speaking aloud without realising it.

'What are you doing, talking to yourself?'

'For God's sake, Adrian!' she shrieked. 'Do you always jump out at people?'

'When you're least expecting it, otherwise it's no fun,' he shot back.

'Very funny.'

Adrian was outside the windows. Behind him a flash of golden lightning hit the sea, releasing a burst of electricity into the water. The sound of the rain on the roof was like a jet engine.

'Well, will you let me in or are you hoping one will hit me?' Adrian looked her straight in the eyes, sheltering under the jacket he held over his head.

'Come in, at least you'll be in the warm here.'

With a shuffle of damp feet across the floor, he immediately went over to the fireplace, his arms outstretched. 'This damned rain caught me by surprise; I told Lea I'd come by to finish the work on the roof, but as soon as I got here it started pouring.'

'What can you do? Summer's over; we can't expect sunny days any more.'

'True, but it has to be said, the end of this summer was a bit crazy; I can't remember such a rainy September for years!' Small puddles of water grew around his shoes.

'It serves you right; that'll teach you to scare me,' she joked, looking at the dripping shirt he wore stubbornly in spite of the shivers he was trying to hide from her. She gestured that he should take it off.

'Excuse me?'

'Take your shirt off,' she insisted and put her hands on her hips and gave him a sly smile. 'I've seen a man wearing less than you are now, so give me your shirt and I'll hang it by the oven to dry. But if you'd rather keep it on and play the tough man, then go ahead.'

'I am a tough man!' he defended himself, slipping it off. He balled it up in his hand and gave it to her, pointing at her. 'You're the one who's trying to corrupt me.'

The rain around the convent intensified and became a grey wall, a screen for Elettra's carefree laughter. 'Stop talking rubbish and at least make yourself useful.'

'This is slavery, Signorina Cavani.'

Elettra glanced at the crate of bruised apples that Dominique had given her a couple of days ago; it would be impossible to sell them, and she was sick and tired of filling jars of jam. She took one to weigh up its uneven roundness, inhaling the scent of wet earth and vanilla.

'Do you like apple cake?'

'It's one of my favourites, why?'

'Then start whipping the cream; if you want a slice you'll have to prepare the butter first,' she replied, sliding a whisk and a bowl of cream towards Adrian, who rubbed his chin doubtfully.

'I'm warning you: I can barely tell the difference between an omelette and a boiled egg.'

Already busy with bowls and ingredients, Elettra turned away from the larder for a moment. 'You don't need any great skill for the moment; all you'll need to do is distinguish between a solid mass and a liquid one. In the meantime, I'm going to get everything else together.'

'This doesn't strike me as an equal division of labour.'

'I didn't say it would be,' Elettra replied, closing the larder door with a nudge of her hip. She combined the egg and the sugar and gradually added the sifted flour, never taking her eyes off Adrian, and when she saw that the cream was starting to stiffen she wiped her hands and wet a clean cloth, moving towards him. 'Now it's time to separate the butter from the buttermilk,' she said, guiding his hand over the cloth. Elettra's touch was damp but firm, and her nearness gave off a bouquet of spices that seemed to confound him. The butter he was holding slipped off the cloth, but Elettra caught it before it could fall back into the bowl. 'Don't rush,' she reassured him, softly, but she found herself closer to him than she wanted; she could almost see the pupils in his chocolate-coloured eyes, but it was Adrian's smile that drew her attention.

'I preferred whipping the cream,' he replied.

Elettra looked down and immediately moved away; she felt uncomfortable but pretended it was nothing. There had always been a boundary between them, solid as a wall, and she found it reassuring to know that neither of them had ever crossed it. After Walter, she had promised herself she'd had enough of men, even though Ruth had laughed in her face when she'd told her, warning her that nothing is for ever. Especially that sort of declaration.

Nonetheless, trusting a man again seemed impossible; she had suffered too much, all the tears she could ever imagine shedding had been spent on Walter, so she didn't have any left for another failed love story. She shook her head to clear her mind of such thoughts and tucked her hair behind her ears. 'Stop complaining and pick that butter up again,' she growled, continuing the joke. Her tone was happy, but something was slightly off and, however slightly, things between them had started to become strange.

'Done.'

'Good. Now squeeze it to get the liquid out, then wash it and do the whole thing again and it'll be ready.' She walked around the table to return to her dough. Adrian's eyes followed her the whole time; Elettra felt them on her when she lifted the bowl of dough to her chest to beat it, when she bent over the cake tin to arrange the apples and give them a generous dusting of sugar and when she was sliding the baking tray into the oven.

They were always on her, whatever she was doing; even in the following days when she was alone in the garden sitting under the lemon tree and he was working somewhere else in the convent, she felt them.

And Isabelle, who returned to the fray just a few days later with her usual mischievous smile, noticed too.

'Adrian seems very interested in you,' she observed, tapping her finger on the bottle of dandelion syrup Lea had made. The syrup was to treat the cough that Isabelle had been suffering for days. 'He comes up with all kinds of reasons to be near to you. He did it the other day when there was the storm, too.'

'Isabelle's right; you seem to have made a real impression on him,' Lea remarked, picking at a bunch of grapes. Unlike the brazen midwife, Elettra heard reproof in her friend's voice. A bitter note that she hadn't noticed before, and that alarmed her.

'It doesn't matter. Even if he is interested in me,' she retorted loudly, 'I'm busy enough trying to solve my own problems, I don't need any more. I've only just broken up with my boyfriend,' she added to dispel any trace of doubt.

'So he's your ex-boyfriend,' Lea corrected, seriously.

Isabelle jumped in her seat, her cheeks blazing. 'Lea, what's that tone for? Since when have you been interested in Adrian?'

Lea replied bluntly, 'I never have been.' Elettra was surprised by the strain in her voice.

Isabelle continued. 'Okay, but listen carefully: two men fighting over a woman can be flattering, but two women, two *friends*,' she specified, 'throwing away their own friendship over a man isn't just embarrassing. It's stupid,' she declared bitterly.

'Well, you needn't worry. Believe me: I'm not interested in Adrian,' Elettra intervened, but Isabelle waved her words away impatiently.

'Even more stupid than fighting over the same man is refusing to be happy with someone else just because you wept over the wrong man. Elettra, splitting up with a boyfriend isn't like losing a husband; you don't need to wear mourning, because no woman should waste time grieving over useless men. Life is for living.' She waggled her finger at Elettra, as Lea angrily stripped grapes from their stalks.

'Even if she wanted to live with Adrian she couldn't anyway; Elettra won't be staying here with us much longer because her mother is dying.'

Isabelle blinked and her hands rose to her chest as she turned towards a bright red Elettra.

Try to stay calm. Elettra repeated it to herself like a mantra, but the midwife's questioning gaze was a beacon shining on her. Elettra wanted to say something, to defend herself against Lea's crude words, but her heart was pounding in her chest, making it difficult to think, and her throat had closed in on itself. Lea had gone too far, revealing details of Elettra's personal life that Isabelle didn't know. She clenched her fists, her throat a boundless desert, dry earth blasted by a murderous sun.

'You have no right to speak about my mother,' she said sharply, her voice hoarse with rage. 'And even less to make statements about her health just because you've probably never had a mother,' she added. She wanted to hurt Lea, to plunge the knife into her flesh and pay her back in her own currency.

Her blow hit its mark effortlessly.

Elettra had buried the blade in an open wound and she had won, delivering the death-blow to her enemy, but she wasn't happy, not if the price she had to pay was the pain they each nursed in their souls. Not if the target was the person to whom she felt closest, who had welcomed her into her home and her life. But Lea had gone too far for Elettra to remain silent.

She continued, 'It's true that my mother is dying, but you have no right to say such things in my presence, as if she were nothing to me. You have no right.' She pointed at Lea before turning her back and leaving the room as Isabelle looked on.

14

Following that afternoon when Isabelle had learned how serious Edda's condition was, Elettra had avoided being alone in the same room with Lea. She preferred to concentrate on baking goods to sell at the market to the last remaining tourists. Despite their disagreements, Elettra was determined to save the convent, even if it would be more difficult without the support of the owner.

And yet Lea had tried to heal the rift.

The very evening of their argument Lea had knocked on the door of Elettra's room to apologise, but she had been left to talk to a closed door for almost an hour. Sitting on the bed against the wall, Elettra hadn't found the strength to open it; she couldn't have done it without attacking Lea, saying even more that she knew she'd regret.

Elettra had a strong sense that Lea had wanted to take revenge on her, to punish her for her understanding with Adrian, for the special way they had of looking at each other, for finding each other even in the morning chaos of the fish market, as they had a few days ago.

It had happened that Friday; she couldn't have forgotten it even if she'd wanted to. She'd gone to the fishermen's jetty with Lea in search of inspiration for a new biscuit to celebrate the opening of their stall and to buy something for lunch, some good fish to treat her friends. The sun was rising up from its bed of fluffy white clouds and the crowd was swarming around the fishermen's crates. There, immersed in the chatter of the market, amongst dozens of people and strong smells, she had let the wind guide her to the unmistakeable scent of Adrian, the mixture of paint and the sea, amongst the gusts of the south-westerly wind. It didn't matter that she couldn't make out his face, because her skin knew before her eyes that he was there.

She'd left Lea to haggle for a red sea bream on her behalf, purchasing it from the fishermen for half the starting price, and she had stood and watched Lea make her way between the stalls with her basket on her arm, looking at the half-empty crates of fish.

Elettra hadn't managed to move a single step. Her breathing had become deeper, almost as if she wanted to trap a tiny bit of that scent with each breath of air, holding it with the beat of her lowered heart rate. Adrian was there, she could feel his eyes searching for her, she read his presence on the faces she saw, in the hundreds of footsteps around her; dozens of pounding sounds on the cobbled ground signalled the hurried rhythm of life taking place amongst the crates of fish and abandoned lobster pots.

And then, finally, she saw him. It was just a brief meeting, but the timing was impeccable; they had both looked in the same direction at just the right moment, they had found themselves in front of each other even in the throng of islanders and tourists. He was sitting on a moped in the company of a friend, but that bright smile and his sea-tangled hair served to confirm something she had been fighting against for weeks.

Alchemy; there wasn't another word to describe that connection, the feeling, the sensation in her head a moment before he entered a room where she was too. A word which Lea must have seen drawn in the tight cord which linked their gazes, and which had made a significant contribution to her black mood.

After a few days, she found the will and the strength to confront her. She asked Lea if her sudden hostility was down to feelings she harboured for Adrian. She'd denied it vigorously.

'You're asking me about something impossible, because love has always destroyed women like me,' Lea had replied cryptically, looking her in the eye for a moment before plunging back into her world of vials and decoctions, far from Elettra and everything else.

Her response had left Elettra with more doubts than ever; but if that was her position, Lea needed to know that she had no intention of giving up her friendship with Adrian.

Their closeness was important because he was one of the few people with whom she could speak freely and who shared her sense of humour; so as soon as she could, she baked a batch of *focacce alle mele* and set off towards his house with her basket under her arm. Since Adrian had appeared in her life, Elettra had felt her connection with the kitchen grow stronger every day, pleasure running over her skin at the thought of the moment he would taste the fruit of her work.

Was this how you felt when you prepared my favourite dishes, when you cooked for your clients? Was it joy you were trying to teach me, Mamma, that love which you found so difficult to communicate in words? Was this why you wanted me in the bakery with you? So I would see that feeding others can make you happy?

She took small steps as she made her way down the steep path that led from the convent to the beach, amongst bushes bare of flowers and berries, now ripped from the branches' embrace by the harsher weather, while to her right the sea crashed against the shore. She knocked hard on the door several times but nobody answered, a possibility she had already considered. So she followed the instructions he had once given her: the key was under the plant pot on the windowsill.

She turned it in the lock and found herself once again in the spartan kitchen where, just a few weeks ago, she had first asked Adrian's help, a time that seemed very distant.

She put her basket on the table, planks of juniper, worn from use and salt water, and the scent of paint tickled her nose, drawing her into the part of the house she had never entered before.

'Is anyone there?' she repeated to chase away the doubt that she might not be alone. Nobody answered.

She left her bag on the table beside the basket and, after a last look around the kitchen, took the first step towards the unknown. In front of her was an old white-painted wooden door that opened into the lounge. Between the whitewashed walls stood a turquoise sofa with a long-fringed blanket on it and a pile of old magazines that served as a table. In the opposite wall was a door painted a sky blue that reminded her of clear days when the mistral was blowing; through there, Elettra guessed, Adrian's secret must be hidden, and that was where she headed, determined to uncover it. She knew that she had no right, but life at the convent had taught her that there was no way of uncovering a mystery without the determination to conquer your own bit of truth. She placed her hand cautiously on the doorknob and as soon as she crossed the threshold she had the sensation of having been catapulted into a parallel world: all the furniture had been piled into a corner and completely covered with a dusty cloth to make room for a dozen female busts that filled the space.

The curtains had been taken down and the sun, risen high, shone in powerfully, filling the room with the violent light of day.

Elettra rubbed her eyes, her reverent gaze barely brushing the creations in progress; she had never been in an artist's studio until that moment, but her presence there made her feel like a defiler, as if she were robbing Adrian of his creativity.

She walked across the floor littered with bags, scalpels and abandoned rags. A golden reflection caught her attention and her eyes flew towards a corner of the room. She made a path through the papers that smothered the mysterious treasure, sketches of studies of a woman's hands and eyes, and there, abandoned in a corner, Elettra spotted a canvas: it showed a boat in a storm: a small human creation against the immeasurable power of nature that was overpowering it.

She picked up the painting, fascinated by the softness of the oil colours applied with fingers, displaying the tragedy of a shipwreck there on a seashore disfigured by a storm surge which had dragged tree trunks and coloured pebbles with it, but she didn't dare touch it because just looking at that boat with its flaky hull and a broken oar brought her back to her own storms.

She put the canvas on a table and continued to leaf through sketches and loose sheets. Everywhere Elettra looked she felt surrounded by a sense of loss; she read it in the shocked faces around her, in the hand stretched towards an unknown elsewhere, in the desperate rolling of the boat tossed by the sea, and yet the hope of salvation lived alongside that desperation. The same will to live that had pushed her to undertake this journey.

She walked silently to the middle of the room and wrapped her arms around herself, trying to relieve the suffering that vibrated between the walls. She closed her eyes for a moment, her head tilted slightly back as she quenched herself on those stories. She inhaled the chalky smell of the dust, of the stone that barely contained the subject matter and those women's faces, replicated over and over.

The floorboards suddenly creaked behind her. She heard heavy steps alongside the noise of the wind.

He was behind her, carrying the scent of the sea; his unruly hair was scented by the warm midday sand, his clothes were impregnated with the now familiar odour of salt and seaweed. When her eyes opened, she realised he had been watching her, and she looked at him, full of embarrassment and stammering words of apology.

'So you've had a look. I hope you like them.'

Elettra nodded and smiled at him. 'They're wonderful pieces,' she replied, gesturing to the array of sketches and busts. 'Are they all your work?'

'They are indeed, they're all my women.'

Elettra shook her head, looking again at the female portraits; at first glance they had seemed to her a gallery of different faces, each a woman with her story to tell, with her own wrinkles and hardships, but on closer inspection she noticed that there was something that linked all of them, a common feature. 'It's strange: the more I look at these faces the more they all seem to belong to the same woman.'

'Touché.'

'Is she your muse?' she asked him. There was something quiet and tender in the way he looked at his creations, a feeling much deeper than the age-old strata that had originated the rock which he'd shaped with his chisel, and she was determined to discover his secret.

'Much more. She's my mother.'

'Really?'

'She died when I was eleven.'

'I'm sorry.'

'Why? You didn't know each other.'

Elettra lowered her gaze, her awkward hands running over the flowers printed on her skirt. This often happened to her with Adrian; when the conversation became too personal he would close himself away behind a smile which excluded the rest of the world. But Elettra wanted to change things, to make him understand that he could trust her, that she would listen if only he opened up. She cleared her throat. 'Is she your inspiration?'

'Do you really want to talk about it?' Adrian seemed surprised. He removed a pot full of pens and scalpels of all shapes and sizes from a chair and sat on it backwards, his chin resting on his folded arms. 'I started to sculpt her face because I was afraid of forgetting it,' he said, his gaze perhaps lost in a distant time, of melancholy happiness that still beat strongly inside him. 'You know, when you're a child you tend to subconsciously select memories; I can tell you about my first day of school in minute detail, but there's no trace of my mother's voice inside my head. I lost it, so I thought I should at least try and capture the rest of her before I forgot completely.'

'Don't you have any photos of her?'

Adrian swallowed, his gaze impenetrable. 'I'd rather not talk about that if you don't mind.'

'Not at all,' she agreed. She looked around, rubbing her arms. She was suddenly uncomfortable there, among the replicas of a woman who had otherwise disappeared. 'I really just dropped by to leave you some *focacce alle mele*. I left them in the kitchen, I expect you saw them.'

'No, I came in the back, without going through the kitchen.'

'Okay . . . well, now you know.'

'Yes, at least I can thank you.'

Elettra blushed. 'There's no need; I brought them because after all you've done at the convent, it seemed the least I could do,' she said, watching him disappear into the corridor to emerge with the basket hanging from his arm.

'I was just doing my job, but I'm very glad you brought me these: I'll probably have finished the lot by this evening,' he said, patting the wicker basket.

'There aren't that many. Have a look, there are presents from the others, too.'

Adrian put the basket on the table and removed the hand-kerchief embroidered by Nicole that had protected the booty of candles, infusions and jars of jam, in addition to the bag of Elettra's *focacce* which filled the air with the cheerful smell of sugar and cinnamon. He rummaged for some time, fishing a clearly labelled jar from the basket. 'Peach and lavender, eh? This looks interesting, but you won't get rid of me by plying me with jams,' he joked.

'No, at least I hope not,' she replied, disorientated. He brushed her back with his hand as he led her into the kitchen. He took the same dark-coloured glasses and bottle of wine from the sideboard that he had offered her the first time, and this time she accepted.

Adrian filled the glasses and sat at the table, his eyes fixed on the knots in the wood. 'My mother was called Anne Morel,' he began his tale after a brief silence. The copper pans hanging from the beams above their head tinkled while the wind outside blew up around the house. Somewhere shutters banged and the sound of hinges in need of oiling reached them.

'Morel,' Elettra repeated, drinking a sip of wine; she'd heard that name before.

'She was the first wife of my father, Bernard Morel. The Parisian who wants to buy the convent and who is working with the mayor to do it,' he hurried to add, beating her to it.

Elettra almost choked at this confession; her wine went down the wrong way and she started to cough. There must be some mistake. There had to be. 'Are you sure it's him? Not someone with the same name?'

'I wish, but it's not.' He played with the now empty glass in his hands, then banged the chipped table. 'Bernard is a real shark, one of the worst. He killed my mother just so he could marry Elodie Laurent, the daughter of the luxury hotel magnate.'

He poured himself another glass of wine and then another, while Elettra found herself shocked into silence. She stared at Adrian with her big jade-green eyes, reading all his bitterness in the scarlet traces of wine on his glass.

'Unfortunately he didn't manage to get rid of me the same way. After his second honeymoon he took me to live with him in the villa belonging to Elodie, who had fallen pregnant before the earth of my mother's grave had even settled, and that's where I stayed until I managed to get out of there. I couldn't stand it,' he told her, swallowing the last mouthful.

To Elettra, who had spent her whole life searching for traces of her father, it seemed absurd that Bernard had let his own son go. 'I'm sorry, but I don't understand: your father didn't try to stop you?' she asked.

He replied with a bitter laugh. 'Are you joking? He'd finally got me out from under his feet; that bastard will have uncorked the champagne.' Dozens of lines appeared around his lips, around his eyes. 'Living with me must have been hell for him; I was the mirror of his regrets, so when I told him that I was leaving he wrote me a cheque and wished me a good journey.'

'And what did you do?'

'What you do in such cases: I travelled the world,' he replied, shrugging as though it were the only possible answer. 'I needed to find peace and truth, because after my mother's death nothing I'd believed in was true any more. The world wasn't what they had told me, and not even how I'd imagined; she'd taught me the meaning of words like loyalty and faithfulness, but there was nothing of the kind in the kisses Bernard would give Elodie, as if he no longer remembered the ones he'd given my mother. And I couldn't accept it; I couldn't stand seeing her memory trampled, so I told myself if that was what the world had to offer me, I'd create a different one for myself, a better one.' His index finger pressed the table top and flashes of purple coloured his cheeks.

Elettra listened to him attentively, captivated by the melodious sound of his voice. She could see that remembering those moments was still very painful for him; he continued to turn the glass in his hand. She cleared her throat. 'So was that when you started to draw?'

'Yes,' he replied abruptly. He ran his hand over his hair. 'At the start I did watercolours and the odd canvas, but then I discovered sculpture. I've travelled the world for years with a couple of coins in my pocket and a desire to belong somewhere, but every place I stopped was the wrong one. I don't even know how to explain it to you, it's a strange sensation that I've dragged around behind me ever since I moved in with Bernard at Elodie's, and it ground me down until I arrived here, even though it's close to my father's home. I like the island, I'm happy here; I immediately adapted to its rhythms, to the locals. But then Bernard arrived and everything changed. The past has returned, and it's brought the anger back with it, and everything I thought I'd buried in the course of my travels around the world. But I don't want to hide any more now; and I won't let him treat you the way he treated me and my mother.'

'Are you saying you took on the job because you wanted to get back at him?' Elettra asked.

'Perhaps to start with, but things are different now. I'm happy at the convent, with you all; I've finally experienced the feeling of being part of something again. Of really belonging,' he explained, making an effort to find the right words.

'And of feeling less alone, I imagine,' she finished for him.

Adrian raised his eyebrows, caught by the dull echo of those last words; they were a fierce condemnation, even if they were dangerously close to the truth. 'Something like that,' he admitted.

She and Adrian had suffered the same loneliness. Elettra had no difficulty imagining him walking along the streets like she did, without ever managing to mix in with people, as if they were both carriers of a bad gene that prevented them from establishing a connection with reality. Each contact caused pain, anguish, disquiet; it had been like that for Adrian, who wandered the world armed with his scalpel, and it was for her, too.

'A *focaccia* for a smile?' Adrian offered her, rummaging in the basket she had brought and pulling out one of the soft discs of dough and caramelised sugar. 'I want to test your mother's theory you told me about last time and see if these are magic too.'

She smiled at him and took the *focaccia* from his fingers, breaking it in two. 'OK, but I don't want the whole spell for myself,' she said. She gave half back to Adrian and he took the first bite.

'Divine,' he said, covering his mouth, ready for more.

Elettra stopped to look at him, her head resting on the palm of her hand. Edda would always prepare these *focacce* at the start of autumn for them to enjoy together, sitting side by side on the sofa with a bowl of soft Chantilly cream. But in that moment, the thought of Edda was a grain of sugar inside her: extremely sweet and evanescent. She resolved to go back to the archive as soon as possible, take some more of the convent's records and examine them; sooner or later she would manage to find something, a name, a number.

She took another bite of the *focaccia*, her mind already on the stairs that led to the secret rooms, but the strong and spicy scent floating in the air spread like a poisonous cloud as the memory of her doomed relationship arose again.

'My last relationship was pretty much like this *focaccia*,' she explained on an impulse, turning her half between her fingers. 'I was the dough, the flour, the sugar and everything else, while he was the final sprinkling of cinnamon. The *focaccia* isn't the same if you take the spice away, but it's still good without it.'

'But I suppose you prefer it with the cinnamon.'

Elettra shrugged. 'I've discovered that there are things I like better.'

'For example?'

'For a long time it was *amaretti*,' she replied. 'I loved how crumbly they were, the crunchiness.'

'But you're talking about them in the past,' Adrian pointed out.

'That's how it was, those *amaretti* were my favourite pastry until I was a teenager. Every year I would make my mother bake them, but I would always complain because they were never the same as the ones my school friends' mothers made. I would get mad at her because she would always add some spice or other or vary the proportions of sugar and egg, making them soft instead of crunchy. It was only years later that I understood that she was trying to make me understand something I didn't want to hear.'

'And then the cinnamon arrived, right?'

'Exactly,' Elettra replied with a long sigh, her gaze fixed on her ringless finger. 'He was the spice that livened up a plain dish; at the beginning it was amazing, but his scent soon vanished. Too soon,' she explained. 'And now it's over and done with.'

Adrian put his weight on his elbows, leaning towards her. 'Don't you miss that hint of cinnamon?'

Elettra looked him in the eyes; they were like great dark teardrops, slanting slightly downwards, but they could see the depths of her wounds effortlessly.

She looked away, uncomfortable, preferring to concentrate on the two halves of the *focaccia*; she looked at the porous dough, the softness, and those brown specks on the crust. 'Do you have a napkin, please?' she asked Adrian, who immediately passed her one.

She spread it on her lap, shook the cinnamon off her pastry and took a bite. She chewed slowly, savouring every crumb; it was tasty, with the right balance of sugar and yeast, like Edda's *focacce*.

It was the perfect pastry, the one she had tried to replicate throughout the previous year: but now she understood that she had lacked the secret ingredient, which she had found, along with Edda, in the convent kitchen. Passion.

She swallowed the mouthful and looked up at Adrian.

'Much better without,' she declared with a half-smile.

15

A blast of icy night air slipped between the nearly closed windows making a piece of metal clatter against the wall. Then, suddenly, a door slammed loudly.

Elettra jumped. The knife she was using to chop nuts slipped from her hands. She needed to ice the biscuits to sell in the market the following day, and once she'd finished she would finally be able to go to bed. It was a huge effort to keep her eyes open, but there were still another two boxes of biscuits to ice before her day ended. Once in bed, if she had the energy, she should go through more of the records borrowed from the archive, searching for her mother's name or some sign leading to her and her mysterious past. She was yet to find a single trace of Edda in those books. She knelt down to pick up the knife, but a glimmer of light on the blade prompted her to turn towards the segment of garden visible through the window.

Elettra gripped the handle of the knife tightly and stood up. She was always very absorbed when she was working, but not this time, and she knew why; it had been the thought of Adrian, those moments spent with him, when they ate *focacce* and talked about the past, that had made her drop the knife.

Foolishness, she thought, shaking her head. She rinsed the knife and turned off the tap, drying her hands on her apron.

She leaned against the table, staring gloomily at the mound of almonds in the corner. She had always been a very reserved person but it was different with him: he hadn't hesitated, and had taken the answers straight from her heart.

She grated that uncomfortable thought away, along with the nutmeg which she let fall into the bowl of ground nuts, then pulled a chair up to the table. She lined up the cooked pastries and dipped them one at a time into the melted chocolate, garnishing them with a generous handful of ground almonds. It took more than an hour to get through them all; each time she dipped one, she remembered part of the afternoon; it had been unusual yet liberating for her to confide in Adrian, but now, as she looked at the pastries lined up on the table and thought about the big day ahead, the smile left her face.

Elettra was afraid, desperately terrified of failing again.

Lea and the others had put so much energy into setting up the stall in the market square, while Isabelle had wandered from one end of the island to the other with her friend Mathilde, spreading the word; their reports were of a region in turmoil at the hands of the mayor's dealings and Elettra was worried about the reaction of the mayor and his friends.

'Don't you worry about those buffoons, they'll always find fault. Concentrate on your job and remember, any publicity is good publicity,' Isabelle had reminded her, raising a toast with her warm cider just a few hours earlier.

Isabelle, Elettra thought with a smile. She was incredibly supportive of a project that many would consider crazy; she gave it all her energy despite being of an age that made strenuous work and long walks exhausting. She could have turned back, but she had taken up the call with no hesitation and addressed the small army that was rebelling against the mayor's dealings.

Isabelle was a fighter, she was the cement that kept that band of rebels together.

Then why don't you want to help me find my mother? Elettra asked herself, thinking back to all the times the midwife had pretended not to hear her questions and when she had used Lea as an excuse to hurry away after Elettra's words had backed her into a corner. She would run, she was always running, like the night when they had met outside the door to the archive, Elettra with her heart in her mouth and Isabelle with a cut on her arm. But Elettra couldn't imagine the convent without her.

She switched off the kitchen lights and set off towards her room, dragging her feet. She was exhausted, her muscles so tight that it was a real effort to move her legs. She rubbed one of her shoulders and embarked on the first flight of stairs up to her room, her head full of her desire to look for Edda again between the pages that waited for her, hidden underneath her wardrobe.

Once in her room she grabbed one of the volumes from the archives, but when she tried to pull it towards her it slipped out of her hands, landing on the floor with a thump. She bent over to pick it up, but just then she noticed a small rectangle on the floor with writing scrawled over it.

'What's this?' she murmured to herself. The writing was on glossy paper that she realised was a photograph, and she turned it over immediately. On the other side she found the faces of three young people in sepia. They were an attractive man and two young women, but the photo had been damaged so that she couldn't see either of the women's faces properly, although she could just about make out a novice's habit on one of them. The age of the photo and their body language suggested the carelessness of a period of their lives Elettra guessed must now be long past. She spotted some writing in one of the bottom corners: *Summer 1952*.

The year before I was born, she thought, fascinated by that sur-prising coincidence. But who are they? she wondered, looking for something in the photo, a shadow of familiarity. All she had to do was turn it over to read the writing; words perhaps written by the very same young nun shown in that moment of joy:

Help me, my God,
Help me to love you how I'd like to, in the
way my habit demands.
Help me to continue seeing you with the
loving eyes of a wife,
And protect me, I pray, from the man from the
sea.
Keep me from his eyes,
Free me from the thought of his lips,
Defend me from the delicate sound of his voice,
And save me from the warmth of his hands,
which have painted your face and the faces of
your saints.
Save me, my God, from this heart that won't
let me breathe.

The photo fluttered to the ground.

So, a forbidden liaison had inflamed the walls of the convent; the seed of an unfortunate love had blossomed in the courtyard, or perhaps the poisoned trace of a woman's betrayal.

What if Edda was the novice who wrote the prayer and she gave up her religious habit for love? Elettra thought. She tried to imagine Edda, with her temperament, submitting to monastic rules and hierarchy, to the hours marked by the bells whose song still echoed in the cloister, but it was enough to make her strike a heavy red line through that theory. Her mother was deeply religious, devoted enough to erect a little altar to her favourite saint at home, but not at all inclined to the blind obedience expected of nuns.

She turned the picture over again to try and glean a clue from the portrait, but it all seemed both familiar and unknown at the same time. She couldn't recognise Edda in the picture. And yet . . . and yet something prompted her to look more closely, perhaps not everything was clear at first glance. Elettra turned the photo upside down, then over again, and reread the prayer, doubtful once again.

Edda probably has nothing to do with any of this, and I'm simply chasing ghosts, as Isabelle would say, she chastised herself, picking up the book and snapping it shut.

Frustration, rage, her body was full of turmoil. Elettra felt the salty fury of the waves crash against her walls. She weakly sought an answer in the candle flame that trembled uncertainly, before a strong gust of wind made the shutters slam, putting out the light and whispering her mother's name.

She took it as a suggestion, a maternal reproof for having abandoned her, for having stopped looking for her in the place where it was easy to find her, to talk.

'You're right, Mamma,' she murmured, stroking the edges of the photo, 'but I'll be carrying this with me from now on,' she added, slipping it into a pocket of her dress and heading back towards the kitchen – towards Edda and her *amaretti*, the pastry that had symbolised her childhood, creating a bridge of almonds and sugar between their existences.

Amaretti

1kg almonds, plus 50 for decoration

50g bitter almonds

800g sugar

200g egg whites

2 lemons (peel only)

1 cup orange blossom water

Mince both types of almonds and combine with the sugar and the zested lemon peel.

In a separate bowl, beat the egg white into stiff peaks then gradually add to the dry ingredients until you have a solid mixture. Leave it to rest in a cool, airy place overnight.

Next day, wet your hands with the orange blossom water then make little balls with the mixture, pressing a whole almond into the centre of each one, and arrange them on a baking tray. Leave them to rest for another four hours then finally cook them in an oven pre-heated to 160°C for around 12 minutes.

Leave to cool.

16

Elettra stood for hours, but there wasn't a single customer. Apart from the odd group of old men, nobody came near their stall; the few who had come down to the square to do their daily shopping had crowded around the fishmongers who were offloading their unsold catch at half price. As for the fruit and vegetables from the convent, carefully arranged and offered at a very competitive price, they received nothing more than passing glances, while the traditional market stalls struggled to manage their customers.

What a disaster, Elettra thought, scanning the faces that hurried quickly past the convent's stand; she had hoped that the novelty would attract the islanders and was determined to take advantage of any curiosity to ask some questions about Edda, but every time she approached someone to invite them to try a pastry or some jam they would move away with an excuse, leaving her with her questions hanging in the air. In the entire afternoon she had only managed to exchange a few words with a pair of old women, both white-haired and wearing black. When she had asked if they knew her mother Elettra had seen the elder one's face light up, and the other elbow her in the ribs.

'My sister is unwell. Please try and understand, it's her age,' the woman had excused them, dragging away her sister, who kept looking back at Elettra. She still had the photo in her pocket, but faced with such coldness she realised that she had made a serious mistake in thinking that these people would help her. Their lips were sealed, at least to her, as were their minds.

She took the almost intact box of *amaretti* over to the wall where Isabelle was sitting. Isabelle had spent the whole afternoon with her eyes glued on Elettra, her tired face heavily shadowed by disappointment.

'You really don't want to give in, do you?' Isabelle goaded her, taking the box from Elettra and putting it down beside her.

Elettra opened her arms, but a bitter breath rose up straight from her soul. 'How could I? This always comes down to my mother.'

'Indeed,' Isabelle agreed, thoughtful, as if turning back the hands of time to a long-ago era. Elettra sensed that thousands of thoughts floated in her mind, along with clouded faces, snatches of names and photos excised from the album of her life. Then, after a deep breath, her mind seemed to return to the present.

'Listen, there's something I need to tell you,' Isabelle began to speak again, playing with the fringe of her shawl, resistant to every attempt by Elettra to catch her eye.

'Go on, I'm listening.'

'Everyone here has a great wish to forget, so don't expect any help from them, nor think they'll come and tell you stories from the past. After my husband died I was practically exiled from the community; they did it to me and they continue to do it to the convent, to the people who once lived there and the ones who live there still. And that's in addition to the fact that strangers are looked upon very harshly here,' she added. 'I know that very well: I had only just left Spain when I arrived here, and despite all the time I've lived here, I've never fit in with the mentality of the place.'

'I'd guessed as much, and we're very lucky to have you. I thank God I met you every day.'

'I know, my girl, I know,' Isabelle agreed, her chest puffed out with pride, giving Elettra a pat on the back which soon became a caress. 'Listen, do you have time to hear an old lady's life story?'

'All the time in the world, I'm afraid,' Elettra replied, looking at the untouched produce on the stall; the food they had prepared, the baskets full of biscuits, jars of honey and syrups to treat sicknesses and ailments. She licked her lips and turned to focus on Isabelle, determined to give herself at least a quarter of an hour's freedom from her problems. 'You weren't born in Spain, were you? How did you end up there?'

Isabelle twisted the hem of her worn shawl, her eyes seeing sepia-coloured days. 'I didn't want to be caged,' she replied immediately. 'My family were fairly wealthy and they were planning a high-class wedding for me, but I was in no hurry to have a ring put on my finger. I was too young and clever to marry the first dandy they suggested, so one evening I climbed out of the window and ran away to Barcelona with the gardener's son.'

'Wow, this is interesting!' Elettra exclaimed, rubbing her eyes, but Isabelle immediately admonished her with a shake of her handkerchief.

'Don't you even think about it!' she defended herself. 'The gardener's son had a face full of pimples and teeth as yellow as lemons; I wouldn't have married him if he was the last man on earth,' she protested with a shudder. 'There was nothing romantic between us. But we were good friends; he was the one who told me about the International Brigades. He used to say that you could do something important to save the Spanish from Franco, and I was so tired of the Parisian conformists that I dived into that adventure without even knowing what a pistol looked like. The first time they gave me one I handed it straight back saying that I couldn't carry it about with me because it was too heavy. A real little city girl with my nose in the air, eh?'

'Not necessarily, perhaps weapons weren't your thing. It happens.'

'But it can't, not if you want to survive in hell,' Isabelle replied, her back straight and her chin held high, ready to face down the memory of hazy years. 'In those days a pistol could save your life, and that's exactly how I met my Juan,' she continued, her voice caressing the memory of a man to whom she'd been married for over twenty years. 'He literally saved me from the bullets. Ours wasn't a meeting to forget.' Her lips produced a smile full of melancholy. She told Elettra about the war, the many friends she had buried, and those who just a few months after their time in Spain had found themselves fighting on two opposing sides, some of them wearing swastikas on their arms. She told her that the Second World War had been a huge dirty trick, as she put it, but she had been able to sit out a good part of it on Titan's Island.

It had been there that Isabelle and Juan, who had lost a leg to a Francoist grenade, had found a bit of peace after the defeat in the civil war; she knew the island well, her family spent every summer there, and once outside Spain it had seemed to her the only safe port where they could seek refuge. They had moved into a small farm with a view of the sea and while Juan had continued to work as a clock mender, 'fixing broken things', as Isabelle said, remembering her husband's own words, she, who had helped so many comrades give birth amongst the smoke and bullets, had started to work as a midwife. They had spent many happy years together, but Isabelle didn't need to add much about her husband's end; the fact that she lived alone was an answer in itself. And the sad downturn at the corners of her mouth was the conclusion.

Elettra looked at the tips of her toes, then up to her knees. There was a wind blowing from the north and she knew it would bring a freezing cold night and storms until the morning. 'Do you miss Juan a lot?'

'Definitely more than you miss Edda,' Isabelle replied, straightening the folds of her skirt with a sweep of her hand. 'When your mother dies it's like the earth is gone from under your feet, but when you lose the only person you've ever loved in your whole damn life it's a completely different story,' she explained. 'When your husband goes to the otherworld it's like you don't have your skin any more, like being a broken doll; you fight on even if you're missing that piece, but you'll never be the same again. It's useless brooding on it now, time can only move forward.' She rubbed her calves, marked by years of climbing the harsh paths of the island, covered in scratches and swollen as a result of her poor circulation. A couple of women dressed in mourning, their faces shaped by the wind, came towards the stall, greeting Isabelle with a timid wave.

Two widows, thought Elettra, jumping to her feet, but her friend immediately stopped her.

'I'll go. They trust me,' Isabelle whispered, moving towards the taller of the two, as the other woman's face blossomed into a huge smile at the sight of the *amaretti* in the basket. Despite her sombre dress, the woman's smooth face, visible through her veil, showed a determined youthfulness.

'She can't be more than fifty,' Elettra thought, noticing her unlined hands. She walked slowly over while Isabelle chatted to her friend and offered her a biscuit. 'Please, try one and tell me what you think,' Elettra said.

The woman looked around, staring at the biscuit with her hands clutched to her chest. 'Really?'

'Of course,' Elettra replied with her brightest smile, shooting a sharp look at the woman from the neighbouring stall who was eyeing up her customer with disapproval. 'It's my mother's recipe, Edda Cavani, who used to live here when she was a girl.'

The woman smiled at her in thanks and took the biscuit, her eyes suddenly bright. 'I used to know Edda,' she murmured, lowering her head as Elettra's heart skipped a beat in shock.

'Y-you u-used to know her?' she stammered, her eyes fixed on the unfamiliar face.

'Yes. We used to take flour to the convent while the nuns were still there. My mother was the miller's wife and when I was little I would often go with her to make deliveries. You know, you don't make much from grain, at least not on this island, so the nuns would always give me something. They'd taken a liking to me,' she explained, a slight blush colouring her cheeks.

Elettra inhaled what felt like all the air in the square; finally, someone who'd known her mother, she could hardly believe it. 'Really? What was she like?'

'She was a girl with melancholy eyes, but a disarming charm,' the woman replied simply, tapping the rough surface of the biscuit. 'She was very beautiful, although her beauty was perhaps a bit wild. And she was proud, fierce, her back was always straight and her eyes were always ready to weigh up every sack that arrived at the convent. An unfortunate girl, even though everybody said her hands were golden,' she added, almost whispering the words.

Elettra nodded, but noted the mention of her mother's misfortune, probably another clue to her past. She began asking further questions, but the woman took up her story from where she'd left off.

'But the old people all remember her pastries; even my grandmother literally went crazy for her almond pastries, and every time Edda was baking the fragrance would reach the church, near the bar. If anyone came near your stall today it's thanks to those pastries;

probably nostalgia for their youth, the years when taking a couple of pastries home with you on a Sunday was enough to make you feel like a lord. After all, the island and the islanders are slaves to the past. We are the hostages and the guardians of our memories.'

Elettra nodded, finding confirmation of the woman's words amongst the grey heads that stood out against the background of the leaden sky; in fact, most of their customers walked with sticks. Elettra began, 'But they alone won't be enough; to get the convent back in order we're going to need the help, the support, of you widows who live on the other side of the island, too. I think this is the first time I've spoken with one of you because you always seem unapproachable when I see you in town.'

The woman looked down, arranging her veil as a stylish woman walked past. She was dressed a bit like Sylvie Leroux and was definitely from the same set. 'We're used to going unnoticed, to not existing. They kicked us out of society years ago and now we want to be left in peace.'

'Then why are you here at the market, *signora*, if you want to be left in peace?' the stylish woman asked, much to Elettra's surprise.

The woman smiled. 'There's no need for *signora*, in the eyes of the town I haven't been a *signora* for many years. I'm just Ada, that's what everyone here knows me as.'

'All right,' the woman said. 'Well then, Ada, why are you and your friend here?'

'Because she asked us to come,' Ada replied, pointing to Isabelle who was busy rearranging the biscuits. 'Marthe and I have known Isabelle for many years, she delivered our children, the ones the storm took away along with our husbands. We have many faults, but we islanders are grateful people.'

'Then help us,' Elettra begged, but just then Ada's friend grabbed her by the arm and whispered something in her ear in the island dialect.

'*Adieu*,' Marthe said, turning to Elettra and Isabelle, and with her hand firmly on her friend's back she moved away, hiding the little white bag containing pastries and honey in the pocket of her dress, while Elettra watched helplessly as the memory of Edda and the chance to save the convent went with her. Having driven them away, the stylish woman gave Elettra a sharp look and walked off.

'Why is it so difficult to convince them, Isabelle?' she murmured, watching them disappear into the alleys that climbed up towards the Titan rock. What Ada had said had left Elettra a little stunned.

'Because they're the strong core, the island's unhealthy heart,' she replied. 'It will be difficult for them to do more than they've done today, given the mentality of the place,' she continued, telling Elettra about a primitive religion, a patriarchal structure of family life governed by legends and superstitions, including those that considered a woman's role in society obsolete without a man by her side, and which condemned the widows of the sea to leper-like conditions.

It was a view of life that left Elettra dumbstruck.

A gust of wind came off the sea, making the lace trim of the stalls flutter.

'Go on, have a biscuit,' she urged Isabelle, but she was immoveable.

'I can't even think of it.'

'Why not? They're very good.'

'I'm sure they are.'

'Well, then?'

Isabelle tugged at the fabric of her shawl, a hint of impatience on her closed lips. 'Because sometimes remembering hurts, that's why.'

'Your husband?'

'Yes, my husband,' she mumbled. 'Juan used to be crazy about the almond pastries they made here at the convent, especially the ones with orange. He always used to say they reminded him of the pastries he ate as a child, that's why he'd ask me to buy a few as soon as we had any money to spare.' She looked down, as the memory became lost in the maze of little sugary cracks. 'He rarely mentioned it, but I knew how hard it was for him living in exile; my poor husband was mending broken things until the day he died, but he was never able to get used to missing his country.'

Their gazes met for a brief moment, but Isabelle's eyes immediately sought refuge focusing on her arthritic hands. Elettra placed a warm touch on her shoulder and she leaned in, as if to smell her breath, and perhaps scent perfumed oranges like the ones she had eaten in great bites, lying on a lawn with Juan and looking up at the Andalusian sky.

'Your husband must have been a good man,' Elettra told her.

'You can be sure of that, my girl,' the midwife replied, knotting the shawl around her wrinkled neck. 'He was a gentleman. An emperor, compared to some who behave like they own the island,' she added, her voice sour with disdain. Isabelle was probably referring to Sylvie; she would make a jibe at Sylvie's expense whenever their paths crossed in town, and when she had Dominique with her, backing her up, she would become unstoppable.

Elettra's gaze fell on the stall; there were piles of jars of jams and boxes of *focacce* with rosemary honey ready to be devoured, but it seemed like nobody intended to undertake the task.

'They don't eat them because they're afraid they'd lose their false teeth, you mark my words,' Isabelle burst out, pointing to an acquaintance who was gazing uncertainly at the pastry that Nicole was handing him. She had returned after hours trekking the paths across the island to offer pastries to the inhabitants. 'And you should stop baking pastries; sooner or later resisting the temptation to buy them will drive them all mad,' Isabelle warned her.

Elettra smiled, gratified by that unexpected comfort, but on noticing that the *amaretto* she had offered the mysterious Ada remained intact, she felt a compelling need for answers.

'I'm just popping away for a moment, would you mind staying here with Nicole?' she asked Isabelle, and hurried off along the path to the countryside.

She ignored the diffident looks of the card players sitting at the bar, the gaze of the women from behind their half-shut blinds and the friends of the mayor waiting for the barber, determined to catch up with her past soon. Ada knew: she couldn't let her go like this, allowing the only trace of Edda she had found to evaporate into the motionless air of the autumn sky.

She left the houses of the town behind her and hurried along the earthy paths that plunged into the wildest part of the island; the Titan in the rock formation was watching over her, Elettra could feel his gentle gaze on her skin. She made her way through the bushes, her ears full of the echo of the sea crashing against the rocks, and finally saw them. Ada and Marthe were walking slowly, dark shadows against the brilliant green of the salt-coated grass. Elettra stopped to catch her breath, leaning against the trunk of a wild pear tree. Her eyes remained fixed on the backs of the two women, depositories of the island's memory, her island's memory, and then Ada turned round. Clearly, she recognised Elettra instantly and made an excuse for her friend to go on without her.

Elettra took advantage of it in an instant.

'You forgot this down at the market,' she said, handing her the *amaretto*.

Ada took it from her hand and smiled. 'You want to know about her, don't you?'

Elettra felt the grip of emotion strangle her words. 'Please,' she begged, her hands outstretched.

'You might be disappointed, I don't know much,' Ada warned

her, accepting her small gift and implicitly agreeing to reveal some of Edda's past.

'Anything you can tell me about her will be plenty.'

Ada nodded and wrapped the biscuit in a handkerchief then put it in her pocket. 'Now then,' she began, 'Edda was a typical Mediterranean girl: big eyes, shapely and with long, dark hair that she always wore loose, without sparing a thought for the abbess's opinion. She was a proud woman, guarded in her affections and extremely wary despite her gentle soul. Many men would have done ridiculous things for her.'

'Well, at least one of them must have won her over, given that I'm here,' Elettra replied, but the widow didn't smile at her joke. Quite the opposite, she suddenly frowned.

'Sometimes it's not a case of winning over but of deceiving.'

'What do you mean?'

'Sometimes we delude ourselves into loving someone but the object of our desire is unreachable; and yet we convince ourselves of having found the right person, we build castles in the air, but just one second thought or a wrong word and everything collapses, leaving nothing but a carpet of rubble. And in spite of loving sincerely, whoever has been deceived sees all thought of a happy life destroyed and lets himself be seduced by the sirens of vengeance.'

Elettra rubbed her eyes; Ada was a bit too cryptic for her taste. 'Please explain, I don't understand; do you mean that Edda was deceived by a man who took advantage of her?'

Ada shrugged. 'I used to take flour to the convent with my mother and every so often I would see what was happening, I would speak with Edda . . . but who gets to decide who's the victim and who's the villain? Assigning the roles is never easy when it's a matter of feelings . . . but yes, your mother has suffered deeply because of a man.'

174

'Who?' Elettra's voice burst forth quickly from her lips.

'I don't know his name, but I know he came across from the mainland. He was an extremely charming man, handsome as a Greek god, who turned half the heads on the island.'

'Including my mother's?'

'Edda was madly in love with him. It was a crazy love, unhealthy, obsessive. The kind that poisons you.'

Elettra moved closer to Ada; things were getting interesting. 'And he didn't return her feelings?' she asked, and Ada shook her head vigorously.

'He couldn't, he was in love with someone else; but someone who could only be his in his dreams.'

'What do you mean?'

'The man in question was an artist, and you know what artists are like: they live on unrealisable dreams.' A gust of wind twisted through the high grass, like the bells of a childhood that was slowly vanishing over the horizon. 'Please excuse me, but it's better if I go now.'

'Ada, wait!' Elettra called after her, but the woman disappeared amongst the vegetation like an apparition, just like a memory, a paper boat carried out to sea on the tide.

'An artist,' Elettra repeated to herself an hour later, surveying the empty square and tapping her index finger against her lips.

She rubbed her arms, looking around in search of Isabelle, but the midwife had already gone while Lea and the others were packing away the tables and chairs, putting the unsold produce back into boxes. She helped them take it all back to the convent, but she didn't say a word; around her was nothing but wind, weak but laden with an invasive damp. The sirocco, Nicole had told her as they went up the street that ran along the seafront, pointing to the clouds sailing in the direction of the coast.

Her project had not been as successful as she'd hoped, and

Adrian hadn't even come; Elettra had asked Isabelle, Nicole and Dominique, but none of them seemed to have seen him.

I'm such an idiot, she thought, looking at a small box of *focacce* she had kept just for him, but when she found herself in the deserted cloister she felt a sadness spreading in her chest. He, too, had disappointed her.

It doesn't matter, we'll try again, she told herself.

She looked up towards the window on the top floor, her head full of Ada's story, and set off for the kitchen.

17

Exactly one week after Ada's revelations, Elettra woke up with an uncontrollable craving for almonds.

To satisfy it, she went to the garden in search of Dominique. Dominique was always reluctant to welcome guests into her domain, but Elettra was surprised not to find her up to her elbows in earth. Usually when she was in a bad mood she would spend entire days digging and hoeing, and she had been in a very bad mood all week since the day of their debut at the market – mostly due to the high cost of the permits they'd had to buy for the convent to be able to sell directly to the public. Dominique ate alone and spoke less often than normal, so much so that even Lea preferred to keep away from her, although she had gradually re-established her harmony with Elettra. That difficult moment, the failure of their plan, had brought them closer again.

'It's best to leave her to herself. She'll start talking again once she's bored of being a hermit, you'll see,' Lea had reassured Elettra at breakfast after she'd seen Dominique heading out of the door.

Having lived with her in close quarters for several months,

Elettra had the impression that Dominique's only aim was to dull her senses with work so as not to think, but Lea had made it very clear she had best keep that opinion to herself.

Perhaps she's just very angry; in any case, the storm is a recent tragedy and pain needs time to heal, Elettra thought, reaching up towards an almond still in its shell. She filled a basket with the small oblong fruits, and when after a while she allowed herself a rest to loosen her muscles, she finally spotted her; Dominique was walking along the strip of unworked land which led up towards the hill, where she had set up the beehives. She seemed to have developed a special rapport with the bees; whenever she was in a bad mood they would buzz around her in swarms but without ever stinging her, like a faithful dog curling up at his master's feet when he senses his sadness.

And there she was, wrapped in a dark and noisy cloud, singing the same old song that Elettra had heard her sing before about a woman who, betrayed by her only love and overcome with rage, poisons him and throws his body into the sea.

Dominique sang those verses with a fiery passion that shrieked across the autumnal greyness of the morning, but Elettra willingly let herself be transported by the song, and using Dominique's voice as her guide, let her legs carry her until she found herself facing Dominique's icy gaze. She had invaded her territory and Dominique wouldn't take her eyes off her until she left.

'You have a lovely voice,' Elettra stammered, breaking the silence of the deserted field as Dominique accompanied her winged friends to their home.

Elettra would have liked to add something, but she fell silent when she saw Dominique frown as she saw her basket.

'I took a few almonds; I wanted to know how it feels to eat something you've picked with your own hands,' Elettra explained in a guilty voice.

There was further silence and a series of suspicious glances from Dominique.

To put an end to that uncomfortable impasse, Elettra turned towards the high grass that was swaying in the wind. She could smell salt on the air, a whiff of sand that gave her a sense of unadulterated freedom, but just one thought of the tarmacked streets of her home city, full of smog and noise, was enough to chase away all joy: sooner or later she would have to go back; and as time passed that day drew closer. And the closer it drew, the more Elettra realised she had absolutely no wish to leave.

The island had a challenging personality, but she didn't want to give in. She wanted to make sense of Ada's revelations, to weave them into the collage of information she had gathered about Edda, the faded trio in the photo and the prayer; the answers were there, she just needed to find the common thread that linked all the clues.

The artist Ada mentioned is probably the guy in the photo, and my mother the girl beside him, she thought, but she felt as though something was still eluding her. What about the novice? What part did she play in all this? If she was the one who wrote the prayer then she must be involved in this business, Elettra guessed, chewing the inside of her cheek, absorbed.

'Is something wrong?'

Dominique's voice startled her, bringing her back to reality.

Elettra stepped back, folding her arms across her chest to protect herself from a question she didn't want to answer; there were huge boundaries to cross, and abysses that would swallow her up in moments.

'Everything's fine. I'm just thinking a bit too much, a touch of nostalgia,' she replied.

'Regretting what's happened without doing anything to change it, that might explain it, mightn't it?'

'Do you think so?'

'"Who wants, takes action, who hopes, dissatisfaction," that's what my grandmother used to say.'

Elettra smiled. 'Well, I'd say I've acted and suffered enough, but it's over now.'

Dominique's gaze ran up Elettra's sides, softened by her flowery dress, slowly rising to her drawn face. Elettra wasn't sleeping much and her Mediterranean colouring only accentuated the violet streaks under her eyes. 'You're more than just worried, though, or am I mistaken?'

'Not at all,' Elettra claimed. 'I don't have a job. Besides which, I haven't the slightest inclination to go back and live in the city, even though I ought to. I felt like I was in a cage there, and ... I know that it's mad, but I feel at home here.' She reached out her arms, embracing the huge cobalt bay which lay below the promontory a few hundred metres away.

'What's mad is making yourself put up with living in a city where you don't belong,' Dominique replied, snapping the wild brambles with her bare hands. She pulled up a branch, then threw it away, turning towards the sea beyond the cliffs.

Elettra brushed her hand against the other woman's matted cardigan, letting it rest on her skin. Dominique didn't show even a flicker of emotion; as if adhering firmly to the role she had established for herself, that of a widow who lived crystallised in the dignity of a pain deeper than the sea.

'It must have been very difficult to live here after the storm,' Elettra murmured.

'The storm has nothing to do with it,' Dominique replied, pulling away abruptly, her eyes glinting with rage. 'It was that evil witch, Sylvie, who ruined my life,' she went on, her voice tainted by hatred. She looked at Elettra for a few seconds, but then slumped down onto a flat rock, her shoulders hunched, as though to protect her from a pain that was still raw.

'My husband cheated on me with her for two long years. When I found out I yelled at him that he disgusted me and that the whole town should know what kind of person he was, but he didn't say a word. He stood there with his hands in his pockets looking at the floor the entire time, but as soon as I called Sylvie a whore he lost it. He silenced me with a single slap. Just one. But it was the first in an endless stream,' she continued, crushing the grass under her rubber boots. Her voice was detached, as if the story was about a distant relative, the kind of tale that clogs up country confessionals. She looked lost in the infinite anguish of a broken heart, and yet Elettra still detected a trace of love in her voice, in the slight hesitation with which she presently pronounced her husband's name. Dominique's lips had pursed, refusing to renew an unresolved pain, but there was something in her, in her twisting hands, that wasn't at peace, and Elettra was sure that it was that love that had survived the betrayal; she imagined that not being able to rid herself of the love she felt for her husband was Dominique's greatest regret. She had tried, but she couldn't silence the suffering woman in love who lived in the shadow of another woman, the icy Dominique, the only one the island now knew.

Dominique clenched her fists. 'Claude had never laid a finger on me in anger before. Never,' she continued. 'But after that evening something changed; perhaps things with Sylvie started to go wrong, I don't know. All I remember is that Claude was angrier each time he came home. I could see he was suffering because of her, that he yearned for that ambitious whore; he pretended it was nothing, but it was pointless. I took the beatings that went along with the drinking bouts as if it were the price I had to pay for coming between them. I put up with living in a cage, one my husband built for me from insults and broken bones.' Elettra's shoulders were rigid as listened to her story. She struggled to believe that two people who had once been in love could turn their relationship into such a maze of bitterness and violence, but Dominique's scars were real.

'I didn't lift a finger for months, not even to defend myself, but one evening I couldn't take the blows and I fainted. When I woke up I couldn't even speak, I only remember the doctor telling me I had a broken arm and a couple of fractured ribs and that I ought to be more careful. I tried to tell him what my husband had done to me, I tried to get help, but when I saw Claude give him a pat on the back I knew that it wouldn't work. Claude had already refused admission to hospital on my behalf, he wanted to make sure I couldn't run away from him. That was when I started to return his hatred.' Dominique looked towards the horizon.

'It took me a while to get better, but once I was back on my feet I was clear about what I had to do. One night I waited for him to go to sleep, then I went out armed with a torch and a couple of old screwdrivers. I walked along the cliff to the fishermen's docks, down along the path that stops by the twisted pine, and I found his boat and tampered with the motor. I pulled wires out at random – in that moment all I could think of was my desire for revenge; he needed to pay for the pain I would carry around with me for ever. I wanted vengeance for my blood that he'd spilled, nothing more. In my dreams I'd often imagined Claude and Sylvie drowning together and I'd enjoyed the image of them floundering in panic, but only he went out on the boat the next day. He said he was going fishing so he could sell a few crates at the market and make a bit of money, but I knew it was to pay for Sylvie's little treats. I didn't say a word, though,' she continued with a lucidity that chilled Elettra's blood. 'I said goodbye to him as usual and followed my domestic routine until the wind began to blow and it started hailing in the afternoon. Then I shut myself up in the house and when Nicole came over that evening to tell me what had happened, I followed her to the café. That was where I learned that Claude had died along with the others, honest family men; he wasn't worthy enough to lick the soles of their shoes. Sylvie was at the bar that evening too, I'll never forget that,' she added with a half-smile. 'She arrived with her husband, her eyes swollen from crying. She said she was overcome by the tragedy that had struck the island, but I knew she'd come to make sure I didn't flip out. She's always been a cheap tart, but just then I didn't know what to do with her dirty secrets. My only worry was the thought that I'd prevented my husband from saving himself. Even I had no idea what damage I'd done to the motor, if I'd done any at all, but I couldn't mention it to anyone without raising suspicions, and especially not without Sylvie finding out. So I didn't say anything, I couldn't.'

Elettra stared at Dominique, uncomprehending, but when she saw her getting up, she took her by the arm. Dominique's eyes were shadowed by a dark night, a black that left Elettra breathless.

'Why did you tell me all this?' she asked, her hand pressed to her chest.

Dominique gave a bitter smile. 'Because fear of the past, of change, shouldn't hold you back. After the storm I had no idea how to move forward without Claude. More than half my home was destroyed and I was so obsessed by what had happened that I started to see traces of what I thought I'd done everywhere I looked. Claude was everywhere, I would hear his voice wherever I went. For a while I tried to resist, forcing myself to remain lucid, but after a few weeks I even started seeing him in broad daylight, amongst groups of people, convinced he wanted to drive me mad. But I still didn't want to let him win, so spent months shut away in my house, until I met Lea.' There was a hint of relief in Dominique's voice and it finally seemed to lose its tension. 'I came to the convent because I wanted to keep to myself, far from other people, and she opened the doors of the cloister to me. She invited me to sit next to the statue of the Saint and ... it seems absurd, I know, but after half an hour I'd told her everything. I told her all of it, about Claude and Sylvie and what I'd done, but in spite of this she didn't judge me or suggest I left. On the contrary, she invited me to move into the convent and share my solitude with her. Do you understand what I'm telling you?'

She stopped and turned to face Elettra, who was listening, mouth open. 'The very person who had least to share with me offered me a roof over my head and the chance to start again.'

The sun had reached its highest point in the sky, casting small shadows. All that remained of the summer was a slight tan on Elettra's skin and an inextinguishable heat that would last for ever. She would never forget it; she had found so much more than she expected in this corner of the world.

'I know I can't undo what I've done, and I'm not seeking forgiveness,' Dominique said. 'That's why I prefer to live at the convent and not in the town; I'm not interested in people's gossip. I made a choice that night and I'm still aware of it even after so much suffering, and I make an effort to live with it because I know I have to. And life means moving forward, even for you, Elettra. Don't let yourself be intimidated by your fears, live. Choose a path and follow it without looking back, but think hard before you choose.'

Elettra looked down and rubbed her eyes, which had been irritated by some dust, and when she looked up Dominique was already several metres away from her.

But her words weren't. They hadn't gone anywhere.

Guelfi

500g almond flour

300g sugar

1 spoon wildflower honey

1 vanilla pod (seeds only)

½ cup orange blossom essence or liqueur

Pour the sugar, honey, vanilla seeds and orange blossom essence into a saucepan and heat until the sugar is fully dissolved. Sprinkle in the almond flour and mix vigorously. Turn off the heat.

Tip the mixture onto a plate and leave to cool.

When the mixture is cool enough to touch, wet your hands with orange blossom essence and shape it into balls the size of walnuts, then cover them with a cloth and leave to dry for two days in a cool, dark place.

Wrap the guelfi in coloured paper, like sweets.

18

Elettra closed the jar of biscuits, exhausted. She hadn't had a moment to catch her breath since she'd got up, and now her morale had plummeted; she had failed and this fact left her sleepless. She put her last hope in Isabelle, who would arrive at the convent every morning to fill her basket with bread and pastries to sell to her acquaintances, and in Adrian with his mania for the sea, who had set off around the archipelago in search of new customers. Elettra had treated him harshly the first time they met following the stall's debut, still angry about his absence, but he'd explained that he had gone to spread the word on the neighbouring islands and lost track of the time.

'But, if you'll let me, I'll make it up to you,' he had added with a smile that offered a glimpse of adventure.

'All right,' she'd replied, accepting the challenge.

A mixture of intense and undecipherable emotions, the memory of the morning they'd spent together in his studio stayed with her.

It was Sunday, one of those island days when the wind, diminished by an unseasonable heat, blew lazily along the coast. She had just finished taking the aniseed *ciambelline* out of the oven when Adrian had appeared in the convent kitchen, armed with his biggest smile, to invite her on a trip round the islands of the archipelago.

'A business trip, to make your delicacies known beyond the island,' he had insisted when faced with her reluctant gaze, sneaking a biscuit from the basket. But what should have been just a carefree day soon turned ugly. Neither she nor Adrian had been prepared for the sudden change in the currents during their journey back.

They had been on the open sea, their prow turned towards Titan's Island; the air brushed their skin and the boat was bobbing on the current. Everything was perfect and Elettra was finally beginning to relax and enjoy Adrian's company when, with a sudden change in the wind, they were left surrounded by waves a couple of metres high. Adrian had grabbed the motor's ripcord and tugged on it energetically to start it, but in vain.

He tried and tried again, but it just wouldn't start: it rumbled and vibrated and spewed black smoke, but there wasn't a movement in the water. Nothing to give any hope that the engine was starting.

'Tell me what's happening, Adrian,' Elettra asked him, her hands gripping the edge of the boat as it bobbed dangerously. He put all his efforts into controlling the vessel and rowing them towards the nearest bay a few hundred metres away, but with the sea growing rougher and rougher, the distance seemed to increase with every stroke. 'We'll be safe once we reach Mermaids' Bay, but these damned currents are making it difficult to get there,' he explained, trying to reassure her as his arms strained to pull the oars through the water and propel them towards the shore. He was rowing at a rapid rate, taking no breaks, but he was soon sodden and breathless.

And the boat was still out in the middle of the sea.

Elettra refused to sit back and watch the situation unfold, so without a word she moved to sit next to him and grabbed an oar, waiting for him to mark time.

'Between us we can do it,' she explained briskly. She tightened her grip and braced her back, trying to ignore the boat's movement beneath her. She needed to concentrate entirely on her own movement, the rest would come; she had watched Adrian for so long that catching the rhythm was easy, but after the first few strokes she started to feel fatigue. Her arms shook and drops of sweat trickled down her back, but she was determined not to give in; she used all her remaining energy, encouraged only by seeing they were closer to the shore when she turned to check. She paid no attention to the sea that continued to batter the boat: her entire being was focused on the shore alone.

A stroke, another, one more, and the boat finally beached itself on the sand.

'Thank you, God!' she murmured, collapsing onto the sand.

Adrian, exhausted himself, rolled over towards her. 'Well, it could have been worse.'

Elettra coughed, massaging her arms which were still shaking from the exertion. 'Give me a warning next time you're planning to go to sea. I'll come up with an excuse to decline your invitation.'

There was silence, as a cormorant flew elegantly above the water.

Adrian folded his arms behind his head, his chest rising and falling rapidly beneath his sea-soaked shirt. 'I see you're still as sarcastic as ever.'

'I am when you try to kill me! Dammit Adrian, that could have ended badly. Really badly.'

He sat up and brushed the sand out of his hair. 'I only wanted to test your spirit of adventure.'

Elettra sat next to him, fighting to free a twig that was tangled in her hair. 'As if.'

'Go on, come here and I'll help you.' She moved closer but the contact between their bodies, still pumped up with adrenalin from the recent danger, threw up a wall of electricity between them. They were suddenly too close, the smell of their clothes mingled, their breath holding the same warm flavour of the life pumping beneath their skin.

Elettra licked her lips, staring at Adrian's mouth; his eyes seemed fixed on hers. It all seemed so natural, so right, the only possibility in that moment; no mental second thoughts, pure instinct.

They leaned towards each other, their lips half open, but they pulled back at the sudden sound of a horn blaring from a boat. It was Adrian's friend greeting them from the bridge; he signalled the end of an adventure that had left bittersweet traces on Elettra's skin.

The trip with Adrian had been crazy, illogical and dangerous. She had promised herself to forget all about it, but Adrian's face, his smell, followed her every moment of the day. He was present even when Elettra discussed financial woes with Lea.

'We're not there yet,' Lea sighed, drawing a line through the black list of her creditors. She'd thought she might be able to start settling her debts and freeing herself of some worries, but the path towards solvency was still uphill. She put the sheet of paper in a folder and closed the accounts book while Elettra gazed disconsolately at yet more boxes of unsold biscuits.

'I don't know what to say. I never thought things could go so badly.'

'Nobody could know how it would go,' Lea cut her off. 'We all knew it wouldn't be easy, but the convent is the only thing we have and the only place where we can live. It's our duty to save it, and I'm sure that we'll find a way to work things out; at least we can afford to fix the central heating with the money we've made so far. As for the rest, we'll just have to have faith. The only thing I'm worried about is time,' Lea continued bitterly. 'Especially because Leroux and Morel aren't backing off. Vincent returned to duty just yesterday; he told me he'd give me time to reflect on his proposition to relocate, but you should have seen his face when I told him that I'd begun the restoration work and I don't intend to leave. He was incandescent, not far off a heart attack.' She burst into sudden laughter that filled the room. She laughed convulsively until the tears ran down her face, until the abyss in front of her wiped all trace of happiness from her face. It was a small victory, but Elettra breathed it in.

'We'll do it, you'll see,' Lea continued as she counted the jars of jam that Elettra had placed on the table. 'Dominique did a great job with the figs we gathered last month: we've got so much jam and dried fruit that we'll be mobbed come November. We'll recoup all our losses.'

Elettra tilted her head to one side, her eyebrows raised in doubt. 'Why? What happens in November?'

'You mean you don't know? Seventeenth of November is Saint Elizabeth's day, and anyway, it's traditional to give baskets of dried fruit as gifts to mark All Saints day,' she explained. She crossed her legs, observing her friend who looked at her, perplexed. 'I thought your mother celebrated the Saint's day, she's a devotee, isn't she?' she continued as Elettra nodded. Elettra had blocked out their family celebrations of the feast days – she'd pushed the memory away while her mother was in a coma, so she didn't have to remember what she'd lost.

'Of course,' she agreed. Each year Edda would prepare hundreds of votive rolls to celebrate the patron saint of bakers, crowns of sculpted bread, spiced bread, twists of pastry and all kinds of sweet treats. It had been real punishment for her fingertips, which always ended up burnt, and was now a sweet torture for Elettra's heart; she was not yet an orphan, but no longer a daughter.

'I'm going out for a moment,' she said.

The air outside was warm, but Elettra didn't take the time to enjoy it; her feet flew along the island's stony paths and her heart, now accustomed to the rough terrain of that wild land, didn't protest in the slightest. Everything around her was calm, waiting. Even the waves silently withdrew from their battle.

But Elettra felt a powerful disquiet run over her skin. After a long walk she found herself outside Gustave's café without realising it. The usual customers were there, drinking beer and wine at all hours of the day, whether it was blazing hot or pouring with rain, and Gustave was always there to keep them company.

The whole countryside seemed to be under a spell; there was an unnatural quiet in the streets. Elettra turned the handle of the door into the bar. 'Sabine?' she called from the middle of the empty room. 'Sabine, are you there?'

No reply.

She tried again, stubborn; she would rather have swum to another island to call Ruth than spoken to Gustave. Her voice faded in the dusty air of the room for a third time, but as she turned to go she heard the sound of hurried steps in the silence. 'I called, didn't you hear me?' she complained as Sabine appeared behind the bar. Elettra went over and froze when she saw the purple shadows surrounding Sabine's eyes. 'Oh, Sabine,' she murmured.

The bar owner's wife was almost swamped by a jumper two sizes too big for her, hanging off her like a shapeless sack.

'Sabine ...' Elettra repeated. 'Is everything okay?'

'I'm very tired,' Sabine cut her off, clearing the bar. She took out a rag. 'How can I help you? Do you want to use the telephone, have a coffee?'

Elettra gestured towards the end of the corridor and said, 'The telephone, thanks.'

'Go ahead, it's free.' As Sabine leaned over the bar and pointed towards the telephone, Elettra noticed a green bruise on her wrist. Sabine's attempt to hide it by pulling down her sleeve only confirmed Elettra's worst suspicions.

'I can't pretend I didn't see that,' she told Sabine as she stood in front of the bar.

Sabine ran her hand through her hair, her eyes turning back to check the door at regular intervals. 'Don't get any funny ideas,' she said. There was a scratch by the edge of her mouth. 'I've been distracted recently; I bumped into the doorframe while I was getting dressed this morning.'

'Or did you bump into Gustave's hands?'

Sabine's face froze, her shoulders suddenly rigid. 'I don't know what you're talking about.' Her fingers frantically searched for glasses to rearrange. 'Anyway, if you need to use the phone you know where it is, otherwise please let me get on. I've got a lot to do.'

'Of course,' Elettra replied, turning towards the entrance of the deserted café, 'they're queuing up outside.' She leaned against the bar; she wouldn't have moved even if Sabine had started shouting. 'Listen, I've seen that bruise with my own eyes, so stop pretending it isn't there; there's no reason to protect the person who gave it to you, it's wrong.' She searched for Sabine's hand and looked softly into her eyes.

'Is something wrong?' Gustave interrupted them, appearing suddenly in the doorway.

Elettra found the answer to that question, to all her questions, in Sabine's terrified face, as she shrank into her sweater.

'Everything's absolutely fine, Monsieur Picard,' Elettra replied with a fake smile. 'I was just ordering a coffee.'

'Ah.' Elettra could feel the man eyeing up the prominent curve of her generous bust, her full lips; he clearly didn't like her or her direct manner at all. He slipped his thumbs into his belt, searching for his wife behind the bar. 'Then what are you waiting for, Sabine? Give the woman what she asked for.' Sabine immediately started the coffee machine. He waited for her to serve it, studying the two women. Elettra and Sabine remained facing each other while Gustave dawdled in the doorway.

Sabine slid the coffee cup across the bar, but as soon as she brushed her customer's fingers with her own she suddenly drew back. She felt something crackle in her palm and her eyes immediately sought an answer in Elettra's.

'It's for you.' Elettra pushed a small object wrapped in coloured paper towards her.

Sabine clutched Elettra's gift in her hand, exploring its roundness; no doubt puzzling at its aroma of almonds and orange blossom.

When Gustave went back outside, she pulled the twisted ends of the paper; tucked inside she found a small ball of almond paste, a little gift that immediately restored her smile.

Elettra quietly watched her friend's response. For once someone had thought of her and her alone. It can't be something that happens often, Elettra thought, gladdened by the smile that shone on Sabine's face.

19

The north wind reached Titan's Island, bringing ice and bad news with it.

Elettra had just finished going through the accounts with Lea, who was suffering a bout of insomnia and had taken to wandering the corridors by night, preventing Elettra from going to the archive. Elettra was terrified by the idea of having to find an explanation for something she didn't want to justify, and the possibility of prompting questions and raising suspicions. Perhaps Lea would have understood, but Elettra reasoned it was only fifty-fifty and she didn't want to put their friendship to the test again when it was already strained by the financial situation with the convent.

'I need some air,' she said, going out into the garden. She wanted to stretch her legs and walk off some tension. She took the road that led down into the town, towards the port, and sat down on a bench in the square to watch the boats in the bay. Watching island life go by at its slow pace provided a sense of calm that seemed to evade her.

'I didn't expect to find you here. It's been a while since I've seen you out and about.'

Elettra jumped and turned round to see Adrian on his bicycle.

'I could say the same of you,' she replied curtly. She had barely seen him since that Sunday at sea, an absence for which she was holding a grudge.

He shrugged, smiling.

'I've been busy,' he replied. He uncapped his water battle and took a sip. 'How about you? Are sales any better?'

The frown instantly disappeared from Elettra's face and she tucked a lock of hair behind her ear. 'Please don't ask.'

Adrian's eyes moved restlessly, tinged with concern. 'Why not? Is it that bad?'

'In two words? A nightmare.'

'That's not good.'

'No, it's not.'

Adrian bit his lip, one hand in his thick hair. There was something magnetic about him; it was in his eyes, his athletic build, his paint-speckled nails and his large hands which contained so much warmth. It was the same warmth her mother had been denied by the artist she was in love with, and which Elettra was being offered spontaneously, if she could only overcome her fears.

'I see, but if you want to talk about it I'm happy to listen. I can keep secrets,' he added, pretending to zip his lips as he got off his bike.

'It's kind of you, but even if I tell you it won't change anything.'

'Give it a try, what will it cost you? Perhaps it'll lift some weight off your shoulders.'

'I'd need to win the lottery for that,' she replied bluntly. 'Do you know any lucky numbers?'

Adrian raised his hands. 'Okay, you win. But my offer's always there.'

He wiped his hands on his jeans and turned the bicycle towards the port. He was about to climb on, but then kicked the stand into place and turned round. 'Do you want to go for a ride?'

Elettra burst out laughing. 'Are you serious?'

'Why, did I say something funny?'

'Yes, you did, after what happened at sea?'

'That was just bad luck, it could've happened to anyone, but at least we'll be on dry land this time. That seems a definite advantage.'

Elettra shook her head; Adrian knew how to get what he wanted. 'All right,' she said, 'but look at it this way: if I agree to get on that bike with you, you might upset one of your admirers or, worse, someone could get the wrong idea. Are you really sure you want to be seen in my company?'

'What do you mean, which admirers?' he snapped.

'Well, artists are very popular guys.'

'Are you jealous?'

'Not at all.'

Adrian snorted and got on the saddle. 'Well, if you've finished talking nonsense then get on. I'll give you a ride to the convent.' He reached a hand towards her. 'Come on, it's not a limousine, but it's got to be better than walking.' Elettra glanced at the path that led to the convent and sighed. In spite of her curt replies, Adrian's offer was inviting. 'Okay.' She got up and gently stroked the handlebar, letting her fingers run over the cold steel. 'It seems I don't have a choice.'

He smiled in satisfaction. 'No,' he replied, 'it seems not.'

He helped her onto the crossbar, making sure she was comfortable enough to last the short journey to the convent. As soon as she felt Adrian's arms brush hers, Elettra stiffened. It was strange to be in contact with a new person – to remember what it meant to feel someone else's body against hers; to know a new breath, a new smell, the scent of the sea and white musk that she now locked away in her mind along with the sound of his voice. She needed to learn these feelings again from scratch, like a new emotional education.

She looked down to watch the path flying by beneath her feet. It was pleasant to feel the crisp evening air brush her cheeks, filling her lungs with the powerful scent of rosemary, and she relaxed until she was leaning into Adrian as he cycled along unknown streets; his skin smelled of sun and exertion, a universe light years away from where she had lived before, but in that moment, as she sat on a half-rusted bicycle that was climbing gruelling paths between juniper bushes and flowering arbutus trees, it seemed she was living another person's life.

All she was, the person she wanted to become, was the woman she'd found on this island, at the convent; she had discovered a new Elettra, perhaps the one suffocated by the restrictive walls of her former life, who hadn't been able to break free in the city. She liked the woman she saw in the mirror in the mornings: courageous, tenacious. Alive.

Someone like my mother, if I wasn't worried by the parallels with her life. What will the future hold if Adrian stays part of my life? she asked herself, trusting the universe for a reply.

'It really is stunning,' she said, leaning her head against Adrian's warm chest and giving her full attention to the majestic view before her.

'So, there are problems at the convent,' Adrian said cautiously, as he followed the road uphill.

'Several, I'd say. Sylvie and Vincent seem to be plotting again. If things go on like this, the mayor will soon be back to enforce the clause in the contract, and Lea will be evicted. She'll have to go, by that point she won't have another option.'

Adrian grunted and replied, 'And what will you do?' He pushed down on the pedals. 'Will you go or will you stay, to see how things turn out?'

Elettra looked at his tensed arms as the earth flew past beneath her feet. She thought about the mayor's threats, the many mysteries surrounding Edda's life, but, most of all, about the convent, and what it had meant and still meant to her. She inhaled, her eyes now turned to the vastness of the sea. 'I'm staying. I'm staying until the end,' she replied. 'I'm one of the family now, aren't I?'

'A fully-fledged member, I'd say.'

'And Lea needs all the help she can get, including mine. Leroux is on the war path, I can't leave her by herself.'

'Unfortunately, I agree entirely: it looks like Leroux is getting angry, and he's like a dog with a bone. The convent is in for a tough time unless we come up with something.'

'You can say that again. And the worst part is that other than Isabelle's extreme measures, we don't know how to stop them.'

'What do you mean?'

Elettra turned sideways to look at him, hiding a smile behind her tangled hair. 'When Lea and I discussed the situation with Isabelle, she suggested threatening the mayor, armed with pitchforks,' she told him, bursting out laughing, and Adrian joined her, throwing his head back.

Elettra paused to observe the small lines either side of his mouth; when Adrian laughed, he laughed with his entire face, and at that moment everything about him, his eyes, his mouth and his cheeks, was laughing.

A few minutes later they arrived at the convent, each absorbed in their own silence; once they were through the gate, Adrian propped the bicycle against a tree, and they suddenly heard Lea and the mayor shouting, rending the air like missiles firing.

'It was stupid to give you time, women like you never learn!' Vincent yelled. He was waving his usual fistful of papers at Lea, who warily watched his every move. 'But you can be sure that things will change around here, really change!' he continued to shout. The buttons of his shirt were strained to the limit, but Lea wasn't intimidated; she stopped in front of him, arms folded, the sleeves of her black dress rolled up to her elbows.

'I'm not afraid of you,' she faced him down, looking him right in the eyes. 'You can come here and yell every day if it makes you feel better, but I won't surrender this place to you and your friend from Paris. The convent is mine, I paid for every last cent of it, and I'd rather blow myself up than sell it to you, so take your damned papers and get off my property.'

'What the hell ...' Elettra murmured, leaning forward, determined to intervene, but Adrian caught her by the arm and shook his head.

'That's not a good idea,' he whispered while the mayor listened to his rival's words in astonishment. Lea was determined to keep up the fight, but the battle against Leroux would be the most unscrupulous one she'd ever fought. She had set herself against the mayor and Elettra was sure he would make her pay a high price for her choice.

'As you wish,' Leroux replied with a smile. He slipped off his jacket, brushed it clean and tightened his grip on his papers, his eyes full of the certainty of victory. 'But you should know this place won't remain your property, as you like to call it, for much longer. You've made a mistake getting in my way, you dear little orphan; you'll never manage to keep it going through subscriptions – and there are no nuns to save you this time,' he warned her. 'Everyone in town knows who you are.'

'We'll see.'

'I wouldn't get my hopes up if I were you, because I swear I'll kick you out of here, whatever it takes.'

He raised his index finger and pointed it at Lea, retreating until he was in the middle of the small square. This time he addressed the whole convent. 'You and the other women who live here are a disgrace to this island, but the moment has come to get rid of the rot. All of it,' he said in a loud voice, making sure the others could hear him too.

Vincent saw the seed of fear in Lea's eyes. His blow had hit the mark.

He gave a last look at the building and slung his jacket over his shoulder. 'See you later,' he said as he headed off along the road back to town.

Lea stayed exactly where she was. Vincent's dig had hit home, forcing her to stumble to the doorway, seeking support from its worn frame. With her hunched back, she was so small and alone that she looked like an old lady.

Elettra sprang forward, but she didn't manage to reach her; Lea had already disappeared into the corridors by the time she got to the doorway.

Defeated, she turned to Adrian, who came over and put an arm around her waist. 'Come on, let's go inside. There's no point staying here.' He led her towards the kitchen. Elettra followed him without protest, her heart crumpling, but when they opened the door they were both shocked to find Nicole sitting staring into space with a blanket thrown round her shoulders; her fists were clenched against her chest and she was crying.

Elettra hurried over to her and took her hands. 'Sweetheart, what's wrong?' she asked, brushing a lock of blonde hair out of Nicole's face. She had to repeat her question at least half a dozen times before Nicole shook herself out of her daze.

Adrian offered her some water and put an arm around her, saying comforting words, but Nicole's breathing became faster and more erratic. 'He says we have to leave,' she whispered. 'He said they'll come back with bulldozers, and if we try and resist they'll bury us along with these walls. He said we can't stay and live here and that if we object he'll have us arrested but if we collaborate he'll help us.'

Elettra frowned, not at all surprised to hear Leroux's threat on her friend's lips. 'Don't worry, Leroux won't do anything,' she told her, but Nicole continued to shake her head, frightened.

'You don't understand,' Nicole insisted. 'If he's said he'll do it, he will. It's happened before, and it was horrible.' Her voice cracked as she fought against a past that was coming back to torment her.

'It won't happen, you have to believe me.'

'But it will!' Nicole exclaimed. She was struggling to breathe again. 'Fabien was Vincent's younger brother, so Vincent was my brother-in-law. He did everything he could to convince his brother and their parents that marrying the dairyman's daughter was madness, but my husband wasn't like him. Fabien wasn't rich like Vincent, in fact he would stay at sea for weeks to earn a bit of extra cash, but he loved me, and that's why he never gave in to their demands. He was a simple person, but Vincent and the storm destroyed everything.'

'What do you mean?' Elettra interrupted, as Nicole's eyes faced the flood of memories from those days once again.

'When they announced on the radio that the search had been called off on that terrible evening, I knew I'd never see my husband again,' she replied. 'Until that point, a part of me had clutched at the possibility that he was safe, but when Vincent came to the bar I understood that there was nothing more to be done. I had become a widow, and so had many others, but it's not the kind of news you fully understand when they first tell you. You need time to get used to the loneliness of an empty bed, a silence in the mornings you used to fill with chatter over coffee, but I wasn't given that time. Vincent came to see me on the very day of the funeral to tell me that I'd have to leave the house. He suggested I stay with my parents for a bit, but when I told him my parents were dead and I didn't have anyone left, he just frowned and told me in no uncertain terms that I had no right to live in the house I'd shared with Fabien because it still belonged to their family. I tried to explain that if he threw me out I'd end up in the street and I even offered to pay him rent, but he didn't want to hear reason;

he told me he wanted to rent the house out to tourists and he had no use for my small change.'

Silence. A bitter smile suddenly appeared on Nicole's blueish lips. 'Do you know how things turned out?' she continued. 'Three weeks after my husband's death I no longer had a roof over my head.'

'What a complete bastard,' Adrian burst out.

'That's absurd,' Elettra said, looking at Nicole.

'No, it's not: that's just how Vincent is. Fabien was the exception, but the desire for money, for power, has always flowed in the blood of the Leroux family.'

Elettra was stunned by the pitiless description of this man. Nicole's story left her full of rage; she felt the need to stop the damage that Leroux had caused, both for Lea and for the other women at the convent.

And for her mother, too, and for herself. 'What happened to you is terrible, but it won't happen again, you have my word,' she reassured Nicole. 'Now go and have a rest, you must be exhausted.' She saw Nicole's warm skin tone return and heard her whisper a 'thank you'.

'It will all turn out fine,' Elettra assured her. She hugged her, and when Nicole left the room Elettra watched the door swinging listlessly. She leaned against the wall and slid down it, her fingers buried in her hair.

'Are you okay?' Adrian asked, reaching a hand towards Elettra, who barely had the energy to look at him. She realised he was offering her much more than his help to get up again; he was giving her the possibility to save the convent and her only option was to grasp it. But in order to do that she had to learn to trust. After one final glance at the flecks of paint on Adrian's fingers, she wrapped her own around them.

'Much better now, thank you,' she replied, although she felt like she was stumbling around in a darkened room. She leaned on his hand for support but when she tried to stand up she wobbled and lost her balance.

Adrian immediately reached out his arms to break her fall, closing in on her, almost up against her lips, which opened slightly at the touch of his warm breath.

She closed her eyes, brushing all reason aside. She had no strength for words to stop him; she would deal with the resulting chaos afterwards, but the confusion she felt in that moment was balanced by the pleasure melting inside her. A kiss, an unexpected intimacy; the taste of new lips and the sea, of a rediscovered liberty that lit a flame in her chest.

Adrian's kiss had cracked the ice. Elettra knew it would be painful, it hurt already, but she hadn't done anything to avoid it. Only when she felt her lips part from Adrian's did she realise that she would never be the woman from that morning again, because, whatever the consequences, that kiss had freed her heart. All that remained of the past was the memory of a misguided love affair.

But just at that moment the north wind blew the kitchen door open, bringing an echo of fear with it. Sabine stood on the threshold, the outline of a woman swamped in a ratty old overcoat. She was panting. Her bloodstained knees were shaking and bruises stood out against her skin like purplish ghosts. 'I can't go back there, I don't want to go back,' Sabine stammered, her voice cracking.

20

Having seen the bruises that had bloomed on Sabine's skin, the map of a marriage from which all love had disappeared some time ago, there was no need to discuss whether or not Sabine should stay at the convent. Nicole prepared a room and Lea and the others gathered what was needed to offer first aid.

Elettra spent hours standing at the end of Sabine's bed, twisting the cloth she had used to wipe the blood from her knees and calm her fever; Sabine was a woman defeated, racked by nightmares, nightmares of a man who didn't know how to love.

The first few days were the hardest; one of Gustave's blows had broken two of Sabine's ribs and the pain was so bad she struggled to breathe.

For their part, Lea and the others avoided making even the slightest reference to Gustave, while Elettra, absorbed by other thoughts, focused on carrying out her work in the kitchen and waiting until her friend was ready to talk. She wanted to continue her investigations, but every time she left her place at Sabine's bedside she felt defeated. She couldn't abandon Sabine, she'd never forgive herself; Edda's life, along with all its mysteries, belonged to the past, but the injuries to Sabine's body were painfully present. All Elettra wanted was for her friend to feel safe, protected, and for nobody in town ever to look at her again with the same gaze they used to direct at her, because she was sure that Sabine would never have withstood the blow.

Framing the days were thoughts of Adrian. He had disappeared after the kiss he'd stolen from her, and Elettra had had problems with her baking ever since; suddenly she couldn't even whip a drop of cream without things going wrong, and preparing a straightforward custard had become pure hell. But in spite of all this, Sabine, when she got a bit better, liked to watch her and Nicole cook together, and found it relaxing to listen to their chatter, reading a passage from the bible she always carried with her.

'Reading the holy scriptures and spending time with you two is the only medicine I need to get back on my feet,' she would often tell them, laughing with amusement at the sight of Elettra's frowns each time the dough rebelled in her hands.

It had been happening ever since she had arrived at the convent, but Sabine was sure she would never forget that last time: Elettra and Nicole were busy preparing *ovis mollis*, a kind of biscuit that had come straight from the young Edda's recipe book.

'Can I sit in here with you?' she had asked them, appearing in the kitchen doorway with a wide smile and the bible pressed against her chest.

Elettra looked up from the dough. 'Of course you can, in fact you should. Come in, sit here with us,' she replied with a quick smile before diving back into the sugary mass that filled the space between her fingers. The dough was too soft, unstable, a couple of minutes in the oven and it would liquefy completely. Elettra huffed, wiping her forehead with her arm. 'Nicole, could you come and give me a hand with these, please? I need your help, otherwise

I'll end up throwing the whole lot out of the window.' She spoke to her friend, while Sabine attentively turned the pages of the psalms. 'I can see you're very fond of the bible,' Elettra said.

'I like the message, the hope I read between these pages. I've had to give it up for too long.'

'Why?' Nicole asked her, tipping Elettra's floury dough onto the work surface.

Sabine stroked the yellowed pages with her fingertips. 'Gustave wouldn't let me go to church, not on Sundays and not on feast days; he said it was a waste of time, and that there wasn't time for the Eternal Father with a household and a bar to run. But I've always liked the sacred scriptures, ever since I was a little girl; reading them makes me feel comforted, understood. At peace.' She shrugged her shoulders while Nicole pulled out a tray.

'Of course, it's not the same thing,' Elettra said, 'but this will help you feel comforted and understood too. Try one and tell me if I'm wrong.'

'Really?' Sabine said, and reached out and took a pinch of the dough in Elettra's hands. The mixture had a sandy consistency; if she squashed it against her palate she could feel the grains of sugar melt instantly, sweet as a memory of summer, while the soft trace of butter and egg yolk hovered in the background. Sabine closed her eyes and pursed her lips. 'Delicious,' she moaned.

'The secret is well-beaten eggs and very fresh butter. And a sprinkling of the magic that seems to have abandoned me recently,' Elettra commented, taking some of the dough to try for herself.

'It's nothing permanent, I hope,' Sabine replied.

'Everything can be cured, even indifference,' Elettra answered, 'you just have to find the right treatment.'

Nicole smiled and put a bag of sugar on the scales; she had found her magic thanks to Elettra and the fragrance of her pastries.

Sabine, on the other hand, continued to stare at the patterns in the tiles. 'It would be nice to learn how to cure indifference, but I'm not sure you'll succeed.'

'Anyone can do it,' Elettra said, folding her arms. 'You have to want it really badly, but there's nothing, nothing, you can't do.' She took a small ball of dough and passed it to Sabine, who looked at her suspiciously. 'Have a go with this.'

'How? I've never baked pastry in my life, I don't know how!'

'Outrageous! All you need to do is stop thinking with your head and use these instead,' she explained to Sabine, taking her hands, while Nicole disappeared into the pantry. 'Let your instinct guide you, play with memories and the evocative perfumes of the ingredients. Listen to yourself and it will be easy, believe me,' she added, rolling the dough between her fingers.

'Okay,' stammered Sabine, staring at the leftover dough in her hand, but when she brought it up to her nose to smell its perfume, she immediately felt drawn to it, lost in the memory of a red scarf that she had put away at the back of the wardrobe. She'd had to hide it in an old biscuit tin, and with time it had taken on the same scent that now impregnated her hand. She had bought the scarf a few months after her marriage, before she began to walk past mirrors without turning to look. Thinking about it made her feel ill, her skin still bore too many bruises, but for a moment that lump of sugary dough had given her back the feeling of a simpler life. When buying a scarf was something normal.

'It smells fantastic,' she said. She let the ball of dough fall into the bowl, while the shadow of the scarf faded behind a closed door in her mind. She stood and watched the mixture swallow up her memories and turned to find Elettra, who was bent over the oven to check its temperature.

'But there's something melancholic about it, too,' she added aloud, and Elettra was not surprised. It was exactly the same effect she felt every time she made these biscuits; all it took was for the essential oil in the lemon peel to blend into the dough to turn back the hands of time and take her back to the warmth of Edda's Dream Kitchen.

'It will all be okay,' Sabine said, her fingers entwined in prayer.

She looked down at the pages of the bible she'd left on the table, and at Nicole's sweet smile and Elettra's warmth, which showed her that the stars still shine even on the darkest of nights.

It was then, she was to tell Elettra, in that very instant, that Sabine understood where her path lay, that she found courage.

She smiled at Elettra, who said, 'What was that? Are you okay?'

'I'm absolutely fine,' she murmured, stroking the cross she wore round her neck as the bells of the church in town chimed the half hour.

21

Elettra pulled her nightdress tight around her as she lay in bed. The storm had caught her by surprise while she studied the photograph of the three young people, Ada's words going round and round in her head; she tried to come up with a theory to explain the information she'd gathered. The man in the photo, she told herself, was the artist the woman had told her about – but then the sudden crash of thunder wiped out all conjectures.

Let's hope the storm doesn't do any damage, she thought, pressing the photo to her chest, afraid. She pulled aside the covers after a second thunderclap shook the convent walls. Feeling chilly, she wrapped herself in her dressing gown and made for the kitchen, in search of something warm to fill her stomach.

Elettra went down the stairs clutching a candle and switched the light on as soon as she found herself in the kitchen. The clock above the door read quarter past four. The others didn't seem to have noticed the storm, there wasn't a sound from their rooms. But hers were fearful footsteps.

A shiver ran down her back as she looked at the door that led to the garden: Dominique's and Lea's wellingtons were missing from their usual place.

They must have gone to check on the animals, she thought, putting a pan of water on the hob. At supper that evening Lea had told her that a couple of the goats were ill, so she assumed that Lea had gone out to check on them.

Elettra waited until the water in the pan began to boil, then turned out the flame and tossed in two spoonfuls of Lea's relaxing lavender, chamomile and lemon balm tisane. She waited patiently, then sweetened the infusion with lemon honey, but just as she tapped the spoon against the mug, she had an idea.

The artist who came from the sea is clearly the key to the mystery, she thought, staring into the darkness; Ava had told her that Edda had gone crazy over an artist who'd come from the mainland, and in the prayer she had found on the back of the photo the novice, she assumed, was asking God to keep her from the attentions of a man whose hands *have drawn your face and those of your saints*. The pieces of the puzzle were slowly coming together, finding their place on the timeline. He's the connection between the two women, a divisive love. He should really be my starting point.

But her thoughts of the past still catapulted her back into the present, to the artist Adrian, who had appeared in *her* life.

Elettra sighed as clouds of steam rose from the pan. There would probably never be an 'us', but Adrian had given her back something nobody had ever given her before that kiss: freedom.

She ran her index finger over the ceramic mug, trying to piece together all the bits of the brainteaser that was slowly taking shape, but she stopped when she heard the sound of rustling.

There was a blow to the door that led outside. Then another.

'Let me see my wife, you whore!'

It was a man's voice, coloured by alcohol and desperation. Elettra backed away from the door.

After a brief silence it started to shake again under a shower of kicks. Rain trickled down the closed shutters. The storm was catching its breath, even the sky was saturated with violence. But it seemed the man at the door could never get enough of it.

Elettra stared at the handle.

'I know you're in there, open this damned door!' the man shouted.

Elettra paled. The man at the door was Gustave, and he was completely out of his mind.

Something seized her and Elettra took a deep breath and moved closer to the noise; she couldn't let fear win again, not any more. Breathing heavily she went over to the door and turned the lock.

'What exactly do you want?' she asked, but as soon as she opened the door, Gustave threw himself at her. She watched as he charged the door so hard that the chain she'd put across for safety vibrated. The links stretched and deformed and Elettra's breathing became harsh. She felt the man's anger blow over her face, which was alight with fear, and the smell of wine that impregnated the air.

'Let me see Sabine!' he shouted, his voice drowning out the thunder, but Elettra didn't move a millimetre. She stood firm with all the weight of her body in spite of the roar of boiling blood in her veins: her legs shook and her vision was clouded by fear, but her lips remained sealed. She gripped the door, ready to slam it closed against Gustave with all her force, and prayed to her mother for help.

'I will only let you see Sabine when you come back here sober, and providing that she agrees, but don't get your hopes up. She doesn't want anything to do with you right now, so get out of here.'

She made to close the door, but Gustave gave it another shove, panting like a raging bull. 'It's not up to you to decide anything, you whore!'

He hurled himself forward again, knocking Elettra backwards as she got up and threw her entire weight against it to prevent him coming in. 'Nor you!' she shouted, pushing with all her might. 'The time when you could beat Sabine is over, and if you don't go I'm calling the police. I swear, if you try and touch a hair on her head, I'll make sure you end up with nothing, and I'm not joking!' she threatened. She pushed, even though her feet were slipping backwards on the floor. It was impossible to stand her ground. He would soon batter the door down and then her only option would be to find something to fend him off. She had already spotted the knife on the draining board and she was ready to use it, but by then he had burst through and had thrown her to the ground. He grabbed her by the throat.

'Leave her alone!' a voice shouted from the other end of the room, as fresh flashes of lightning split the sky. 'I said, leave her alone!' Sabine shouted. Elettra quickly realised her mistake.

Gustave turned to the side and let go of Elettra's neck, but as he faced Sabine he seemed not to recognise his wife; there was nothing left of the woman she'd become following their marriage, the one with the limp hair and tatty clothes.

Sabine wasn't wearing the rags in which she'd fled from him, nor the evidence of his rage. She was a new woman, one who was ready to challenge him. There was no fear in her proud eyes, but he didn't give up. 'You're coming home right now, we're getting out of here,' he ordered with his usual intimidating tone, but when he turned at the door, his fists and lips clenched, Sabine hadn't moved a step towards him. She had stayed where she was.

'No.' Sabine spoke her refusal loudly, with an authority she had never possessed before.

Gustave opened and closed his mouth like a fish, shaking himself, clearly registering his wife's reaction. 'All right, you've made your scene, but now we're leaving. This place stinks of depravity,' he said. He shot a poisonous glance at Elettra and spat on the floor. It was obviously an ultimatum.

But it was up to Sabine to choose her destiny; she took a deep breath and turned away without a word.

But Elettra could never have imagined the violence that it would unleash.

Overcome by rage, Gustave grabbed Sabine by the hair and dragged her out of the kitchen as Elettra fought to free her.

Elettra shouted, kicked and followed Gustave outside to the old chapel, then, overwhelmed by a wave of hate, she threatened him with a lamp that was kept lit all night outside the chapel door.

'Get out of here!' she shouted at the top of her lungs, trembling. All she wanted was to keep Gustave away, for him to stop shouting at Sabine and leave, but as she stood with her back against the door, she realised that Gustave had let go of Sabine, and saw his huge, dirty hands reaching for her instead.

Everything seemed to contract, becoming a black haze, while the crunch of windows and the bitter smell of smoke did the rest.

Then there was nothing but darkness, deep and profound.

Then flames exploded in the chapel and immediately crossed the threshold, setting fire to the trunk of the jasmine tree that covered the convent's façade. In just a few moments the fire engulfed the wall in a scorching embrace and reached the abandoned cells on the top floor.

Dozens of explosions followed as Nicole screamed. She had woken up to find herself surrounded by flames; her yelling came through the broken windows and the sound of other footsteps were audible over the howling of the weather.

It was Lea, appearing out of the darkness along with Dominique and Isabelle.

'My God, Joséphine!' screamed Isabelle, running towards the burning building with Lea on her heels.

'You take care of the others!' Lea shouted to Dominique before disappearing into the smoke on the stairs.

Elettra rushed after Lea and Isabelle, groping for the handrail. The only thing guiding her through the smoke and crackling was Isabelle's voice, urging Lea to move.

'There's nobody up there!' Elettra shouted, but they didn't hear her. Meanwhile, down below, buckets of water and a driving rain were pouring onto the flames, depriving a fire hungry for life of nutrients.

The three women dashed up the stairs that led to the top floor in just a few minutes, rubbing away the smoke that burnt their eyes and throats, but as they drew closer to the old laundry the air became so thick and bitter that Elettra lost sight of Lea and Isabelle.

She found them again as soon as she climbed the last stair. They were struggling with the lock on a door at the end of the corridor, from behind which came the cries of a frightened animal.

Finally real, the woman who had filled Elettra's dreams screamed in terror beyond the door; Elettra opened her mouth in a mute cry, pressing her hands together to hold back the memory of all those nights, all the times she'd felt like a visionary when she heard that voice. But she had heard the voice, there was no doubt about it.

She tried to make her way through the smoke as Lea's trembling hands undid all the locks, and when Lea and Isabelle finally shoved the door open, a cloud of black smoke filled the corridor. The forbidden room had been opened.

Elettra hurried inside with them, and she saw Isabelle taking the pulse of a woman in a nun's habit who was moving on the bed as though she were having convulsions.

'Joséphine, that's enough!' Isabelle told her, but when the nun turned towards the door and saw Elettra, a hoarse, heartrending cry came from her lips. 'For God's sake, Joséphine, stop that!' Isabelle shouted, her face red, as Lea sobbed at the woman's feet.

A woman, then, and not a ghost. A nun.

'Ed-da ... Ed-da,' she repeated, staring at Elettra, her voice a muddle of strangled syllables. It only lasted a moment, then the body wrapped in the cocoon of fabric began to contort again, a victim of the spasms once more. Isabelle turned towards Elettra, her face coloured with fear of a kind Elettra had never seen before. 'Get out of here!' she thundered, enraged.

'Get out of here!' Elettra kept hearing the words in her mind until Isabelle and Lea, who carried the unconscious nun in her arms, re-emerged from the smoke that enveloped the convent.

Elettra walked towards them, her face plastered with ash and tears in spite of the surge of adrenalin still in her body. She moved slowly, one step after the other, an automaton devoid of all will. She just had time to look at the expression on the nun's face, finally calm and relaxed. Her face was distorted, her lip twisted up to the left in a permanent grimace, the visible scars of an illness, but although they were marked by age, her features still had a refined beauty, a timeless elegance. She was the portrait of a wounded angel with broken wings.

Elettra extended a hand towards the woman, who was now trapped in the arms of an unnatural sleep; she could still see the searing power of her eyes, in her ears was the echo of Edda's name, shouted into the flames.

'Who is she?' she asked Isabelle, who stood a step behind Lea, who, hearing her friend's voice break the silence, turned to face her, chocking down a sob.

'Do you really have no idea?' Lea replied as Elettra's arms collapsed under the weight of further questions and Isabelle took a deep breath, trying to convince Lea to take the woman away, far away.

'This is not the moment, Lea; anyone could see her, let's go. We need to take her to safety and call the doctor,' Isabelle told her again, pushing her forwards, but Lea didn't move a centimetre. She continued to stare at Elettra, her arms holding a secret that had now been revealed.

'She's my mother, the last abbess of this convent.'

Vino alle rose di Edda

1 litre white Muscat

200g rose petals

2 spoons honey

Carefully wash the rose petals then delicately pat them dry.

Pour the petals into a bottle, cover with wine and honey and leave to infuse in a cool, dark place for around a fortnight, taking care to tip the bottle upside down twice a day.

Filter the wine and serve chilled.

22

Ashes and shattered hopes; that was the aftermath of the fire that broke out in the convent. Dominique and Nicole spent hours cleaning the areas the fire had reached, and by the time they'd put everything back to how it was, their hearts were full of soot. The flames had entered their souls, too, burning until the very last moment of that hellish night, tearing away all their hopes. Two years earlier the water had taken their loved ones, and that October night the fire had robbed them of their future, consigning them to darkness.

It was that darkness in which Elettra had found the answers to Lea's secrets. Lea had lied to her: the abbess was alive. She was not the legend Sabine had described to Elettra. She was Lea's mother. Elettra had done nothing but talk to Lea about Edda but Lea had never spoken a single word of her own truth.

It was a deep crack in their relationship, in a friendship in which Elettra had invested so much. She realised that Dominique and Nicole had betrayed her too; they knew about the abbess's existence and they had never said a word to her. Elettra knew she hadn't been entirely honest with them, either, not telling them what she discovered about her mother, but those were just suppositions, clues, and there was the threat telling her to maintain her silence. But Lea was the person who had hurt her most of all.

'Stop behaving like capricious little girls,' Isabelle suddenly told them, gathering Elettra and Lea in the dining room. She told them to sit down, but when they both hesitated she raised an eyebrow, staring at them. 'Now what's going on? Are you so childish that you don't even want to be in the same room?' Isabelle seemed to have aged by a hundred years since the night of the fire. Her skin appeared tight on her bones and her reddish eyes seemed tired.

It was a poisonous atmosphere and Lea had tried to rebel, staring at the midwife with a hostile glare. 'Well, why did you make us come here?' she asked, looking her right in the eyes.

'It's simple,' Isabelle replied, opening her arms, 'because I'm fed up of all this deceit. I'm sick and tired of fighting a battle that isn't mine and indulging other people's whims. I've done it up until now, but it's time you knew the truth. The whole truth.'

'What truth?' Elettra burst out.

'There is no truth,' Lea interrupted, trying to silence Isabelle.

'Not even you know the whole truth, my girl. And you should remember that I delivered you with these hands, so I'm authorised to give you a slap with them as well, if necessary,' Isabelle said sharply.

Finally, the moment had arrived when every question would have its answer, every puzzle its solution: Elettra had so many of them, so many secrets. 'Go on, then: tell us,' she urged Isabelle under Lea's hostile gaze.

Isabelle knotted her fingers together, breathing deeply. 'I haven't been entirely honest with you.'

'I'd guessed as much.'

'Why, what did you tell her?' Lea interrupted.

'Me, nothing. I asked Ada to do it for me.'

'Ada?' Elettra repeated, astonished.

'Exactly,' Isabelle admitted. 'I know, I must be mad to have done something like that, but I couldn't bear it any more. I couldn't keep pretending not to know and inventing accidents to prevent her finding out the truth about your mother. About everything,' she corrected herself.

Elettra gasped and thought of the path she'd undertaken to discover her mother's life, the clues and the reticence every time she spoke of her, Isabelle's sarcastic comments and about the night she must have followed her to the abbess's archive. 'How could you do such a thing, Isabelle? I trusted you.'

'Unfortunately I had to, because I had to stop you going where you shouldn't. But believe me, if it was down to me this story would be over in a flash.'

Elettra looked first at Lea, then at Isabelle. 'I can't believe what I'm hearing.' She was soon cut off by Isabelle's raised hand.

'Not everything is as straightforward as it might seem, Elettra. There are so many things you don't know, and which you need to be told.'

'Oh, really,' Elettra spat. 'Now I deserve answers, now that it's too late?'

Isabelle looked her in the eyes, her arms rigid at her sides. 'It is never too late for the truth.'

'What truth, what the hell are you talking about?' complained Lea, breaking in between them. 'First of all, tell me who Ada is and what she has to do with us, but, more importantly, Isabelle, I want to know what story we're talking about. Because when I asked you whether you knew Elettra or her mother you told me very clearly that you knew nothing about them. I need to know what's going on. Whose side are you on?'

Isabelle clasped her hands in her lap, her gaze lowered; Elettra could tell this leap in time required a lot of strength.

Elettra slipped her hand into her pocket and clutched the photo, but something told her not to reveal it, not yet. 'Isabelle,' she said again.

'All right, all right,' Isabelle gave in. 'Everything started just before the war, when the convent was at its busiest. I had recently arrived from Spain with Juan and we were trying to settle in, to make friends, like you do when you arrive in a new place, and so we started to come to the convent like everyone in town. We all came here to buy bread and pastries, and that's when I met Edda,' she said, looking at Elettra, who immediately straightened up in her seat. 'I think she was working at the convent as a lay sister, a kind of young housekeeper, or perhaps she was just one of the many girls whose large families freed themselves of them by sending their daughters to religious institutions or to work in factories. I'm not exactly sure. But your mother wasn't like the others. Edda had a gift.'

'A gift?'

'In the kitchen,' Isabelle replied naturally.

'She was a real marvel and breads and pastries were her speciality. She had worked side by side with the convent's old baker for years, learning the basics of bread-making from her, but she soon surpassed her. Unlike her mentor's efforts, there was something magical about her creations that spoke to the soul and healed every wound.'

'Where does my mother come into all this?' Lea asked, staring at Isabelle with her arms folded and a confrontational expression on her face.

Isabelle clenched her fists. 'Joséphine was Edda's best friend,' she replied briskly. 'Those two were inseparable, I remember it well. A bit like you two, if you'd only stop fighting.' Lea and Elettra exchanged a quick glance for the first time since the night of the tragedy. 'They were almost the same age, just a couple of years between them, with totally different family backgrounds. But that was the good thing about the convent: it levelled out any differences. Whether you were a countess or a pauper it didn't matter: in here everyone was equal,' she explained. She poured herself some water. It was difficult, terribly difficult, to continue, but when she saw Lea and Elettra sitting in front of her twisting their hands out of the corner of her eye, she knew she couldn't stay silent any longer. 'They lived in harmony for years, during and after the war. They did everything together, they cared for the garden, tended the goats, and they would go down to the sea to bathe, ignoring the edict of the abbess at that time, who was for ever having to come up with new punishments for them. There wasn't a day when they didn't get up to something, or a summer evening when you wouldn't find them out there on the terrace looking at the stars. They even built themselves a kind of house in the tree by the river, and they carved their names into the old lemon tree in the garden to celebrate their friendship.'

Elettra jumped. She remembered that carving well, but something wasn't quite right about that idyll, or Isabelle's grave voice. 'If they were such good friends, why was part of the writing scratched out?' she asked. The photo started to pulse in the pocket where she kept it, as though it were alive.

'Everything was fine until the summer of 1952. A season the elderly like me will never forget.'

'Nineteen fifty-two, did you say?' Elettra repeated, her eyes wide.

'Yes, why?'

Elettra took the photo from her pocket and showed it to Isabelle. 'Does this mean anything to you?'

Isabelle looked over but Lea interrupted straight away. 'Excuse me, but would one of you be so kind as to tell me what's going on?' Neither Elettra nor Isabelle replied. Isabelle took the photograph from Elettra, stroking the yellowed paper. Perhaps there was a trace of a carefree smile on one of the girl's faces, and the man in the middle was clearly leaning towards her, his arm around her waist. She stroked all three faces with her finger and returned the photo to Elettra.

'They took it at Mermaids' Bay. It was a sunny Sunday, as hot as hell.'

'I'm not interested in talking about the weather,' Elettra said.

'I know.'

Elettra could see all her uncertainties vanish and nestle into the warm bed of the story, the story of the family she'd never had. She traced the edges of the photograph with a bitter smile; that sepia-coloured rectangle held the germ of a suspicion.

'That's the three of them, isn't it? Edda, the future abbess and the artist,' Elettra said.

Isabelle nodded.

'What's going on, Isabelle?' Lea thundered; her certainties had crumbled inside her and the earth had started to tremble in her world, too. She turned to Elettra, an echo of the fire in her eyes. 'And you,' she stammered, 'where did you get that photo?'

'I found it. In the archive, a few days ago, before Sabine came to the convent.'

'What?' Lea exclaimed, furious. 'Who gave you permission to rummage through my mother's papers?'

Elettra stiffened her back and raised her chin. 'You, with your reluctance and your continuous evasion of my questions. I asked you for help, but you were so afraid I might uncover the truth that in the end I decided I'd have to find the answers for myself, and so I did, in spite of the letter. And the threats,' she added.

'What do you mean, what threats are you talking about?' Lea asked.

'Those damned notes I sent her,' Isabelle suddenly interrupted.

Lea stared at her friend, dumbfounded.

'You?' murmured Elettra, her forehead creased in surprise. 'Impossible,' she stammered, her gaze lost, empty; she felt like she was trapped on a rollercoaster whose gears had stuck, leaving her to ride endlessly. Names, faces, smiles and words whirled around in her head, as she tiptoed hesitantly through a cloud of unanswered questions. 'Was it you outside my door that night? Was it you who left the note?'

'Yes,' Isabelle confessed. She turned to Lea, wrong-footed, unable to outline a story her friend clearly didn't already know.

'How could you?' was all Lea asked, as her voice struggled against tears. 'How could you do it?'

'It was Joséphine who asked me to, even if I didn't agree,' Isabelle explained. 'She was the one who went crazy as soon as she saw Elettra in the cloister and smelled the perfume of Edda's baking again. At first she seemed furious, she did nothing but complain and throw things, but when I went to see her a few days later, I found her in the grip of a deeper melancholy. She was crying desperately and repeating her friend's name.' She brought her hands up to her face. 'She's been consumed by a battle between her two selves for weeks, divided by the great, huge love she felt for Edda and bitterness at the life she herself had wasted. It was hellish, believe me.'

She wrapped a ribbon around her finger as she thought back over the last months. 'From the moment Elettra crossed the convent threshold, Joséphine started to talk about the past, it was all she ever seemed to do; she was convinced that Elettra was Edda, or that Edda had sent her. But she was afraid that Lea would suffer if everything came to light and the truth was revealed, and the last thing she wanted was to cause her daughter pain,' Isabelle continued, staring at her hands. 'It was complete folly,' she shook her head. 'You should have seen her, Elettra; she would rock back and forth for hours imagining your reaction, staring vacantly at the sea, and a moment later she would start to cry again and shout desperately from her bed. Night and day, from that point on,' she concluded, her eyes fixed on Elettra, ignoring Lea's fiery glare. 'But I couldn't play her game and humour these whims, that's why I asked Ada to tell you what she knew about Edda. All I wanted was for this whole thing to finish as soon as possible, because I couldn't bear to see you wandering around this island any more.'

Elettra shook her head. 'Incredible. It's ridiculous that it's come to this.'

'Unfortunately, the situation is very complicated,' Isabelle tried to explain.

'I bet she was the reason you changed the subject every time I asked you about Edda.'

'Yes,' Isabelle admitted, but before Elettra could go on the attack, she stopped her by raising a hand. 'But when Lea told me that Edda was dying, I said that was enough. Since then I haven't listened to Joséphine any more because I think she needs to yield to illness, to death; it may be the last remaining mystery, and we have a duty to respect it.' She paused. 'I spoke to Joséphine about it that same evening, but learning about Edda's condition has only worsened her own.'

'Why, what's so wrong with the abbess that she's hidden away and locked in a room?'

Isabelle tried to meet Lea's eyes, but she suddenly turned away, angry. 'Joséphine suffers from a form of dementia triggered by the stroke that paralysed one side of her body a few years ago. Since then she's alternated between moments of lucidity, now increasingly rare, and others when she's like a girl again and she completely loses her sense of reality. She's capable of anything in those moments, even hurting herself, which is why it's necessary to shut her in her room. To protect her.'

'Well, that doesn't seem to have been your first priority recently, given what you've done behind her back. But how could you, Isabelle?' Lea said, her voice barely a whisper. 'How could you do this to my mother?' she repeated. 'She's ill, she doesn't realise what she's doing, what she's saying, but you haven't done a single thing to put an end to this folly.'

'I know.'

Elettra felt the floor tilt as she sat next to Lea. It was all a lie, the result of a manipulation which had caused the line between right and wrong to become a hazy concept, an indistinct margin between the two sides of the same story. 'Lea's right,' she interrupted their exchange. 'It really is very difficult to understand the reason behind all this; why so many secrets, Isabelle?'

'Because Joséphine has done so much for me in the past,' Isabelle admitted, put on the spot by Lea and Elettra. 'Whether you like it or not, I'm in her debt, and there are some things I don't forget. Joséphine helped me a lot after Juan's death and even during his illness; she wrote to bishops and high-ranking church officials to get me medicine for him when he started having trouble with his heart, and she was the only one who reached out to me and helped me to keep the house going when everyone else looked the other way. She's done so much for me, I couldn't turn my back on her.' She was holding herself rigid in her seat so as not to let the emotion and memory of her husband's death get the better of her.

'You two have so few years behind you, you just wouldn't understand,' Isabelle continued. 'You can't know what it means to lose the person you love more than life itself, who is your life, and how tightly you hold on to every little hope. You can't imagine how grateful you are for a hand on your shoulder to instil you with a bit of courage, when all you want is to point a pistol at your temple and end it all.' She stared blankly at the two women in front of her. 'I'm bound to Joséphine by a deep gratitude and I'm not embarrassed to admit it. That's why I didn't back down when she asked me to help her. I did what I had to, I wrote those notes and I led you off-track, Elettra, even though, as I said, I didn't agree; in my opinion that story is dead and buried and remembering certain things is pointless.'

'What things?' Lea and Elettra both asked desperately.

'Edda and Joséphine fell in love with the same man, that's what this is all about,' Isabelle admitted. 'They were both around twenty, it was hardly surprising that something like that should happen, but things were more complicated for Joséphine; she was supposed to take her vows, she was destined for the religious life.'

'But that wasn't the case for my mother.'

'No, not at all; Edda wasn't a novice.'

'But what exactly happened?'

'Marte – I only know his first name – came to the island to restore the fresco of the nativity in the chapel,' Isabelle continued her story. 'The Curia sent him here in late May with the task of repairing everything that the bombs had destroyed. A mammoth job,' she went on, 'and since the island didn't yet have a boarding house, the nuns decided to host him at the convent in a ground floor room and made him Edda's responsibility. She was to take care of him and provide everything he needed to work at his best, but she only had to see him once to lose her head completely, and it was understandable: that boy was divinely handsome, his hands were always stained with colours and he had an enchanting smile. He was shut up in the chapel all day painting, and only occasionally, when the sun was setting and the light became too poor, would he take his boat and go and explore the neighbouring islands, or go down to the beach for a swim. But whenever he was at the convent he was always ready to lend a hand.'

'A gentleman,' Elettra observed.

'Indeed,' Isabelle agreed. 'I think he knew how handsome he was – he was a real hit with the women of the island who suddenly started to visit the convent en masse – but he didn't seem to give much weight to it. His true beauty, which was the cause of this whole disaster, was the goodness of his soul. So it's obvious that meeting a man like that must have been a huge shock for a girl like Edda who was used to living a very sheltered life, barely even greeting the wizened old parish priest. She fell in love immediately.'

'But Marte didn't return her feelings, did he?'

'It's a bit more complicated than that. Edda was always fluttering around him, she made her best pastries for him, she washed and ironed his clothes fresh for each morning. She pampered him as if he were her husband, and in return he thanked her, offering to carry heavy loads for her and helping her in the kitchen every so often. He was the one who gave her the recipe book; he made the notebook with his own hands after trying Edda's pastries, so that whatever happened her recipes wouldn't be forgotten. And so she'd remember him.'

'I'm sorry, but where does my mother come into all this?' Lea interrupted impatiently. 'It sounds like those two made the perfect couple, didn't they?'

Isabelle studied Lea. 'Marte fell in love with Joséphine. It was a lightning bolt,' she declared. 'It took just a fleeting encounter in the herb garden to light the fuse; but although she was very taken with him, she was defenceless, like Edda, after a life lived very much on the margins. Joséphine turned him down in the name of her holy vows. She felt the weight of her family's expectations and the commitment she'd made in God's sight. The poor thing spent several terrible weeks consumed by regrets.'

Elettra put the photo on the table, turning it face down. 'Then I suppose she was the one who wrote these words.'

Lea's eyes fell on her mother's elegant handwriting and Elettra didn't need to ask any further for confirmation of the truth; it was enough to see her friend's eyes widen and her skin flush, as Isabelle's eyes softened at the memory of long ago days.

'Joséphine wasn't just struck by Marte's charms, she returned his feelings. Look here at her words, this prayer; they speak very clearly,' Elettra said, turning to Lea and Isabelle. 'The poor girl,' she murmured. She put the photo on her knees. She felt uncomfortable beside Lea who was looking around her, stunned, but she needed to know, however painful it was, because she had never come so close to the truth before.

Edda was just a step away now.

'What happened next?' Elettra continued, looking Isabelle straight in the eyes. Isabelle shrugged.

'Edda found out about Marte's feelings for Joséphine, and as always tends to happen, jealousy, mixed with the fear of losing her best friend, got the better of her. She did all she could to keep them apart, and when, on Edda's advice, Joséphine destroyed all Marte's hopes, Edda slipped into the hole she left in his heart. It happened during the celebrations for the feast of Saint John, I remember it as though it were yesterday.

'There were bonfires all along the coast that night. We burn great fires of Saint John's wort, which grows along the cliffs, in honour of the Saint and at midnight we jump over them to drive off bad luck and make a wish,' she explained to Elettra. 'Marte had been rejected by Joséphine that day and he was devastated, so Edda suggested he go down to the beach with her to see the fires to cheer him up. She made rose wine for the occasion and took it with her as she went down the path to the beach with Marte. What with the wine and a delusion of love, the rest isn't hard to guess: two minuscule cells found one another inside your mother's body, and so you were conceived. I was the only one she told, just before she left the island,' Isabelle added quietly, softly, as Elettra's eyes filled with emotion. She knew what Isabelle was referring to, she had read the recipe for the wine in Edda's notebook, but it was all so new to her, so confusing! She finally had a father, a name to go on, a man who, somewhere in the world, might be dreaming of having a daughter to embrace, while she wanted nothing more than to pronounce those two syllables she'd been chasing since childhood. Papa.

A long silence filled the room, punctuated by the glances Lea and Isabelle continued to exchange.

'He can't have been that distraught, if all it took was a bit too much to drink for him to go to bed with someone else,' Lea observed. 'Now I understand why my mother never mentioned him to me; it was too depressing to remember a man like that.'

'Pain is the answer to your question, nothing more,' Isabelle said. 'In any case, after that night he really was distraught,' she continued, 'so much so that as soon as he regained his senses he begged Edda to forget all about it; he told her that he considered her a good friend, but that there could never be anything more between them. It was a very hard blow for Edda.

'At that point it was Edda herself who offered to accompany the abbess to Rome for medical treatment; she needed time away from the convent and from Marte, she could no longer live under the same roof as the man who'd broken her heart. But while she was in Rome, Joséphine, who knew nothing of the events of the feast of Saint John and missed Edda's company, gave in to the voice in her heart. I witnessed the first kiss she shared with Marte myself,' she told them, smiling sweetly at the memory. 'I was just there, in that very spot,' she said, pointing to a patch of shade beneath the colonnade. 'I'd come by to drop off a clock Juan had mended and I spotted those two behind a column, illuminated by the light of the moon. They were pressed together, she in her novice's habit and he in his usual paint-stained shirt; it was such a tender kiss, and a story of doomed love. Marte was so in love with her that he wrote verses for her, hiding them on the chapel floor.'

'Are you sure?' Lea objected.

'It's a genuine declaration of love!' Isabelle replied, getting up to show them so they could see for themselves.

They approached the chapel in silence and were confronted by its scorched façade. Isabelle walked briskly along the central nave and turned to face Lea and Elettra when she reached the pews that were once reserved for the novices. 'Look,' she said, moving aside the blue runner that covered the writing, 'read it for yourselves, then tell me I'm imagining things.'

Elettra obediently followed the line of Isabelle's outstretched index finger; the Latin quotation *Amor vincit omnia* wound through the decorative polychrome marble. Beneath it another smaller text read:

My
Affection shall
Remain
True
Eternally

An admission, a declaration of love, that left Elettra dumb-founded. A love so great couldn't be opposed or conquered, so it was natural, she thought, that of the two it was Edda who gave in.

She opened her arms, her eyes flooded by a painful truth. 'Why did my mother get in their way? Their destiny was already clear, nobody could have changed the course of events,' she murmured, her eyes fixed on the coloured marble, on those letters carved by a man in love with a woman he couldn't have, and her voice full of compassion for Edda and her unhappy heart. 'Why did she want to hurt herself so deeply?' she asked herself, as Isabelle placed a comforting hand on her shoulder.

'Unfortunately it didn't end there,' Isabelle replied, her voice serious, and she sat down on the pew between Elettra and Lea, who followed her like a silent shadow.

'One day Joséphine wrote a letter begging her family to free her from the obligation to take her vows. She asked her parents for permission to marry Marte, the man she loved; she dreamed of a life with him, a family, and she was tired of living their love in secret. Edda found out about their relationship on her return from Rome. It was Joséphine herself who told her everything and it was her biggest mistake.'

'Why?'

Isabelle sighed heavily. 'Edda seemed crazy in those days, she said she wanted to stop cooking and she was always in a bad mood, so one morning Joséphine suggested she join her and Marte on an excursion, convinced that it would help her relax. That was when the photo was taken. The only one of the three of them together,' she told them.

Lea finally understood why her mother had insisted so firmly on staying at the convent, making her buy the building even when it was falling to pieces; she wanted to live and die in rooms full of a lost love, which she had never managed to forget. A poisoned love that joined Lea and Elettra in an unbreakable bond, transcending time, forged in the breath of that summer.

'What happened next?' Elettra insisted.

'A disaster,' Isabelle announced.

So, an untreatable emotional wound had prevented Edda from marrying and finding new love, Elettra thought. As a result she had preferred the solitude of her kitchen in the city and that was why she had spent years trying to keep her daughter away from other people: she wanted only to prevent her from experiencing the same pain. Edda wanted to protect her, just like any other mother.

Urged on by Elettra's gaze, Isabelle sighed. This was the hardest part to tell, the most painful. She sought Elettra's hands. 'Edda shut herself up in her room until the evening of the feast of the Assumption, when the nuns traditionally brought pastries and bread to church to be blessed and then offered them to the faithful who'd joined the procession. At midnight there were fireworks over the sea. The whole town gathered on the beach that night, including the nuns.' She ran a hand through her silvery hair.

'Everyone was there, everyone except Marte, whom Edda had asked for an explanation that same evening. One of the nuns told me that Edda had decided to leave the convent, break all ties with her past and start again somewhere else. She was so furious that she had even decided to stop cooking and had gone as far as hiding the recipe book in a corner of the oven so that nobody would notice it and it would get burned as soon as possible, although not that evening. She chose her own territory for that last meeting with Marte, the only place she felt confident: near the convent bakery. I don't know exactly what happened, or whether she wanted to tell him she was expecting his child, but they had a violent fight; Edda upended everything, including the tables and chairs. She was furious, hurt at having been deceived and giving herself to a man who had begun a relationship with her best friend, who, furthermore, was destined to become a nun. She accused him of wanting to deprive her of her closest friendship, a sacred thing, but when he tried to fight her off, he accidentally knocked over a lamp. And there was a fire as tall as the building. It only took a few minutes for the entire convent to become an enormous castle of flames and everyone ran up from the beach to put it out, armed with buckets and water. It was hell, real hell,' she told them, her voice still full of ashes, bitter cinders that had clumped together within the walls of a heart that guarded too many secrets. The secrets of two friends divided by their love for the same man.

Silence suddenly fell on the room. Only Elettra, whose mind continued to rush towards the truth, couldn't stay quiet; she had been kept silent for too long, and her dry throat demanded sips of truth, however bitter it might be.

'My father died in that fire, didn't he?' Elettra murmured, conscious of the reply she was about to receive. But she asked all the same, determined to free herself of every shadow that hovered over Edda's past and her own life, but the reply was silence. An oppressive silence to confirm the worst of her suspicions.

'They brought his body out the next day, there was nothing they could do,' Isabelle finally admitted.

Elettra's face contorted into a sob and as she faced the pain of a broken dream, Lea reached for her hand. The father Elettra had only just discovered had died before she had entered the world, and Edda had been in a coma for a year now; she had no family left.

'Edda left immediately afterwards, she didn't even stay for the funeral,' Isabelle continued. 'She took the first morning boat, and nobody here on the island heard anything more from her. As for Joséphine, she was racked with pain after she found out about her friend's betrayal and locked herself in her cell for days. She refused to eat or drink, hoping to die, until something made her review her plans.' She paused, and slowly turned to look at Lea's tense face. 'You,' she said softly. 'Her love for Marte had found a refuge inside her body; a life the size of a cherry was growing inside her, the memory of a love destined for immortality. Helped by the nuns she carried the pregnancy to term in great secrecy, and when you were born she was forced to come up with a surname for you like they did for all the other orphans so it wouldn't be linked to her.'

Elettra rubbed her eyes, pale faced, then stared first at Isabelle, then at Lea. 'All right, but if we're both that man's daughters, then we . . . ' she stammered without managing to finish her sentence.

'Yes,' Isabelle interrupted her, looking at the two women sitting together in front of her. 'You two are sisters.'

Lea was her sister, or half-sister, but her blood in any case.

Lea, to whom she had immediately felt so close and whom she'd risked losing because of new secrets that were rooted in the same past as their mothers'. But things wouldn't carry on like that, the story would never be repeated.

A lump filled Elettra's throat, exploding into a sob. Her hand squeezed Lea's tightly, and she turned towards her in search of consolation for a devastating loss.

The tears and crying continued, and after that outpouring Isabelle told them how the tragedy had marked Edda so deeply she had cut all links with the island, while Joséphine had begun her life as a nun which, following her secret pregnancy, had limited itself even more firmly to the confines of the cloisters until it entered into legend. The old midwife added that long years of silence between the two women followed that summer, until Edda, unable to live with her remorse and pain at the loss of the person whom she had considered a sister, had started to send money to the convent, hoping to bring about a rapprochement with her friend. Money which Joséphine passed on to her daughter, as if to compensate her for the absence of her father, of whom the other woman had deprived her.

'I probably shouldn't have told you all this. Joséphine made me promise to keep it to myself until I saw Juan again on the other side, but I couldn't stay silent and watch the past come back and divide you like this so stupidly.' She looked up at the two sisters. 'You're not Edda and Joséphine, you're the future, and perhaps the future of this island. You had the right to know the truth, especially given your shared interest in Adrian.'

For a moment Lea glared at Isabelle, but Isabelle quickly continued, ignoring any protests.

'I've seen how you look at him, Lea, and I was afraid. For weeks I've felt like I was reliving the past, I could see the same seed of poison in your eyes that infected Edda's heart, but I wanted things to go differently this time at any cost. There's been too much pain, and so I've told you everything; the moment has come for you to turn to the next page of the book that Edda and Joséphine began writing.'

'Your reasoning is spot on,' Elettra interrupted, 'except for one

234

small detail: Adrian is not a problem. He hasn't been so far and he never will be, because if I had to choose between him and my sister, I wouldn't hesitate,' she added, although she lacked the courage to look at Lea, who didn't dare raise her head.

Now she could see it; Lea finally saw how she'd behaved, the icy looks and poisonous words, turning her back when all Elettra needed was her support, nothing more.

A sister's support.

'I need to be alone,' Elettra said soon afterwards, struggling to her feet. She left the chapel, weighed down by the story.

It was too much information and too much truth in one go for someone who had always been starved of both. A mountain had collapsed on top of her and she was struggling to breathe.

She left Isabelle and Lea behind the closed door, and out in the cloisters was forced to shield her eyes from the light of dawn. She tasted the salt of tears again, and buried them under her confused thoughts. Her existence had appeared from nowhere, linked to the thread of a mother who had both given and taken away everything possible. She was at risk of falling into the void again if she didn't react somehow.

Elettra went over to the well in the centre of the cloister, looking at her reflection in the little circle of water where a flower bobbed peacefully. Inside the well was the reflection of pain, the face of a broken woman, disfigured by time.

'What else is going to happen to me?' she asked the air, bitter with ashes. Nicole, who'd arrived unexpectedly, looked at the woman reflected in the well and gave her a smile that struck her with its sweetness. The only verb carved on Nicole's soul was 'to love'.

'The Saint,' Nicole murmured, pointing to the statue disfigured by the fire. 'She'll help us, she always has. If we clean her up again she'll save this place, she'll save us from Vincent.'

Elettra turned, perplexed, but when she met Nicole's eyes,

illuminated by a special light, she understood that she couldn't fight destiny. 'Exactly,' she said, heaving a long sigh with the gloomy certainty that this was just the beginning. 'Vincent will be the first to turn up as soon as word gets out.'

And she was right.

The next day when the sky still showed traces of the dawn, Vincent came speeding through the gates of the convent with Bernard and a couple of cronies in his black car.

'Now you'd better explain what the hell has been going on!' he thundered, slamming the door. 'I want to know how all this happened!'

He pointed towards the chapel that had been ruined by the fire while Lea, hurrying from the garden, ran to meet him and block his path; she felt a duty to protect Sabine's secret, which had been at the root of the disaster.

'It was an accident, a broken lamp.'

'Don't you think you can get away with an excuse like that,' Vincent replied, examining the faces of the widows who seemed to close ranks with their friend. 'I've tolerated your wild life until now, but enough's enough.' He turned to his companions, gathered in a tragic silence. He threw a glance at the Saint and another at the walls blackened by the flames, the grave expression of one bearing bad news on his face. 'Our island has put up with all your strange ways, but this is too much.'

'I've told you that it was an accident,' Lea retorted. 'The same thing happened at the dairy last winter.'

Vincent stroked his chin with his fingertips and gave a satisfied smile. 'One of Marcel's outbuildings caught fire, but this is the island's patron saint, they are two completely different things; you have a duty to take care of her, and look what you've done to her,' he said, urging his associates to come further into the cloister. 'Look, look what this bunch of madwomen has done!'

He raised an arm in the direction of the Saint, while a murmur of indignation bubbled up around him. Bernard took advantage of the moment to move away from the little crowd while the mayor continued. 'The truth is that you're a disaster for this island, you've even destroyed the statue of the Saint!' Elettra watched the scene, ready to give the mayor a piece of her mind. She had swallowed Vincent's accusations one after another, but he'd crossed the line; she knew the mayor had no say when it came to the convent, but she wouldn't listen to another word without fighting back, so went and stood in front of him, ready for a challenge.

'If you knew the meaning of the word honesty, you wouldn't bring the saints into this, Monsieur Leroux. And as for you,' she continued, turning to Leroux's faithful sidekicks, 'you wouldn't be here to applaud like performing seals.' She folded her arms across her chest, eager to let it all out and show that man exactly what she thought of his business dealings. She moved close enough to him to be able to smell the masculine fragrance of his aftershave.

'We all know that it wasn't devotion to the Saint that brought you here, Monsieur le Maire, but your desire to get your hands on the convent to the detriment of its legitimate owner and those who live here.'

'That is pure conjecture!'

'Monsieur Leroux, be honest; I understand you want to defend your honour, but at least have the decency not to offend the intelligence of those present,' she replied with a glance at the people gathered around them. 'It's clear that if Lea doesn't find sufficient money to rebuild you will force her to sell, drawing on the contractual clause that obliges the owner of the convent to take care of its structure, but it seems you're not the only shark on the hunt for this prey. You're interested too, aren't you, Monsieur Morel?' she continued, glowering at Bernard, who stiffened as though someone had just poured a bucket of ice-cold water down his back. Elettra, on the other hand, could feel herself burning with rage; she couldn't take any more of Vincent's arrogance, nor could she stand Lea and the others accepting any more of his insults without reacting. The fact that that man claimed the right to mistreat her sister, well, that was beyond the pale.

Because Lea shared her blood; she'd felt an intense connection to those sapphire eyes right from the start. Lea represented all that was left of her family, and it didn't matter that there were cracks in their relationship and bridges to rebuild, because she was ready to defend her happiness at any cost. The bond that joined them would overcome the obstacles of the past that had divided their mothers. Elettra had understood this the moment Vincent had stepped forward, bandying insults about Lea and the convent: Lea was her sister, and now Vincent had another enemy to fight.

She took a step towards the mayor, her hands clasped beneath her breasts and an intentionally affable smile on her face. 'I'm terribly sorry to say this, but I believe the moment has come for you to go back where you came from,' she continued. 'As you know, the convent is private property, so, if Lea wants you to leave, she is within her rights to throw you out.' She dramatically changed her tone of voice, while her eyes sought her sister's. 'And believe me, if I were her I wouldn't give it a second thought.'

'As you wish,' Vincent replied, raising his hands, 'but you can be sure you won't get away with this,' he warned her cryptically. 'You'll see, Signora Cavani ...'

'Signorina, please.'

'Signorina,' he indulged her, 'unfortunately you don't seem to have accepted the reality yet; this is a community of fishermen and the elderly, and we all know how attached people become to tradition in such places.' He took an immaculate handkerchief from his pocket and pretended to wipe the dust from his face. 'What do you think they'll say when I tell them that a gaggle of incompetents has let the island's patron saint burn like a bale of hay?' He smoothed his moustache, but the dark twinkle in his eyes was the worst response that Elettra could have hoped for.

'Well, *signorina*, I'll tell you: they'll get angry, very angry; I can just see the line outside my office asking me to take the Saint away from you and free the convent and the island from your presence, it's just a question of time. Soon nobody will want anything to do with you, and then baking biscuits to charm the sympathies of a couple of pious women won't be enough because, you see, *signorina*: on my island, it's not the women who are in charge.' Leroux searched for a hint of uncertainty in Elettra's glare, but faced by her blazing eyes he turned his back and walked stiffly back to his car, which set off towards the gates, leaving a trail of dust behind it.

Elettra watched the car disappear in a reddish cloud. It was happening again, like a film she'd seen before. She watched the horizon become as clear as she wished her days were; this would be an uphill struggle. The only consolation was the presence of the sister which destiny had given her. The past had divided their mothers, but after the encounter with the mayor she was more convinced than ever that it was their duty to write a new page in that story.

'Thank you,' Lea whispered, rubbing her shoulder against Elettra's, still tentative after Isabelle's revelations and the discovery of the truth she had kept hidden from them. Perhaps she was afraid of a rejection, but instead she found Elettra's hand in hers.

'You're my sister, and it doesn't matter what's happened or may yet happen between us, because I will be on your side for ever and always. Always, whatever happens.'

23

In all the shock of what had happened over the past week, Elettra had been unable to reach Sabine who had returned to work. Elettra had visited again and again but no matter what time of day, she only ever found Gustave's menacing face behind the bar. But she didn't give up.

The bar's clientele were full of disapproving looks but also desire provoked by her presence. Sylvie's friends spread rumours about her but it no longer bothered her. Let them think what they want, she repeated to herself, walking along the streets with her head held high, unmoved by the eyes that remained glued to her. Nothing they did could upset her any more. But those revelations, Edda's story and all its consequences, the loss of her father and the discovery that she had a half-sister, were truths it took time to digest.

How much pain, how much suffering have you had to take, Mamma? she stopped to think, standing on the other side of the street with her hand pressed to her heart as she stared at the striped awning of Gustave's bar. Like you, Sabine. Why did you come back here? She was still pondering this when she entered the bar and was finally met by someone other than Gustave. She stopped frozen in the half-open doorway, a smile lighting up her face.

'Sabine,' she murmured, bringing a gust of freezing air from the alley in with her; the temperature was plummeting, the weather forecast had announced ice and a leaden sky for the whole week. She tightened the shawl Lea had given her, her hands clutching the handle of her bag; it was cold outside, but inside the bar was even colder.

The shining glasses were arranged on the shelves as usual, rigid and opaque from the cold, and opposite her was the usual Sabine, wearing shapeless clothes with a rag over her shoulder, rapidly moving her fingers.

She worked in silence without even the crackle of a radio to keep her company; the sound of her thoughts seemed sufficient to fill the entire room.

Elettra rubbed her numb hands buried deep within her shawl and approached. 'Sabine?' she murmured again.

She continued drying glasses with her head lowered. 'Would you mind closing the door? It's cold, the heating's not working.'

There it was again, the voice full of terror that took Elettra's breath away.

'It seems to me that the heating isn't the only thing that's not working,' Elettra replied, noticing the same old traces on her friend's face; violet marks staining her skin and the defeated expression that was like a blow to her stomach. 'It isn't too late. You can still come back to the convent, if you want.'

'No.'

Elettra sprang back; she looked for Gustave in the room, the only explanation for Sabine's blunt reply, but the still air betrayed his absence, there was no trace of him. 'What do you mean, no?'

'That I'm grateful to you for not telling anyone that it was Gustave who caused the fire, but I'm not coming back. I'm staying here.' Sabine tossed the rag onto the bar, her face hidden by the hair that fell forward over her cheeks. Elettra was speechless.

'What did he say to convince you to stay? That he wouldn't hit you any more?'

Sabine's fingers tightened around the cloth, which dripped with a beige liquid. 'He promised me.'

'And you believed him?' Elettra burst out. She was stunned, caught between rage and astonishment. 'How is that possible, after everything he's done to you? How can you believe him after he dragged you home like an animal?'

'He's given me his word.'

She barely whispered it, her eyes were lowered like someone who doesn't have a choice. Elettra wanted to take Sabine by the shoulders and shake her until all the false promises Gustave had made her fell to the floor, but her hands remained powerless, tucked inside her shawl. She was angry but there was a part of her that still viewed this woman with tenderness, the victim of a game with no rules.

'Words are like the wind, Sabine, and Gustave's especially so.'

'Perhaps, but I don't have a choice, Elettra. I have to believe him.'

'No, you don't have to, dammit!' Elettra shouted, thumping the bar. 'The world is full of choices, and even if you make the wrong one it's not the end, but you can't let a single mistake ruin your life. You don't deserve this unhappiness. No one deserves this,' she insisted. Her mother's story, that love sunk by a glass of wine and the coloured lights of a summer festival, echoed in her ears.

For a moment their eyes met; everything was clear from the words they'd exchanged and the exasperating resignation of a woman who was renouncing her future.

Elettra shook her head, imploring, while Sabine hung hers, aware of and guilty about her surrender. She picked up the rag to rub away the ring a glass had left on the bar, but it wasn't going anywhere. It remained soaked into the wood, having penetrated too deeply to be removed by the wipe of a sponge.

'Tell me about the fire instead. I heard that the statue of the Saint is almost destroyed.'

Elettra stared at Sabine, her lips half open in an unspoken protest; there was no point insisting, if Sabine didn't want to reclaim her own life, she had no choice but to give in. 'It's all true, but the Saint isn't the only one left in pieces after the other night.'

'Why, what's happened now?'

It was difficult for Elettra to explain something that she herself hadn't fully processed yet; the multiple implications of a sibling relationship born from the tragedy that had invaded her life before it had even begun.

She had a sister, and she would have to come to terms with this reality one day; but Lea hadn't trusted her, hiding the presence of her mother, and Elettra had lied to her in return: a labyrinth of secrets that had only caused pain and tears.

Suddenly tired, she perched on the nearest bar stool; she hadn't been able to sleep following Isabelle's story, but the insomnia was nothing compared with what Edda had suffered for years. An unspoken pain which lacerates the flesh.

She took a bank note from her wallet and put it on the table.

'I'll tell you everything, but I need a coffee. Make it a double, and a strong one at that.'

Sabine put the money in the till and started the coffee machine. 'Go ahead, I'm listening.'

An hour later Elettra was drinking the last sip of her now cold coffee.

'That's impossible,' Sabine murmured; what Elettra had just told her couldn't be the truth. Sabine explained that so many times she had disbelieved Vincent for accusing Lea of being the illegitimate child of the last abbess. And yet Lea really was the daughter of the woman whom the entire island had believed dead for years, and she was Elettra's half-sister.

Elettra realised her friend was as shocked as she was, but hurt, too.

Sabine stretched her arm across the bar to squeeze Elettra's hands.

'Perhaps Lea just wanted to protect her mother, that's why she didn't say anything,' she hypothesised. 'After all, she's had to go through absolute hell ever since she was little, due to all the stories about the abbess.' She faced Elettra. 'They've always spoken badly of her in town, believe me: they've never been kind. They treated Lea as if she were some kind of black sheep, and even though she's gone to great lengths to earn their respect, it hasn't made the slightest difference. But you're sisters; that must mean something, mustn't it?'

Elettra shrugged, wounded. 'Of course, but it hurts to know that your own sister doesn't trust you, after everything I've done for the convent. I'm not like them,' she said, gesturing towards the street and the people who walked by wrapped up in their woollen overcoats. 'I would have understood and I would have helped her to keep the secret, to care for her mother, but she didn't trust me. Why didn't she, Sabine, can you explain it to me?' Elettra asked, her hands clenched on top of the bar.

'Because she's suffered, Elettra, and once a person's been hurt, even if they still want to believe in people, they always carry the pain of the original wrong inside them. Perhaps Lea wanted to tell you thousands of times, but she simply hasn't done it. Can you blame her?'

Elettra looked down, tired and despondent. Sabine's logic made sense, but it was difficult to entirely accept the affection she had felt and still felt for Lea, because she had started to see her with different eyes. A deep rift had opened between them, but she knew it wasn't an incurable wound; understanding and forgiveness would be enough to go beyond it and see the good they could still do and share. 'No,' she admitted. 'I can't blame her.'

Exhausted, she watched the daylight fade on the dusty floor of the bar while Sabine went about her tasks, glancing regularly towards the door. Just the wind rustling in the street seemed to put her on alert.

'You ought to leave Gustave. I'm serious,' Elettra said, for at least the dozenth time since she'd arrived at the bar, but each time Sabine had frozen in the middle of the room and leaned her chin on the broom handle. Elettra moved towards her, hoping for a miracle; there were no words in her friend's clouded gaze, just the faded images of days poisoned by rage.

'I know.' Those two words carried awareness, and the bitter conviction that she didn't have a choice. There wasn't one, not in her world.

She's probably the wiser of the two of us, Elettra thought without surprise.

'Sabine, is there anything I can do to convince you? Anything?' Elettra pleaded.

Sabine touched her hand and looked straight at her: 'Not right now.'

She turned to look at Sabine as she went out into the street, keeping her eyes fixed on the glass door of the bar; Sabine lived in a reality she would never understand, but that was okay. She could have gone on pressing her for ever, but Sabine would have held her ground; however insecure she might seem to others, she wasn't ready to leave the world she had clung to since she was a little girl, so Elettra had to respect her choice.

'If you ever do change your mind ...' she said, intentionally leaving the sentence hanging before setting off on her way back.

Her time with Sabine was over and so were the words she had to spend on her cause. She pulled the shawl tightly around herself, rubbing her numb nose against the warm wool while her thoughts bounced quickly between memories of the last few months, stopping at Adrian's warm lips.

If she closed her eyes she could still remember the taste of the sea and that damp contact between their existences, but she immediately disengaged herself from that memory; she didn't have the strength to weather further storms. I need to put an end to this stupidity and concentrate on the future, she scolded herself, trying to chase such regrets from her mind. Sooner or later she would have to go home, a prospect that left her breathless because she didn't have the least desire to do so; at the convent her mother was beside her, even if most people didn't understand how, and so was her sister. At the convent Elettra felt like she had a family for the first time in her life.

She kicked a stone that rolled to the opposite pavement, where a man's powerful voice boomed. Hearing that distinctive accent combined with the intense odour of lily of the valley cologne made Elettra feel as though she'd been stabbed by a blade; it was Vincent again with his slippery words, standing on the stump of an old tree to whip up the crowd, promising work and wellbeing for the whole island with his heartfelt words.

'We'll get through this difficult period, and we'll get through it thanks to Monsieur Morel's project,' Vincent exclaimed, pointing his index finger towards the sky. 'But to do this, to convince Morel to invest in us and give a new boost to the island's economy, stagnant for too long, I need your support. We have difficult decisions ahead of us if we're going to build the hotel, move the Saint to the chapel in the church so we can all finally come and pay her homage, and build the golf course that will bring in tourism and important income. You know I'm referring to the current inhabitants of the convent, but we must all be ready to make small sacrifices if we want to save our community. For my part I promise to undertake the impossible until everything works out with the least upset, but I won't be able to help you by myself. I need you with me to do this – only we can save the island. Together!' he exclaimed while his minions burst into fervent applause, trying to encourage the crowd.

A sorry sight, Elettra thought, examining the faces of those present. The islanders weren't the type for public displays of enthusiasm, but she read the first chapter in a story of a defeated future in their faces tanned from a life at sea; poverty and the scarcity of fish they all lamented had crushed the religious devotion of even the oldest fishermen, the heads of families who found themselves humiliated by smaller and smaller catches. In other times they and their wives would have fought against the mayor's hunger for expansion, but the impossibility of putting two meals a day on the table was the stumbling block wearing down the island's spirituality.

Defenceless, Elettra watched the little crowd nod their heads in response to Vincent's promises and leaned against the chipped wall of an old building.

The past was here again, like a shawl wrapped too tightly around her.

Elettra stirred her spoon in her bowl, blowing on her minestrone. 'Vincent's turning the people against us, and the worst thing is that he seems to be gaining support for his project. We need to come up with something fast, otherwise things will go very badly,' she continued, while Lea handed out slices of toasted bread.

Dominique took one and broke it in half. 'So he's not as stupid as he seems. He's realised how to win over the fishermen, pretending to be one of them, and you can be sure he'll succeed. The locals have had empty stomachs for months now, and crucifixes don't provide food.'

'The fishing really is going through a bad patch; the boats come back lighter each day,' Lea added. 'I can see them from the field where I go to gather herbs for the infusions; the coast stretches along from there to the port, and it's a worrying sight.'

Dominique glanced up from the edge of her plate, bringing a spoonful of soup to her lips. 'If I know him as well as I think I do, that scoundrel will play on their desperation to get what he wants, and the only ones who'll put a spanner in the works are the few elderly men left in town who still have their wits about them; I don't think they and their wives will be jumping for joy at the idea of the hordes of tourists the hotel would attract, if it does get built. But the others are still a big problem; they're so desperate that they'll have no scruples about hounding us out of here if Vincent can convince them it will result in new shoes for their children, and by the time they're left empty-handed it will already be too late.'

'What do you mean?' Lea asked her.

'Someone who's lived a life at sea can't learn to build walls overnight, and that Morel doesn't strike me as someone with time to waste on teaching our fishermen construction techniques.' She broke up her bread and let the chunks fall onto her plate. 'Vincent and his friend will make them all believe they need construction workers and want to source them locally, but I'd bet my life that once they have the green light they'll give them all a kick in the backside and outsource everything to a specialist company.'

Nicole jumped up from her seat, her face flushed from the steam rising from her soup. 'If that's the way things are then we should warn them!'

'Why, do you think they'll believe you?' Dominique replied with a bitter laugh. 'So what shall we do? Wait for the mayor to chuck us out?'

'We don't need to worry, Nicole, the situation isn't that serious yet; Vincent and his friends can kick up as much fuss as they want, but nobody can chuck us out. I'm the one who bought this place, it's my name on the deed of sale.'

'True, but let's not underestimate the situation; when Vincent puts his mind to something, he always gets what he wants in the end,' Dominique replied, reaching out a hand for another slice of toast.

Elettra listened to the conversation in silence, her fingers entwined in a prayer that nobody seemed to hear.

'Dominique isn't entirely wrong,' she said eventually, speaking up between one silence and the next. They all turned towards her, waiting. She turned to Lea. 'If Vincent manages to prove the convent is too rundown, and I don't think that would be difficult given the effects of the fire, you'd find yourself forced to carry out restoration work immediately.'

'I know, but I don't have enough money at the moment. I've barely got two coins left to rub together,' Lea replied.

Nicole clutched the crucifix that she wore around her neck, her eyes bright with hope. 'And what if we couldn't do those restoration works, if we couldn't find the money? What would happen then?'

'We'd have to find somewhere else to live, because as far as the mayor's concerned, the convent can be knocked down. If Lea doesn't honour the contract, it would be simple for him and Morel to confiscate it,' Elettra replied. She paused, her heart in her mouth as she faced her friend's bright eyes. 'I'm sorry, Nicole, but the situation is serious.'

'It is,' Lea echoed her, collapsing into a seat. 'It seems like

Vincent's got our backs against the wall,' she added, drumming her fingers on the table; she couldn't seem to stay still. 'I can't believe what that worm's done to me.'

'I wouldn't raise the white flag quite yet,' Dominique objected unexpectedly. She balled up the napkin beside her plate, pushing her chair back. 'It's true that we don't have long, but let's not waste that time whimpering. Life has thrown worse at us than that puffed-up idiot's threats, and I think that if we've managed to keep our heads in a storm once, we can do it again. We need to fight for this place.'

'How?' moaned Nicole, while Elettra silently tried to transform Dominique's battling spirit into something more concrete. It was the right approach to take, she could already smell the fresh scent of change on the air, but the weight of the tension was too heavy for her to think clearly. She implored the silence for scraps of insight, and then, suddenly, she had a brainwave, as unexpected and blessed as a storm after a drought.

It seemed ridiculous not to have thought of it sooner.

'We'll reopen the island's old bakery,' she suggested, immediately capturing the entire table's attention. She ran her hand quickly through her hair, her fingers itching to grasp the ideas as they emerged from between her dark curls and shape them into a plan. 'Every time I go to Sabine's I hear the older generation complain about the endless increase of the price of bread, mainly due to the cost of the fuel necessary to transport it from one island to another. If we started producing it here again we could charge a fair price and the convent would become a focal point for the whole island again, just like it used to be. If we reopen the bakery and produce bread here, nobody could chuck us out, not even Leroux.'

'What makes you so sure about that?' Dominique challenged her.

'The fact, Dominique, that nobody, but nobody can free themselves from their own past, so let's take advantage of it; we'll start producing the convent's historic bread and pastries again,' she replied, looking Dominique straight in the eyes. Elettra's own eyes contained the will to do it, to get to work and win out over the greed of a man set on handing the island's history over to a stranger intent on turning it into a money-making machine.

'You think we should reopen the bakery?' Lea echoed her.

'It's the only viable option to save this place,' Elettra insisted, noticing her sister's worried look. 'We'll start the restoration work in time for the feast and could have the grand opening on the seventeenth; after all, Elizabeth of Hungary is the patron saint of bakers, and reopening the old bakery in her honour seems perfect.'

'I think it's a good idea, too. A great idea!' Nicole supported Elettra, clapping her hands.

'Reopen the bakery,' Lea murmured.

'It would help us find the money necessary for the restoration and create a steady stream of income that would give you a bit of breathing space. We need to restore the statue and the convent before Leroux makes his move, but reopening the bakery first will win the sympathy of the older generation. As the mayor himself admits, they make up the majority of the island's population and evoking a piece of their youth, when life was better, will guarantee us their support,' she replied. 'Adrian could give us a hand with the initial work. The ovens weren't damaged and it would be enough to tidy up the parts of the convent worst hit by the fire. I think this is the route we should take.'

Dominique folded her arms. 'I don't think it's a good idea; when we sold pastries at the market it was a disaster.'

'You're always the same old pessimist,' Nicole grumbled.

'It's different this time; we're not talking about baking a couple of loaves, but giving these people back their past, a dream,' Elettra replied; she could feel the energy of a new plan vibrating in her hands, a hope born of the ashes of a disaster. 'We'll show the islanders that their land is alive and that their people don't let themselves be conquered by adversity, and we'll also give the fishermen hope; the convent and its bakery aren't just a source of earnings, but also, and more importantly, a symbol for the entire community. Reopening it shows that when they work together people make a difference and that a sense of community still exists on this island, and it's a strong one. This time Sylvie's poison won't stop us.'

'What makes you think it will be different?' Dominique pressed her.

Elettra turned towards the cloister, her finger pointing towards the rectangle of light through the window frame. 'She does,' she replied, pointing to the Saint. 'It will be thanks to her that we regain the clients that Sylvie and her cronies lost us last time.' They would fight for the convent, for the Saint and for all those women whose souls had been healed within those walls. 'If we all play our parts the rest will happen naturally. Nicole and I can take care of the baking; water and flour are my elements, and she is an outstanding student. Between us we'll do a great job,' she added, winking at her friend, who smiled broadly in reply.

But Lea still seemed distant, her arms folded and her face pale. 'Do you think it will work? I mean, do you really think we can regain the islanders' good will?'

'Why not?' replied Elettra. 'If what Vincent said about these people is true then we have a chance, we just need to convince the old men and their wives. After all, how many of them have prayed at the feet of the Saint for their loved ones to come home safe and sound after a storm? How many of their sons, brothers, husbands and lovers have been helped by the sisters who lived at the convent, by the Saint herself? How many offertory loaves have been baked in these kitchens on behalf of souls lost at sea, and how many more wedding banquets have been prepared in here?' The others looked at her with bewildered eyes. 'All I'm asking you to do is think, just for a moment: the convent, along with my mother's pastries, was the heart of this island for years and people still remember both today. This place has withstood the seasons, the passage of life itself, for decades but the tragedy of the sea and Leroux's handiwork have caused all this to be set aside and forgotten. We'll give this island back its heart; it's a forgotten heart, trampled and salt-crusted, but still beating, so it's our duty to give it back.' She stopped for a moment to catch her breath and at that moment, sweet as a caress, an intense fragrance of aniseed spread through the air. Nicole had mixed it in with the sugar for the *sablé* biscuits she'd made for Isabelle, but Elettra could smell it so strongly it made her suspect intervention of a different kind.

Her legs trembled in hope.

'I've seen all the offerings at the feet of the Saint with my own eyes, and I've touched proof of these people's faith with my own hands,' she continued, showing them her hands criss-crossed by intricate lifelines. 'The islanders will never let her be removed from the cloister, because the convent is her home and this is where she should stay. Where she will stay,' Elettra concluded, her hand banging down on the table. She had done what she could; now Lea and the others had to make up their own minds.

'I agree,' said Nicole.

'Lea?' Elettra's voice called her, ready to drag her back out of the sad thoughts of the summer of 1952.

It was the first time Elettra had called her by her name since the fire. Elettra was still hurting, but even in the darkest moment, when the future was just a dark chasm, she was there to offer Lea her help, by her side once more.

'I'm with you,' Elettra's sister whispered in reply.

Pane di Ognissanti

1kg flour

600ml mosto cotto, plus extra for the icing

180g starter made with 50g fresh brewer's yeast

200g walnuts

75g hazelnuts

75g almonds

1 cup brandy

1 orange (peel only)

1 lemon (peel only)

Aniseed, cloves and ground cinnamon

1 small cup coloured sprinkles

Soak the raisins in the brandy, slowly adding warm water until they are completely covered.

Heat the mosto cotto and combine it with the flour, then slowly add all the other ingredients except the coloured sprinkles. Knead thoroughly for some time until the dough is smooth and fully combined, then leave it to prove in a warm place for two hours.

After proving, divide the dough into four pieces. Shape them into loaves, then cover with a cloth, insulate well and leave to rise for a day and a night.

At the end of the rising period bake the loaves for forty minutes at 180°C with a pan of water in the bottom of the oven.

Once they've cooled, dip the loaves in mosto cotto a couple of times then decorate with the coloured sprinkles.

Leave to dry then serve.

24

On the island the days grew shorter while the bad moods at the convent only increased, like dough rising out of control. The rebuilding work progressed slowly and Elettra spent most of each day in the kitchen teaching Nicole the secrets of baking and hoping to avoid Adrian.

She felt trapped every time he caught her eye, and when it happened she would see the proof of her own inconsistency blossom on her skin; she avoided him, yet she often found herself wandering the convent in search of his scent. It had happened to her just after sunset the night before; she knew he'd already left, but she'd been unable to resist the urge to go into the room where he'd been working all day, searching for traces of his scent in the air heavy with the smell of fresh paint. It was there, Elettra could sense it, as welcoming as an embrace, but still something she continued to flee.

She was aware that her attitude was unfair, but she couldn't help it. They still had a lot to say to one another, even though her discoveries regarding her mother's past – her love for that artist, Marte, who'd got her pregnant and then abandoned her, denying any tenderness that had existed between them – made Elettra feel immersed in a suffocating symmetry. She had no intention of following in Edda's footsteps so she fought with all her might against her growing feelings for Adrian because she knew she needed to keep well away from that path if she valued her wellbeing. And she wasn't ready for a confrontation with him, not yet, so, rather than facing him, she preferred to immerse herself in Edda's recipe book, trying out the recipes with Nicole, whose new-found skill continued to astonish her.

'You have to keep the recipes in here, not on paper,' her mother had been for ever telling her, tapping her temple with her index finger. 'You don't write cookery down, you feel it, and the paper won't help you a jot if you don't know how to use these,' she'd admonished Elettra, showing her her hands, which were already swollen with arthritis. But now, after years of false starts and silences, Elettra had found nothing less than Edda's first recipe book; a gift straight from a magical past where Elettra anxiously sought her mother. All she wanted was to have her with her a bit longer, long enough to heal the rift and restore the harmony between them. Or, if she only had the courage to admit it, perhaps for ever, to have a piece of her that nothing and nobody could ever take away from her. Not even the past.

'What delights are you baking today?'

Elettra slammed the notebook shut and raised her eyes to the still soot-stained ceiling, biting back a cruel comment. The one time she wasn't thinking about him, Adrian had decided to turn up in the kitchen!

'*Pane di Ognissanti*,' she replied brusquely. She went round the table, sweeping up crumbs. She wanted to busy herself with some little task, but everything she needed for her baking was behind Adrian. On the other side of the trench dug by her pride. Perfect, she thought, her forehead creased by a frown, still embarrassed by the kiss they had shared.

'*Pane di Ognissanti*,' Adrian repeated, turning around, intrigued by the pans she was gathering on the table. 'The bread of the saints,' he continued, watched by Elettra. She focused on her recipe, but was still aware of his every blink. 'What are the ingredients?'

She folded her arms and took a deep breath. This was her territory, she was safe amongst the sugar and the flour, but conversation had never been her strong point. She gestured to the crowded row of ingredients gathered on the table, hoping that they would speak for her. But Adrian wanted to hear her voice.

'Dried fruit and *mosto cotto*. You can see the rest for yourself,' she replied reluctantly.

'Is it one of your mother's recipes?'

She stiffened, her hand on her hip. 'What makes you think that?'

'Well,' he began, slipping his hands into his pockets, 'since we found that book of recipes, you must want to have a go at them . . . after all, you're more than capable. I think you've inherited the same gift as your mother,' he said, smiling at Elettra's confusion as she wiped the rest of the flour off the table.

She hated to admit it, but she was intrigued by his manner, especially the way the skin around his mouth folded when he smiled. And those eyes that just riveted her every time. This is exactly what you don't need, Elettra, she scolded herself, washing her hands.

'Yes, it is one of my mother's recipes,' she admitted, drying her hands on the dish cloth.

She missed Edda, terribly: she often lay awake at night trying to remember what life with her had been like and how it would have been if her mother had stayed on the island instead of leaving, a question she often pondered in the darkness of her cell when everyone else at the convent seemed to be asleep.

Much simpler was the answer she always came up with, imagining baking the same bread with a young Lea beside her while Edda watched to make sure they didn't make a mess of it and gave them handfuls of coloured sprinkles to scatter over the glaze of the dark, autumn-scented loaves; if her mother had remained at the convent Elettra would have had a friend to play with and share everything with. She took a handful of flour and scattered it over the work surface while the *mosto cotto* syrup warmed on the hob. It would have been exciting, she thought, for someone who had always lived under maternal surveillance; with Lea, she would have had the childhood she had dreamed of as an adult, and perhaps even the father she had sought for years amongst the men waiting at the school gate at home time.

She shook her head, her hand pressed to her forehead to block out the pain, the same one as always, but as soon as she saw Adrian studying her she turned her back on him.

'What's up?'

'Nothing, why?'

'I don't know, you tell me. If you don't want me under your feet just say so; don't sulk at me.'

'It doesn't matter,' she said. Faster than normal, she grabbed a couple of jars of spices from the rack, reviewing the recipe aloud. 'Aniseed, cinnamon and cloves,' she repeated like a lullaby.

'Okay, message received,' Adrian gave in. He made as if to leave, but stopped on the threshold, his head hanging. He tapped the toe of his shoe on the floor, then walked around the table and stopped behind her, his hands in his pockets. 'It's about the kiss, isn't it? Because I disappeared?'

Elettra's face opened in a brief smile, while her fingers automatically played with the labels on the jars. 'Not at all,' she replied, trying to sound distracted.

'If that's what it is, I can explain.'

'You artists are all the same, you don't need to explain anything to me.'

'You artists?' he repeated. 'What do you mean, Elettra?'

She sighed. She had absolutely no wish to talk about Marte, her mother and the mirrored life in which she felt trapped, but Adrian didn't seem likely to let this go.

'I'm telling the truth,' she told him, but, as always, he continued to hold her gaze, so Elettra wiped her hands on the dish cloth again and exhaled noisily. 'I guess you want to know the whole story.'

Adrian looked around, bewildered. 'I'd really appreciate it, because, to be honest, I don't understand what you're saying. What story do you mean?'

'Mine, Adrian. Mine, the story of my mother and this place,' she said, gesturing to the white walls and then beginning her tale. The words flowed spontaneously but reluctantly; Elettra forced herself to stare at the recipe she was making, her head lowered, closing her eyes tightly when emotion got the better of her, but when she steeled herself to look Adrian in the eyes, she read a combination of bewilderment and sadness there, and felt what she most feared in her soul: deep down he was like her father, his behaviour was proof. He had shown himself to be unreliable with his continuous disappearances, and she had no intention of ending up like her mother. More than anything, she wanted to stop talking and cook.

'And there you have it, the truth,' she finished, brushing hair out of her eyes. She would have liked to take all her ingredients and get to work, letting her hands move freely, wearing herself out, concentrating only on the bread and pastries for the feast, but seeing Adrian there, with the scent of his skin stamped on her mind to remind her of what she couldn't allow herself, was a torture. The memory of that kiss, the taste of his lips and his arms that had held her in a way she hadn't dreamed possible, was torture. 'Anyway, we're adults, not a couple of fourteen-year-olds. It was just a kiss, no great tragedy.'

'Just a kiss,' he echoed her. His voice had become hoarse, Elettra could sense strong undertones like saffron. She carefully stroked the glass belly of a jar, her shoulders hunched.

'Exactly. Just a kiss,' she replied. She had said it; she had thought about it for days, but when she had least expected it the truth had slipped out of her mouth.

A stony silence followed her words, broken by the normal sounds of the convent: the endless gurgling of water in the rusty pipes, footsteps on the floor above and the noise of the hoe Dominique was using to weed the orchard. Elettra peered at the intense blue of the sea through the small window in the outer wall. She had been down to the shore a lot in the last few days, to a small, secluded bay reached by a twenty-minute walk along a path winding through mastic bushes. She would spend hours there with her knees tucked up to her chest, sitting on a granite rock and watching the sea washing against the stone, listening to the repetitive gurgle of the water. Since Isabelle had told her about the summer of 1952, the currents had also invaded her body, drawing the profile of a rugged coast and pointed cliffs on her soul. Like the bay, small yellow flowers grew there in spite of the harsh soil, although Elettra didn't like to acknowledge them.

'I suppose you feel like an independent woman now. You've got what you wanted without owing anyone anything, because nothing touches you. Well done, good job.'

'What do you mean?' she stammered, pushing the cupboard closed, her cheeks flaming. She didn't like Adrian's tone at all, but judging from his angry gaze he wasn't going to back down.

'Why, do you mean to say that's not the case?' he continued. The hands Elettra liked so much were hidden in the pockets of his jeans, clenched into fists. 'I was useful for getting your ex out of your head, and now you've done that ... well, now you can get rid of me, too, right?'

Elettra looked over her shoulder, astonished. She twisted the floury dish cloth between her hands then dropped it onto the table. 'That's not the case, and it's not straightforward,' she defended herself anxiously, while Adrian's gaze seemed to seek out the words she couldn't say.

Their eyes were locked, drawing her towards him.

'If I've misunderstood things, tell me why you avoid me, why you behave as if nothing happened between us.' He moved towards Elettra but when she drew back he stopped where he was. 'And if it's true that I'm wrong and that damned kiss and your ex have nothing to do with it, then tell me what I should make of all this.' His voice was bubbling with anger, demanding answers she didn't have.

Elettra looked around, holding her breath. She dug into every corner of her subconscious in search of the right words, then she grabbed a handful and tossed them across the room. 'It's not because of Walter,' she stammered, 'and it's not because of you.' Her hands were clutched against her chest in an effort to control her increasingly harsh breathing. It was difficult to speak with a man in front of her asking for something she had been seeking for so long. She had regretted meeting Adrian only that summer so many times during her solitary walks through the convent corridors; if their lives had crossed paths a few years earlier everything would have been different, easier. A perfect match.

But things hadn't turned out like that, and it was impossible to go back. Edda's stroke and its consequences had turned her into a tired, disillusioned woman, honing the many sharper aspects of her character, but that was life, her only life, and she just had to play along.

'I can't change what I've become, and you can't do anything about it.'

'You can't know that.'

'Yes, I can,' she retorted. 'Perhaps I could have been a different person if my mother hadn't had that damned stroke and I hadn't had to take over the bakery instead of focusing on what I wanted to do with my life, but things went differently from how I'd hoped, how I'd dreamed. Everything went very differently,' she remarked. She was digging up something she had promised herself to leave behind, and once it came out it would only cause trouble.

But Adrian wanted to know; well, he asked for it. 'You have no idea who I was before nor who I am now, so don't tell me that there's still time for me to become a better person, because time is the one thing I don't have.' She leaned on the table, the back of her hand pressed to her lips. She wanted to stop talking, thinking, fighting. All she wanted was a moment of rest from Adrian's eyes, just a bit of peace.

'What you're saying makes no sense.'

'Yes, it does,' she replied in a tired voice, but he shrugged.

'You're telling yourself a bunch of lies so as not to face reality.'

'You know reality, do you? You know so much about me that you can judge my life?' she snapped. She had had enough of this pressure. She was confused and afraid, but she felt like she wasn't allowed to be these things. Furious, she brushed a lock of hair out of her eyes. 'You don't know what my life's been like these last few years and you don't have the slightest idea what I've been through since arriving here.'

'You're right,' he nodded, his voice suddenly friendly. 'I've no idea what you've been through, so tell me. I'm telling you I want to know, that's why I'm here, but you're so obsessed with your dramas you don't listen to anyone but yourself. And you certainly don't listen to me.'

Adrian was determined not to understand, it appeared. He didn't see that she didn't want to face these issues. She was sure that continuing down this road would lead to one of them getting hurt, and she was sure it would be her; it was like a film scene her mother had already played out.

She looked up at him as he stared at her, arms folded. It was too late to go back.

'You want to know what my life was like? Do you really want to know, Adrian?'

He looked her straight in the eyes. 'That's why I'm here.'

Elettra bit her lip as her heart seemed to play a troubling tune. The figures of Edda, Joséphine and Marte were taking shape in her head, along with the bakery, her childhood and the stroke that had turned everything upside down.

'It was hell,' she replied through clenched teeth. 'You don't know what it means to wake up every damn morning without the least idea what you'll do that day, because your life and your family, or rather your mother, have fallen to pieces. You don't know how frustrating it is fighting against a sense of failure or how much the fear of not getting myself together terrified me.' Her eyes filled with tears. 'And you don't know how hard it is for me to accept my mother's past,' she said, her fist clenched against her chest once more. She had said it, finally; she had found the courage to admit that the idea of summer 1952 oppressed her, that she was furious with Edda for depriving her of a father and with Marte for preferring another woman to her mother, leaving Edda to come to terms with a love she couldn't deal with. It left her feeling divided, at war with herself.

'All I dreamed of was a normal life, like everyone else's; I imagined ending the day rereading an article to go to press. Waiting for my husband to come home from work. I would make him dinner, a good dinner, or perhaps we'd go out. I fantasised about calling my mother and how we'd go to hers for Sunday lunch every so often. That was what I wanted, nothing more; a night at the theatre, perhaps a trip abroad, a few carefree evenings with friends. A child, yes, but not immediately, perhaps after a few years, and instead I've got nothing, because overnight I suddenly found myself in a nightmare; first my mother, then the bakery. But okay,' she said, backing away, her hands raised, 'I'm big enough to accept that things don't always go how we want them to, and I know I can get over it all, however difficult it is, but it's pointless pretending this hasn't changed me. The girl with all those dreams has been gone some time, and she won't be coming back.'

'You talk as though you had no choice but to become something you're not.'

'Perhaps that's true, I don't know,' she replied. 'In any case, I have no intention of turning back, there's no point. I'd rather concentrate on the future, on the life I have now, and try and improve it, but the time for grand dreams is over. Everything I've experienced is inside me, and it can't be erased, it's not like changing channel. I don't work that way,' she finished, pointing at herself, her eyes clouded by a sudden fragility. She was looking at Adrian, but she didn't see him; in front of her was just the confused map of her life and the chaos of the last few months.

But when she saw him take her hands she felt her stomach twisting.

'I'm not Walter, and I have no intention of hurting you.'

She shook her head, defending herself, her hands raised to enforce a distance that would let her breathe. 'It's not you,' she whispered. She pressed her palms together, her thumbs sealing her lips.

One minute. She just needed sixty seconds to scrape her courage together.

'What is it, then?' Adrian asked.

'The problem is me and everything I've lost, my mother and her secrets,' she admitted, exhausted. 'I have too many things to get back and so many more to understand, so there isn't space for anything else at the moment. And I doubt there will be for quite some time,' she added, her palm against her chest, listening to her angry heart. It rebelled, kicking against her, but Elettra was impassive. It was the right decision for her, the only one possible; Adrian represented a past from which she wanted to distance herself, a life that had never belonged to her, no matter how much she wanted it, which she did; she wanted Adrian and a life with him, but she knew that letting emotions get the better of her would turn back the hands of time to that terrible summer.

It was a mistake she couldn't afford to make.

She remained standing motionless, breathless; waiting for something, any kind of reaction. A word would have been enough, just one, to break the curtain of silence between them.

'All right.'

Adrian sounded as if he more than anyone needed to be sure of what he'd said. Then he put his hands back in his pockets and walked out the door, his footsteps the only sound.

Elettra watched him walk away, without the strength to speak further. All she noticed was that he leaned forwards as he walked, as though he had the weight of the world on his shoulders.

'So, what's cooking today?'

Those four words hit her back as though someone was shaking her.

She grasped the table for support, while Nicole's serene expression lit up the walls of the kitchen with fresh light. 'Hey, is everything okay?' She met Elettra's tense expression, a portrait of surprise and dismay, with alarm. 'I'm late because I stayed in the chapel longer than normal,' she excused herself.

For a moment Elettra couldn't remember why Nicole was there, then she suddenly remembered the previous evening when she had promised to show her some recipes. She forced a smile and picked up the pan she'd used to warm a sticky liquid, gesturing Nicole towards a couple of bowls beside her. She had a second batch of *pane di Ognissanti* to prepare and almost all the ingredients were on the table.

'Come on, let's begin,' she said, moving over to the work surface.

She ground the cloves in the mortar and poured them into a bigger bowl with the other spices, then added the flour and a pinch of salt, finally adding the grated orange zest that slid reluctantly off the plate. Elettra swirled the pan of *mosto*, which soon gave off the thick, slightly alcoholic fragrance of fruit fermented in the sun.

'What now?' Nicole asked her soon afterwards, gesturing to the loaves they'd just shaped while Elettra checked on the ones she had already left to rise.

Have I made a mess of everything? she asked herself before meeting Nicole's angelic smile.

'Now we wait,' she said. 'All we can do is wait,' she added, covering the bread.

25

Elettra had spent hours outside the closed door, or passing – sniffing the air in search of a sign, a trace – but she was yet to find the courage to knock. Lea's mother had lain two floors above her, having fallen into a stupor ever since the day of the fire. At first it had been Lea who'd asked her to delay their meeting, but Elettra felt there was something else. Every time she touched the handle she was filled with the feeling she was doing something wrong, that there had to be a better time for this encounter.

Her body told her to be patient, but she wasn't made for waiting; the present was in hot pursuit so she didn't have time to waste, and she decided to act that morning.

She had got up early, much earlier than the still-rising sun, her legs full of the urge to go where she had been asked not to. She went down to the kitchen and took a couple of the *guelfi* biscuits, which Lea had told her were the abbess's favourites, from the jar and then went up the stairs that led to her room.

Elettra needed to look that woman in the eyes and ask her to forgive her mother. She needed that forgiveness; she wanted it for Edda, to finally put an end to the past, and she needed it for herself.

She gently pushed the half-closed door and tiptoed into the room, which was as bare as all the other cells. The bedroom contained only a wooden table, a chair and an enormous crucifix, standing guard over the spartan bed. The air was stuffy and smelled of illness: the acidic aroma of a battle-weary body and bandages soaked in alcohol-based herbal solutions.

In the background, a splash of colour contrasted with the white walls: the sea that had given and taken so much in Joséphine and Edda's lives.

'May I come in?' she murmured, aware she shouldn't wait for an answer.

Stretched out in the bed of timeless-smelling linen sheets, her wizened hands clasped as if in prayer, the abbess was a slight figure wearing her dark habit. At the creak of the door her eyes had focused on her visitor, the profile of a past she had been awaiting for a long time and which she greeted with a weak smile. Her smile seemed to come from the afterlife, a sensation that froze Elettra's blood.

'You didn't need to worry about me, dear,' she murmured, a courtesy that calmed Elettra's racing heart.

'I'm Elettra Cavani, Madre,' she said quietly. 'I'm Edda's daughter.'

'I know who you are,' Joséphine replied, lifting her hand from the covers. 'I've known since the first moment I saw you. Did you know you're beautiful? You look just like her, you've even got her hair,' she continued, her gaze seeming to caress Elettra.

It could only last a moment, Lea had warned her. She had advised that her mother's moments of lucidity were like comets that burnt out in a brief explosion. Elettra just needed to hold her hand, still capable of feeling heat and of clasping the hand of a frightened young woman who had undertaken a long journey to find her, to make peace with the past.

'Why?' Elettra whispered. She had so much to ask her, a whole life to ask about, but that single word slipped from her lips before she could think. Isabelle had given her version of events, but Elettra needed to hear them from the woman her mother had loved, and perhaps still loved, like a sister.

'Why did you try to obstruct me? Why didn't you want me to learn the truth about Edda and her past?' she asked, as Joséphine's porcelain face morphed into an ecstatic smile.

Joséphine tried to turn over and stretch her other hand towards Elettra, but her gesture failed.

She spoke softly. 'I was afraid. I was afraid that so much pain would have ended up destroying everything, and you would hate me as I hated you. I hated you and loved you, I have since the beginning, but I would never have wanted to cause you so much pain.' Joséphine seemed to fish each word out of a pool of tangled thoughts and memories. 'I never wanted you to suffer as much as I did, and I was so happy and so angry when I saw you in the cloister! You were a vision. A marvellous, tremendous vision that broke my heart.' She looked at the ceiling, her eyes perhaps fixed on the memory of the day when the daughter of the past had entered the convent and their lives had crossed paths for an extremely brief, yet fatal moment.

Elettra lowered her head, her fingers searching for purchase amongst those words, heavy with meaning. Love and hate had left their mark on the lives of her mother and the abbess, and neither of them had emerged victorious from the confrontation.

'Madre,' Elettra whispered, leaning towards her, determined to bring an end to Joséphine's story, but Joséphine ignored her; she continued to look at the white wall above her head.

'When I heard you were dying, when Isabelle told me, oh my God, I thought I'd die too. I wanted to die too,' Joséphine continued, clutching her fist to her chest, her eyes misting up. She was talking to Edda and Elettra together, it seemed, her mind unable to distinguish between them.

Elettra's hand reached out to comfort her; her heart racing, her whole body shaking. The abbess's pain was real, a laceration of the soul that Elettra wanted to heal, that she needed to see cured for both Edda's peace of mind and her own.

'Madre,' she murmured again as the woman moved away from her, seemingly towards horizons without time or colour, where everything was light.

'Peace,' the nun murmured, reflecting. 'It was lovely to lie stretched out on the terrace in the evenings. The sea looked beautiful from up there,' she whispered, giving voice to the images that crowded her mind. Blurred, timeless moments. 'Two girls with a basket of apricots under our arms, running flat out to the water's edge to roll around, shrieking and laughing on the sand, washed by the gentle touch of the waves on which the orangey fruit bobbed happily ... Evening, two women sitting at the same table look at one another without saying a word, their eyes reddened from crying ...

'Edda,' the abbess whispered in a child's voice, letting Elettra feel the pain in her chest. Her eyes were full of the need to speak, to halt the flow of memories and grab the words that floated around her. 'I was so stupid, so stubborn,' she said, letting the hatred flow out of her clouded heart. 'Oh, Edda!'

She groaned, her fingers tense and her eyes and mouth wide open, unable to articulate more than noises, while Elettra stroked her forehead, trying to calm her. It was Edda she had seen, Elettra was sure of it; it was Edda the abbess fled from in those visions, from the poisoned fruit of jealousy that had broken their connection, and yet she still wanted her old friend at her side.

'Forgive her.' A request suddenly slipped from Elettra's lips, a prayer that gave voice to heart-rending pain she read on the abbess's face, the same pain that tortured her mother.

Finally, it was all clear.

Finally, Elettra understood that strange dance of half-clues; it was the love Edda and Joséphine shared that fought to break the crust of bitterness and return to the surface to breathe, seeking absolution for the errors of the past through a timeless journey.

'Forgive Edda,' Elettra repeated softly. She begged Joséphine's forgiveness on her mother's behalf; forgiveness for not understanding, for letting jealousy destroy a sacred link, for being unable to rejoice for her friend.

For an extraordinary love that had blossomed in the cloister of that same convent.

It was then, when Elettra spoke her mother's name, that the abbess uncovered her wrist to show her the scar of an old wound.

'Edda, my sister,' Joséphine murmured as tears blurred her vision and her lips opened at the memory of two girls. 'We made a blood pact on the terrace of this convent, lying on our backs, looking at the stars and eating lemon sweets.' By her expression, the flavour still lingered among her tarnished memories, the taste of the sun carved where not even illness could reach it.

Lea walked confidently into the room and leaned gently over her mother's face, brushing her forehead with a kiss. Then she smiled at her and turned to face Elettra. Joséphine, Edda, Lea and Elettra; the women whose lives the past had woven together with wefts of secrets and sugar, and who once more breathed the same air between the walls of an old place.

Lea reached out a hand in search of her sister's, while squeezing her mother's feeble fingers with the other. She squeezed both tightly in silence as her thoughts flew to a woman lying in a hospital bed many kilometres and yet just a step away from them.

'Peace,' she whispered as the sun blessed the new pact, giving them the golden sparkle of the sea, filling the room with a new light which smelled of lemons and rediscovered affection.

The past was healed, the hands of time were back in synch with life.

26

The days flew by following Elettra's encounter with the abbess; time seemed to knot all the threads back together again to weave a plot in which the two sisters could write a new page in the family story. Yet there still seemed to be a cloud overshadowing Elettra's days and her smile: Isabelle.

Things had changed between them: the laughter was no longer carefree, the jokes less amusing. Only crumbs were left of the relationship they had shared, just a few words exchanged in the corridors, but in spite of the initial rage that had compelled Elettra to distance herself from Isabelle, Elettra really wanted her friend back. Isabelle was the voice of her conscience, unbiased and honest; she couldn't bear to lose her.

'You have to eat at least one of them if you want to make peace with me,' she said, bursting into Isabelle's house one Sunday morning with a jar of *amaretti* in her hands.

'Elettra, listen to me; you know I don't eat pastries, but I'm begging you to understand the reasons why I did what I did.'

'Look, Isabelle, this is the point: I'm not interested in the reasons any more. It was painful to learn the truth like that, but I know it now and I've even discovered a sister, so there's no point mulling over the merits or otherwise of certain choices. I don't want to risk losing a friend because of a mistake, which we all make, every day. But your silence hurt me, and there's no use denying it,' she explained, taking the paper lid off the jar. 'You owe me for hiding the truth, and this is how you can repay me. The time has come to lay the past to rest and move forwards. And that goes for both of us,' she explained, as Isabelle faced her, mouth open, shocked by her young friend's initiative.

In any other situation Isabelle would have snapped back at her, the words already there on the tip of her tongue, but perhaps her conscience told her to keep quiet and obey Elettra's request.

'Peace?' she asked, fishing an *amaretto* out of the jar.

'Peace,' Elettra agreed.

Isabelle broke it in two and inhaled the scent of almond and orange blossom, of Juan's kisses.

'My Juan ...' she murmured, rediscovering a smile with the first mouthful.

'Well?' Elettra asked, curious.

'I hope you're planning to bake these for the grand opening in honour of times past. Adrian and I are arranging plenty of publicity; people are expecting something special. And you need *pane all'anice*, I'm sure about that; they were all crazy for it back in the day.'

Elettra looked down, Adrian's name had made her jump, but Isabelle had begun a fresh assault on the biscuits. Elettra said, 'How do you think the townspeople will react this time?'

'They're damned credulous idiots who cling scarily tightly to the priest's skirts; it's difficult to convince them to give you a second chance, especially the older women. Those dried out old crones can't accept widows taking part in the life of the community; in their opinion, once you lose your husband you should shut yourself up in the house until it's time to carry you out of it.' Isabelle brushed her hands to get rid of the sugar. 'They tried to make me do the same after my Juan passed away, but I made it very clear that I've no inclination to live as a recluse. I wanted to stay here because this is where our memories are, and I wouldn't leave if they threatened me at gunpoint. You can't stop living, you shouldn't. We have obligations to the people we lose, if we really love them. And I really loved Juan, and I will continue to do so, even if he's nothing but a handful of dust now.'

Elettra felt her friend's worried gaze fall on her. She knew she looked tense, her eyes were circled by shadows and she dragged her feet. Did Isabelle think all these responsibilities were too much for her?

Isabelle cleared her throat. 'We'll do it, you'll see. With a bit of diplomacy I'm sure we'll manage to make the medicine go down,' she said, but Elettra just arched a sceptical eyebrow.

'Do you have a plan?'

'Of course I do! I was in the war in Spain and I've fought against this self-righteous crowd a lot longer than you have: making plans is my specialty.'

'Your optimism is impressive, Isabelle. You ought to stand for mayor at the next elections,' Elettra mocked her, but Isabelle remained unmoved.

'If we can assure these people that you will resurrect the heritage of the nuns and live in the convent to take care of the Saint, we won't have any trouble. Anyway,' she continued, picking at the sugary crust of another *amaretto*, 'you ought to prepare plenty of these special pastries. The people are looking for something that will take them back to the good times, when the convent was still active ... When Edda delighted us with her masterpieces,' she added cautiously, but Elettra was not upset by the reference. She had forgiven Isabelle the moment she read sincere penitence on her face, when she had heard her speak about the death of her Juan; she would never feel bitterness towards such a loyal friend who had promised to honour a debt from many years ago. Elettra knew Josephine had done much for Juan during his illness, and in return Isabelle had felt bound to Joséphine's wishes and secrets.

'Don't worry, they'll get their trip back in time. Provided the Lerouxs don't put a spanner in the works.'

'You can be certain they'll try, but this time they won't manage to ruin everything. If fortune really is a turning wheel, it'll be our turn to rise sooner or later.'

Elettra sighed, trying to rid herself of the nerves that had tormented her stomach for days. 'I really hope so, Isabelle; if I were to fail again, Lea would never be able to resist Bernard and Morel's attacks, and she would have no choice but to leave.'

'Knowing that those two are in cahoots worries me a bit, too,' Isabelle admitted, chasing a crumb around the jar. 'Adrian told me that once this Morel sets his heart on something, he gets it sooner or later. He's an old-school businessman, he won't give up easily.'

'Exactly,' Elettra replied. 'It doesn't seem a promising start.'

'I know, but we shouldn't let that scare us; we can't assume things will go wrong just because there are a couple of sharks lurking around. Not even they are safe in the ocean.'

'What do you mean?'

Isabelle shrugged. 'It's not long until the grand opening, and it's not a given that things will remain as they are. There might be a few surprises. Nice surprises.'

Elettra's forehead creased. 'What exactly do you know, Isabelle?'

'I don't know anything at all,' Isabelle defended herself. 'I'm only saying that we need to be optimistic, and Adrian thinks so too. We need to keep trying until the very end,' she declared, which seemed to put an end to the conversation. She brushed the crumbs off her chest and drank a sip of water. 'Ah, I forgot to warn you that you'll have to do without Adrian for a while; he's had an accident,' she said, but she didn't have time to finish her sentence before Elettra leaped in.

'What's happened?' Elettra clutched a hand to her chest.

Isabelle looked down, a victorious grin on her face; as if she knew she'd hit the target, her instinct far from rusty. 'He hurt his leg falling off a ladder and now he's got a bump on his head, but it's nothing serious. His ankle's badly sprained, though; when I went to see him it was swollen up like a balloon. Very impressive.'

'When and where did it happen?' Elettra asked.

'You're asking a lot of questions for someone who's not the least bit interested!'

'Don't be stupid,' Elettra defended herself. 'Adrian has a job to finish; we can't mess up.'

'Are you sure that's the only reason you're worried?'

'I really don't need this, Isabelle,' she sighed.

'I know that you don't want to hear it, but I know why you're worried. About Adrian, I mean,' she added, rubbing Elettra's arm. Elettra tried to pull away, stubborn in the face of her words. 'Adrian isn't Marte, sweetheart; he is truly in love with you. And don't tell me you don't feel the same way.'

Elettra looked around, huffing. 'Do we really have to talk about it?'

'It's only the advice of an old madwoman, but it's genuine and you know that. Don't let Edda and Joséphine's past influence your future.' Isabelle studied Elettra, looking her in her eyes. 'Your mother's life, with all its mistakes and poor choices, is hers alone; it has nothing to do with you, and you shouldn't let it influence your decisions. You're a different person, Elettra, and so is Adrian. He adores you, even the rocks that make up the island can tell, but he won't wait for ever; nobody can endure an eternity of rejection.' She sighed deeply and released her grip, stepping back. 'Think about what I've told you, but don't think of Adrian too much when you're baking, or the bread will be ruined!' she warned Elettra, whose cheeks were as red as apples.

'Don't worry!' Elettra reassured her, disappearing out of the door, wrapped tightly in the winter coat Lea had lent her.

It was true, Adrian wasn't like Marte; they were two very different men, and yet Elettra remained hostage of the ghosts of a past that didn't want to set her free.

She went into the old chapel in search of silence and comfort. She re-examined her journey to Titan's Island and her relationship with Adrian, but still all she saw was an inverted version of her mother's past. Perhaps there had been something between him and her sister; it was obvious that Lea felt more than friendship for him, but the way he looked at Elettra was unique.

Thirty years or so later, the roles seemed to have been reversed. Odd, isn't it? she thought.

Amor vincit omnia, said the writing above the declaration, a promise that prompted a fearful smile.

Her father had just been a man in love and, however hard it was to accept that the woman he'd loved was not her mother, Elettra understood that the time had come to accept it. He had been in love with Joséphine, but that didn't mean if he'd known about Edda's pregnancy, he wouldn't have cared about her baby. Perhaps he would have loved Elettra, perhaps he would have been proud of his daughter with her olive skin and the aquamarine eyes she'd discovered she'd inherited from him.

She ran a hand through her hair and read the sentence again, a warning or a message for a life to be built free of the past.

The moment for reflection was over: she and the others had a convent to save.

She joined Nicole in the kitchen and worked with her non-stop until late afternoon; together they had baked at least a dozen batches of bread and biscuits. But her head was somewhere else completely and often her assistant had to save their baking from her continual distraction. Elettra didn't know how or why, but she had ended up putting an egg in the rosemary bread instead of the almond biscuits.

'You'd better take over, I just can't get it right today.' She finally gave up, after burning a tray of meringues. She would have thrown it all away if she could, but they had limited resources and no margin for error. The only thing that had come out absolutely perfectly for her these last few days were the *pani all'anice*, which were on the table, lined up and covered with a white cloth to prove. When they were ready she put some, the best ones, in a basket which she studied for a long moment before taking off her apron. She asked Nicole to tidy the kitchen and went to the doorway, her basket hanging from her arm and a pot held against her hip. 'I'm going out, see you later,' she told her, disappearing into the golden light of the sunset.

Walking the dark paths of the island with a pot of hot broth in her hands and the basket hanging from her arm was hell, so she gave a sigh of relief when she made out the outline of Adrian's house a hundred or so metres away. She arrived at the door, hidden by the skeleton of the bougainvillea, to find it ajar, and when she went in she found a sliver of light seeping into the living room. There was someone in the back, in the studio.

So he's at home, she thought, placing the warm soup and the pastries on a tray, but when she entered the studio she found herself facing something that shocked her.

Adrian wasn't in the room, but right in front of her was another Elettra; her face made of stone, shiny and polished, but it was *her*, it had her eyes. Elettra stiffened to find herself in that stone reflection. She ran her index finger over those pearly lips, as full as her own but bloodless, and she struggled to find herself in them. The sweetness of the eyes was disarming, painfully distant from the woman she had become.

Elettra looked around, drowning in the folds of her coat, her head buried between her shoulders. Adrian had robbed her, stolen part of her, the most fragile part she had tried to hide. Adrian had seen something in her that she was afraid of but still wanted to touch again, just for a moment, long enough to remember what it had been like living with herself.

She studied the bust, full of a strange disquiet; the answers she needed were locked in that face which mirrored her own, but she didn't have the strength to confront them. The truth was there, though, staring at her with an insistence that made her legs shake.

Perhaps Adrian truly loved her. Perhaps that was why he hadn't opposed her refusals even though he'd looked into her soul. Isabelle was right; but Elettra wasn't ready to accept it, ready to return a feeling that had hurt her so deeply in the past. She had had to forget what it meant to be loved in order to survive, the pain of abandonment had been too agonizing to bear.

She rubbed her arms, beset by her old fears, and, shaking her head, looked back at the face of the stone woman smiling sweetly at her. It was all so damned complicated.

Then, unexpectedly, Elettra heard a sound from Adrian's room. She carefully turned the handle, her heart beating like a drum. He was stretched out on the bed with his eyes closed. He was asleep but restless, mumbling complaints between closed lips.

'No!' he shouted suddenly.

'It was just a bad dream,' Elettra reassured him.

His breathing laboured, Adrian stared at her in confusion and ran his hand across his hot forehead, his eyes flitting from one side of the room to the other.

'What are you doing here?' he asked brusquely. He leaned up on his elbows to get up, but Elettra put a hand on his chest, pushing him back.

'Don't even think about it,' she said firmly. 'Getting up won't do you any good, so lie back down.'

Adrian obeyed her, obviously enjoying the touch of her warm hand, its outline pressing itself on his skin.

'There are lots of things that won't do me good, but the situation won't improve if I languish away here,' he protested, but she was unmoved.

'There's no danger; a sprained ankle isn't the end of the world, you'll soon get better.'

'It's a shame there's not much time. You might not have seen him around, but Vincent won't have given up. If that bastard has guessed something's wrong and if I don't get on with my work, he'll be the one laughing at us. And you can be sure they won't hesitate if my father's involved,' Adrian added. 'It's a mystery why they haven't already made a move to survey the convent and certify its state of disrepair.' He glanced at the disorder in the room, at the covers on the floor and the cassettes scattered on the empty side of the bed. He turned his head to look at the floor and picked up some papers.

'I've brought you something to eat. Nothing special, but I hope it will cheer you up.'

'That would take a miracle.' He seemed unable to stop provoking her; she had hurt him, yet she was sitting there as if it were nothing, bringing him dinner like a good neighbour.

Adrian had had to abandon his sculptures in order to help her and the convent and only now did Elettra understand what a sacrifice that was for an artist. She had asked a lot of him, perhaps more than was right, given their relationship. She went back into the kitchen to get the food, cutlery and crockery. She arranged it all on a tray, then removed the plate she had used to keep the soup warm. The air was immediately filled with the rounded, velvety smell of simmered vegetables.

'Here we go. I hope it's not too salty,' she added. Sitting beside him, she watched him eat his dinner in silence; he didn't look up from his plate and she didn't dare try to catch his eye.

To fill the time she poured herself some water, but instead of drinking it she held the glass against her chest. Silences were habitual for her; in the last year she had spent hundreds of afternoons sitting beside Edda, the time marked by the dripping of the tubes into her veins, remembering every minute, every day lived and lost, squandered by pride.

'Is everything okay?'

Adrian asked her at least four times, but Elettra refused to answer him. Isabelle's words were in her head, along with the writing on the marble that had become an obsession. Perhaps Isabelle and Marte, with their blind faith in love, were right; there was no sense fighting the past, it wasn't her life. She needed to stop living as her mother's reflection.

'Adrian,' she murmured with an effort after a long silence. Her hand found his face in a caress and her eyes were full of all the sweetness she had never allowed herself to show before. Her look spoke, conveying what words never could, trapped as they were at the back of her throat.

Adrian guessed the truth with a smile, leaning towards her in search of further contact. 'Elettra, I . . . ' he whispered, but he was silenced by her lips, by the heat of her hand as she pulled him towards her.

A heavy kiss: heavy with life, with meaning, with fears that slowly vanished. Their bodies immediately entwined in an instinctive embrace, reclaiming contact after such a long time, while their lips quenched one another's thirst, pressed together in a pact that broke with the past for ever.

Elettra felt her body vibrate at Adrian's touch as he traced new shivers onto her skin, their rough breathing growing hotter with every touch.

'Every time I sculpted your face in stone I imagined touching you, what it would be like to hold you against me and stroke your skin, but now, doing it, feeling you alive between my hands, it's completely different,' he murmured. 'You're the best work of art anyone could ever create.' His hand slowly slipped under Elettra's shirt, sliding over her burning skin, but the door flew open as he went to pull her against him, filling the room with ice.

The wind blew under their clothes, separating them.

'What the hell's going on?' Adrian jumped to his feet, but it only took a single step to make the room spin, flinging him back on the bed, his hand reaching for his face as he tried to stop the roundabout in his head. Elettra groped her way to the light switch by the door and felt her heart skip a beat when the lamp's filament lit the corridor. There in the middle of the doorway, between the two milk white walls, stood Lea, her face a mask of shock and her eyes full of terror.

The slim legs emerging from her mud-stained skirt were clearly shaking. She was struggling to breathe, as though suffocated by words.

Elettra remained motionless, her breath catching in her chest, until her sister's eyes filled with tears.

'My mother,' she whispered.

'Your mother?' Adrian echoed her, obviously surprised.

'What's wrong with Joséphine?' Elettra said.

'She's just fallen into a coma,' Lea replied, covering her face with her hands and beginning to sob.

Elettra clenched her fists and closed her eyes.

Edda, Joséphine: the synchronicity of two imperfect souls that chased one another along the path of time.

Marzapane di Edda

480g peeled almonds

20g bitter almonds

500g sugar

100g egg whites

1 small cup rose water

Food colouring

Grind the two types of almonds and the sugar together until they resemble flour.

Whisk the eggs until white but not fully firm, then add them to the mixture along with a couple of drops of rose water. Knead vigorously until you have a smooth, compact block.

Colour as you choose and model into the desired shape.

27

Lea was in a terrible state by the time the doctor left in the middle of the night. She had been the one who'd found her mother unconscious on the bed. The body of the woman she'd loved and protected for years had given up. No spasms, no reactions, not even to Lea's voice when she kept gently calling her. There was no longer any trace of tenderness on Joséphine's face, everything had been frozen by the desperation of a heart that had suffered in the shadow of the cloister for years.

Lea insisted that the doctor, who had always visited her mother in secret, treat her at the convent, but as he closed his briefcase he told her that there was no cure to halt the degenerative progress of the illness, and, based on his experience, her mother didn't have long left.

This prognosis left Lea with a big black hole burrowing voraciously into her soul.

That was when her face became clouded by grief. Terrified by the idea of losing her, Lea didn't leave her mother's bedside for a second from the moment the abbess's eyes gave in to the blank sleep of the coma.

In an attempt to comfort and support her sister, Elettra began going to pray at a spot on the shore named Scoglio della Speranza, Hope Cliffs. Isabelle had told her that the women had been going there for centuries to scan the horizon in search of their loved ones' boats, their hearts swollen with fear, and radiant wives had greeted their returning husbands from those cliffs.

That edifice standing above the sea had been a junction of hopes and tears for years; Elettra couldn't imagine a better place to pray for Joséphine's recovery.

She hated admitting it, and she couldn't do so in Lea's presence, but a bit of her was relieved to know that the abbess was now resting serenely; her condition had worsened over the last few days, and the spasms, genuine fits of convulsions, had become more and more frequent.

'Now you're close to her,' she murmured, thinking of her own mother. 'You two have always been close, you and your friend,' she said, swallowing back tears as she remembered the sight of Lea's distraught face.

Elettra was suddenly filled with a need to know that her mother was all right; it would be enough for someone to tell her that her condition was unchanged, because just the thought of Edda lying in a satin-lined coffin with a crucifix in her hands kept her awake at night.

Back at the convent, she put the almonds on the work top and ground them into flour. She knew that making lunch wouldn't help because nobody would eat it, Lea and the others barely ate enough to keep themselves going, but a glance at the calendar that morning had reminded her she had no time left to lose so she decided to continue with the work for the grand opening.

She looked at the empty bowl for a long time, listening to Adrian's rhythmic banging in the distance; he had returned to work at the convent a couple of days after the abbess fell into a coma, but every so often Elettra would see him clinging tightly to the ladder and clutching his forehead so as not to fall. He was by no means fully better but he was there to fight alongside her and Isabelle, their most stalwart supporter. Isabelle was hurting too, she had wept like a baby when she saw Joséphine, but she hadn't abandoned her.

Elettra picked up the bowl of sugar and poured in the almonds, combining them with her hands; it was pleasant to feel them against her palms and gradually give in to their perfumed oil, but she shivered when she had to add the chilled stickiness of the egg yolks to the mixture and they slipped, liquid, between her fingers. She tightened her grip, letting the damp from the eggs seep into the sugar; this had always been one of Edda's jobs, but Elettra had had to start making marzipan by herself.

She plunged her hand into the yellowish mixture, her mind drifting. Going back to carefree feast days, when the window of the Dream Kitchen was full of little coloured fruit, was like breathing fresh air: Elettra still remembered the pyramids of jars full of tiny marzipan creations.

Edda used to work for nights on end to make them, her glasses often slipping down her nose as she clutched her delicate paint-brush between finger and thumb, but when Elettra insisted on staying up to keep her company, her mother would tell her in a voice somewhere between tender and authoritarian to go to bed because she needed to go to school tomorrow.

'Don't you want me to turn the radio on for you?' Elettra would suggest, determined to wangle a little longer with her mother, but Edda would always shake her head.

'I'm fine like this, I'm not afraid of spending time with myself,' she would reply with a slight smile.

Elettra didn't understand what she meant, so she just agreed.

Elettra couldn't have known it then, but she would never forget the image of Edda leaning over a ball of marzipan in her colour-stained apron, her gaze caressing her little creation, ready for another sleepless night. Another night of thoughts held back by duty and yawns, fighting against ever-darker hours.

Elettra shook off a shiver that ran up her spine.

She quickly finished kneading the ingredients, dusted the work surface with sugar and turned out the mixture, which she covered with a cloth. She could still feel the shiver and it left her with no desire to work alone in the kitchen. The thought of Joséphine, of Lea's desperation, had filled her with a compelling urge to go to Sabine's, to call Ruth. She wanted to hear her friend's voice telling her that her mother was all right.

That everything would be fine.

At the bar, Elettra dialled the number and waited patiently for the connection. A dull sound, then another, and in her mind the summary of the speech she had prepared.

'Hello?'

'Hey, how are you?'

'Hello, stranger!' Ruth trilled. It took her just a couple of seconds to get over her surprise, then she began a detailed summary of the local weather and her love life. She eventually moved on to Edda, telling Elettra she was stable, but that she'd been having blood pressure issues recently.

'Nothing alarming,' she clarified when she heard Elettra gasp down the line. 'The doctor's prescribed her new medication. They're going to run some tests on Wednesday to see if the treatment's working.'

There was silence apart from the artificial crackling of the telephone wires in the background and a series of held breaths.

'By the way, when are you thinking of coming home?'

Silence fell again, broken by Sarah's distant laughter.

'I went to your house today to collect the post and ... oh God, I don't know how to tell you, but I've already found letters from the bank twice now.'

Elettra shook herself. The word 'bank' still sounded as terrible as when she'd left. 'Go ahead and open them, I won't keep any secrets from you.'

'I know, but these are delicate matters, I'd prefer you to read them in person.'

'Get one of them and tell me what it says,' Elettra ordered. Her voice was different, her tone calm. She swallowed. She was trying to stay afloat, but every time she raised her head something pushed her back down, where she no longer wanted to go. In spite of the months that had passed, the Dream Kitchen continued to swallow up money and hopes. Most of the outgoings, Ruth told her, were on the pitiless demands for interest payments, but the diminishing sums left in the bank were not her only worry.

Faced with this darkly shaded outlook, Elettra's future seemed blacker than ever.

'Hello? Are you still there?'

'Yes, yes, I'm here, Ruth,' she replied, disorientated by a maze of numbers and interest charges.

'So, what do you want to do? Are you coming back or staying?' Ruth pressed.

A pointed silence fell between them, the words remained hanging on the line. It was the wrong time to tell Ruth everything, she couldn't do it over the phone.

Elettra looked around; Sabine was the only person in the bar, sweeping the floor like she did every afternoon. 'I'm staying. I'd rather be here a bit longer.'

Ruth stammered. 'Are you sure?'

Elettra smiled; she knew she would have to think seriously

about a return date sooner or later. She would have to find a job as a baker, or perhaps take up pen and paper and knuckle down like she used to in the old days when she worked at the newspaper.

Elettra fantasised about the possibility of putting everything that happened down on paper, telling the story of Edda and her life, but it was a distant dream. Her here and now was in that deserted bar, in the connection she had developed over the summer with a land as harsh and intense as her mother, with the rebellious breeze that had filled Edda's lungs, and later her own, with the sea. Her life was the convent, the bread and the spices for her pastries, reopening the old bakery so as to give the island back a fragment of its history, and cancelling out the insult of the fire.

The convent was under a dark cloud to which only she and Isabelle refused to submit. It was Isabelle who had decided to break the veil of silence during lunch the previous day.

'Listen for a moment,' she demanded, tapping the edge of her plate with her spoon, 'I understand that this isn't a happy time, but I've got news for you: the calendar doesn't give a fig about disasters. There's less than a week until the reopening of the island's bakery and unless you plan to pack up and give in to Vincent, you need to lose the long faces and roll up your sleeves. Do we or do we not have a convent to save?' she urged them, her hands firm on the table top and her voice like a general ready for battle.

It had been a risk, but at least she'd managed to get their attention; in fact, all eyes had been on her.

'Elettra can't do everything on her own, and there's a huge backlog of work to do. The chapel and the cloister need cleaning, the finished produce needs packaging and that poor statue needs a good clean. We can't allow ourselves the luxury of moping, otherwise we might as well hand the keys to Vincent. And, furthermore,' she added, 'I don't think Joséphine would want to be evicted. She hasn't spent years fighting tooth and nail to protect this place to throw it all away, so I think that instead of spending all day despairing we should also get cracking for her sake in particular. Joséphine doesn't deserve to lose her home, not like this.' She exchanged a quick glance with Elettra, who was sitting on the other side of the table and gave her a grateful smile. Isabelle was brusque but effective: a born motivator.

'Isabelle's right,' Elettra agreed, turning to her sister, her hand reaching out for Lea's, squeezing it tightly. She was ready to fight.

And so were all the others.

In fact, the convent seemed to be imbued with fresh energy following Isabelle's tirade.

The corridors were suddenly alive once more with the coming and going of footsteps, and the ovens filled the cloisters with aromas and stories from the past.

Nicole and Adrian threw themselves wholeheartedly into the restoration of the statue of the Saint, while Dominique, armed with buckets and damp cloths, cleaned the chapel on top of dividing her time between caring for the vegetable garden and the bees.

Lea offered to prepare an inventory of the produce for sale; she didn't have the strength to work alongside the others and talk about this and that, not yet. She needed time for herself, for her pain; she didn't ask for more.

Elettra caught her sister's eye at the bottom of the stairs – Lea with a notebook under her arm, and she with a basket of lemons against her chest – she studied Lea's emaciated face. Elettra had so much to say to her, but the words died in her throat when she heard Lea panting as if breathing were the most thankless task in the world. She went on her way, her thoughts skipping between her sister's pale face and nostalgia for her mother.

Elettra looked out of the window, towards the blue that moved beyond the white frame; it was majestic, but there was something sinister about the power with which it played with the boats, making them rear up one moment and plunge down the next. And heavenly: the wild sight of the sea, with its waves following one another and releasing crests of white spray, left her breathless.

She prayed for the same strength as those waves, to be able to loom over the man who planned to defeat them.

She took a deep breath, her eyes closed, as friendly fingers brushed her shoulders, sliding gently along her arms.

'Well then, shall we get to work?' said Isabelle.

Elettra smiled. She set the basket on the table and knotted the shawl around Isabelle's hunched shoulders as she studied her, as feisty as ever. She squeezed the fabric, which smelled of ashes and chopped wood, tightly between her hands, then let the wool slip between her fingertips.

'Of course, I'm just about to start, there's nothing stopping me.'

28

After a final burst of frenetic activity, the dreaded 17 November arrived. The day of the feast of the Saint, of the reopening of the bakery, of reckoning.

Overwhelmed by preparations, Elettra hadn't had a chance to spend more than a few seconds with Adrian since the day the abbess had fallen into a coma, but she felt a shiver run up her legs at the thought of what would happen once that day drew to an end, when the pressure was off.

She still hadn't given any thought to afterwards: should she go home or stay on the island and pretend to herself that she had plenty of time to make life decisions? And Adrian, what role would he play? Was there any kind of future for the two of them?

Baking was the only thing that could calm her down, so, driven by the need to be active, she had opened the window and let the salty air sting her cheeks as she gathered all the ingredients on the table.

She had decided to prepare *pani all'anice* for the feast, and plenty of them; she owed it to Edda and everything she had learned at the convent. Baking the bread that had set her on the trail of this magical and mysterious place was a kind of tribute to her mother and the gifts of the past, to the sister she had discovered and the love she felt surrounding her between these walls.

It was genuine, palpable; she could feel the heat just placing a hand against the wall.

Elettra had tried to infuse this love into every crumb of dough, into every movement with which she kneaded the warm mass, into the spicy, alcoholic aroma. She had worked through the night, until the dawn surprised her. She woke with her arms crossed at the table, propping up a head that was growing as heavy as her heart, which wouldn't let her stop thinking of Adrian; she had tried burying herself in her work, but his lips remained on her skin in spite of her fatigue.

Now she sat on a chair waiting for the bread to rise, her arms wrapped around her knees and her gaze upturned to the dawn. When, after long hours full of thoughts and hopes, she had finally baked them, those little green seeds had worked their magic once again.

Elettra started dozing at the table and began to dream of an explosion of perfume, which floated out of the kitchen, snaking across the floor to the window, and from there following an imaginary path that connected the town to the convent. It was an extremely long rope between the kitchen and the handful of angry souls, hurt and disfigured by the sea, but not ungrateful.

The sweet and melancholy scent of the bread had flown on the wind, reaching the centre of town in the blink of an eye. Having scaled the bell tower, it had rung the bell of memory for the many souls that lay behind dark curtains; one chime had followed another and the houses had all lit up at once like an enormous nativity scene, from the main streets to alleyways even the priest and the forces of law and order had forgotten. There were flickers of light everywhere, comets from a past which filled young men with white beards with the liveliness of a rediscovered light-heartedness, and the promise of days yet to come.

The whole island and all its inhabitants were joined in a single breath and a single heartbeat that night.

Time had been destroyed, defeated. The hands had been halted at midnight while the past travelled the streets, whistling happily, stroking the stray cats that slept curled up against the closed front doors and sprinkling handfuls of memories and summer scents like confetti at the carnival of life.

'A magical night,' Elettra had whispered. It was the life in which Edda was simply the mother she loved, and whom she had never wanted as much and felt so close to as she did that night. Edda was there in her kitchen, with the magic of her secret ingredients and everything they had never said to one another but they had now finally found the courage to confess, speaking through creams and doughs.

It was now very clear to Elettra that this was the power of her family; everything was in the flour and sugar, in hands able to read people's souls.

Because nothing is more magical than a chocolate biscuit.

'I love you so much, Mamma,' she murmured, blowing a kiss to the stars, where she knew she'd find Edda.

'Elettra?'

She raised her head, as the enchantment of the dream slowly dissolved before her eyes. She inhaled the fresh smell of bread rolls as she woke up at the table. She turned to locate the source of the voice, although it was unmistakeable.

Adrian must have iced them while she slept. Their scent had a different note, woody and manly; the smell of Adrian, of those eyes that looked at her admiringly despite the fact that the rest of his face remained hurt and closed.

Have I ruined everything? she asked herself in the brief interval of their silence, but he didn't give her the chance to read the answer. His eyes looked elsewhere, towards the sea beyond the shut window.

'Did you do that?' she asked him, pointing at the window.

'It was too cold, I didn't want you to get ill,' he replied, but the sweet, caring way he spoke those words cut her like a dagger. 'If you mean the bread rolls, I decorated them how you would have done. I hope I haven't messed it up, but I didn't want to wake you.'

'Thanks,' she nodded, still befuddled, dazed by the steaming cup he slid under her nose. Coffee.

'I thought you might need something strong.'

Elettra inhaled the intense aroma that reminded her of melted chocolate. 'If I could wake up like this at home every morning, I'd get on a plane this evening,' she said with a laugh, trying to shake off the lingering shadow of her dream. She had said it as something to say, but the frown on Adrian's face made it clear she would have been better off staying silent. He had been kind and worried about her, and she was thinking of leaving.

'Adrian,' she murmured, deciding to be strong and clear, but when she looked at his face his expression was already distant. He rummaged in an old leather briefcase and took out a dozen crumpled sheets of paper. 'What are those?' she asked. She leaned over to try and read the text but Adrian's large hands hid it all.

'The proof we were looking for to ... Ah, perfect, you're here too!' Adrian greeted Lea who'd just appeared at the door, pale and skinny. He drew up a chair for her and spread the sheets across the table, moving Elettra's now-empty cup. It was a brisk gesture, echoed in his newly evasive gaze, but Elettra chose to concentrate on the papers he was showing them and save her question for later. There would be plenty of time to clear things up once the day was over.

'So, what did I miss?' Lea asked, studying the papers. She rubbed her eyes and picked up a sheet, trying in vain to decipher it. She read a few lines full of numbers, and gave it back to Adrian. 'Tell me what these are, please; I'm so tired it'll be a miracle if I don't fall asleep too.'

'These are the documents that will help us catch Vincent out and foil his scheme,' Adrian replied calmly, grabbing their attention immediately. 'Do you remember the mayor's plans?'

'How could we forget?' Elettra snorted, folding her arms.

'Of course,' Lea nodded.

The clock chimed the hour. The island seemed to be holding its breath along with the two sisters.

Adrian placed both hands on the table. 'I've discovered something important. My father had no intention of giving the contract for the construction of the hotel to local companies and employing the islanders. He'd made an agreement with Leroux to split the state funding for local redevelopment between their own interests as soon as they were granted it – the contracts would go to my father's friends. After the payment of a bribe, of course.'

'Oh my God,' Elettra whispered. 'We had our suspicions but we didn't have proof.'

A heavy silence fell in the kitchen, as if the words needed to settle.

Lea remained seated for a few minutes. Adrian continued to scan the papers in search of new explanations and Elettra stared at the *couronnes* of sweet raisin bread that were rising by the oven. Everything seemed so complicated, but in the end it was as banal and straightforward as the ingredients in the *couronnes*: greed was at the heart of Vincent and Bernard's project, like flour was at the heart of her baking.

'What should we do?' she said.

'I need to search for more information,' said Adrian.

It was all too much for Lea who was looking increasingly pale and fragile. She made her excuses and returned to her mother's bedside. Elettra told her she understood and would let her know if they found anything.

'Everyone needs to know what kind of man Vincent Leroux is, but if we mention this your father's name will come up too, and I don't know if . . .'

'If what?'

Elettra looked up at the ceiling, her fingers entwined. 'If you could stay involved.'

'I wouldn't worry about it. My father never does anything in his own name, he uses his second wife's: she's the one with the capital. It's Elodie's firm that would make an agreement with Leroux, my father's just a minority shareholder. And anyway, I'm just Adrian to the people around here.'

'What if the connection came to light anyway?'

He shrugged. 'I can say the shared name is a coincidence, or just admit that yes, that worm is my father, but whether or not I feel hurt by the whole thing is none of anyone's business. What matters is that Vincent and Bernard leave you in peace, and if this is the only way to give them that message, then fine. We didn't start this war.'

It was simple, in spite of its harshness. As she listened Elettra wanted to add that she cared whether or not he felt hurt, but she kept quiet.

'Okay, fine, but what's our next move?' she asked, as Adrian walked back and forth behind the table, his hands in his pockets and a vague look in his eyes.

'I've no idea, but we can't wave this paperwork under people's noses without a plan.'

'Why not?'

'Because it wouldn't have the same emotional impact, and we need that too. We're gambling everything on these documents, we can't overlook the smallest detail.'

Elettra slumped into her chair, her mind in turmoil. Adrian was right. 'Can I ask how you came to have these documents?'

'Why?'

'Because I can't think of anything for the "great revelation" so I'd rather think about something else than circle it pointlessly.'

Adrian shook his head, apparently amused, and leaned against the table. 'Let's say I had to suffer a bit to get them, but it was worth it.'

Elettra raised her eyebrows.

'I went to find my father at the hotel, but I made sure he was out first.'

'You stole them?'

'I don't break my leg for small fry,' he said, crossing his arms.

'So you didn't fall off a ladder, like Isabelle told me!'

'No,' Adrian smiled, shaking his head, 'although for a moment I was afraid I'd break my neck jumping down from the balcony. Perhaps I should thank her for the fact I'm still in one piece,' he added, nodding towards the statue in the cloister. 'The Saint probably protected me; after all, it was for a good cause, wasn't it?'

Elettra followed Adrian's gaze out towards the cloister, which was bathed in morning light; the Saint, the reason why she'd set off on this journey months ago, had powers unknown to the sceptics. 'Yes, perhaps she did,' she murmured, her eyes tracing the statue's serene face and the open arms where she would have liked to take refuge.

29

Elettra opened the freshly painted convent gate; Adrian hadn't had a chance to put a layer of anti-rust on first, so he'd had to do his best covering the ravages of time with a bit of varnish.

Not much later a small crowd started coming through; at the head of this improvised procession was Isabelle, decked out in her Sunday best. She was radiant in her turquoise shawl, her combatant's eyes two flames that lit up her face; she was proud of herself and she made no effort to hide it. Behind her were gathered the women of the town, the elderly followed by the younger ones, their heads covered and their hands clasped in prayer.

Elettra and Lea stood next to each other, and heard a murmur of *Ave Marias* recited using rosaries made of shells and pebbles from the beach. They were all in black, as always, and they looked up towards the cloister.

'It's the tradition for them to be the first to pray at the Saint's feet and honour her with flowers,' Lea had explained in response to Elettra's perplexed expression.

'Why?'

'Most of them are widows, mothers or sisters of someone lost to the sea, and as an island that made and still makes its living from fishing, people respect their pain. The community lets them pray alone before the main event. On this island pain is considered something strictly personal, to experience in silence.'

Elettra nodded, fascinated by the magnetism of those faces heavy with experience, and thought of Sabine, of the way she had tried to rebel against tradition and how she'd been left alone.

Everyone in town had pretended not to see her bruises, her pain. 'I'd say it's a very deep-rooted tradition,' she commented pointedly, but Lea shrugged.

'That's the way we're made, reserved and solitary.'

Selfish, I'd say, Elettra thought, but she kept quiet. She preferred to set aside her passing ill-temper and search for Sabine amongst the unfamiliar faces, but she was startled to find instead the one person she would rather not have seen: Vincent and his sharp little smile were there, to watch a failure from which the convent would never recover. He had come alone, he hadn't even troubled Sylvie.

He really can't see us as much of a threat, Elettra thought. She tried to stay strong but she soon looked away, irritated; she would have given anything not to have to see the mayor's face again. She couldn't have known that destiny was paying particular attention to her voice that day.

Elettra mingled with the crowd so as not to have to see him again, waiting for the women in black to finish their solitary prayers; there were only a few innocent gusts of wind to trouble the high clouds and, from there, the sea was like a sleeping giant.

Then a gust of wind suddenly blew down the convent corridors, snatching her breath.

'Come quickly!' shouted a voice from the cloister.

Elettra felt a flutter in her chest.

The crowd at the gates suddenly turned towards the cloister, pushing and shoving; a nervous shuffling of feet stirred up the dust again and Dominique's flowers were trampled beneath rubber boots.

Lea and Elettra exchanged a worried glance and ran towards the cloister, where they found a woman on her knees at the feet of the Saint, her arms raised towards the statue and her hands full of sheets of paper from the basket at the Saint's feet.

The very same ones Adrian had brought up to the convent a few hours earlier, and placed carefully in front of the statue.

It was a perfectly planned scene, Elettra decided, smiling at the memory of his words.

In the middle of the crowd, Vincent paled. He knew those letters well, copies had been sitting on his desk for weeks, and suddenly they had turned up here.

'What the devil . . . ?' he murmured, loosening his shirt collar.

A trickle of sweat ran down his deep red face. He walked over to the statue with long strides, pushing all in his path out of the way, but when he tried to snatch the papers out of the woman's hands, Isabelle got there first and thrust them at old Dupont, the oldest of the fishermen and a local hero during the last war.

'At least we can be sure they're in safe hands,' she declared loudly while the crowd held their breaths and the aroma of aniseed from the baskets of bread at the Saint's feet drifted merrily before the people's worried faces. The old partisan was an institution and a symbol of integrity on the island; he hadn't bought himself a drink since 1945 and there wasn't a Sunday when his friends didn't bicker over who was inviting him over for lunch. Nobody would question his word. But given the serious expression on his face, tanned by a life on the waves, everyone imagined that rather than a miracle, he believed the Saint brought tidings of fresh punishments, or that someone was trying to denounce the evil-doing of one of the islanders.

Elettra watched the scene breathlessly, subtly turning her gaze to Vincent; the triumphant smile he'd been wearing just moments before had withered on his round face.

There were a couple of minutes of calm as the convent held its breath along with the man who quickly read the documents.

'This man is a thief: he's schemed for months to rob us of the convent, of the Saint and of our lands, and all in order to profit off the backs of us fishermen, who no longer know how to feed our families while he grows rich in the blink of an eye,' Dupont thundered.

Dupont's finger pointed directly at Vincent as the air rang with the ignominious accusation of betrayal. Each word pronounced in the silence of the cloister was like a rock hurled at him, a verdict whose fulfilment would involve much more than a few years in jail.

The papers were passed from hand to hand amongst the men attending the festival, leaving a trail of angry resentment behind them.

The ink on those pages revealed a truth that had been manipulated and kept quiet for months to the whole island, a truth Vincent could no longer flee.

All the deceits had been brought to light, there were no lies left to defend.

After Dupont's fiery words, Vincent had no one left to count on, least of all Bernard, who had suddenly become unreachable; perhaps he had been the one to betray him. The mayor was so scared at that moment that his only thought was of saving himself. He had tried to deceive a lot of men, too many to appease with words. Fleeing, escaping, must have been his only thought, the only option for a life now shrouded in shame.

'Two years ago, the day before the storm, the remains of a boat shipwrecked on this coast ten years earlier were found in the Saint's hands,' Lea told Elettra, seeing a question form on her lips at the sight of some women kneeling to thank the Saint. 'Many women interpreted that discovery as a sign, a warning to keep away from the sea, and some of them convinced their husbands to stay at home at least on the following day. There were furious rows and slammed doors in more than half the houses the night before the storm, but those few men who listened to their wives and didn't go out to sea were saved, and even today they come with tears in their eyes to thank the Saint for preserving their lives.'

'They ought to thank their wives, not the Saint,' Elettra objected, earning a glance from her sister, who turned towards the throng of people around the statue. Elettra felt more and more a part of this island, but there were still some attitudes that she couldn't fully grasp. 'What did I say wrong this time?' she asked Nicole, confused by Lea's reaction, as a hand rubbed her shoulder.

'The people of this island never forget a good turn, but the men always think twice if it's a woman to be thanked,' interrupted a voice behind her and Elettra's face lit up as soon as their gazes met.

'Sabine!' she exclaimed, throwing her arms around her neck, happy for this small miracle. She squeezed her tight and kissed her; her friend still had her air of suffering and bruises hidden under an overly long coat, but she was smiling.

'We're a stubborn, moody people, but we know how to be grateful.'

'So you can be sure that you'll find the offertory box full by this evening,' Isabelle added, handing them each an *amaretto*. She kept the largest for herself, looking around in satisfaction. In spite of the distraction when Vincent had taken centre stage, the reopening of the old bakery seemed to be winning approval.

In fact, after an uncertain beginning, the space in front of the convent had filled with people, each with their own opinions on the scam Vincent had been plotting.

'A dirty trick!'

'An outrage!' they thundered, waving glasses of wine in the air and clutching samples of the *pane all'anice* Nicole and Lea were giving out to all and sundry, renewing the magical promise of the evening.

There were sweet and savoury delicacies everywhere, arranged in baskets, and hampers of every size and shape, along with platters of meringues, *grissini*, almond brittle and *amaretti*, and smaller jars containing every kind of almond sweet Elettra had been able to find in Edda's recipe book.

The convent courtyard was soon so full that it was hard to walk around; the whole island seemed to have been drawn to that jewel set in the Mediterranean scrubland by the magical cookery of a girl who, many years before, had transformed spiced bread into a promise, a token of pure and unconditional love.

Love; that was the ingredient that had long been missing from the island, among the people who finally exchanged smiles over *amaretti* and biscuits.

'Excuse me?' Lea heard frequently, stopped at every step by the elderly, often the oldest couples on the island, who took advantage of the party to apologise to her for years of unkind words that nobody had wanted to challenge, preferring to give in to the flattery of the gossip spread by Sylvie.

'It doesn't matter, not any more,' she would reply each time, 'what matters is knowing you're here to fight beside us to protect the Saint from the entrepreneurs and reclaim our old bakery together. Do you remember what it was like?' she would ask them. They would smile at her with a renewed empathy, talking at length of their memories of distant days, when the convent bakery was a bustle of chatter and laughter and life moved slowly, governed by the tides; when Titan's Island was just a piece of land like any other, without scars or the memory of tragedies that divided people instead of reinforcing the old feeling of solidarity amongst the fishermen.

The old resentments had vanished, washed away by the first

hesitant smiles, becoming a renewed harmony instead in the pleasure of laughter shared over biscuits and bread rolls.

The island was finally free of the ghosts of the past, of a dark tragedy, and so were its people.

Alone among dozens of strangers, Elettra took a bite of the *amaretto* Isabelle had given her, looking up to watch the evening fall over the island. A string of coloured lights lit up the port like a nativity scene, while behind her, wrapped in the darkness, the Titan in the rock kept watch over his kingdom. Facing him, minute by comparison, her arms outstretched in an embrace, was the Saint, protector of the island and Elettra's own life: everything had turned out for the best, or at least it was on a hopeful path. She realised that ever since that statue with her smile had come into her life, things had changed, she had changed. It wasn't a question of faith, more an energy that she felt emanating from the Saint; there was a bit of magic in what had happened to her in recent months. She could have missed out on meeting dozens of people whom she now realised she couldn't live without.

Including Adrian, perhaps the most important of all, if only she'd let herself admit it.

She sighed, stroking the sugary surface of the biscuit with her finger.

There really was something magical about that evening, something that once again, as always, took her back to her mother; it was the perfume of almonds, the salt sea air, the coloured lights and the people devouring oregano *grissini*, one of Nicole's specialities, and the *pane all'anice* Elettra had prepared, while the lemon trees released their summery fragrance into the air in spite of the November evening.

Everything was perfect, the likelihood that the convent would be saved grew as metal clinked into the donation box that Isabelle cradled like a newborn, but there was still something missing.

'It looks like things are starting to head in the right direction,' murmured Adrian, putting his hands on Elettra's shoulders. They were warm and smelled of sand and paint. Elettra inhaled those fragrances combined with his and gently nodded as he leaned towards her, his faint smile like a question. 'Is something wrong?'

'No, why?'

'You're acting strangely. You don't seem to be having a great evening.'

Elettra looked away. She concentrated on an elderly couple sitting on a bench, trying to share a marzipan apple; aged by the years, their hands trembled visibly, like laundry forgotten in the sunshine. They were perhaps ill, but she was moved to see them laugh in amusement when the half of the sweetmeat the woman was about to give her husband ended up in crumbs on his trousers. Elettra looked at them carefully, trying to dig into their daily lives to see what was missing from her own. She explored their eyes, the tenderness of their glances, while she felt the earth crumble in her chest and the bitter taste of her solitary life.

'Do you fancy a stroll?'

Adrian's voice pulled her back to the present, where she stood beside the man who was once again offering her his upturned palm, impervious to her rejections. To accept, to refuse; those verbs seemed nothing more than a jumble of letters.

'All right. Shall we go towards the cliffs?'

It wasn't nearby, not without the light of the sun to show the path between the bushes, but it was the first place that had sprung to mind; the light and all those voices were becoming unbearable. There was too much joy around, too many smiles.

'If you like.'

They set off in silence, walking side by side.

Adrian didn't even try to make conversation; Elettra clearly wasn't in the best mood, and he appeared to be in a hurry to get there. They made their way between dry branches, the roar of the sea their only guide along the stony paths, and when they arrived at the clifftop and began the descent towards the beach, the sky surprised them with a flash of its best silver. The line of the coast was an enormous dark curve against the blue. Adrian jumped down from a heap of seaweed the currents had gathered and helped Elettra to do the same. He wiped his hands on his jeans and looked up towards the stars.

'I've tried to learn the names of the constellations dozens of times, but I've never managed it,' Adrian said to fill the silence, but Elettra didn't reply. She watched him out of the corner of her eye, hugging herself to stave off the cold. She regretted coming down there. Wrapped in her cardigan, she hunched her shoulders to keep warm. Perhaps later she would ask him to lend her something warmer, after all, his house wasn't that far away.

'Did you do it to impress the girls?'

'What?'

'Learn the names of the constellations. It's a good idea, very romantic. A guaranteed winner.'

Adrian shook his head at her jibes, but it seemed he'd learned that the best way to avoid conflict was to ignore them. He wrapped his own jacket more tightly around himself, his cold-reddened hands thrust in his pockets. 'Yes, but I've had better luck with art,' he admitted with a half-smile. 'I've never had to pay my models.'

'Were they all that eager to take their clothes off for you?' The sharpness of her voice revealed the shadow of jealousy triggered by his comment. She turned away without giving him a chance to reply and continued walking along the dark sand, inhaling the ocean.

Adrian joined her, his feet sinking into the sand and the hint of a smile on his soft lips. 'I get the feeling that someone's jealous, but I never said I was interested in nudes.'

''Very funny,' she replied without stopping; if he really wanted to talk to her he would have to keep up, and, naturally she wasn't going to make things easy for him. 'Lots of artists get into it to see naked girls. Isn't anatomy the first thing artists study?'

Adrian stopped short, and after a couple of steps so did Elettra.

'The first thing an artist studies is what's inside a human being. The form is just a reflection of the self, and is rarely faithful,' he replied seriously. His voice had softened, becoming warm and sweet like an old ballad. It was comforting, so much so that for a moment Elettra closed her eyes to enjoy it. The sea at their feet flowed in various directions, disorientated by this night without a North Star. She looked up to the sky, fascinated by the enormous ochre-coloured crescent moon. Soon there would just be a shadowy gap, the new moon, in its place. She slipped off her shoes and put them on a rock, heading towards the water's edge. She felt as unsettled as the sea that night; she had had everything but she didn't know anything any more. Lea was probably counting the donations now and weeping with happiness, but deep down, Elettra still felt on edge.

A single step and she would fall into the void, unless someone pulled her away from the edge.

Adrian's arms slipped around her waist, brushing against her. Elettra felt his breath caress her hair. His shirt was still paint-marked, dirty with colour like she imagined her father's must have been years before. She would have to make peace with his ghost sooner or later. One day, perhaps, but not that night.

Elettra relaxed into the embrace, without even resisting; it was warm, familiar, something she suddenly realised she missed terribly. She closed her eyes and threw her head back against his shoulder.

'What is it?' he murmured in her ear, but she heard her own voice break, while she instinctively reached out towards the hand that was searching for hers in the dark. All she could do was hold and squeeze it.

Her life could be here, on this beach, with Adrian; she could risk being happy with him, finally serene, and perhaps that would be enough for her. All she had to do was grasp what was being offered and give in for once. Just once.

She relaxed against Adrian's chest and raised his hand to her face. The sound of the sea was a vortex and all Elettra could hear was her and Adrian breathing.

'Adrian, I don't . . . ' she stammered, but he silenced her with a kiss, the sweetest she had ever received. She opened her lips, sealing an unconditional pact. She sought the heat she lacked in the taste of him, transforming the sweetness into a voracious hunger, while her hands slipped quickly up his back, clinging to the soft cotton of his shirt. They slid under the fabric, across his burning skin, and she dug her fingers in. She wanted to feel him, to blend into him, to meld into his flesh until she disappeared, until she didn't remember who she was. Her only wish was to close her eyes and wake up in a life where there was no longer a place for the painful deceit she'd been carrying with her for months.

A home, a warm place for herself.

She let him lead her through the night to his door, to the fresh sheets in his bedroom where she lost and found herself again as time ticked by. Feeling his lips brush her breasts, linger over her stomach and then slip down to her groin left her gasping. Her breathing accelerated and then became a passionate moan. She gripped Adrian's hand tightly as she felt him move inside her until she became lost in breathing, in a pleasure where she rediscovered herself, the woman she thought she'd lost. She arched her back, brushing her lips against his, her eyes half-closed among waves of sweet abandon.

Adrian, the man in that bed, his legs entwined with hers, inside her; he was what she was looking for, the balm for her restless soul. Adrian was her home, the only walls among which she could lay down her weapons and give herself a chance.

She surrendered to pleasure and then pretended to sleep in order to avoid words, to avoid being forced to analyse what was in her mind; it had happened and that was that, it was pointless trying to explain. She entrusted everything else to time, and to the night the task of hiding the fears that slithered in under the doors.

But Adrian wanted her still; he sought her with the same hunger, the same need that Elettra felt blossom inside her again, too. Their hands sought each other, their breathing accelerated by the urgency required on such a fragile night. The spell could break at any moment in the light of the morning, of that treacherous sun that would be back to illuminate the bay and their lives. But the night, that was still theirs, and they could still trap it between the sheets in a bed where a man and a woman had blended their dreams.

The impulsive and unexpected pleasure morphed into languid abandon. Adrian's warm body stretched out beside her own, tangled in her hair, trapping her in an embrace.

I could stay here for ever, she thought, her eyes bright.

She felt Adrian slowly fall asleep, while she reached for the sheet with her fingertips. She turned towards the window that faced the coast; she could see the lights of the convent still shining in the distance.

She imagined Nicole, Sabine, Isabelle and Lea toasting the success of the evening and the Saint, who had protected secrets and uncomfortable existences for years, watching over the island from her stronghold above the sea. They would have dedicated this victory to Joséphine and exchanged amused looks at her and Adrian's absences, but their spirits would be too high for them to notice another absence, more serious and dangerous . . .

*

Lea and the others wouldn't have heard a familiar rumble going down the mountain and snaking through the high grass until it reached the sea; the hard heart of an unforgivable act, of a fragile mind, beaten and betrayed by life. They wouldn't have heard Gustave's muffled cries ringing through the silence of the town's dark streets. They would have continued to laugh under the sky of coloured lamps that Adrian had arranged in the cloister, the good food and noisy company would have done the rest.

Only much later, under a night sky, would the wind bring the voice of the law to the convent – and later still would it cross Elettra's path.

Only as the cloister was emptying would a boy wearing a serious expression and a policeman's uniform make straight for Sabine to tell her the news.

'I'm sorry to have to tell you this, Madame Picard, but your husband has just been found dead.'

Dead. Those four letters echoed in Sabine's head like the sound of a pinball machine.

She stepped back. 'It's not possible,' she said, staring at the policeman, waiting for a retraction.

There had been no mistake. Gustave really was dead.

A shower of questions rained down on her: where had it happened, and how?

It had to be her fault, of course. Would Gustave still be alive if she hadn't snuck out to go to the festival, leaving him to suffer yet another hangover?

But she had had to leave, she told herself, she needed to leave those walls that stank of alcohol and bad moods. She'd walked out of that door because she couldn't stand him railing against the world any more; her ears needed some peace. But once outside, she hadn't felt relieved as she had hoped; she knew that, sooner or later, she would have to go back, the prisoner of a marriage that stifled her.

It was her husband's fault, hers ... even she didn't know who to blame.

She sobbed as a terrible question formed in her mind: why didn't Gustave love her? Why did he care more about the bottle? Why did he turn on her?

'Insects. Monsieur Picard's death was caused by insects,' declared the policeman. Gustave had been found stretched out in the heather that grew abundantly in the lands around the convent, near Dominique's beehives.

Lea and the others, who'd run alongside Sabine, tried to prevent their friend seeing her husband's body, but when she insisted and found herself in front of Gustave's corpse, she felt her blood freeze. She stared at the lifeless body of the man she'd married, trying to unravel the emotions warring under her skin; her oppressor lay rigid and defenceless on the ground, yet she felt nothing.

It crossed her mind that he could no longer harm her now, that there would be no more bruises to hide, but when she looked for confirmation in Gustave's half-closed eyes she was overcome by a powerful wave of nausea that forced her to move away in search of air, her stomach burning.

For a moment, just one, she felt lighter, but she couldn't accept that this was the price for her peace, because there had been a time when Gustave had meant the world to her, even if he'd never loved her.

'He's feeling off, he's not himself,' she would repeat as she stood in front of the mirror trying to hide the bruises, trying to strengthen herself to withstand day after day of violence.

And now they were telling her that he was dead, killed by the poison of countless hundred insect stings, but, in her heart, Sabine, like the other women from the convent, knew the truth.

Only Dominique's bees could be responsible for this tragedy, Dominique who had come to the bar on the day of the festival to beg her to leave 'that worm'; that was what she'd called Gustave. Dominique who had paled, fists clenched, at the sight of Sabine's scratches, who had helped her escape from a Gustave who'd been drunk since midday and go to a party that she hadn't yet attended herself.

Sabine saw her face again as she stood in the channel the rains had worn between the brambles, and then her husband's; it took just a couple of seconds for her to be overcome by horror again, because she couldn't forget any more.

But the people of the town gathered around her were still astonished by what had happened to Gustave. They looked at one another dumbstruck, their mouths half closed as they endlessly stammered the cause of death the pathologist had just announced.

'Let's go to my house, they won't disturb us there,' Isabelle suggested, her arm stretched out to protect Sabine from everyone's stares.

'That would be best,' Lea agreed before saying goodbye and walking away into the darkness. Her voice sounded worn, matching the look on her ashen face. She had given Sabine a comforting hug then turned immediately towards the sea, but she hadn't wanted anyone to go with her. 'It's something I have to do alone,' she explained when Nicole offered to accompany her. 'I haven't seen Dominique since early evening.'

Lea walked along the coast path, pushing past bushes that crowded the path, ignoring the hostile eyes of the stray dogs along the way and the howling wind coming off the sea, which now gurgled restlessly, but as soon as she walked through the convent gate she felt a shiver run through her.

The tables full of pastries, bread and jams still stood on the piazza, the skeletons of the burnt-out lanterns bobbed, blown by the wind, while the undertow filled her thoughts with thunder.

Lea slipped into the convent, hurrying towards Dominique's cell; if she was in some way the architect of this tragedy, Lea was bound to find clues in her room. She rifled through her friend's papers, upending the mattress and emptying the wardrobes, but she found nothing; Dominique's rage seemed to have disappeared, along with all trace of her.

Lea went through the drawers one last time and found a hand-written note with that day's date between the pages of an old bible. It was the confession she'd been searching for.

She collapsed into a chair, Dominique's letter between her shaking fingers, a handful of hurriedly written lines asking forgiveness of the one person who'd had the courage to believe in her and whom she had deeply disappointed.

I am not worthy of your friendship, my soul must seem a muddy mire to you, and I know this to be true myself. So I have decided to leave and never come back, but I've let destiny run its course first: I refused to help Gustave, I let him die from the stings of my bees.

That brute turned up early in the evening, during the celebrations, as I was checking on the beehives in the field. I needed to slip away for a moment for quiet and he came with an evil glint in his eye, accusing me and the rest of you of brainwashing Sabine and ruining his life. You should have seen him, he called me all kinds of names. He was ranting like a madman until suddenly, all at once, the bees started to buzz more loudly around me, as if to create a protective barrier, but the more I told him to calm down, the more he raised his voice, and my little warriors closed ranks. I could tell there was something strange in the air so I told him to go, that it was dangerous to stay, but, as usual, he didn't listen. Then I shouted at him to leave me alone and to leave Sabine in peace once and for all, and in that very moment Gustave wrote his own death sentence by doing something he should never have done: he hit me so hard I fell over.

Believe me, I don't know how it happened, but as soon as my body hit the ground the swarm that had been around me moved away towards him, enveloping him in a cloud of poison. It's difficult to understand exactly what happened, everything was complete chaos in that moment, but in spite of the deafening buzz of the bees, I could distantly hear Gustave's voice begging for my help, weeping and despairing, but I didn't lift a finger to help him. I couldn't, not after what he did to Sabine and the convent. Yes, I turned my back on him. I let the bees kill him, I let them carry him away, otherwise our poor Sabine would never be free of that monster. And they did it, they defended Sabine and me as nobody ever did before.

I already know you'll condemn me, but I'm not sorry I rejected that worm. Perhaps one day you'll understand that cruelty is a necessary evil, but Sabine's bruises are not. They are

*preventable, but Gustave didn't spare her a
single one when he was alive.*

*I'll catch the ferry soon, but I want to thank
you all again before disappearing from your
lives; you've been everything to me, more than I
can say. I'd like to say something to each of you,
but you know me, so be content with a thank you.*

Be happy and pray for me.

Dominique

Feeling empty, Lea reread the letter dozens of times.

She refolded the paper, slipped it silently into her pocket and said a prayer; wherever Dominique had gone, the guilt for what she'd done would follow her.

Elettra was already awake when dawn arrived.

The images of the night before blended together; everything seemed crazy in the light of day. She had gone to bed with Adrian convinced it was the best thing she'd done in recent months, but now she wasn't sure. As soon as she'd opened her eyes she'd remembered that there wasn't room for a relationship in her life, but when she asked herself why she'd let herself go, she'd heard the word 'loneliness' bobbing to the surface like oil on water. She hadn't let selfishness stop her, because for once she'd wanted to put herself first. She'd needed to feel loved and she had sated herself on what he'd offered. The morning light had re-established the old boundaries.

She stirred the spoon in the cup, reliving the last few hours. She had felt good with him, she couldn't deny it; with Adrian it had felt like coming home, even if she'd never had one.

It had been *normal*. She had imagined her life would be extraordinary, not normal, when she was struggling to make it as a journalist, working sixteen hours a day, running from one side of the city to the other, notebook in hand, to catch the day's headlines before going back to an empty house in the evenings. But perhaps she had realised within the sparse walls of the convent that deep down she no longer wanted to become the extraordinary woman. It looked like what made her different was being able to produce a *couronne* loaf and spend her life by the side of the same man. Perhaps *that* was the real challenge for her.

She frowned, trying to come to terms with the concept and apply it to her life: ever since childhood it had been anything but normal. Her existence had always been littered with adjustments, chases and departures, but that morning she realised she was tired, she needed rest. Sitting in Adrian's small kitchen she found herself wanting something ordinary, and everyone else could go to hell.

All she wanted was to feel free to be herself, without any need for masks or filters; normality meant not having to fight for something or someone but living, simply, in harmony with herself and others.

She tried to stitch those words together with the feelings she had experienced that night, but a dangerous vertigo made her stop. She looked up, her cheek propped up on her hand; she was thinking too much for this early in the morning, she needed to clarify her thoughts. She took Adrian's jacket and left him a note next to the breakfast on the table, closing the door behind her.

'Fresh air, at last,' Elettra said, savouring the salty morning breeze. She didn't need to look twice before running towards the sea. She pulled Adrian's jacket tight around her and the crumpled paper in which she'd wrapped the *pane all'anice* for the festival poked out of the pocket: it still carried the scent.

She smiled.

318

Once she would have considered it a sign from her mother, a clue to follow to find her, to uncover that mysterious past that continued to evade her, but sitting on that cliff looking over the sea she understood that that period of her life was over. She had followed the past for too long, now it was time to live in the present.

When Adrian found Elettra's note he put it in his pocket and thumped the table. He'd been had again, like a fool.

'You shouldn't smack it so hard; hands are essential for an artist.'

'What are you doing here?' Adrian was instantly on the defensive, surprised to see his father on the threshold; he didn't have a meeting scheduled with him, not in the immediate future.

Bernard didn't seem at all surprised by his son's icy welcome. He took off his hat and placed it on the table, ignoring the cutting look Adrian gave him. He'd expected it from the moment he'd decided to visit him. 'I dropped by to say hello.'

'You shouldn't have bothered.'

'I'm leaving; I don't know when we'll see each other again.'

'Since when has that been a problem? We haven't seen each other for years.'

Bernard folded his arms, holding back a bitter laugh. 'You never let up, do you? A good sign, it means you haven't lost your grit.'

'Should I? If it makes you happy I'll leave you in peace. In fact, look, you can go now if you want.'

'But you dropped by my room when I wasn't there, didn't you?' Adrian turned slightly, alarmed.

Bernard ran his index finger along the edge of the table, stopping a dozen centimetres or so from Adrian. 'I know very well that it was you who stole those documents.'

'I'm not a thief.'

'Only because I didn't report it. I knew it would lead to you.'

'If you suddenly feel I've done you an injustice, you could have reported it. It's your right.'

'Don't you wonder why I decided to stay silent instead?'

Adrian crossed his arms. 'Perhaps you had second thoughts and realised it wouldn't be to your advantage. As far as I know, the agreement with Leroux wasn't as transparent as you made everyone believe.' He gave a challenging smile. 'Am I right?'

Bernard looked him right in the eyes, puffing out his ample chest. 'No, not at all. I didn't report you for your mother's sake.'

The air became leaden. Adrian's arms suddenly tensed. 'You shouldn't even speak her name. She has nothing to do with this, so if you've nothing else to say, the door's over there,' he roared, pointing with his arm.

Bernard followed the line of Adrian's index finger without moving a muscle. 'But she is connected to you. She would never have wanted you to end up in jail.'

'Get out.'

'Whether you believe it or not, this whole sequence of events, the fact that you live here, finding you again, made me think of her. I've reconsidered my life, our family.'

Adrian felt his jaw contract. 'Don't make me laugh! You don't know the meaning of the word "family".'

'Now you're being unfair. I've made mistakes, but that doesn't make me a monster.'

Adrian nodded and began to walk around the room, his hands in his pockets. 'Really? So you're trying to tell me you don't remember anything about cheating on my mother with Elodie, how much you made her suffer? Perhaps you've forgotten the day she died, when she couldn't bear the weight of your squalid affairs any more and had a heart attack? Don't you even remember that, Papa?'

Bernard stroked the brim of his hat. The fabric yielded gently under his fingertips, while his son's poisoned words seeped in. Adrian still hadn't forgiven him. 'I did her so much damage it ended up killing her, I know that; I couldn't escape my guilt even if I fled to a desert island, but I can't go back in time. Anne is dead, and I've realised too late that I didn't deserve a woman like her, like I didn't deserve to have a son with her. We've been at war for years, but today I'm grateful for this business, even if it's fallen through. If I hadn't accepted Vincent's proposal I wouldn't have seen you again.'

'Sure,' Adrian replied icily. Time passed, endless minutes he prayed would slip by faster; he wasn't comfortable with his father, each time he saw him again he remembered his psychiatrist's leather couches. He'd hated that woman, or at least finding Bernard or Elodie sitting in the waiting room afterwards, confident that his rage was a sickness that could be cured with a box of tranquillisers.

Adrian sprang towards the door, his shaking hands hidden in his pockets.

'Listen, let's give up and say our goodbyes.' He turned the handle as his father's face paled into a weak smile.

'I think Anne would be proud of you. Do you know you look like her?'

Adrian slumped imperceptibly, his hand over his mouth to hold back a swear word; it was a low blow. His mother was still an unresolved pain despite the passing of the years, but he wouldn't let Bernard use her death to score points against him.

'What did you come here for?' he spat.

'To tell you I understand why you sabotaged my project and that I don't harbour any hard feelings. And I want you to know I'm sorry for the pain I caused you and Anne. If there was a way to go back, I'd change a lot of my past.'

'Fine, you're forgiven. Now go.'

Bernard faced the door as he put his hat on. He took a last look at Adrian, who glared at him with angry eyes, and smiled. 'And I came to tell you I'm proud of the man you've become.'

He said nothing more.

He walked towards his hotel to settle his bill and collect his post. Elodie had sent him a copy of the biopsy and a fact sheet from a highly regarded clinic for oncological medicine in New York. He would study it all calmly, once he was on the ferry.

30

Elettra curled up under the covers, her knees pressed against her chest.

December had arrived on the island, covering it in its cloak of ice and rain; drops fell from the gutter and the scent of damp earth was all round. Elettra loved that pungent aroma.

Lea's story of the night of the festival had initially hit her like a landslide as she listened teary-eyed, her breathing ragged. Her throat was too tight to admit air or voice thoughts, but in the following days she kept asking her sister to tell her further details of what had happened. Almost a month had passed, but Elettra couldn't resign herself to it, couldn't accept the fact that death had knocked at their door again to cause havoc, even if it was Gustave. She'd told Lea she didn't want to see anyone, all she wanted was some peace in her room; that small damp room had suddenly become the only refuge where she could breathe, where she could rediscover her centre of gravity.

She'd spent days stretched out on her bed listening to the sea, the symphony of the storm and the sound of Adrian's words. He had come back to the convent each day to see her and Elettra was grateful to Lea for not letting him come up, she wouldn't have known what to say. Now she searched under the covers for Adrian's jacket, which she wrapped around herself to sleep; it still held the scent of his skin, the heat of an unforgettable embrace. She inhaled until her lungs were full of his smell, and took the wrapper she'd found that evening out of the pocket; that little square of crumpled paper had led her to the truth, it was her lucky charm. She held it to her nose, seeking traces of the scent of *pane all'anice* in the brightly coloured wrapping.

She left her room and went to the cloister. Months ago she had set off for Titan's Island convinced she'd rediscover her mother there, hoping to ward off the fear of losing her and protect her memory with new memories, but she had wound up finding an even more precious gift on that harsh island: herself.

She'd made peace with her fears on the island, with an identity she'd long sought but been denied. Elettra had fought for years; every morning she would find something wrong with the woman she saw reflected in the mirror. Before getting on the ferry she no longer knew what she wanted from life, but then, standing facing the sea after her night with Adrian, she did.

'You told me so many times not to mind what people say, and, more importantly, to stay true to my own conscience, but I never listened to you. I thought it was more important to gain people's approval, to find a love from men to replace what I hadn't received from my father, and to flee from them when things got too serious out of a fear of suffering. I kept making mistakes even though you tried to show me the way, but you know what I'm like: I need to learn from my own experience. Yet you tried all the same, you never gave up,' she murmured, her mind's eye tracing Edda's face.

She had finally solved the puzzle, and she was grateful to her mother for guiding her here, to this forgotten corner of the world, following the trail of her *pane all'anice* that had also turned out to be Adrian's favourite. Edda had accompanied her on this solo voyage so Elettra could come home and acquire the peace she lacked.

Edda, Clara, no one she'd met had fully opened the door to reveal her mother's past but they showed a way to discover Elettra Cavani, the woman who was sitting in the cloister while the air danced with the fragrance of caramelised apples and sea salt to a tune from Nicole, who was busy with the morning chores. Nicole had spent the last couple of weeks moving the larder to the wing where it had originally been housed to make running the bakery easier, and she'd spent days going up and down the stairs dragging bags of flour and sugar. That morning she was carrying a sack of icing sugar on her back, but on hearing Elettra's voice she had come to the window, asking whether she'd prefer her to leave it in the kitchen.

'Do you need it for today's biscuits?' she asked, poking the sack with her finger, but when Elettra nodded and she went to put it back, a long tear appeared in the strained fabric, releasing a white cloud into the cloister. 'No!' shouted Nicole, trying to close it, but it was too late: thousands of sugared crystals flew through the cloister like a miraculous snowfall, causing Elettra to fling open her arms in amusement. Drops of sweet talc-like powder spread through the garden, settling lightly on the Saint's face and the branches at rest for the winter, and Elettra smiled as she watched the immaculate snowfall that fell through her hair.

She closed her eyes, her hands outstretched and her heart beating in time to the pulse of the cloister around her. It was the blessing she'd been waiting for, a long-awaited sense of peace finally arriving on an ordinary December morning.

Finally, Elettra felt alive.

She inhaled as much of that feeling of beatitude as she could, but rapid footsteps and laboured breathing soon clouded her sky.

The white storm was interrupted and she opened her eyes again; Adrian stood panting in front of her, his expression serious.

'There's a Ruth who called for you. A phone call. It's urgent.'

Just a few words, but they left her breathless.

She grabbed Adrian's hand without thinking and followed him to town, to the telephone at the end of the corridor in the bar. She was so distracted that she didn't notice Sabine sitting behind the bar beside Isabelle, who was holding her hand. Elettra was unaware of anything but her legs stiffening with every step that took her closer to the handset, like a reluctant animal outside the abattoir door. Something in her head told her that once she crossed that threshold there'd be no turning back.

She lifted the receiver, but her hands shook so much she had to use both of them and squeeze it tightly in order to raise it to her ear. There was a crackle of crossed, worn lines, then Ruth's upset voice on the other end of the line.

Her typical 'bad news' voice.

'Elettra, is that you?' she asked hesitantly. She'd recognised her before she even opened her mouth; Elettra could almost see Ruth leaning forward and rubbing her eyes in the effort to work out whether the breathing was her best friend's.

Elettra felt her eyes fill and her surroundings blurred. 'Yes, it's me,' she confirmed, her heart pounding in her chest.

Ruth held her breath for an endless moment, interrupted only by the bitter thunder of a sob. She didn't say anything else, there was no need.

Elettra's eyes closed, letting a tear trickle out.

Edda had gone. Her mother was dead.

31

Elettra glanced at the suitcase open on her bed, her mind whirling; her thoughts were a collage of hazy images arranged haphazardly along the timeline of a hellish day. She didn't know how, but after Ruth's phone call she'd found herself in her room at the convent with a suitcase to fill and her eyes overflowing with tears. Adrian hadn't left her for a moment and she was soothed by his low voice coming from downstairs. It hadn't been a hallucination, she really was back there.

Ignoring her thumping headache, Elettra tried to piece together the fragments of Ruth's call, the few syllables she'd managed to get out of her; Edda's condition had worsened in the early hours of the morning, but nobody had answered when her friend had tried to call the bar to tell her.

Sabine had slept at Isabelle's every night since she'd become a widow; she was still frightened to confront the bed where Gustave's body had been laid out. There was still too much pain to process.

'Damn it!' Elettra exclaimed, hurling a blouse into the suitcase with all her strength. She needed to let off steam, to unload the rage that was boiling her blood, but as she looked at the crumpled fabric she realised that the hate inside her had no source. It wasn't her fault Edda had died and she couldn't do anything about it. Even if she'd caught the first flight, she would never have arrived in time to say goodbye to her.

But anyway, she asked herself, curling up with her knees pressed together and her eyes full of tears, what difference would it have made?

Edda had never woken after she'd fallen into the coma, so Elettra had had to content herself with what was left; her memories, Edda's smile, the gift she'd given her by leaving crumbs of herself along the path to the convent, and all her secrets. Perhaps, she thought, that was the best way her mother could have said goodbye to her. Without drama.

'Just how you wanted,' she murmured. Letting go of her would not be easy, Elettra thought as she clutched Edda's old exercise book.

She'd had plenty of time to prepare for it, the doctors had been clear from the outset that Edda's condition was serious, but that was only one of the lies she told herself; faced with the enormity of death, with the mystery that had left her an orphan, Elettra felt overwhelmed by sadness.

She slid down to the foot of the bed, her hands covering her red face. After more than a year of silence, Edda wasn't there any more, she would no longer be able to hold her hand, nourish the hope that her eyes might open again one day. She'd known it would never happen, but she'd soothed herself with the fantasy. Part of her felt she had a right to that fairy tale.

'Hey,' a brief syllable and the warmth of an embrace.

Elettra sagged into Adrian's shoulder, already exhausted by a suffering that felt like it was just beginning. She would have liked to be strong, but she was tired of pretending.

'I'm coming with you. Pack your case and let's go.'

'No, you really don't need to.' A conditioned reflex pushed her back into her old habits. She wiped her face to dry her tears, but he looked her straight in the eyes and took her hands.

'Don't even think about it,' he said, serious. 'I won't let you push me aside again and deal with all this on your own, so don't play superwoman, not with me. I know who you are, and I also know you're too proud to admit that you need someone by your side, that you need me.'

'Ruth's a good friend,' Elettra babbled, trying to free herself, but Adrian held her hands more tightly.

'Ruth isn't me,' he insisted with such strength in his voice, in his hands holding hers, that Elettra realised she didn't want to resist any more. She wound her fingers through Adrian's and raised them to her chest. She had to try, to try and trust him, even if she was afraid.

'Okay.'

'Okay?'

'Yes. Go and get the tickets for the ferry, I've still got a couple of things to do,' she continued, watching him move across the room until he disappeared into the corridor. When she finally heard him go down the stairs she squatted down by her suitcase. She was exhausted, and the knowledge that this was only the beginning was not comforting. With an effort she finished packing and went upstairs, straight to the terrace; she would say goodbye to the convent from that magical place that overlooked the whole property and had given her such wonderful evenings.

Elettra had spent an entire summer talking to Lea there, their eyes fixed on the sunset and the cicadas chirping in the warmth, reflecting on her eccentric life and on Edda's. She would carry the scent of the flowering wisteria that grew across the convent's façade with her for ever, along with the sea breeze that filled the whole convent and the memory of two girls stretched out on the ground eating apricots and using their infinite imaginations to come up with new constellations.

Elettra filled her lungs and her mind with those fragrances, with the many evenings spent in this maritime oasis. When she left the terrace behind her and went back inside she found herself facing the half-open door of the abbess's room and she felt rooted to the spot.

After one last moment of hesitation, she went through the door.

Joséphine's room was in darkness; the curtains were drawn, and the only light in the spartan cubicle was the soft glow of a forgotten candle left alight on her bedside table.

The abbess was stretched out on the bed, thinner than ever. Her once beautiful face had shrunk to show her increasingly prominent bones. Her skin had become extremely thin, the fragile structure of a back-lit leaf. Elettra gently dabbed at the sheen of sweat on Joséphine's face, but when she took the tissue and patted her blood-less lips, she felt two icy hands clasp her face. She held her breath, stifling a cry. Surely Joséphine couldn't really be waking up, coming out of a coma.

'Edda, is it you?' the nun asked in a rough, faded voice. She seemed to be speaking from a distant place, so distant that her voice ware barely audible. She was looking for her friend Edda, the woman who, more than any other, had been close to her at difficult times. Elettra's eyes clouded and a lump formed in her throat when she heard her speak her mother's name; it took all her self-control not to pull away and weep, and when she raised her hand to touch the abbess's, Joséphine lost consciousness. Her butterfly hands fell to the rumpled sheets and her lips remained open in an unheard prayer.

Elettra stayed to watch her, holding her breath. Joséphine appeared dead, but the sheer thought left Elettra frozen; she wasn't ready for another tragedy. Not like this, not that day.

She stepped away and ran to the door, yelling Lea's name and bringing her running up the stairs.

'Your mother's worse,' she told her darkly, and from then on she counted every single hour of that horrible night like those of a difficult birth.

As she sat on the plane that carried her home, just the thought of that night made Elettra teary. Her hands searched for something to occupy themselves and her thoughts were reduced to scraps of paper scattered across the smooth floor of her mind. She would have liked to stay by Lea's side, but her blood prevented her; her mother was on the other side of the sea and it was a pain she had to face head on.

She leaned her head back against the upholstered seat, watching the line of the horizon tilt outside the window beside her.

She smiled as she looked down at Adrian's hand held in hers. Earlier, sitting beside her as they waited for their flight to be called, he had promised to be there for her; he didn't care where or how, as long as she let him into her life.

'Let me in, let me take care of you,' he'd implored her in the middle of the departure lounge, begging her to let herself be loved.

Elettra had listened in silence, astonished; she couldn't understand how he could love her so much, what had clicked inside him to make him turn his life upside down for a woman he barely knew.

But perhaps, she'd told herself, handing the boarding card to the air hostess, that was what living meant. Perhaps she'd come closer to true love than she'd thought.

Still dazed, she'd settled into her seat, and she'd continued to watch Adrian from there as he spoke to the staff, joked with his neighbour and arranged the blanket over her legs when she'd said she wanted to rest. He hadn't moved even when she'd fallen asleep on his shoulder, and he'd hugged her tightly when the outline of the city became visible. He'd known this would be the hardest day of her life before she was even aware of the knot forming at the top of her stomach as she heard the smooth voice of the captain announce their imminent arrival.

He'd known, perhaps because he truly loved her.

Ruth was waiting for them impatiently behind the barriers.

She was wearing a sombre expression, but her face lit up as soon as she spotted Elettra. She couldn't hold her tears back any longer and ran to embrace her.

'I'm sorry,' Ruth murmured into Elettra's ear, but she wasn't listening; she was so happy to see her again.

'I know,' she replied quietly without for a moment imagining that her friend's words could refer to anything else than her bereavement but, having arrived at the clinic and been confronted by the truth, she felt faint; Edda's body had already been placed in the coffin in preparation for the funeral due to take place the following morning.

'Everything happened so fast,' Ruth apologised, gesturing to the dark wood just visible at the end of the corridor, which was lit by two lamps. 'Unfortunately the company didn't have any other styles available. I know Edda wasn't a fan of mahogany.'

Elettra silenced her with a nod, following the nurse to a small door. A man in a blue uniform with a long white beard led her into the room where her mother was; he asked if she needed anything, offered his condolences and took his leave as soon as she shook her head.

Then she turned to Ruth and Adrian. She wanted to spend some time alone with her mother, she said, her eyes bright, but as soon as she heard the door close behind her the binding that kept her emotions in check gave way and she collapsed beside Edda's body, once full of life, now an empty cocoon, trapped in a dream from which she would never wake. She leaned over her expressionless face to kiss her forehead; she'd often kissed Edda during her coma, but feeling the chill of her cheeks left her paralysed. There was no longer warmth inside her, nor the vitality Elettra had always envied her. Just a cold body Elettra didn't know at all.

'Goodbye, Mamma.'

She whispered those two words, wiping away her fast-flowing tears. Edda looked serene, as though the deep wrinkle that had carved a groove across her forehead for the past year had never existed, and she looked splendid in her blush-pink dress, which Elettra had bought her.

Edda would always be beautiful, her charm would never fade, but she was dead: those words chased each other round Elettra's head in a suffocating repetition.

She took a deep breath and stroked Edda's hands, smaller than she remembered them, a smile colliding with the wall of pain that immobilised her. There were no crucifixes or prayer books with Edda, she'd never needed them; for Edda, her saint was enough, so Elettra placed the necklace with the medallion from the convent between her slender fingers.

Finally, she gave the faces of Saint Elizabeth and her mother one last kiss.

She dug in her bag for a tissue, but her fingers met a different, more rigid, resistance: the notebook full of recipes she'd found at the convent.

Elettra took a long look at its flour-marked edges, the clots of pastry that stuck the faded pages together, and arranged it beside her mother. 'You were right, you know. I need to stop following the rules other people have written for me, even yours, and trying to please others at any cost. I've lived like that for years and I've always been unhappy, so the time has come to learn to keep the recipes in here,' she whispered, tapping her index finger against her temple. 'All of them, even the ones you didn't want to teach me,' she added, biting her lip as Adrian, who'd silently re-entered the room, slipped his hands around her waist.

She brushed one with her fingertips then nodded. Three men dressed entirely in black were at the door armed with a dark briefcase. 'I'll just be a moment,' she told them. She went over to Edda's body, and she slipped the photo from that magical and terrible summer, the summer of 1952, which had dictated the course of their lives, between the pages of the exercise book. 'I've brought you Joséphine's forgiveness, Mamma, and mine. It's not your fault Papa died, nobody's angry with you for that any more,' she whispered, kissing Edda's forehead as fresh tears welled up from her chest.

A pointed cough.

'Elettra,' Adrian murmured, and she nodded. The moment had arrived.

Oppressed by their presence, the words, everything she'd wanted to tell Edda, shattered.

She, Ruth and Adrian were invited to leave the room.

They enclosed Edda in a container, but Elettra knew she wasn't made to be imprisoned; the few times they'd discussed the subject, when they heard of a high-profile death in the papers or a customer's passing, Edda had always reiterated her wish to be cremated.

'When the time comes, I'd like you to scatter my ashes in the Mediterranean; that's where I belong, along with all the others like me who come from the sea,' she'd told her. Elettra hadn't understood at the time, thinking they were just the words of a romantic woman, but her journey and the stories from the convent had shown her how deeply rooted that request was in her family's origins.

The next day when the men from the undertakers handed her

the urn containing Edda's ashes, Elettra found Adrian's hand tight in hers, offering comfort.

As it had throughout that brief journey.

Incapable as Elettra was of expressing herself in words, his loyalty prompted fresh tears.

'Adrian,' she stammered, when the station wagon with the name of the undertakers on the side pulled out into the morning traffic. Ruth joined them as he pulled the key to her saloon car out of his pocket and opened the passenger door.

'Get in the car, you're very tired and we've got quite a drive ahead of us,' he said, stroking Elettra's face.

Ruth took her friend by the shoulders, realising she was on the point of collapse, and sat beside her. 'Don't worry, I'll take care of her.'

It was a journey of just over a hundred kilometres, far enough to reach the nearest port, and Elettra slept the whole way. Her body seemed to have imposed a forced rest that prevented her from thinking. Edda's urn was beside her.

'Look, we've arrived.'

Adrian's voice pulled her across the blurred edges of a dream, giving her a view of the port. Ships were docked just outside the fishing harbour, ready to depart for exotic destinations. Beyond them was nothing but the open sea.

When they reached a deserted beach, Elettra got out of the car and pushed back her hair. The wind was blowing towards Titan's Island; the sea would soon carry Edda home.

The moment to bid her goodbye had come, and this time it would be for ever.

She opened the urn, her face shrouded by profound grief; she'd wanted to keep Edda with her a little longer, to feel like the two of them still had time together.

She glanced at Ruth, who nodded in silence, smiling at her; she would be there, she'd never leave her on her own, but that morning Elettra felt like the only survivor of a tragedy.

She turned to Adrian with her heart in her mouth and unsteady legs; she wasn't going to manage it, if all that was left of Edda was a handful of powder, if an urn was all she had left of her now she was preparing for a new life. But this was the route her mother had chosen, and she needed to respect that.

She took a deep breath, but when she felt the tears blur her vision she hung her head. 'I can't do it,' she murmured, defeated. She closed the urn again and squeezed it tightly, her arms clinging to a mother she didn't have the strength to let go of.

A herring gull glided along the shore, filling the air with its cries.

The sun was high in the sky, the wind a caress that gently surrounded her, guiding her hand towards the task that awaited her. Nature, life, perhaps Edda herself, was asking her to let her go, to return her to the sea that held out its foamy arms towards her. Elettra shouldn't be afraid, she seemed to tell her; she wouldn't be alone, not any more.

'Mamma,' she whispered in tears, and then a fresh hint of that magical aroma of aniseed filled her lungs with hope. It came from Adrian, Elettra could sense it emanating powerfully from his skin.

Adrian, her home. Her hope for the future, for all the thoughts behind her eyes, amongst the folds of a soul that was finally at peace. Adrian, Edda's last gift, the most precious. The most sacred.

The one man, the only man, who'd filled the word 'us' with meaning.

Elettra looked at him, her hands clutching the urn stretched out towards him. 'You said for ever, didn't you?'

'Elettra, I will always be with you,' he replied, surprised.

'Swear it. Swear to me that you won't go too,' she whispered, her cheeks streaked with tears.

'I swear to you,' he repeated, stroking her face. 'I'm here now, and believe me, I've no intention of going anywhere,' he added with a smile, trying to imbue her with the security she'd always lacked, forced as she was to live with no roots apart from Edda. He brushed her hands gently, reinforcing the sincerity of his words. 'Believe me,' he repeated, 'because I love you.'

Elettra sighed. She glanced at Ruth, then her eyes met Adrian's again as a stream of powder was released into the sky, dancing amongst the colours and perfumes of a homecoming.

Nuvole di Elettra & Adrian

500g sugar

5 egg whites

1 handful dried apple slices

1 pinch salt

1 orange (zest only)

1 lemon (zest only)

1 spoon coloured sprinkles

Whip the egg whites, sugar, salt and citrus zest into stiff peaks. The mixture is ready when you can turn the bowl upside down without it moving.

Add the dried apples and pipe into small cloud shapes with an icing bag.

Scatter them with coloured sprinkles and bake for 75 minutes at 100°C.

The clouds are ready when the outside is hard but the middle is soft.

EPILOGUE

Elettra pushed the squeaky door that led onto the terrace and it flew open to reveal the line of the coast, brightened by the fishing boats that had just gone out to sea.

Lea was busy taking the laundry down and pieces of fabric of all colours and sizes still hung on the line, stretched out to catch the last rays of the sun. She was singing as she always did when she was alone, and a white cat had wrapped its tail around her legs, purring as it rubbed its head against her.

'That's enough, Meringue!' Lea giggled, playing peekaboo with the cat from behind a pair of white pillowcases, but when she saw Elettra she dropped the basket of folded laundry, which fell to the ground and scared away the cat.

'Lea,' Elettra greeted her, walking towards her.

'Elettra!' Lea exclaimed, radiant, running to hug her. She squeezed Elettra tightly and kissed her on both cheeks, happy to see her after her long absence. 'I'm so glad you're back, how are you? When did you arrive?'

Elettra took Lea's face between her hands and smiled at her. A year had passed since the day she had last set foot on the terrace, but everything there seemed unchanged, even though nothing was the same as before. Lea had opened all the rooms in the convent and enlarged the bakery so it now had an area for displaying and selling the produce.

'I've only just got here. Adrian's stopped to speak to Nicole for a moment, but I came straight up to see you. I knew you were here, I could hear you singing from the garden,' Elettra said, smiling at the blush that spread across her sister's cheeks. The sky was fading into the sunset and the scent of the lemon tree facing out over the coast filled the velvety evening air with sweetness. After a moment Elettra felt herself fill up with memories of last summer, of the nights they'd spent laughing and counting stars; back then she didn't yet know that Lea was her sister, but she'd known they shared a rare affinity.

She closed her eyes while the ferry merrily greeted the people gathered on the pier, announcing its departure to the fishermen in the bay.

'I really missed the convent,' she said.

'And I missed you,' Lea whispered, taking her hand. 'Especially when, after Edda died, Mamma died too ...'

Elettra held her tightly, continuing to stare at the horizon. 'I know. I know,' she repeated, her voice full of emotion at the memory of those tear-filled days. 'Joséphine and Edda live on inside of us, but life goes on, Lea, and we can't keep looking back towards the past. Our mothers did it for too long and it almost destroyed them.'

'Elettra?'

'Yes?'

Lea stood in front of her sister and took her hands. There was a new urgency about her, a need to confide, to be open like before. To create that special bond that connects two sisters who only met as adults. She bit her lip, her foot tapping impatiently against the cracked tiles of the terrace. 'There's something I need to tell you. Something I've been meaning to tell you for a while, but I haven't found the courage to do it.'

Elettra smiled, she knew what Lea was talking about, she'd learned to read her months ago. And she knew exactly why she was embarrassed, why she licked her lips, why her hands twisted the sleeve of her flowery dress. She smiled and tilted her head to meet Lea's eyes. 'There's a man in your life now, isn't there?'

'He's called Antoine and he works in the bakery. And there's something else.'

Lea looked down and placed her hand gently on the slight roundness of her stomach.

Elettra stepped closer to her and gently lifted her chin until they could look into each other's eyes.

Edda, Elettra, Joséphine, Lea: in spite of the passage of time and the generations, destiny continued to draw parallel paths for them to follow along the journey of their lives.

'I'm calling mine Edda Joséphine. What are you going to call yours?' she asked, her hand stroking her own gently curving stomach.

ACKNOWLEDGEMENTS

Every novel is a journey, and like every expedition it requires the presence of travelling companions. *The Little Italian Bakery* has been very lucky in this respect, because mine have been the best.

The first of this long stream of thank yous goes to Laura Ceccacci and that first coffee in damp mid-January. I didn't just find an agent at that table, but a precious friend, too. You took me under your wing when I felt lost and alone and nobody believed in me and you've welcomed me into your life. You're a special person and if I've never told you out loud it's just because I cry easily. It's much better to put it in writing, at least then you won't see me drowning in tissues.

There was once a young girl who would set off to Sardinia each summer with a bag full of Garzanti Elefanti children's books, dreaming that one day she would find her name on a book cover alongside that publisher's. Thank you to Elisabetta Migliavada for making that dream come true. Thank you for the advice, encouragement and chats. Thank you for your time and patience, for the sweetness of your smile, which caused all my fears to crumble away the first time I set foot in the Garzanti offices; my knees were shaking when I walked into your office, but my heart was as light as a feather when I left.

Thank you to Adriana Salvatori, just Adriana to me, whom I've come to know and consider a friend. Thank you for your patience in putting up with my slowness and for making Elettra's story better. Thank you for your humanity, for the little gestures: simply thank you. If you hate me for all the times I made you reread and correct the manuscript, I'll understand!

Thank you to the entire fantastic Garzanti family: the warmth with which you've welcomed me can only be compared to a hug. It's the warmth of a family to which I hope I deserve to belong.

Thank you to the whole amazing Laura Ceccacci Agency to which I'm honoured to belong, and in particular to Cristina Caboni, true friend and 'fairy godmother'. Your friendship is very important to me, as are your advice and the calm and uncondi-tional affection you've shown me so many times during this long journey, always rock solid but never ostentatious. You're a special woman.

Further thanks to Francesca Saitta, Maria Antonietta Azara, Loredana Rei, Francesca Romana Pirolli, Flavia Cingoli, Massimo Guiso, Antonino Manfré, Mariantonietta Carbone, Paul Burger, Maria Domenica Meloni, Ghita Montalto, Anna Rita Felici, Franca Marzi, Eliana Castellazzi, Lidia Mangiatordi, Luca Lo Iacono, Pierpaolo Fadda and all those who've supported me on this journey, to those with us and those now gone. For reasons of space I can't name you all, but I thank you. Thank you to all the readers out there, the greatest support for any writer, whether aspiring or multiple prize winning: without you even the most beautiful words would be nothing but dead letters.

Thank you to the booksellers, who love stories however many we write for them. They are the guardians of this magical world of ink and imagination. My heartfelt thanks to you.

Thank you to Sardinia, my mother's home, which has inspired the places in this novel and enriched all my summers with the song of the mistral and the scent of the sea, filling my eyes and soul with beauty.

Finally, special thanks to my family and in particular to my maternal grandparents, Matteo and Rosalia: I never had the honour of knowing you except through other people's memories, but if there's a dash of your marvellous island and its magic in this book, it's because of you. I've loved it since I first saw it in photographs along with your faces and your genuine smiles, typical of people with open hands and simple hearts. I send you a kiss and pray it reaches you up in the clouds.